LADY'S CHOICE

"You say you shot this man in self-defense, ma'am?"

Jessie said, "Yes."

The lawman hunkered down by the cadaver to gently roll it partway on its side. "This man never took no lead in the front of his shirt. He was shot in the back, at close range." He got back to his feet, his gun still out, as he stared warily at Jessie. "We'll be going over to the town lockup now, ma'am. I'd sure feel silly handcuffing a woman. So you just come along like a lady and—"

"On what charge?" she cut in.

To which the town law soberly replied, "Murder, of course. Did you really think you could back-shoot Judge Reynolds, an elder of our church, and get out of it? We got you, ma'am, dead to rights. If it's any comfort, Utah Territory gives a convicted murderer the choice of hanging or a firing squad."

TABOR EVANS

LONGARM

AND THE
LONE STAR FRAME

JOVE BOOKS, NEW YORK

LONGARM AND THE LONE STAR FRAME

A Jove Book/published by arrangement with
the author

PRINTING HISTORY

Jove edition/October 1988

ISBN: 0-515-09752-7

Jove books are published by The Berkley Publishing Group
200 Madison Avenue, New York, New York 10016.
The name "JOVE" and the "J" logo
are trademarks belonging to Jove Publications, Inc.

PRINTED IN THE UNITED STATES OF AMERICA

10 9 8 7 6 5 4 3 2 1

Chapter 1

Longarm could recall setting his battered alarm clock for early, but not this early, dammit. It was still dark outside, and for some reason the fool clock seemed to be on the wrong side of his bed this cold gray dawn.

Still half-asleep, the tall naked deputy reached a long bare arm out to silence the obviously malfunctioning contraption or, failing that, hurl it across the room, which usually shut it up for a spell. But as his big sleepy paw came down on something a lot softer and warmer than any brass alarm clock ever made, Longarm blinked himself wider awake to chuckle fondly and say, "Well, howdy, pard. For a minute, there, I thought I was in my own furnished digs up the alley."

The lady he'd just woke up in bed with giggled and moved his hand down her curvacious nude torso to an even more inspiring point of contact as she did him the additional favor of turning off the alarm on her side of the bed. It was only fair, since it was her alarm clock as well as her bed. Longarm remembered why they'd set it so early by mutual agreement. It was payday. So he meant to get to the office earlier than usual. But no man born or mortal woman was about to just get up and go after waking up in such stay-in-bed company.

As he began to stroke her to full attention, she cuddled closer and moaned a string of singsong love words whose exact meaning was sort of Greek, or more like Cantonese, to Longarm. But he could grasp their meaning well enough as she spread her petite thighs and commenced to move her com-

1

pact hips in a pleading manner. It just wasn't true what they said about Chinese gals, even when they were pretty as old Ching Mi, and one woman moved a lot like any other when she knew what she wanted.

Not wanting to pass up such an opportunity, and aware he did have to get to work *some* damn time today, Longarm rolled into the notch of Ching Mi's tawny thighs and upthrust pelvis, which made her come at once, and didn't leave him all that far behind. For she was one of those naturally lusty little gals a man just couldn't seem to get enough of, and vice versa. He'd lost count of the ways and means by which he'd had her before they'd agreed to set the alarm early in hopes of doing just what they were doing some more. He knew there was no way in hell he was going to get to the office on time this morning, payday or not.

But it was still dark out when, having gotten their second wind and deciding to go dog style, again, his Oriental hostess arched her spine with a sigh he took at first to be the result of how deep she could take it, this way, and told him to hurry, adding, "You gotta come right away and get dressed and outta here befo' goddamn sun *he* come, too! You no remember what you promise about my reputation?"

He didn't answer. He was too busy pounding his way to glory. But he knew what she meant and, as usual, women were always more pragmatic about sex, even when enjoying it.

The pretty little waitress from the Golden Dragon obviously *was* enjoying it, and he knew he could get her to give him some more if he wanted to be piggy. But he had assured her, during the considerable wrestling it had taken to get her in such a state of reckless enjoyment, that he understood her position. Or, to be exact, the position she was in with both her race, and his, when she had her hair up and her skirts down.

The Chinese Riots of the 1870s were hopefully a shameful memory of the past. But there were still a lot of hard feelings on both sides, and they did not include or approve of the hard feelings he and this pretty little China doll were enjoying at the moment.

Longarm wasn't worried about himself. He'd proved on

more than one occasion he could take care of the bullyboys inspired by radical racist orations. It didn't take much to crawfish a wolf pack out to prove its courage by ganging up on unarmed Chinese, one at a time. But while Longarm was one large, armed white man few street toughs were up to messing with, this pretty little waitress gal was a heap smaller than he was. Even if some red radical didn't hit her with a horse apple to protect the jobs of true-blue Americans just off the boat, she could wind up fired by her Chinese boss for forgiving true-blue Americans, of any kind, in such a friendly fashion. So once they'd somehow wound up on the bedside rug with her on top, and neither seemed up to coming again right away, Longarm didn't argue when Ching Mi disempaled herself to flop facedown across the bed, sobbing to herself about something in singsong Cantonese.

Longarm knew better than to argue with a gal suffering cold-gray-dawn considerations, even when he understood what she might be bitching about. So he rose, enjoyed a quick whore bath at her corner washstand, and proceeded to get dressed.

It didn't take him long, even though he had the whole damned suit of tobacco-brown tweed he always wore on payday to get into. He rose to stomp on his low-heeled army stovepipes, strapped on the .44–40 double-action gun rig he wore cross-draw under the tweed frock coat, and reached for the battered brown Stetson he wore with a Colorado crush. Then he cleared his throat and asked the still-nude lady on the bed if there was anything he could do for her, now, or if she was just crying because it felt so good.

She sobbed, "Oh, why oh why I act so crazy just because you got big shoulders and wicked smile? I never been wicked befo'. Now how I gonna stop, poo' me?"

Longarm could see her silvery form more clearly now. So he suggested, "Try to keep it in mind that I'm sort of large, even for my breed, and that I've had to arrest many a white man for killing his woman. See you tonight, when I drop by for some more chop suey?"

She gasped, "Oh, no! Don't you come Golden Dragon no more after what you do last night to me! How I gonna facing

3

such a customer without I blushing like a rose! You *got* your forbidden fruit for dessert, bad boy. We gotta cut this crap befo' we get killed by vigilante boys! Promise me you never come Golden Dragon again?"

He said he did and put on his hat. But as he turned to go, the pretty waitress turned over, sat up, and pouted, "Goddamn, don't you wanna *argue* about it?"

Longarm answered, "Nope. It hurts like fire to say adios for all time to such a pretty little thing, Miss Ching Mi, but I told you last night, as you were telling me how unwise it might be to enjoy forbidden fruit for dessert, that if you'd only try it and then tell me you didn't like it, we'd say no more about it."

By this time he had his hand on the knob. So Ching Mi had no choice but to say, "Oh, shit! Wise man saying, after loaf cut, one more slice no big deal. I get off same time tonight. You better wait outside on Cherry Creek bridge, right?"

He chuckled fondly and told her, "Maybe. I told you when you asked how come I hadn't been by in a while, before we got around to discussing dessert, that I travel some in my job." She pouted and demanded, "Goddamn, you wanna make more nice-nice with me tonight or not? What you think I am, goddamn free and easy girl?"

He smiled crookedly down at her to remark, "I had to work like hell, as I recall. But, like I said, my whereabouts at a given moment can be a sometimes thing. I *hope* we're staring at an off-duty weekend and, if we are, one can only pray we both survive it. But my boss, Marshal Vail, has upset my weekend plans more times than he has any right to, when you consider what Justice *pays* a poor, hard-up deputy. So, in sum, I'll get back to you as soon as I can. If you have a better offer between now and then, don't let me stand in the way."

For some reason that made her throw a pillow at him, hard. So he ducked out into the hallway, which was still mercifully dark, and didn't encounter any other early risers as he left via the back door of the somewhat squalid rooming house. His own hired digs were just up the way, since both nonwhite and underpaid residents of Denver were expected to bed down on this unfashionable side of Cherry Creek. But Longarm didn't head for home. He was already up and reasonably clean, and there were limits to how many times he wanted to sneak in and out of back doors on the same fool morning.

His attempt at discretion came to an end as he left the alley running behind Ching Mi's block. He ran into a Denver beat cop walking his rounds with unseemly diligence despite the ungodly hour. The copper badge recognized Longarm, which may well have prevented him from demanding some explanations, but prompted him to ask Longarm, "Out to change your luck?"

Longarm sniffed in a dignified manner and replied, "I was just investigating a possible federal offense, Muldoon."

To which the copper badge answered, with a knowing grin, "Sure you were. Any man can see we're only six or seven hundred miles from the border, and them Chinamen will sneak across every chance we give 'em. Was we investigating that plump little gal as works for Lum Fat's laundry, or the Widow Chang, who runs that novelty shop down to Wazee Street? I hear they both like big men."

Longarm took a brace of three-for-a-nickel cheroots from a vest pocket and offered one to Officer Muldoon as he sincerely assured his fellow peace office that he had never had occasion to even flirt with either of the ladies just mentioned.

As they lit up, Muldoon commented, with a thoughtful frown, "I might have knowed a wiseass like yourself would have tumbled to the fact that that Arapaho breed gal, Alice Yellowpony, wasn't the prim and proper little church-choir gal some take her for."

Longarm recalled the lady in question. For he'd often seen her passing by his own rooming house with her nose in the air and a psalm book clutched to her otherwise interesting breast. He took a thoughtful drag on his smoke before he said, "I reckon a man walking a beat with a healthy interest in country matters don't miss much, eh?"

Muldoon, in Longarm's opinion, smoked too fast on a cheroot that cost so much, as he confided in a dirty-little-boy tone, "All Injuns like music. But when she ain't showing off her high soprano, old Alice is said to enjoy low life as much as the rest of us. So, fess up, Longarm, how was it?"

Longarm repressed a grimace of distaste as he replied, "You're taking the name of a lady in vain, Muldoon. You have my word I have never even heard the lady in question sing in church. Ah, which church would that be, by the way?"

Muldoon said, "First Baptist, on Walnut Street. They let anybody in, the fools. But, no shit, Longarm, if you weren't messing with any of them free and easy gals on that block, what *were* you up to just now?"

Longarm smiled mysteriously and said, "Nothing that comes under the jurisdiction of Denver P.D. I pack a federal badge, remember?"

Muldoon did. He also recalled how another Denver beat man called Nolan had wound up with sergeant's stripes after backing Longarm's play during a burglary attempt at the Tabor mansion. So he stood there staring wistfully after the tall federal lawman as Longarm strode off toward the Cherry Creek bridge.

By this time it was light enough to see colors, and the night aboard a Chinese waitress after a supper of Chinese food had left Longarm hungry as a wolf. He knew nothing edible would be available this far from downtown Denver. But he still kept an eye open for a place that just might be open this early as he clomped across the wooden foot bridge and headed for Larimer Street. The Golden Dragon was out of his way by a block, and he knew they didn't open before noon in any case, since hardly anyone he knew ate Chinese food for breakfast. As he passed a not-yet-open corner cigar store, he suddenly recalled a bitty Mex bodega up that side street. He'd never yet passed it to see it closed, so he nodded to the wooden Indian on duty in front of the cigar store and swung that way, stomach growling.

As he approached the gay red and lime-green awning he saw the bitty bodega was indeed open for business. He was too hungry to worry about sitting down to be served. Like most such neighborhood establishments, they'd likely have tortillas, cerveza, and maybe some cheese they were willing to sell by the slice, and a man who couldn't fashion his own sandwich on the fly with a beer bottle in one hand wasn't really hungry.

6

As he approached, he saw that the owner, a fat old Mex, seemed to be waiting on another customer ahead of him. So Longarm paused to admire a banana stalk hanging from the awning out front as the Mex went on jawing with the other man, a sort of rat-faced gent sporting a straw skimmer, a striped summer jacket, and a diamond pinky ring that was just too flashy to be real.

How another hungry early riser dressed was none of Longarm's business, of course, but he couldn't help overhearing some of the flashy dresser's conversation with the somewhat confused old Mex. Like Longarm, the bodega owner was perhaps beginning to wonder why the dapper stranger wanted to be so good to him so early in the morning.

Longarm had an advantage on the Mexican victim of the old but seldom failing Gypsy Switch Con. As a lawman, Longarm was of course *supposed* to know more about such business transactions than the average citizen. So when the gent in the striped jacket got to the part about the Mex allowing him to hold some money in trust, if they were to be such trusting pards, Longarm tapped the con man on the shoulder, smiled pleasantly down at him as he turned, and planted a stinging left hook in the center of his innocent rat face.

It felt good, to Longarm. The recipient of his solid blow went down, of course, and then proceeded to imitate a stuck pig that had somehow learned to cuss in English.

The startled Mex, who'd been in the process of making a lot of money with the help of a man now sitting on the damp sidewalk, cussed Longarm in Spanish and added, "Have you gone loco en la cabeza, señor? For why did you just hit my friend in such a manner?"

"It's the only way I know how to hit with my left," Longarm replied. "It's dumb to lead with your right. He's not your friend, Viejo. So listen sharp while I explain some other facts of life to the scumbucket. Are you listening to me, scumbucket?"

The man he'd just downed stared in wonder at his own bloody fingertips as he marveled, "You split my lip, goddamn you. I've a good mind to have the law on you, cowboy!"

Longarm chuckled fondly down at him and said, "I'm

sorry about that. I was aiming to bust your nose. But you flinched at the last. You must be used to getting sucker punched by now, Rom. So while we both know you ain't about to go anywhere near the law, I'd best advise you I happen to *be* the law!"

As the gypsy began to protest his innocence, Longarm cut in with, "I ain't done yet. Lucky for you I'm federal. My boss would chew my ass if I drug such a petty crook to work with me. But, speaking purely as a private citizen of these United States and a resident of this fair city as well, I'm telling you flat out that you and your little game ain't welcome in these parts. So why don't you do yourself a favor and get out of town before we meet again? It's only fair to warn you I wander all over town, a lot, and that every time I see you I mean to bounce you on your ass until you get my message, hear?"

The one he'd knocked down might have. But before he could answer, an Irish brogue to Longarm's rear yelled, "Longarm! Duck!" Then, since Officer Muldoon's warning was punctuated by the sound of gunshots—three, at least—Longarm dove headfirst at the portly old Mex in the doorway. The two of them wound up on the sawdust-covered floor inside. Longarm was on top. So the skinny old Mex lady who tore out from the back with a broom got a few good licks in before Longarm could roll out of the way and, as the Mex sat up, she hit *him* alongside the head hard enough to make him call her awful things in Spanish. So she stopped.

By this time Longarm was back on his feet with his own gun drawn. He crouched in the doorway with the muzzle of his .44-40 trained on the scene out front in hopes of making a lick of sense of it. Doors and windows were popping open up and down the narrow street. Some men, a lot of women, and a mess of kids were hollering fit to bust. The con man he'd sat on the walk was still there, now stretched out total, with his face in worse shape than Longarm recalled putting it in with his fist.

Officer Muldoon was striding across the street toward them, his billy in one big fist and smoking six-gun in the other as he called out, "Are you hit, Longarm?"

8

The taller and leaner federal lawman rose to full height and stepped gingerly into view as he called back, "Not by anything more ominous than a broom. What in thunder was all that noise about just now?"

Muldoon said, "You can't see him from there. He's behind that big cottonwood tree across the way. He was drawing a bead on your back from the cover of the tree when I seen my duty and done it. Now it's your turn to tell me just what we've wrought here this fine morning. For my precinct captain will be vexed as hell if I can't offer him at least a few words of explanation for the shooting of these two darlings!"

Longarm kept his own gun out—it was that kind of neighborhood—as he quickly moved over to the nearest corpse, dropped to one knee, and patted the striped jacket down for hardware.

To his considerable relief, he found a bitty .32 whore pistol tucked in an inside pocket. As Muldoon joined him, Longarm rose to hand Denver P.D. the dangerous weapon, saying, "It's a good thing I saw him going for that gun as you threw down on him, pard. To tell the truth, I didn't think he wanted to make a fight of it. But we live and learn."

Muldoon shrugged and replied. "Oh, well, I had my gun out in any case, and I've heard it's not a good notion, once shooting starts, to leave anyone on the other side feeling left out." Then he added, "Jesus Mary and Joseph, will you look at them kids!" He turned to head back across the street, waving his billy as he roared, "Leave that dead man's boots alone, you scamps! Have you no shame and can't you see they're evidence?"

By this time police whistles were tweeting in the distance. So as the kids ran off, jeering, but at least moving in the right direction, Longarm turned to the old Mex and his wife, now staring thunderstruck from the doorway, and said, "It's likely to get even more confusing to you folk before it gets less. So I'd best explain what just transpired here."

The Mex said he sure wished *someone* would. So Longarm told him, "I don't want to know how that con man was putting it just before I spoiled his play. We both know he sold you a bill of goods that called for a little larceny in your soul."

The Mex started to protest. Longarm shushed him with a wave of his .44-40 and said, "Pay attention. I'm federal, not state or city. So I just don't care whether the two of you were fixing to get rich together by collecting a reward on a wallet he just happened to find on your sawdust, or whether he'd convinced you a smart young gent like you could make a lot more money, on the side, selling something less wholesome than groceries at such a handy location. As I walked up, he'd already gotten you to the gypsy switch. The two of you were to each chip in a nice hunk of cash for him to wrap in a kerchief and hold as security while his pard and fellow gypsy ran whatever errand the three of you were to get rich on, right?"

The older man frowned and said, "There *was* another hombre with him just before you came to join us. I had forgotten all about him."

Longarm sighed and said, "I should have my head examined for a piss-poor sense of timing. I hadn't heard the whole pitch. But I should have recalled the details of the way the game works. I reckon the shill spied *me* first, then ducked across the street to act as lookout, and we all know how *that* developed."

Longarm holstered his gun as he spotted more copper badges in the distance and continued, "Suffice it to say, what I busted up works like so. The one con artist stays with the mark, that's you, and after his sidekick fails to return in a spell, he hands the security bundle to you, since by this time he knows he can trust *you*, and lights out to see what could be keeping the *other* rascal. Assuming you're the average mark, you'd wait some more before, when *neither* came back, you'd get about to opening the package. You'd figure that if something had gone wrong, the least you were entitled to would be your own share back and, assuming you're human, you'd sort of hope they'd never come back so you could keep that *other* sucker's share."

"I am a man of honor," the old Mex protested.

Longarm just smiled thinly and replied, "Whether you are or not don't matter with the gypsy switch. Either way, when you open the carefully tied kerchief, you find *all* the money

10

somehow turned to newsprint. It's such a simple trick that I'll be switched with snakes if I can see how grown men and women can fall for it. But they do, over and over. That's how come I wasn't even paying the attention *I* should have to the details just now."

As if to remind him of his own lapse in underestimating the desperation of small-time crooks, Muldoon rejoined them with a sergeant in tow. So Longarm had to spell it all out again, albeit fellow lawmen were able to grasp things quicker and clearer. It wasn't too clear whether the old Mex had figured it out yet or not. But it didn't matter when the sergeant clapped Muldoon on the back to say, "Sure and all's well that ends well, and it's a grand job you just did, Muldoon. But I still don't understand how you happened to be on this side of Cherry Creek when you came to the rescue of this federal man in dire need."

"I knew he was on a case," Muldoon said. "He told me so. I'd say I just proved to everyone's satisfaction that while Longarm likes to work alone, he may not always be as able to cope with dangerous criminals as he'd have us think. For the one across the way had Longarm dead in his sights when I swung yon corner, just in the nick of time!"

The sergeant stared morosely down at the closer cadaver as he observed, "That likely accounts for the way his lungs wound up plastered to cottonwood bark. Whatever might have possessed you to blow half *this* one's skull off, Muldoon?"

Longarm, who'd had to explain such tedious details a mite more often, chimed in with, "He was reaching for a Harrington Richardson .32 when your man fired first. Show the man the gun, Muldoon."

As the somewhat trigger-happy beat man did so, another copper badge joined them, saying, with a jerk of his thumb, "I recognize the face of the one across the way in connection with a tintype in our rogues gallery, Sarge."

He grimaced down at the one at their feet and added, "This one would be tough for his *mother* to recognize now. But if they was working together, I'd say our Muldoon just depleted the Wicked Watsons some."

The sergeant brightened and asked, "Are we talking about

11

that clan of Scotch gypsies wanted in many a state and territory for shearing sheep without a permit?"

"We are," the other copper badge replied with a nod. "This'd be the first time members of the band resorted to gunplay, as far as we know. So, judging from the results, I'd say Muldoon may have nipped a new disgusting habit in the bud."

Longarm read newspapers too, so he knew what they were talking about now. He said, "It was likely just panic, or a sudden rage occasioned by my setting an elder of the tribe on his ass." Then he caught himself and shut up. For while the Wicked Watsons were, according to the *Denver Post*, a wandering band of petty thieves and swindlers, he owed Muldoon. The nosy and officious bastard had not only saved his life, but tipped him off to three whole neighborhood gals he'd never even considered before!

The sergeant shrugged and said, "Well, the meat wagon ought to be on its way by now. Soon as we tidy up here, what say we all go down to headquarters and put the sad story down on paper for the nitpickers."

Longarm swore softly under his breath, but saw he had small choice in the matter. For although, next to mucking out a stable, nothing was more tedious than producing a sworn deposition tight enough to satisfy your average coroner's clerk, he knew he had to make Muldoon look good enough to run for governor, should he ever lose his more honest job.

★

Chapter 2

By the time Longarm left Police Headquarters it was almost noon and he still hadn't had a bite to eat since that chop suey the night before. So, seeing as he was going to get hell in any case, Longarm stopped by the Parthenon Saloon near the Federal Building to see what they had on the free lunch buffet at the end of the bar. The salty offerings of the day consisted of ham, pig's knuckles, head cheese, and German-style potato salad someone had put too much salt in as well. But he'd been aiming to wash it all down with a few schooners of needled beer and, looking on the bright side, he knew his boss, Marshal Vail, generally went home for lunch instead of paying for it with the hoi polloi from the nearby federal offices.

So Longarm felt sort of cheated as well as chagrined when, just as he was starting to feel human at one end of the bar, old Billy Vail in the flesh bellied up to the mahogany beside him, saying, "I heard. How come you let Denver P.D. have the credit? And what in thunder is that shit you're eating, old son?"

Longarm washed down the last of the pig's knuckles and potato salad he'd been gnawing before he replied soberly, "I had to let the town law have the Wicked Watsons. I didn't even shoot *one* of the rascals. Even if I had, since when have petty con games been federal?"

The older, shorter, and much dumpier Vail shrugged and said, "Every little bit helps, and that gang does like to cross state lines some. But what's done is done. I was *hoping* I'd

13

find you here about now. Would it help if I had the boys paint a stripe all the way from your rooming house to our office? You sure seem to have a tough time finding the place before the working day's half shot."

Longarm grinned sheepishly and reached for a smoke as he said, "I know it's payday, boss. I was up at the crack of dawn, I swear. But then I fell in with wicked company, and you know how picky the county coroner is when you don't cross every *t* and dot every *i*."

Vail drew a bulky manila envelope from under his own frock coat with a weary sigh, and placed it on the bar between them, saying, "You'll find your wages and expenses for the month in there with your travel orders. I told you the last time you up and vouchered a hotel honeymoon suite as a legitimate expense that the paymaster was raising hell about your honeymooning in the line of duty. So this time you're getting six cents a mile and a dollar per diem, and I don't want no argument about it, hear?"

Longarm lit his cheroot, shook out the match, and said, "It was worth a try. How come you're sending me out in the field some more? It feels like I just got back here, and I had, ah, sort of planned on spending the coming weekend here in town."

Vail tried not to smile as he replied, "I'll bet you were. You spend more time in bed than at the office when I don't give you something to keep pure. We're sending you down to the Four Corners country again. By we, I mean Justice and the B.I.A. Lord only knows what might happen if the *War Department* gets wind of Indian trouble while President Hayes is fighting 'em on military appropriations this session."

Longarm took a thoughtful drag on his cheroot before he said, "I know where the Four Corners are, sort of. It's easier to find where Utah, Colorado, New Mexico, and Arizona come together on the map than where they might on barely surveyed high desert. It's a heap easier to get lost down there than it might be to find enough Indians to matter. The Indians living in cliff dwellings stuck to the canyon walls ain't been living for some time. I met a few more lively ones the time I got to chase Iron Shirt down that way. But hardly enough to interest the fool army, even if they'd been acting meaner."

Marshal Vail nodded and said, "I know it's hard and mostly useless country. That's doubtless why the B.I.A. has set most of it aside for Ute and Navajo."

Longarm whistled softly and said, "I'd like to be excused for the rest of the afternoon, boss. I know the way you get appointed an Indian agent is by voting the right ticket and writing fifty words or less on the topic of Hiawatha. But you'd think even the B.I.A. would know what an explosive mixture Ute and Navajo make. The only thing them distinctly different brands of noble savages have in common is a mutual dislike, going back to before Columbus took that wrong turn on his way to India. If I were running the B.I.A., I'd want Ute and Navajo reserved a heap of miles apart, not shoved together cheek-by-jowl in country where food and water problems can lead to down and dirty fighting among blood relations!"

"You ain't running the B.I.A., more's the pity. That may be why they asked for you, by name, to have a look-see at whatever seems to be ailing them fool Indians this summer."

"Don't the Indians know?" Longarm asked.

Vail replied with a growl, "If any *white* man knew, there'd be no point in my sending you, damn it. All the B.I.A. knows for sure is that both the Ute and Navajo seem mad as hell about something."

Longarm blew a thoughtful smoke ring and tried, "I only know a few words of either lingo. How could the B.I.A. know the two nations are at odds if they don't have some agents who know more about Ute or Navajo than me?"

"You know how hard it is for *any* white man to get a red-skin to say what's got him prune-faced and beating on his damned old drum. The Indian agents down that way can't even get them Ute and Navajo to cuss each other no more. They say both breeds seem to be avoiding all contact with whites, and you know how serious *that* could read, don't you?"

"I do. It could mean an arrow up my poor white ass, and I'd take that serious as hell. How come you and the B.I.A. like me so much, boss?"

"Someone with your experience in dealing with redskins

has to contact 'em, find out what's gong on, and see if you can keep a lid on whatever it is until the B.I.A. can fix it."

Longarm snorted in disgust and protested, "Why not ask me to walk on water while I'm at it? You know the trouble I had tracking down Iron Shirt that time, and that was a case of white on white. How in thunder am I supposed to tree even one Indian in canyon country he knows better than me, let alone two whole infernal tribes? You don't know them parts like I do, Billy, and *I* hardly know enough of them to matter. It's a pure maze of flat-topped wooded mesas cut up into a great big jigsaw puzzle by canyons great and small. They only have the main canyons on the fool map. I found me a whole dead city one time where the map shows open range. That's what the survey crews call county-sized hunks of real estate they never got around to, open range. I'm more likely to lose myself than find any Indians who ain't aiming to be found down there, Billy."

"Try to be careful. You know I love you like a son, old son. Your best bet would be by rail as far as Durango. I had old Henry in the front office route you that far via the Denver and Rio Grande and the narrow-gauge through Wagon Wheel Gap. Once you detrain at Durango you'll be able to requisition a government mount at the Ute agency just four or five miles south."

Longarm finished his beer, put down the schooner, and picked up the big envelope, saying, "It sounds like a fool's errand, but if I wasn't a fool I wouldn't be working for you. I'd best go home to my furnished digs and start packing."

But Vail said, "I wish you wouldn't. The matter is urgent and you got a train to catch within the hour."

Longarm protested, "Dammit, Billy, I just hate to ride bareback and, even then, not in this sissy suit you make me wear around the Federal Building. I'd have dressed more cow and drug saddle and Winchester after me this morning had I known you were in such a hurry to get me scalped, but—"

"I don't think Navajo scalp," Vail cut in, adding, "Ute sure do, of course. So be careful. I want you aboard that next D and RG. That's an order. The Indian pony won't cost anything. Bill us for a sensible saddle and saddle gun, pick up some trail duds over in Durango, and we'll pay for 'em as long as you go easy on woolly chaps and sateen shirts, hear?"

"Have you ever had the feeling you were being sold a gold brick by a pal, old pal?"

Vail looked innocent as he replied, "I don't know what you're talking about. Don't you want to work for me no more?"

Longarm said, "I reckon it beats herding cows, but—"

"But me no buts and make sure you don't miss that train," his boss cut in.

So Longarm left, muttering to himself as Vail regarded his departing figure with an expression of high pleasure and low cunning. Then Vail glanced up at the clock above the bar, knowing it ran a quarter hour slow lest paying customers miss that last one for the road, and hit the road back to the Federal Building.

The noonday sun was warming things up a mite, and as the thickset U.S. marshal moved up the granite steps on his stubby legs, he was inclined to regret not having ordered at least one beer back there. But slick timing had been of the essence and, if he'd timed it wrong, he was in deep dung indeed.

Old Billy Vail was red-faced and puffing by the time he'd made it to his office on the second floor. As he entered the waiting room he cast an anxious eye on the pasty-faced young dude who played the typewriter for him and asked, "Is she here yet, Henry?"

His employee and fellow conspirator smiled and murmured, "I sent her into your private office to wait, as instructed, sir."

Vail beamed down at him. "Keep up the good work and someday you'll have your own private pencil sharpener, Henry."

The wan youth looked sort of wistful as he replied, "I'd rather be a deputy someday, sir."

Vail didn't answer. Everybody seemed to want to tell him how to run the outfit these days. He bulled on into his oak-paneled inner sanctum, glanced at the banjo clock on one wall, and saw to his relief that by this time Longarm would be

17

almost to the Union Depot, if he didn't run into a pretty gal or an ugly outlaw along the way. He removed his hat with a flourish and turned to the pretty gal seated in the leather chair near his desk. "I'm sorry if I kept you waiting, Jessie. I got tied up down the hall in court and—Land's sake, if you don't just keep getting prettier every time I lay my poor old eyes on you!"

Jessica Starbuck was used to being told she was beautiful, and brought up well enough to accept the compliment with a gracious smile that could be read any old way a man wanted to take it. She was glad Uncle Billy, as she thought of the gruff old bear who'd once ridden with her late father, hadn't repeated that dumb observation on how she'd *grown* since last he'd bounced her on his knee. Uncle Billy had, in fact, done exactly that more than once in his Ranger days down in Texas, when the world was younger and Dad was still alive. But since then a lot had happened, and her dad's old pal knew it. Dad was gone, cut down in the prime of life by crooks out to grab his Starbuck Enterprises and, to keep the empire he'd built in the family, his daughter had cut a few men down as well.

She hadn't held on to Starbuck Enterprises by gunplay alone. So she waited until the stocky marshal had moved around behind the desk and taken his own seat before getting down to business.

Vail didn't really want to get down to business just yet. So he made a grand show of lighting one of the expensive but pungent cigars he admired as he admired his younger guest.

He knew her age, give or take a few years, but Jessie was one of those fine-boned beauties who could pass for anything from sixteen to thirty-six, depending on how she wanted to be taken. At the moment she looked, say, twenty-five, with her honey blonde hair pinned proper under a ladylike straw boater, and her mighty feminine but rawhide-tough figure dressed for town in a summer-weight Paris frock that was either gray or lavender, depending on how the light hit it. The only thing that gave the show away, and then only to a keen-eyed old pro like Billy Vail, was the pair of gunmetal spurs she wore on cordovan footwear that looked a lot more Justin than high-button. He knew she always packed a gun. He wondered idly where and what caliber as he stalled for time with his smoke.

He knew he was pressing his luck when Jessie asked flatly, "Where is Custis, Uncle Billy?"

Vail took a drag on his cigar, glanced at the clock again, and told her, "Longarm's out of town at the moment, honey. I fear I'd already sent him out in the field before your night letter was delivered by Western Union this morning."

Jessie swore—under her breath, of course—and added, "We need him badly. We don't have much time, either. When do you expect him back?"

"Hard to say with Longarm. But let's study on your night letter a spell, little darling. Don't you still have that big Japanese on your payroll if you want somebody bent all outta shape for you?"

Jessie frowned. "In the first place, my friend, Ki, is my *segundo*, not an employee. In the second place, he's only half Japanese."

"I know. But he still knows all them Japanese tricks if you need a door opened, sudden, with a foot or anything *else* he wants to put through it. Why didn't you bring old Ki along if this fool notion about lost Indian gold mines is likely to call for rough stuff?"

"Ki's at the hotel with the girl I wired you about. Honestly, Uncle Billy, did you read my message at all?" Jessie sighed.

Vail had. Longarm's remarks about him being a fool for paperwork were not without foundation. *Somebody* in the outfit had to do the less interesting chores. But to give himself more time, Vail allowed himself to seem more foolish than he really was by saying, "I read it. Can't say it made much sense to me, even reading it twice. Maybe you'd best fill me in some more, honey. You lost me when you got to the part about wanting to help some Paiute gal find her white daddy's mine near the headwaters of the San Juan."

Jessie took a deep breath in order to keep her voice lady-like. "In the first place, the mine's not lost. We know where it is, between the Chaco and the Mancos, close to where they come together to form the San Juan. In the second place, Victoria Miller is not what I'd call a Paiute gal. Like Ki, she's half American. You know how the law reads on that, Uncle Billy. Dear Uncle Quanah Parker is living white these days."

Vail smiled thinly and said, "It's certainly an improvement on the way he was living as a war chief of the Comanche, before he figured he was half white. I follow your drift on this breed gal you've adopted, Jessie. I'd say that if federal law could overlook a pure white Mormon having a dozen wives, it would have no call to deny a lady with some Indian blood her own gold mine. But if you say you know where her property is, and you got that big tough Ki to back your play, why in thunder would you need Longarm?"

"Two reasons. We don't know who we're up against. All Victoria knows is that her father was working a rich vein, lonesome, when he simply vanished from human ken. Victoria was in school, back east, boarding with white relations she and her father took for friends, until the money stopped coming. They threw her out. She had to go to work as a domestic servant. Fortunately for her, I needed a maid when I was back east last year on business, and I hired her from an agency."

Billy Vail leaned back in his swivel chair to say dryly, "That's when she told you she was an Indian princess with a gold mine, and of course you took her serious?"

"There's more to running my late father's vast holdings than riding and roping." Jessie shook her head. "Naturally, I have business contacts all through the west, and a lot of places you'd be surprised about. I got in touch with the Bureau of Mines. There *was* an Isaak Miller, and he did have an Indian wife—lawfully, by the way—and he did indeed sell high grade, once a year, through the Provo assay office, until he just stopped coming out of the desert a few years ago."

Vail nodded soberly and said, "Making your former maid his lawful heir, whether he's really dead or not. So who's disputing her infernal claim, honey?"

"That's the second reason we need Custis to help. I didn't simply verify the girl's story. I sent some good prospectors who've worked for me in the past to go have a look at the property. Twice. Neither party ever returned. That's why Ki, Victoria, and I don't want to enter those canyonlands without a damned good guide as well as a fighting man. A while ago, when Custis was, ah, visiting me in Texas, he told me about a case he'd worked on down that way. Ki may be able to pass for an Indian better, but Custis really has a way with them and, well, he already knows the Indians down in that area."

"How do you know it was Indians who vanished the gal's father? Indians don't get as excited about gold as some. Sounds more like claim jumpers to me."

Jessie nodded and said, "That's exactly what Ki thinks. Victoria is not as sure. You see, one of the reasons her father sent her east was that she *was* Paiute, or partly so at any rate, and the Indians her father had to deal with near his mine seemed to have it in for Paiute."

"I'm glad I ain't no Paiute. I've always considered 'em harmless enough. But everyone else seems to want to use 'em for target practice."

Jessie glanced at the wall clock this time before she told him, "Victoria says her mother's folk have ever drawn fire because they're not so good at shooting back. But, getting back to the fortune her white father may have left her, whether Isaak Miller was killed by Indians or claim jumpers, Custis would be able to find out, wouldn't he?"

Vail studied the ash on the end of his cigar. "If anyone could, he'd be the one, most likely. Now I want to tell you something, Jessie Starbuck, and I want you to listen sharp."

She said she would. So Vail said, "For openers, what's between you and Longarm ain't none of my business. But I sure have caught hell from Washington for some of the *other* games you cute little kids have played in the past. I don't know how to put it polite, but U.S. Deputy Custis Long works for the Justice Department, not Starbuck Enterprises."

She blushed just a shade and almost snapped, "You're right. I'm a grown woman and Custis is surely old enough to vote. So how we feel about one another is nobody's business but our own!"

"I ain't finished. I don't think even Washington cares about Longarm's personal life. What the First Lady, old Lemonade Lucy Hayes, don't know, won't hurt her. But they did get vexed, and told me so in no uncertain terms, the time you, Ki, and Longarm invaded Mexico and almost got us into another

21

war with the same. You diverted my deputy entirely from the case I'd sent him on and, before it was over, the three of you had massacred half the Mexican army, with artillery, for God's sake!"

Jessie grinned like a mean little kid and said, "We thought it was only fair, Uncle Billy. They'd only hauled those big guns up to shoot at *us* with. Besides, in the end Custis resolved the case neatly, with all the bad guys you'd sent him after dead, remember?"

Vail looked disgusted and replied, "Along with a mess of either innocent or not-so-innocent Mex rurales and federales. The point is that I have orders from Washington, *direct,* not to let you and Longarm get within a country mile of one another if I can help it."

Jessie glanced at the clock again. Then she heaved a gallant but defeated little sigh. "In other words, as soon as you knew I was coming to Denver to look Custis up again, you sent him out of town."

It was a statement, not a question. She started to rise. Then Billy Vail said, "Sit down and pay attention to your elders, you willful child. I'll tell you when I'm done, dammit."

She sat back down, but said reproachfully, "I don't need a glass of orange juice to get the bitter pill down, Uncle Billy. I'm a big girl now, and if Custis isn't here he isn't here."

"I was about to tell you where he is, or will be," Vail told her. "You understand, of course, that while we both know I can't give a direct order to a pesky woman with no sense of proportion when things get a mite noisy, you've been *told,* and *warned,* what a dim view I take of my hired help behaving at all noisy in your company."

She said she'd try to be good, if ever she and Longarm met again. So Vail growled, "Good. This very morning, just after your night letter arrived, I got a really dumb request from the Bureau of Indian Affairs. I don't work for them any more than I work for Starbuck Enterprises. So, as both requests read dumb as hell, I was fixing to toss 'em in the wastebasket together. Then it occurred to me that here was a fat cat in Washington asking me to send Longarm on a fact-finding mission to, guess where?"

22

"Not the Four Corners!" she cried with delight.

"You peeked. Anyway, like I said, I can't help you look for lost gold mines with any of my deputies. So if I ever find Longarm got together with you and that homicidal lunatic Ki again, I'm likely to get mad as hell. So, should you run into him down in the Four Corners, don't you dare lead him down no more primrose paths, hear?"

Jessie leaped to her feet and moved over to give Billy Vail a big hug as he rose from behind the desk. "I knew we could count on you, Uncle Billy. But just where in the Four Corners did you send Custis? It's big country, you know."

"A lot of it's mighty empty, as well. If I know you and that rascal deputy of mine, you won't have too much trouble bumping, ah, noses. Just remember, under oath, that I begged and pleaded for you to stay the hell away from him and didn't even tell him you was coming."

She dimpled at him. "I have to dash back to the hotel and start making travel arrangements. I guess over the South Pass and down the Mormon Delta would get us there about as fast as anything, right?"

Vail looked away as he murmured, "One way's as hard as another getting to a place one just can't *get* to from here."

She started to leave. Then she turned in the doorway to ask him thoughtfully, "Uncle Billy, if you hadn't had that request from the B.I.A. as an excuse, how would we have ever managed it?"

He told her, "We'd have thunk of something." She pecked him on the cheek and left, laughing.

Vail went back to his desk and sat down, feeling older. He was a happily married man, most of the time, but there was nothing like having a pretty young gal kiss you, meaning it innocent and no doubt expecting you to feel the same, to make a man aware that he wasn't getting any younger.

He'd just gotten his smoke going again when young Henry came in to ask, "May I put that request from the B.I.A. back in the files, sir?"

"I already did. Only wanted a couple of dates and such. Have you typed up that letter approving their dumb notion?"

Henry said, "I have. But, no offense, there's something I

23

don't understand here, sir. That request from the B.I.A. has been sitting there unanswered for a good three weeks and—"

"I never answer 'til I'm goddamned good and ready!" Vail cut in. "Let that be a lesson to you, Henry. Never throw a scrap of paper away and never write one 'til you have to. A man just never knows when he may need some paper to cover his ass."

"If you say so, sir. It was my understanding you meant to *turn down* that B.I.A. request as both dangerous and unprofitable."

"I was," Vail said, "'til I saw some *profit* in helping another government agency out, while doing a little favor for the daughter of an old pal. Don't try to understand me, Henry. Sometimes I get so slick I surprise myself."

Chapter 3

The luxurious suite of rooms that Jessie had hired at the Palace Hotel overlooked the entrance of the Union Depot across the way. Her "Uncle Billy" hadn't thought of everything. But Victoria Miller didn't know Longarm on sight, and the somewhat mysterious Amerasian called Ki was shaving in the adjoining bath in any case. His ancestry was almost as confusing as how he'd wound up in the American west, and so the tall and muscular Ki—or Kiai, in his mother's lingo—had to shave as often as most white men.

He was shaving carefully, aware he wouldn't get the chance to do so with hot hotel water for a spell, once Jessie got back with that mighty handy but somewhat annoying Longarm. The notion of pressing on into Indian country that Longarm knew, *without* him, had never crossed Ki's mind. Aside from being tall and tough, the two of them had nothing in common but a mutual regard for the honey-haired Miss Starbuck. Ki knew human nature, including his own, well enough to grasp the simple fact that it was just how *much* Longarm regarded Jessie, and vice versa, that made it hard for him to take the dry humor and West-By-God-Virginia twang of the slightly taller Custis Long. But Ki had to admit they made a good team in a fight and, so far, they'd avoided fighting one another, serious.

Taking a last lick for luck with his straight razor, retempered in the Nihongo way by a man who knew his steel, Ki regarded his freshly shaved face in the mirror as he wiped the lather off with a wet towel. He made sure he got it all. The warm water he got on his chest didn't matter to a man stripped to the waist as much as soap itch under a shirt might on a long train ride in high summer. Ki was only interested in looking halfway presentable. He no longer worried about looking sort of odd to American eyes. Looking sort of Occidental to his mother's people and sort of Oriental to his father's people had only confused him when he'd first come to America as a young adult. He knew that in a pinch a man as big and tough as him could pass for either, if he insisted, and to the credit of his father's folk, Americans weren't quite as race-conscious as most Japanese, which had been one good reason to leave Japan in the first place.

He fit in better, here, to the extent any person of mixed blood could feel he fit in anywhere. His English was perfect. He could sound like a Texas good old boy if he wanted to, and few Texans were impolite enough to comment on the features of a man who, for all they knew, could be a mighty tall Texan with Comanche blood. It seldom occurred to anyone to take him for part Chinese, since intermarriage between whites and Orientals was forbidden by statute law in most western states, while Japanese were still rare in *any* state. So most pure Americans had to see Ki in action before they sensed that whatever he might be, it sure didn't act *human* in a fight.

Ki, like Longarm, suffered no false modesty about his fighting skills. He was segundo and bodyguard to Jessie Starbuck for one good simple reason. Alex Starbuck, Jessie's late father, had been a good friend of Ki's own American father, and he'd wanted a damned fine fighting man on his payroll to begin with. Ki seldom thought about the way being the product of two distinct fighting breeds made him a bundle of dismal surprises to any man dumb enough to start up with him. For, almost without thinking, Ki accepted both the frontier code of his father's people and the Bushido code of his mother's samurai clan. There was a lot to be said for both, and both could get a man killed if he didn't temper them with common sense. Ki did. So whether he ripped out your heart with a bowie knife or busted your neck with the edge of a horny palm depended more on opportunity of the moment than philosophical soul-searching on Ki's part.

Ki wiped himself dry and moved out to the sitting room to get a fresh shirt form his bags atop a wall table. Victoria Miller was lounging on a chaise near the window, smoking a corncob pipe. Ki knew that wasn't any good cause to dislike a pretty gal. So as he buttoned his clean work shirt on he tried to decide just *why* she made him feel uneasy.

Like Ki, the erstwhile lady's maid was obviously a neither-nor. Her features, set in a heart-shaped face, were Caucasian as well as comely. Her cheekbones were perhaps a mite high, and her dark eyes were perhaps a mite almond-shaped for a white girl's, but what gave her maternal ancestry away the most was her blue-black braided hair and copper-tan complexion. Ki had no way of knowing that back east, where Jessie had first hired and then sort of adopted the pretty little breed, Victoria had been subjected to much less polite questions about her ancestry. For she'd been working at the time in tidewater Virginia, where white folk were less used to meeting Indians, and memories of the War Between the States were still fresh. It wouldn't have mattered as much, to Ki, if the girl had been what Virginians put delicately as a lady of color. He just knew, or felt he knew, she was trouble that his real worry, Jessie Starbuck, had no business involving her self with.

As Ki tucked his shirttails in and moved over to the window seat, Victoria stretched her petite but voluptuous young body, as if luxuriating in the new blue summer dress Jessie had bought her, and said, "I'm bored. How long are we supposed to wait up here in these stuffy old rooms, anyhow?"

Ki parted the lace curtains to gaze down at the sunbaked street outside. "Until Jessie gets back, of course. We told you she had to go see that marshal pal of her father's at the Federal Building. She'll be back when she wants to be back. Meanwhile, if you think it's hot up here on the fourth floor, the noonday sun is baking the pavement down there hot enough to fry tortillas brown."

"Pooh, I hear there's a grand view of the Rocky Mountains from atop the capitol hill, here in Denver. It would be cooler up yonder, wouldn't it?"

Ki said, "It's not that high, and the sun's coming straight down, everywhere. But ask Jessie when she gets back, and if there's time, I'll take you both up there and let you sit on the cannons the Colorado Volunteers brought back from the war. There's two of them. I'd rather sit on the grass in front of the State House, if it's all the same to you."

The pretty half-breed knocked the dottle from her pipe into a heavy glass ashtray near the chaise, and might have refilled it from her fringed leather tobacco pouch had not Ki told her, "You should not smoke so much but, if a lady has to smoke, she does not look her best smoking a corncob pipe. I suppose it's all right for a woman to smoke those French cigarettes, as long as she does so in private. But, please, a corncob pipe?"

Victoria put the pipe aside with a little bee-stung pout. "I've never been able to afford high-toned smokes," she explained. "Like I told you, the relations I was boarding with back east cast me out before I was old enough to smoke anything. It was a good thing for me the north had won the war by then. For my cousin, Lavinia, kept calling me a darkie and might have sold me as a slave if she'd been able to."

Ki turned from the window to regard her curiously. "I think you're feeling more sorry for yourself than the law would have allowed, even if the South had won. Your late father's kin were just being dumb. You're not that dark. You could pass for white, if only you'd learn to act more ladylike and get rid of that chip on your shoulder."

"Easy for *you* to say. I've noticed you ain't exactly white, but nobody would ever take you for a darkie. What are you, anyway? I heard you and Miss Jessie talking a funny lingo the other night through my bedroom door. I thought it sounded Chinese, at first. But it wasn't as singsong. I know it wasn't Ho. I remember some of my mother's lingo. You ain't part *Navajo,* are you?"

"Not hardly." Ki chuckled. "The Na-Déné tribes left Asia quite some time ago, though you wouldn't be the first to notice the similarity of speech patterns. Jessie and I speak Nihongo—you'd call it Japanese—when we don't want others to understand, or when I'm explaining a fine point of the martial arts to her."

"That's crazy. I can see you ain't pure white. But are you trying to tell me Miss Jessie ain't? Land's sake, that girl has blonde hair and green eyes, even if she is more suntanned than my snooty cousin Lavinia might approve of. Cousin Lavinia never goes out in the sun without her fancy parasol, and still puts bleaching cream on her ugly face every night before she goes to bed. But I guess I can tell a white gal with a suntan from an infernal China doll!"

"You might have just insulted both the ladies of China and Dai Nippon. They may look alike, to you, but where I was born, Chinese and Japanese got along about as well as Sioux and Crow, or Paiute and Navajo."

"The Ute hate us just as much, and they speak the same lingo as us, almost."

Ki never let information that might come in useful, later, get by him. So he raised an eyebrow and asked, "Almost?"

The half-Paiute girl explained, "Most everyone out where my mother hailed from speaks the same basic Ho, save for Apache and Navajo, who make no sense at all. But the different Ho nations can tell friends and enemies apart by their Ho *accents*. Just as an English-speaking white can tell a Texan from a Yankee or an Irishman from a Scotchman, see?"

Ki said, "I do, now. It gives me an idea as well. Could you put on a Ute accent if you were translating for us in Ute country, Victoria?"

She frowned and said, "Call me Vickie. It don't sound as snooty. I don't know how to talk Ute. I told you my poor mother was Paiute, and I barely remember the way she talked her own lingo. She died when I was eight or nine and, even before she did, my dad and her spoke mostly English. Dad could talk lots of Indian dialects. He was smart as anything. But, like I said, he felt more at home with English, and a good woman does what she can to make her man feel at home." She thought and added, "To tell the truth, my Paiute is sort of baby talk. I'd never be able to make sense to a Ute, Shoshone, or Bannock."

Ki insisted, "But you just said it was all the same basic language. As I now recall, Comanche, Hopi, and even Aztec are related to Paiute. I know lots of Americans who can sound like an Englishman, Irishman, or whatever, if they put their minds to it. So why couldn't a girl who speaks Paiute sound like a Ute, with a little practice?"

Victoria's expression indicated she wasn't used to thinking all that hard about anything, and didn't enjoy the effort. She said, "Silly, there's no way a Paiute could get to practice a Ute or Shoshone accent. A Texan may be able to talk to a Yankee long enough to imitate him, now that the war's been over a good while. But, you see, Ute don't just talk a mite different than Paiute, they kill 'em on sight. I've never held even a short conversation with a Ute gal my age. I just know from my mother's side that they speak Ho funny. I don't know what it sounds like."

"Why couldn't it work the other way, then? How would a Ute know you were a Paiute, if you didn't say you were? How well could a given Ute know the accent of a folk he never spoke to all that much?"

She said, "He wouldn't have to. Unless a stranger spoke just the way his own dear mother taught him, he'd know he was talking to a *saltu,* which means stranger. And while his momma was teaching him to talk anything, his uncle was teaching him to treat *any* strangers he might meet mean as anything."

Again, Ki's quick mind picked up on what some others might have missed. So he asked, "Why his uncle and not his father?"

Victoria regarded him with the expression of a schoolmarm wondering why a student so long in the tooth couldn't seem to grasp long division. "Don't you know *anything* about Indians? I was raised more white. For none of my poor old mother's brothers would have anything to do with her, once she married a saltu. But among all Ho speakers, it's not the father's duty to raise such kids as he might father here and there. A Paiute knows, for sure, who his or her *mother* has to be. The mother's brothers know for sure that kids their own sister had have to be his blood relations, so—"

"Right," Ki cut in, "I'd forgotten how many Indian nations are matrilineal. It sure helped Texas settle down when our Quanah Parker recalled his dear old mother, Cynthia Parker, was a white captive, and that maybe he was fighting on the wrong side, after all. No doubt she'd had more to do with raising him than his Comanche father would have and so, once he noticed the Comanche kept losing anyway . . . Hold on, I see Jessie down there now, and she just turned into the Union Depot. I don't know what Marshal Vail might have told her, but she has to be buying railroad tickets to go with his advice."

Relieved to get the chance to change a subject she found a confusing bother, Victoria said, "Good. I can't wait to get going again. What's the story between you and her, anyway?"

Ki turned a blank gaze on her to reply, "Story? I thought I told you, coming up from Texas on the Denver and Rio Grande. It's not all that complicated, ah, Vickie. When I decided to come to the States, I naturally looked up an old friend of my American father. Alex Starbuck had a finger in many a pie, and that included his import-export business to the Orient and just about anywhere else he wanted to send his clippers. We took an instant liking to one another and he hired me as a ranch foreman, not too long before he was murdered by business rivals."

Victoria sighed wearily and said, "I wasn't talking about how you got the job as Miss Jessie's bodyguard, Ki. I was talking about how close your two bodies might get when you ain't on duty."

Ki stiffened. His face went wooden. Then he said, "I'd say that was none of your damned business if it didn't look as if we'll be stuck with one another's company for a spell. For the record, I'm Jessica Starbuck's second in command, body-guard, and, I hope, her best friend. That's *all* I am to her. It's all I ever can be. It wouldn't work any other way, and we're both adult enough to understand it has to be that way."

"How come? I know the two of you spend a mess of time alone, while she's out chasing bad men as the lady vigilante. Are you trying to tell me the thought's never once crossed your mind, camped all alone with her out on the romantic moonlit range?"

Ki contented himself with cursing softly in his mother's language before he took a deep breath, let half of it out so his

31

voice wouldn't betray his emotions, and said, "Try to understand. I came to work for Starbuck Enterprises while Jessie was a teenager. We hit it off at once because, aside from her being a damned likable girl, she'd been raised by a Japanese housekeeper, spoke Nihongo like a native Japanese and, well, I was sometimes sort of homesick."

Victoria smiled knowingly and said, "That's what I meant. How long did it take you two kiddies to get around to playing doctor in the hayloft?"

"Baku kimuzukashi," Ki snapped, "it was nothing like that at all. When old Alex was murdered, Jessie had to fight for her far-flung inheritance against an army of hired guns. Before it was over a lot of men were dead and some others had begun to know her as Lone Star. Partly because she fought mostly alone, Texas style, and partly because I'd taught her how to hit silently, at a distance, with a star-shaped *shuriken.* Tucked in her hatband, a shuriken looks something like a lawman's silver star, until she lets fly with it and . . . All that's neither here nor there, Vickie. The important point is that I'm just her backup, as ferocious as the situation may call for, but platonic, the way it has to be between a highborn lady and the one man she can depend on, *always.*"

Victoria shrugged and said, "If you say so. I still don't see why. Don't she have any boyfriends at all?"

Ki looked as if he'd been slapped with a wet rag and was trying not to show it bothered him as he answered stiffly, "Both of us have natural appetites. But, working together as we do, our relationship has to be that of, well, a devoted brother and sister, see?"

"No. I never had a brother. But I once caught Cousin Lavinia playing doctor in the attic with Cousin Fred, and it looked to me as if they sure enjoyed it. What's so wrong with brothers and sisters having fun together, anyway? I mean, I know the Good Book says it's wrong. But it don't explain *how come.*"

Ki grimaced. "Sometimes I think that's where the religion of my father's folk slipped up. The Eastern sages took more time *explaining* the wages of sin instead of leaving it up to Jehova to deal with via thunder and lightning. Incest isn't wrong because of the act, itself. It's the sticky situations it can lead to that's made incest a sin to almost every society on earth." He smiled wearily at her and added, "Next thing I know you will be asking me why women aren't allowed to join armies. Just take my word for it that people fight better, side by side, when sex is not on their minds."

Victoria shrugged and said, "Well, it ain't my problem. I guess if she don't want you playing doctor with her, she'd have small call to get upset with me if *I* sort of let you examine me now and again, right?"

Before Ki could answer, if there was a sensible answer, they both heard Jessie calling from the other room, *"Anata wa doko ni imasu ka?"*

Ki called back, *"Aisatu,* we're here in the sitting room, Jessie." He repressed the urge to add they were playing doctor, since she'd apparently gotten back just in time.

Jessie came in waving the string of railroad tickets she'd just purchased across the street and said, "We have less than an hour to catch our train to Utah Territory. I just got Uncle Billy to tell me where Custis Long is heading and you only get three guesses."

Ki rose from his window seat with a puzzled frown, saying, "I wouldn't be surprised to meet that man anywhere, Jessie. But isn't Utah out of our way if we're going to the headwaters of the San Juan in the Four Corners country? I've been going over the maps and railroad timetables. We'd make a lot better time if we took the Denver and Rio Grande southwest and changed to the narrow-gauge to Durango."

Jesse said, "I know it's out of our way as the crow flies. But the law's not run by crows. We have to deal with some paperwork with a county judge before pressing on to the Miller mine in the canyon country. My legal staff says, and I can see why, that it would make little sense to just *locate* a gold strike we already know is there. We have to sew up a proper claim for Victoria. It was one thing for her late father to wander out of canyons with a burro-load of color. But the poor girl wouldn't be in this fix if he'd thought to file his claim properly with the territorial and federal authorities before he chose to vanish on us all."

Ki didn't argue. He knew Jessie hired lawyers with the same care she used to hire cowhands, clipper crews, or, come to think of it, half-Oriental segundos. As a man of action as well as a man of mostly Shinto legal education, Ki was content to let the Texas law firm of Peters and Cohan worry about the pestiferous small print it took to get things done in this country. One of the few things Ki and Longarm had ever agreed on was that it sure took a lot of small print to just act natural without getting in trouble with some nit-picking pencil pusher.

Jessie was saying, "Now that we're leaving the confines of civilization I think I'll travel in more comfort. It'll only take me a moment to slip into my range duds. I'll be right back."

She didn't order Ki to make sure everything else was packed. One of the nice things about Ki was that he didn't have to be told to do things. He just did them. Sometimes before she could stop him. But as she went into her own hired bedroom to change, Victoria followed, asking if there was anything she could do to help.

Leaving the door ajar—a lady didn't have to worry about Ki peeking—Jessie shook her head as she unpinned her hat and golden hair to let it fall comfortably down on her shoulders. She told the little breed, "I can manage faster on my own, dear. You might want to slip that travel duster I bought you on over that dress, though. We've a dusty and sooty ride ahead of us."

Not turning to see whether the erstwhile maid was taking her advice or not, Jessie shucked the expensive town dress as if it were corn husk and moved to the nearest chest of drawers naked as a jay, save her low-heeled riding boots and garter holster.

Victoria watched with some awe. She was more accustomed to the sight of nude flesh than most girls. But she knew that most of them felt the need of considerable whalebone to maintain the figure current fashion required. Jessica Starbuck's firm young torso hourglassed in a way the fashion plates in *Leslie's Magazine* considered just right, without a bit of artificial help.

As Jessie opened a drawer to slip on an expensive but practical silk riding shirt, Victoria asked cautiously, "Don't you wear no underthings, my lady?"

"Not in high summer, heading on to desert country. And I wish you'd stop calling me my lady, dear. I told you we were friends now, and for heaven's sake, you own a gold mine!"

As Jessie slipped into a dark-green riding skirt as well, Victoria gulped and said, "If it's still in the family, you mean. How come you're doing all this for me, Miss Jessica? I mean, I knew you were going to be a nice boss as soon as I came to work for you. But you're a high-toned lady, with lots of business of her own to tend and I . . . I'm just a half-breed orphan gal."

Jessie picked up her Stetson, but put in on only to let it hang down her back as she turned, smiled simply at the not-too-bright and sometimes annoying waif as she told Victoria, "You're a human being. You need help. I have the time and the means to help you right now, and maybe that will make up for the time I've been too busy fighting for my own rights to worry all that much about others." She took her six-gun rig from the bedpost she'd hung it on the night before as she added with a roguish grin, "I'd feel silly with a lady's maid in the gold-mining business and, to tell the truth, I need the exercise. Now that I've about taught the men of this man's world not to mess with me, Starbuck Enterprises is nearly running itself, and I have to consider my figure. You'd better cover that figure of yours with something more practical for a long train ride. So get a move on, dear. We don't have all day."

Jessie strode into the other room, her hand-held gun belt swinging at her side, to ask Ki, "Am I likely to meet Jesse James in the parlor car or do you think I'd best carry this in my carpetbag along with my other feminine notions?"

Ki took the six-gun from her to pack it in the carpetbag atop the side table, saying, "You look sort of Calamity Jane for the main line as it is, and you can get at your side arm almost as fast if you keep this bag on the seat beside you. I just had the hotel porters carry our saratogas over to the depot and check them through. So all we have to worry about is this hand luggage, and I have three hands, at least."

Then Ki cast a wary eye at the door across the room and told her softly, in Japanese, "I would find it most desirable if you would stay here in Denver, since I can't seem to get you to forget this affair entirely, Jessica."

She replied in English, "Keep your voice low and let her *guess* we're talking behind her back. Don't *tell* her. I don't want to argue about it, Ki."

"I do," he said. "I still don't buy her story and, even if it is true, I could make better time forging on alone while you enjoyed the sights of Denver and—"

"Are you saying you can outride me?" she cut in with a frown of mock severity. "I've seen the Tabor Opera House and the Rockies from the State House steps already. Even if I hadn't, there's more to securing Victoria's inheritance than proving her father struck color somewhere between the Chaco and the Mancos. Along with my gun in that bag, I'm carrying the properly typed-up papers my lawyers prepared for at least one Mormon judge to sign. Peters and Cohan assured me the circle Isaak Miller drew on that penciled map he sent Victoria just before he vanished should be close enough, in unsurveyed land, for a rustic J.P. Once we have a notarized claim to wave at anyone we catch anywhere near the strike—"

"Jessie," Ki cut in, "that map could be a fake. You don't really know that girl. Everything she's told you could have been cut from whole cloth."

Jessie shook her blonde head and insisted, "I'm not really that stupid. I didn't take her story at face value, even though she seemed a simple, trustworthy soul the day she came to work for me. How many times do I have to tell you I had my lawyers verify the existence, and prosperity, of Isaak Miller in Utah mining circles? It's common knowledge he had an Indian wife and prospected all over the Great Basin. He was last seen, flush with gold dust, in the Four Corners country. How would a simple servant girl I met in Virginia, just outside

Washington, make up a story like that, even if it *didn't* check out?"

Ki said dryly, "Permit this simple servant boy to point out that servants working out of an employment agency near the capital of the United States wind up in lots of places, overhearing lots of conversations. Say a prospector named Isaak Miller did exist, until he hit pay dirt and somehow didn't seem to exist anymore. Who's to say that girl's really his daughter?"

"Me," Jessie said. "I paid good money to find out as much as I could, on paper, before we saddled up and rode. Peters and Cohan will no doubt send me one whopping bill at the end of the year but, meanwhile, working with Utah associates who'll likely cost me dear, as well, they were able to get copies of marriage and birth certificates that back Victoria's play. Peters and Cohan cut paper sign for me back east, too. It was easy enough to track down the relations of a reasonably well known old-timer. They sent a private detective to ask discreet questions around the neighborhood. Isaak Miller did have a sister, and she in turn had a son and daughter named Fred and Lavinia who have an interesting history of their own."

Ki smiled crookedly and said, "Vickie told me they were fond of one another."

Jessie shrugged and said, "They weren't too fond of Victoria. The neighbors distinctly remember a young woman of suspiciously dark complexion for those parts, who seemed to be treated as a member of the family until Isaak Miller's sister died, and then as a sort of house servant until, as best the neighbors can recall, she wasn't there anymore."

Ki snapped Jessie's carpetbag shut as he observed, "If the whole neighborhood knew that much, who's to say some *other* gal with a dark complexion and a vivid imagination couldn't have heard it, combing some gossip's hair, and decided it sounded a lot more glamorous to be a disinherited gold miner's daughter than just a, well, whatever she really was? Did Peters and Cohan send you any tintypes to indicate what the real Victoria Miller might have looked like?"

Jessie told him not to be silly. Then Victoria, who'd come

37

in from the next room, dressed in a bulky tan travel duster and a pout, said, "I heard that, you mean-hearted old thing, and I ain't about to budge one inch further west with folk who think me a lying colored gal!"

Jessie assured her, "Don't be silly, Victoria. Nobody's said any such thing."

But the pretty little breed pointed a finger and a scowl at Ki to insist, "*He* did, and all this time I thought he was nice. I never asked you to help me find my dad, Miss Jessica. You offered. I guess I can get suspicious about strangers myself, if that's the way you want to play. I've wondered more than once how come folk I barely know seem so anxious to find my poor old dad's gold mine. But I was raised more polite than this fool Chinaman!"

Jessie sighed and told the upset girl, "Ki's paid to worry over me like a mother hen, Victoria. You mustn't take him all that serious."

Victoria replied, "Ma'am, when you've had blood kin call you a darkie and throw you overboard to sink or swim, you learn to take folk serious. I ain't going out in no damned desert with no damned Chinaman who says I can't be trusted. You've been real good to me, Miss Jessica. But I ain't fixing to stay where I ain't wanted. So I'll just take off this duster you gave me and be on my way. I have to go back in the other room it take it off. I ain't wearing nothing under it. You can come along and make sure I don't steal that nice dress you bought me. The duds of my own I brought along to dust in will suit me just fine 'til I can get a job here in Denver, hear?"

Jessie stamped her booted foot for silence and said, "We don't have time for all this foolishness. We have a train to catch. Ki, tell the girl you're sorry, and if she won't come along like a lady, pick her up and carry her."

Ki laughed despite himself and said, "She called me a Chinaman, more than once. So I'd say we were even. How about it, Vickie? Is the war over for now?"

The little breed pouted some more, but grudgingly allowed they had a truce, at least until he said mean things about her again. So Ki didn't have to carry her to the depot after all and,

38

in a way, he wondered if he hadn't been too hasty in making up with her. For packing a wriggling vixen who was bare-assed under a thin poplin duster might have been interesting and, either way, he still didn't trust her as far as he could throw her.

Chapter 4

The first leg of Longarm's trip, aboard a real train, would have been sort of tedious even if he'd had company. It was worse riding on a hardwood seat alone, with a mean little kid up ahead shooting every cow they passed with his grubby finger and a nasal cry of *bang bang*.

But all bad things, like all good things, have to end some damned time. So, to Longarm's great relief, the mean little kid and his ugly mother didn't transfer to the narrow-gauge to Durango with him.

The seats were no softer, and narrower besides. The mountain combination ran on tracks a bare yard apart, and so the rolling stock had to be built skinny with seats obviously meant for one fat ass or two midgets. The one Longarm found by an open window would have suited him and maybe that mean little kid about right. But Longarm had his doubts when a not-bad-looking but sort of heavy gal asked him if the little patch of varnished wood left over was taken. Longarm rose politely to his feet, ticked the brim of his Stetson to the lady, and told her, "I'm game if you are, ma'am. Before you take me for a badly brung up brute, I'd best explain it's my considered opinion that you'll enjoy the ride better if I sit by the window."

She looked mildly displeased. So he said, "So be it, then. After you, ma'am." He watched, bemused, as she slid in to hog the open window and most of the seat.

Save for being pleasantly plump, to put it politely, the gal was a handsome brunette with sort of Latin features. She was dressed in good taste, save the sort of bird's nest, bird and all, she'd pinned atop her upswept hair. The dress was summer-weight peach gabardine. He doubted it would be as peachy by the time she made it to Durango. He'd taken a window seat knowing soft-coal smoke couldn't really do much to tobacco-brown tweed.

All the other passengers, mostly male, were dressed for sensible train travel as well. But it was a mite late to tell a lady who'd already taken him for rude that she ought to take her dress off. So he just sat down beside her, sort of, with a leg out in the aisle to brace one buttock above thin air as the narrow gauge started up, and up—it was that sort of a railroad. They'd have never built her narrow-gauge if there'd been flatter ground to lay tracks across.

She didn't grasp this right away. Perhaps because of the awkward moment and the way the rolling wheels beneath them sort of tingled her hip against his, she stared out at the passing scenery intently, until it soon commenced to get more interesting by the moment.

The rail line, like the mining camp ahead, was brand new. Neither would have been built in such bumpy country if hard-rock mining didn't call for lots of rocks. The grade averaged nine degrees, and the roadbed was cut into hillsides a lot steeper. To her credit, she didn't let on it was unsettling her until they rounded a sharp turn and she found herself staring out at a heap of high altitude, with a white-water stream winding like a cotton thread through the canyon below, and not so much as an eagle's feather between the windowsill and it.

She didn't outright scream, but Longarm got her message when her big butt came close to setting his on the floor. He cleared his throat and said politely, "That was why I suggested you might be more comfortable on the aisle side, ma'am. We wouldn't have found this seat at all if others who travel this route more regular didn't have delicate feelings, too."

She turned to him with a shudder to say, "My Lord, you'd think they'd put a guardrail or something between us and that awesome drop. Is it like this all the way?"

41

"No, ma'am. There's some steeper cliffs up ahead. As for guardrails, even if they did any good, there'd be no place to put 'em. It takes an expensive heap of dynamite to cut this much of a shelf in granite. So the cross ties are wedged solid against the rock on one side and sort of, ah, hanging out a mite on the other."

"I think I'm going to be sick," she sobbed.

"It's likely the altitude. The thin air up here makes lots of folk uncomfortable. Try to breath faster than you might back home and, if you feel faint, put your head down on my lap. I won't take it personal."

She laughed despite her now sort of green complexion and told him, "I might. I don't even know you, sir. I'm Peggy Gordon, by the way."

"In that case I'd be Custis Long. I reckon you get asked a lot whether they named that song after you or vice versa, eh?"

She sighed and said, "I'm hardly *that* old. I don't even know who the Peggy Gordon in that old Scotch song may have been, but my folks were really named Gordon, and I guess they had no imagination when it came to making up new names for baby girls."

He chuckled and said, "I never would have picked out Custis, had *I* had any say in the matter. You want to change seats with me, Miss Peggy?"

"I'm not about to stand up until this fairground thrill stops somewhere on level ground. I don't think it would do any good, anyway, now that I know what's out there. What good would it do me to be sitting on the aisle if even one of those bitty wheels under us jumped the track?"

He was too polite to explain that on hastily laid narrow-gauge it was usually the *track* that jumped off the mountain. He was glad she didn't want to change seats. It was nice to see she understood the facts of life, too. He didn't blame her for not wanting her big ass half out in the aisle. It was tough enough for him to ride this way, skinnier, and they still had a considerable ways to go.

As if she'd read his mind, or hip, Peggy Gordon asked if she was by any chance crowding him and, without waiting for him to lie, did her best to scrootch over a mite. He found he could just get both halves of his butt on the seat by shoving his hip harder against hers than he'd have dared, had they not introduced themselves to each other. She blushed becomingly and murmured, "Well, I certainly don't have to worry about falling out now, and, oh dear God, how did we get out here in the middle of the sky?"

He soothed, "We're still on the tracks. It's not all that unusual to see clouds below you, once you're this high in the mountains. I remember a time, down to the Mogollin Rim, I got to watch a whole thunderstorm from the top side. It sure looked odd, having a God's-eye view of thunder and lightning while I drank canteen water with a hot desert sun beating down on me. I'm more used to such goings on now than when I first came west after the war. The hills where I was born didn't get such unusual weather and, there you go, we're out of that clouded-over canyon and things look normal again."

She gulped and replied, "If you call a drop-off like that normal you surely must have been out this way a while. My people missed the war. I had no brothers and my father was too old for the draft of sixty-three. What about you, Custis?"

He yawned, on purpose, and said, "I wasn't drafted. I was too dumb to wait 'til both sides got that desperate. I forget a lot about my misspent youth. My most pleasant memory of the war was coming out alive at the end."

"Don't you even remember which side you were on?" she asked.

"I reckon I could if I studied on it. I don't choose to. There were good men and bad, and a lot of boys too young to die on both sides of that fool war. As far as I can see, it's been over a spell. But many, from both sides, still recall it as yesteryear, nursing the hateful memories as if hate was heroic. I have to travel a lot all over this country, so I've found it best not to indulge in old war stories."

He found they could both ride more comfortably if he put one arm up on the seat behind them. She didn't seem to mind. But he was careful not to touch her shoulders more that he had to as he said, "Most old war stories are old bore stories in any case. I've always suspected the good ones you hear are pure bull. So let's talk about you, Miss Peggy. How come you're

43

bound for Durango? No offense, but you don't look like a mining man."

She laughed girlishly and replied, "Neither do you. I'm on my way there to apply for a job with the city government."

He frowned thoughtfully and said, "Correct me if I'm wrong, Miss Peggy, but the last time I passed through Durango they just didn't have a city government. It's a mining camp, not a real incorporated township. There's a county sheriff, I know, and the usual miners' vigilance committee, but—"

She cut in with, "They've just filed for incorporation as the township of Durango. It should go through this year, if not next year, at the latest. Meanwhile, as they wait for Denver's final approval, they've already begun to set up a provisional administration and, well, you know what they say about a girl getting in on the ground floor."

"That ain't bad advice for a boy, either, if he needs a job. I'm sure glad I met up with you, Miss Peggy. Like I said, it's been a spell since last I passed through the sprouting tent city up ahead. Maybe you can help me get my bearings as I get set up in Durango for the next leg of my trip."

She stared right at him thoughtfully as she said, "I've never been to Durango. But I'm still glad we met. What did you mean about a next leg. Won't you be staying with us in Durango a while?"

When he said he wouldn't be for long, Peggy Gordon reached demurely up to take his hand off the seat back and cuddle it to her soft shoulder as she sighed and said, "Oh, dear, you don't give a girl much time to move in on you, do you?"

Considering how she'd kissed him, French, without being asked, the first time their train had run through a dark romantic snow shed, Miss Peggy Gordon sure seemed reluctant to take her duds off by broad daylight. Longarm had had no trouble getting her to check into the Uranium Inn with him. She'd just stood there as if butter wouldn't melt in her mouth while he signed them in as a couple of Browns, since Smith seemed sort of unimaginative. But when he got her and her bags upstairs to the fine corner room with bath he'd booked for them, she ran over to the window to peer out at the grimy little mining settlement as if she thought they were in Paris and she didn't want to miss a lick of it.

He put her gear down and proceeded to shuck his hat, coat, and gun rig as she marveled about some distant smelter stacks and asked, "What's uranium, dear? I mean, I know it's some sort of metal, and I know they mine it here, along with gold and silver. But what's it good for?"

"Not much. They use it to make that Tiffany glass that looks like someone spilled coal oil on water. It's a by-product of the vanadium they mine here. They smelt both out of an ore they call caronite. The vanadium's what they're really after, of course. You can make mighty fine springs out of vanadium steel and, speaking of springs, would you like to take a bath with me before we try out the springs of that big old bed?"

She turned to stare in apparent dismay at the brass bedstead taking up a good part of the room. She still kept her dumb hat on as she asked, "Just like that? With the sun still shining in at us?"

"It wouldn't be coming through the curtains so hard if it wasn't fixing to set any minute. I'll take you out to supper, first, if you're really hungry, but . . ."

"Was that a crack about my figure, you brute?" she demanded.

He tried to look innocent as he replied, "We ate on the train less'n an hour ago. I'm sorry if I failed to feed you enough. But it was your notion to refuse that second helping."

She glared at him and snapped, "In other words, you bought me one meal and now you think I owe you my all? You men are all alike!"

He picked up his gun rig and strapped it back on as he told her, "No we ain't. Some of us enjoy kid games and some of us don't. I'm sure sorry I read your smoke signals wrong, Miss Peggy. I can see you're blushing schoolgirl, now. Most often, when a gal starts the rain dance on her own, it's been my experience that both parties had a right to expect some rain. But I stand corrected and, what the hell, as long as this room's paid for, one of us ought to get some use out of it."

He was putting on his coat again when she came unstuck to ask him where he thought he was going. He told her, "I just told you. It's all yours. You're dead right. Buying a gal a meal and a hotel room for the night doesn't give a man no call to mess with her if she doesn't want to be messed with."

He put on his hat. She rushed over to grab his lapels as she pleaded, "Please don't go, Custis. You know I never flirted with you to take advantage of you."

He couldn't go with anyone that heavy hanging on to him for dear life. But he said, "I don't know what you wanted of me, Miss Peggy. I don't suspect you know either. I never have and never will make any secret of the fact that I enjoy making love to women. All the alternatives are sort of disgusting. But if I have to play kid games to get my lovings, I reckon I'll just go find me a kid, so . . ."

"You bastard!" she sobbed, dragging him toward the bed by his lapels. "First he says I'm too fat, and now he says I'm too old for him! I'll show you who's the young and frisky one around here, you brute!"

So she did. Longarm probably could have kept her from hauling him across the room and throwing him down on the bed had he wanted to. But she wasn't that old or fat, so who on earth would have wanted to?

His hat fell off, of course. But it felt sort of dumb to be fully dressed, gun rig and all, as the big brunette, still wearing her bird's-nest hat, rolled atop him, hoisted her now somewhat sooty but still peachy skirts, and braced a stout thigh out to either side as she unbuttoned his fly, hauled the contents out still half soft, and proceeded to have her way with him.

It must have felt as good to her as it did to him, judging from her joyous moans as she moved up and down on what was now at full attention. She gasped, "Oh, you're so big. I'm afraid you'll hurt me if you go too deep."

To which he could only reply, "Don't bounce so hard, then," though his heart wasn't really in it, and she obviously liked what was in her too much to take his warning seriously.

He came in her, fast. She said that made two of them. But when he rolled her on her back and tried to undress her she protested, "No! Not until it's dark, dear!"

46

He didn't ask why. He sat up and started shucking his own boots and duds, allowing them to fall wherever they had a mind to as she stared up adoringly from under her silly hat. Then, ready for action again, Longarm moved her skirts as far out of the way as she'd let him, and it was even better this time with him on top. She didn't need a pillow under her to take him at an angle of sheer perfection. She raised her heroic thighs, mostly encased in fishnet stockings and frilly garters that made his bare hips itch, and dug her nails into his bare back, crooning, "Oooh, you feel so . . . so *naked*, darling!"

He laughed, kissed her, and said, "I am naked, and if you had a lick of sense you'd be naked, too. This is a hell of a time to be modest, Peggy. It ain't as if we're strangers now, you know."

She sobbed, "Oh, I'm starting to know every inch of you and it's all too good to be true. But I don't want you to laugh at me, and you would, if you saw me naked."

He started moving faster in her, insisting, "This is no laughing matter. What are you afraid I'll see? Making love with your duds on is a crime against nature, honey. Would *you* care right now if you suddenly noticed I had two heads or a brass ring in my nose?"

She moaned, "No. I already knew you were a bull, and I'm coming again and, oh, damn, it *would* feel even better if we were both stark naked, but for Christ's sake don't stop!"

He didn't. He couldn't have. But then, as they lay panting in the pleasant afterglow, he brushed a stray tress that had come unpinned away from her moist forehead, kissed her gently, and murmured, "That *hat*, at least, has got to go. It makes me feel bashful to have stuffed birds watching me at times like this."

She didn't argue as he unpinned her hat, put it aside on the bed table, and allowed her lush black hair to cascade in inky streams across the white linen. But as he began to unbutton her bodice, Peggy said, "Wait, darling. It's almost sunset out there in the real world now, and we have all night, don't we?"

He wasn't ready to think that far ahead yet. He kissed her soft throat—a double chin could be sort of cute if a lady didn't overdo it—and said, "I was hoping we could let ma-

47

ñana worry about itself. But, since you brung it up, honey, I told you aboard the train that I have to ride down to the Four Corners and see what the Indians are upset about. It ain't my own desire. I wasn't looking forward to it, even before I met you. It's my job and, looking on the bright side, as soon as I find out what could be spooking the B.I.A., I'll be coming back this way. To tell the truth, I got more leeway getting back to Denver than I do leaving it." He reached for her bodice again as he added, "I might be able to steal more than one night next time if you really admire me."

She moved his hand away firmly, but laughed as she told him to hold his horses and let her up a minute. So he did, assuming she either had to take a leak or, better yet, wanted to undress herself. But she surprised him by reaching down to open one of her bags on the floor and producing what sure looked like a pint of snakebite medication. She rejoined him on the mattress, handing him the bottle with the suggestion he open it, any way he knew how, fast. So he bit the cork with his teeth, and once he had it out the results were pleasant enough, albeit unexpected.

He handed her the bottle, wheezing, "Good stuff. I fear I ain't used to more than a hundred proof without a chaser, though. What is it? It sure ain't Maryland rye."

She took a good swig, braver than most gals or many a man might have been, and said, "Malt liquor. Not that sissy blend they sell as Scotch whiskey on this side of the pond. My people keep in touch with the old country."

Longarm tried another swig, found it easier to take, now that his gullet had been anesthetized, and said, "You're right, I've been served Scotch before. Thought it tasted sort of la-di-da with iodine thrown in. This stuff's better. How come rich folk in this country think it's more fashionable watered down?"

She sipped some more before she shrugged and said, "My father says it's because all Saxons are sissies. I think it may be because Americans drink more, in bigger glasses, to be sociable. The real stuff comes off the copper meant to be taken a wee sip at a time. The Scots are slow and steady drinkers, not once-a-week drunks. A few drops of the Speyside Creature, as

48

they call it, will cure the common cold and convince a poor crofter wearing wet wool that he's warm and dry. But it is strong stuff and not meant for careless drinkers of the Dodge City variety."

Longarm took another belt, smiled sort of silly, and said, "Lord have mercy, if they'd been serving this proof at the Long Branch the night John Wesley Hardin rode in, it might have saved some lives. I doubt even Hardin could have hit the broad side of a barn with a skin full of this stuff."

"I know. I should have had some sooner. For, somehow, that soft sunset light coming through the curtains now just looks romantic rather than revealing. I don't know why I was so bashful before, do you?"

"Nope. I wasn't bashful to begin with. Can I help you out of them duds, now?"

She rolled off the bed, stood there swaying slightly until she got her balance, and said, "Weeeh! I don't need any help with this damned fool dress. I don't know why I ever put it on in the first place."

And then she took it off, along with the silk chemise she had on under it, as Longarm gravely set the bottle aside. For, if there was one thing he didn't want to be it was too drunk to take full advantage of the natural bounty Peggy Gordon offered now. He'd been braced to keep from laughing at a fat girl in the altogether. But to his delight, she was more awe-inspiring than amusing, standing there in the soft gloaming light with nothing on but her black net stockings and high-button shoes. For, as was the case with her dawning double chin, old Peggy was at just that delightful stage between well padded and too well padded. Sort of like old Venus de Milo might have looked had she gained ten pounds and got her arms back. But he forgot all about marble statues as the big brunette climbed back in bed with him to take him in her living loving arms, and legs, to start all over with him, as if from scratch. She seemed to take it as a compliment when Longarm took longer, despite his renewed inspiration, to climax in her that way. She seemed to be coming almost continuously, now that she'd gotten over her first shyness. When they finally had to stop for a breather, and some more malt liquor, Longarm said,

"I wish I had some of this stuff to take out in the desert with me. You're right. It's just the stuff for anything that might ail you."

She cuddled lovingly against him, murmuring, "I have another bottle, still sealed, dear. You can take it with you into the wilderness if you promise to think of me, and remember me, every time you, ah, treat a snakebite with the Speyside Creature."

He patted her big bare shoulder fondly and said, "Lord knows they have snakes where I'm heading. But what about you, honey? I wouldn't want to deprive a lady of her down-home tonic."

She toyed with the hair on his chest, saying, "I don't need anything that strong when you're not here, silly. It makes me feel wild and wicked, and you wouldn't want me feeling this wild and wicked with anyone else while you were away, would you?"

Longarm didn't answer. He had to study on that. She was a good old gal and a damned fine lay as well. But there were gals and then there were gals in his tumbleweed existence. A very few he knew might have been able to tie him down, if a man who packed a badge for a living had the right to be tied down to one gal and possible widow. This particular gal wasn't Jessica Starbuck, Kim Stover, or even poor dead Roping Sally, all of whom left a man feeling mighty wistful when the time came for moving on. He had to reconsider coming back by way of Durango if old Peggy was starting to take this slap and tickle so serious. He didn't like to hurt any gal if he could help it, and most were smart enough to understand recreational loving from the real thing. Had he said anything, so far, to give her the notion he thought he had a hold on her, or vice versa? He didn't think so. He was careful about making commitments, even when he was coming. But the trouble with fornication for fun was that not everybody played by the same rules, or understood them.

As a lawman, he knew all too well how good dirty fun on the part of one man or woman could lead to hurt feelings and even a killing rage on the part of another. He recalled that poor old bastard in Sitka who'd blown away his young wife, her casual pickup, and himself, just because he couldn't understand that the flighty little gal he'd insisted on marrying up with didn't take her wedding vows as serious as he had. He could have had her for the asking without marrying up with her. Lots of other men had. She'd doubtless died bewildered, unable to understand why her man was so upset at her for giving her hot young stuff to others any time he wasn't using it himself.

Beside him, Peggy murmured, "Penny for your thoughts?"

"I ain't brooding, honey. I was just now thinking about other folk. Wouldn't this world be a nicer or at least a safer place if we really could reach each other's minds for a penny?"

She snuggled closer. "I'm an open book to you, in every way, dear."

"Not really. I know your sweet hide pretty good now, and I mean to know it better as soon as I can catch my second wind. But nobody ever knows, for sure, what's going on inside another's *head*. We come into this world locked up inside our own skulls and go out the same way. Maybe that's why we like to screw so much. It's as close as we can ever get to another human being, and it still ain't really that close. With luck, we may get to know ourselves, in time. We never really know another. We just get to try. But that can be fun, too, so let's not worry about it."

She began to walk her fingers down his belly as she asked him, "What do you think I've been holding back from you then? Aside from a weight problem, I mean?"

He chuckled. "Nothing sinister. I was sent to pry into Indian affairs, and you don't look Ute or Navajo enough to matter, no offense."

"If you must know, I get my olive complexion from a Spanish grandmother. The story is that a Highlander serving with Wellington in the Peninsular wars brought her back from Spain. You're probably right about old war stories, though. I never met her. My parents moved to America in the fifties, before I was born."

"I noticed you talked natural. I wish you'd quit thinking I'm making veiled remarks about your charms, little darling.

51

First you worry about me thinking you're too hefty, and next you're worried about your fool complexion. I like you fine, just the way you are. I wasn't prying into your past when I said you'd have a hard time passing for an Indian. I don't look like an Indian either, and you don't hear me arguing about it, do you?"

She'd worked her free hand down to a sort of distracting position by then, and proceeded to distract him while she told him, "You're dark as some Indians, where the sun can get at you. But don't ever show them all this body hair if you want to pass for Apache."

He moved his own hand down to explore her body as well.

"Wait. You still haven't told me what you suspect me of, Custis."

"I was hoping you'd turn out to be a sex pervert," he replied in exasperation. "Why is it that every time I let someone know I'm a lawman they think I suspect them of something? You ain't been up to any federal crimes of late, have you, honey?"

"No, but while we're on the subject of perversion, pass me that bottle and I may be able to get up the nerve."

So he did, and she did, and while what they wound up doing was not a statute offense under federal law, there were at least a few states where they could have wound up in jail if they'd been caught at what old Peggy called some experiments she'd always meant to try.

From the way she did 'em, Longarm found it hard to believe she'd never acted so shocking before. But what the hell, it felt better when a lady committing crimes against nature knew what she was doing.

The Buscadero Kid was hardly a kid these days. He'd made it past thirty by noticing early on that the owlhoot trail he rode was a business for serious adults. So the lean and mean Buscadero Kid never drank in any establishment where he couldn't keep an eye on everybody coming and going.

Longarm wasn't looking for the Buscadero Kid as he came through the batwing doors of the Argentina Saloon, Men Only. He was looking for directions and maybe a shot of Maryland rye to wash the aftertaste of all the malt liquor off his sleep-fuzzed tongue. So when the Buscadero Kid spotted Longarm in the mirror above the bar, the results were a mite less predictable than usual. The Kid had the edge of total surprise, or as total as Longarm ever allowed himself to be surprised. Nobody but a suicidal lunatic ever strode into a strange saloon in a tough little mining camp expecting to be greeted with three rousing cheers. So Longarm was wide awake, despite the early hour, and the Buscadero Kid made the mistake of spinning away from the bar *before* his gun had cleared its low-slung holster.

He still might have made it, had not Longarm assumed at a glance that any obvious gunslick slapping leather in the vicinity of a well-known lawman had a particular target in mind.

Even so, it was close. They both fired at the same time. The Buscadero Kid's .45 round punched a hole through the space Longarm had been filling a split second before. The Buscadero Kid had as naturally crabbed to one side as he drew, but Longarm anticipated the southpaw's crab to the right instead of to the left and so, this time, the move that had carried the left-handed killer through many a gunfight failed him.

Longarm's .44-40 slug took the Buscadero Kid just over the heart and tore out back, taking a strawberry froth of lung tissue with it as it smashed a bottle behind the bar but mercifully missed the more expensive mirror. Longarm's second shot struck lower and stayed in the Kid's torn-up guts. By the time Longarm could have shot him again, the Kid was facedown in the sawdust, drumming with one boot tip like a stomped sidewinder.

As the smoke began to clear, Longarm saw he seemed to be all alone in the dinky little saloon. So as long as he had the time he proceeded to reload. He'd just gotten five in the wheel again when the white-faced barkeep cautiously raised his bald head from behind the bar, staring at Longarm in dismay.

Longarm said, "I'm the law, friend. Could you tell me who that may have been that I just shot?"

The barkeep was either short or not yet ready to rise to his full height as he replied, "He was trouble I surely wish you'd have gone someplace else to finish. For, lawman or not, you just went and killed the Buscadero Kid, and his pals ain't going to give a fig about *your* side of the story!"

Before Longarm could answer, a trio of armed men came busting through the batwings. All three were wearing county stars. So while Longarm had the drop on them from where he now stood in a gloomy corner, he only said, "Put them guns away and I'll do the same. I'm Deputy Marshal Custis Long, and this'd be a hell of a time for any of us to make mistakes."

The senior county deputy, a man a little older than Longarm, and hence wise in the ways of the world, quickly dropped his Colt '74 to a more polite position and snapped, "Easy, boys. I do believe this must be the one and original Longarm."

So *they* got polite, fast, as well. Then the man in charge told one of his backups to block the doorway and keep the rest of the town out there until he could get a handle on the situation. As his order was obeyed, he moved closer to the body on the floor, holstered his side arm, and marveled, "Jesus H. Christ, that would appear to be the one and only Buscadero Kid, and you say you took him alone, Longarm?"

The younger lawman nodded soberly and said, "I had to. Nobody offered to help. He drew on me as I came in. He must have thought I was after him. I wasn't. I'd heard of him, of course, but so far he'd never committed a federal offense. There ought to be a federal open-season on hired guns. But there ain't. I reckon Uncle Sam expects state governments to do *some* of their own chores and, correct me if I'm wrong, but didn't that old boy on the floor build most of his rep shooting others of his ilk for a modest fee?"

The local lawman nodded. "He was mostly a bounty hunter, they say. The Texas Rangers wanted to talk to him about bushwhacking some unwanted gents out of season. But, like you said, he mostly confined his disgusting habits to Texas. We'd heard he was here in Durango, though. The sheriff said to give him a day or so and maybe he'd move on. We was hoping he might, without any gunplay."

The backup on the older lawman's far side said, "He must have come here to meet someone. Or to wait for someone.

54

You reckon it could have been you, Longarm?"

Longarm put his reloaded gun back in its cross-draw rig. "I got to study on that. *I* didn't know I was coming here until just before I left Denver, yesterday. On the other hand, the B.I.A. asked for me by name. So somebody must have expected me to show up in these parts, even before my boss did. I thought we'd about cleaned up the old Indian ring in the years since poor old Grant left office. But now and again I run across holdouts, still trying to get rich by crooking the Indians. Then again, the Kid could have been here on other business, spotted a known lawman, and the rest was guilty conscience."

From behind the bar and his once more normal height the barkeep exclaimed, "The owlhoot Longarm just treated so cruel was in here last night, with two others wearing their guns as professional. We try to run a decent establishment, here. So I would take it kindly if you'd all clear out, and take that dead boy with you, before his pals come in here wearing war paint!"

The older local lawman growled, "Shut up, Herb. You mess with La Plata County and you won't have to worry about strange gunslicks. You'll be out of business."

He turned back to his backup. "Jim, pat him down for whatever he has on him and, even if we don't find a murder contract on him, there may be enough money to bury him."

The more youthful Jim moved to hunker down above the dead man, asking, "Who gets this keen double-action .45, Uncle Jake?"

The older and doubtless nepotistic deputy looked uncertainly at Longarm, who said, "I have no use for it. A .45's all right for saloon fighting. But it's a bother when a man packs a .44-40 Winchester as well as a six-gun. It's all yours as far as I'm concerned, Jim."

From the way the kid grinned as he helped himself to the dead killer's weapon, Longarm felt it safe to assume that if he hadn't made a friend, at least he hadn't made an enemy.

Uncle Jake, if that was his name, said, "All right, we'll get Billy out front to send someone for the undertaker. We can worry about the coroner later. Doc's out of town at the moment. Had to ride up to Rockwood to set a fool woman's leg

55

right. You'd think any stockman dumb enough to put a woman on a mean bronc would at least know something about setting busted bones. But that's the way some gents are, I reckon."

Longarm said, "Hold on. I'm on a mission. How far would this Rockwood be and how much of a delay are we talking about, ah, Jake?"

The county lawman shrugged and said, "The distance ain't hard. Rockwood's an easy day's ride up the Animas. How long old Doc means to be there is tougher. I reckon it depends on how stove in that stockman's woman might be."

"He had forty-two dollars and change on him," young Jim chimed in. "Nothing to say what he was doing here, though. I'm sure old Doc will see it as guilty conscience, like Longarm says, and he's surely due back within a day or so."

Uncle Jake nodded and said, "Yep, busted legs ain't hard to figure. If mortification sets in, there's not a thing any doc can do for you. If it don't, it just heals natural, once it's been set and splinted right. Either way, old Doc's sure to be back this side of, say, Wednesday, Longarm."

Longarm shook his head and said, "There has to be a better way. I can't hang around here half a week, dammit. Isn't there someone else I can clear this shoot-out with? I heard you had a municipal government up here in Durango now."

Uncle Jake shook his head soberly and said, "You heard wrong. They keep jawing about incorporating. They've even elected a few provisional town officials. But, until the State of Colorado approves the motion on paper, our so-called mayor and aldermen are just playacting."

The barkeep yelled, "I'm going to tell the city council on you if you don't get that dead bastard and the man who killed him out of my saloon, Jake Foley."

The county lawman shot him a weary look. "You just do that. While you're at it, tell 'em about that young runaway boy you've been keeping so tender, out back. Did you really think the county don't hear about such disgusting habits, Herb?"

That seemed to shut Herb up pretty good. Uncle Jake turned back to Longarm and went on, "Even if there was a city government, the county would surely bust your ass, or try

56

to, if you left before the county coroner said you could ride on. I sure hope we have a friendly understanding, Longarm."

Longarm nodded silently. It was a pain in the ass, but things could have been worse. He might have wound up stuck here for days with no company and, what the hell, a few more nights in the sack with old Peggy wouldn't be too heavy a cross to carry.

Chapter 5

Longarm would be neither the first nor the last to observe that law officials, high or low, could be hard to come by west of the Continental Divide. For as Longarm was exhausting the possibilities of Miss Peggy Gordon and her last pint of malt liquor in Durango, Jessie and her party arrived in Salinas, Sevier County, only to be told that since the rails now ran even farther up the Sevier River, the officials she really wanted to see would doubtless be in Richfield, now the county seat.

There followed some blistering telegrams to Jessie's Texas law firm, and another sunbaked wait on an unshaded railroad platform for the next train to Richfield. Once aboard it, however, Jessie could take some small comfort in the consideration that the extra twenty-odd miles by rail might, in the end, save them all some hot, dusty riding. It was Ki who pointed out they could save themselves a full day in the saddle if, once they'd taken care of the legal aspects of securing Victoria's inheritance, they went on by rail as far south as Marysvale, the end of the line near a Mormon mission to the Paiute. For like many an experienced world traveler, Ki understood that it just wasn't true that a straight line was always the shortest distance between two points, except on a flat paper map.

Jessie had been around, herself. So the two of them killed some of the short but tedious run from Salinas to Richfield by planning the harder going, once they left the comforts of the Mormon Delta.

Said delta was really more a long stringbean of once desert

land, hard won by hand-tooled irrigation canals and ditches that took advantage of a complex natural system of desert ridges and seasonal streams running more or less north and south down the axis of Utah Territory, or Deseret, as most Mormons still preferred to call it. Ki's original suggestion was that they load up on all the water their pack mules could carry and push east across the high and mostly dry Colorado Plateau from the last sure summer water south, then day-camp around Bryce Canyon. It was Jessie who pointed out they could wind up having to cross some other impressive canyons going that way. They were both a mite surprised when Victoria, who'd apparently been staring out the open window half-asleep all this time, turned to them to say, "You want to ride south from Marysvale, packing light, along the shady banks of the upper Sevier, three or four hours' ride, to the Kingston Trading Post. From there you ride up a wash, due east. There may be water in it, but it's never too deep at this time of the year. When you reach the next north-south basin, maybe two hours' ride, you swing south to where some saltu, neither Ho nor Mormon, have a little mining settlement. I don't remember what they are mining there. It was not gold. It sounded like monkies."

"Antimony?" Jessie suggested. Victoria shrugged and said, "Maybe that was it. It's not as important as the water they have there. It's good water. So there you want to fill the water bag with as much as the mules can carry. Because from there to the Green River, eighty-odd miles to the east, there is nowhere to seek water."

Ki, who'd of course studied his pocket survey map before he opened his mouth in the first place, said, "I'm not sure I follow you, Vickie. Anyone can see the directions you just gave allow for some mighty dry riding. But what's wrong with following the Escalante River, just to the south. The map says she runs all the way from the ridgelands west to east."

Victoria grimaced and said, "It does. I thought you wanted to do some riding, not mountain climbing. It would be easy enough to follow any number of washes down to the Esca- lante. But don't you know what Escalante means?"

Jessie nodded soberly and said, "Ouch. To be called 'hard-climbing' in canyon country, a river would have to run through some steep grades indeed."

Victoria nodded and said, "The canyons of the Escalante are not as famous as those of the Colorado, but that is only because they are narrow, dark, and gloomy. The Spanish lost interest in them early when they found waterfalls around almost every bend and no place to walk dry-shod between. My mother's people learned a long time ago to stay out of canyons if they wanted to go anywhere in a hurry. The flat-topped mesas between canyons are easy to travel, as long as you bring plenty of water. It's not all bare desert between here and the Four Corners. There is plenty of juniper, some piñon pine, and here and there even a water hole this late in the year. I think you could make it in three or four days to about where my dad's claim has to be."

Ki observed, "You keep saying Jessie and me could do all these wonders, Vickie. Weren't you planning on coming along?"

"I don't know. I'm still thinking about it. I don't like to be anywhere I'm not welcome."

Jessie nudged Ki to silence him as she told the sullen little breed, "There'd be no point in our finding your mine for you if you were pouting somewhere in a corner, dear. All three of us go or none of us go. Let's talk about the how, not the who. I like your notions of beelining across the flat tops until that gets us to the Green but, isn't that likely to involve some steep drop-offs from juniper flat to white water, dear?"

Victoria said, "Sure. The Green cuts deep as it can get almost all along its length. That's why few Ho and even fewer saltu have ever lived along it. But my route meets the Green where its awesome banks rise neither as high as the Orange Cliffs to the north or Kaiparowits Spurs to the south. There's more than one trail a horse or mule can follow down to that stretch of the Green and it runs there broad and shallow, for the Green. Climbing the far side, into the clay hills just north of the San Juan, is even easier, even if we do have to start keeping an eye out for those pesky Utes from there on."

Ki suggested, "Utes seldom ride south of that east-west mainstream of the San Juan, do they?"

But Victoria knocked that notion down with, "No, but Navajo do and, while I hate too say a good word about my Ute cousins, Navajo are even worse to run into. They're more two-faced than Apache, not one bit nicer."

"Your suggested route seems shorter, in any case, Vickie," Jessie said. "I'm surprised you recall the country so well from your girlhood. Was that Mormon mission your mother's original home?"

Victoria shook her head and said, "No. Those Mormons don't even spell Paiute right. My mother's people were the Corn Creek clan. My father's people called them Digger Indians. But he never did. I want to find out who killed my father. I want to pay them back as my mother's people would."

The sometimes rather ferocious Jessie knew just how the daughter of a murdered father felt about such matters. So to cheer Victoria up she pointed out they didn't know for sure her father had been murdered, saying, "Many a prospector has died of more natural causes, alone in rough country, dear."

To which the other girl replied, "I'm not sure I'd feel any better if he'd fallen down into the pumpkin or been eaten by ants. For it would fret me more, in the end, if we never found out what really happened to him."

Ki raised an eyebrow and asked how dangerous pumpkins might be in the Four Corners country. It was Jessie who explained, "That's what the Indians call the orange rock our own geologists refer to as the Navajo Sandstone. It's almost a mile thick in some places, and since it's pumpkin-colored, and sort of swiss-cheesed with sinkholes, caves, and crevasses, Custis Long once told me they called it *going into the pumpkin* when someone got down into that orange confusion, on purpose or by accident."

Ki grimaced. "He would. Longarm's always been given to colorful speech. Meanwhile, this train's slowing down. So if we're not about to be held up, we must be coming to a town."

They were. As Ki helped the two ladies down to the sun-silvered wooden platform the fair city of Richfield used as its answer to Union Depot, the baggage smashers were already unloading Jessie's saratogas from the baggage car up ahead.

Jessie looked around for a welcoming committee, or at least a messenger boy, because she'd wired her intentions to her law firm well ahead of this arrival. But if Peters and Cohan had contacted any associates here in Richfield, they had to be mighty ignorant of local railroading. From where she stood in the hot sunlight, she could see just about all there was to see of the little and not too old town. The main drag was little more than a business block. She assumed the rich fields had to be the irrigated croplands beyond the frame residential buildings huddled around the modes business center. The most imposing building in sight was obviously a Mormon temple or tabernacle, set back on its own little manicured grounds, and not too large to begin with.

Ki waved two small boys and a yellow cur-dog closer and bet them two bits they couldn't find anyone to carry all this baggage to the Mountain View Hotel. He lost when they were back within minutes with some sturdy teenagers and a middle-aged drunk who no doubt needed the money more than they did. So Jessie led the grand procession to the nearby establishment she'd wired down the line for reservations.

Inside, the old lady behind the reservation desk allowed she'd received the wire indeed and that she was pleased as punch to let her whole top floor for two dollars a night. Ki supervised their baggage up the staircase with Victoria's help, and while Jessie signed them all in, the little old lady leaned across the counter to whisper, "That boy of yours isn't a Chinaman, is he?"

Jessie said, "He's not a boy, he's my segundo. He's not Chinese, either. Would it really matter to you if he was?"

The little old lady shook her sky-blue head of hair and told Jessie, "Not to me, personal. I'm a Saint, and you surely must know The Church of Jesus Christ Latter-day Saints hold all human beings, whether ignorant of The Book or not, to be equal in the eyes of our loving Lord. Why, the Prophet, Joseph Smith, even teaches that the so-called Indians are lost children of Israel, confused as some of the poor things may act at times. But you see, there be others in this settlement, gentiles, ignorant of our prophet's teachings, who might not approve of my allowing a Chinaman to bed down under my

62

roof or even eat at table with other white folk. Night riders lynched a poor Chinese cook up the line a year or so ago, and I try to run a nice clean and quiet hotel here. But if you say he ain't a Chinaman, that's good enough for me."

As Jessie finished with the scratchy hotel pen and handed it back to her, the landlady whispered, "What is he, really, some sort of half-breed?"

Jessie told her that was close enough and the old woman smiled smugly and said, "Well, that's all right, then. I guess I have the right to hire a bed to a lost child of Israel. Is that dark little gal his woman, then?"

Jessie said dryly, "They're still working on it. I have to look up a Judge Reynolds, here at the county seat, ma'am. I don't suppose you know him?"

The old woman brightened and replied, "Indeed I do. For he's an elder of our church as well. You say you have business with him, Miss Starbuck?"

"I do. My law firm wired him I was coming and, to tell the truth, I expected someone from his office to meet my train. Could you tell me how I might go about getting in touch with him, ma'am?"

The older woman nodded and said, "Indeed I do. If he's in town, I mean. You see, Elder Reynolds serves as a circuit judge as well as our town J.P. and, heavens, he's such a busy man. If he's in town right now, you'll either find him at home or, more likely, over at his office. You can't miss it, dear. You just walk over to the first corner barbershop you come to, go up the side stairs, and you'll find his name in gold on one of the doors on the second floor. I can't say which one. But there can't be more than four office suites up there and, as I said, they all have writing on their doors."

Jessie thanked her and went upstairs to fill Ki and Victoria in. As she got out the legal documents she wanted a Utah magistrate to approve, Ki offered to go with her. But she said, "Sometimes a girl can draw more flies with honey. I was just told this town is on the prod about gents of Oriental appearance."

Ki smiled thinly and said, "Maybe I should take up chawing and spitting. What if I just tagged along as far as the nearest saloon covering our old judge's door?"

She shook her head and said, "It's hard to find a saloon in Mormon country. They don't even hold with drink as strong as tea or coffee. Go easy on chewing tobacco around them while you're at it. I don't want you lurking ominously in a strong town, and I hardly need backup against an elected official my own lawyers know and approve of. I'll strap on my six-gun if you're worried about me walking a block or so in broad daylight, all right?"

Ki nodded grudgingly, and so Jessica Starbuck proceeded to rig herself, though not with a shuriken star in her hatband this time, and went back downstairs with her .38 Special strapped around her green-skirted hips.

It was special in more ways than one to Jessie. Her father had ordered Colt Arms of Connecticut to make it special for his daughter's eighteenth birthday. He'd discovered on a business trip east that Colt was about to come out with the double-action improvement on their tried-and-true Colt '74, or Peacemaker, and so, like Jesse James, Billy the Kid, and a more wholesome young man called Longarm, old Alex Starbuck had grasped at once what an edge double-action would give a man, or woman, in a rapid-fire contest. For the reliable, nearly indestructable and hence most popular Peacemaker had to be cocked with one's thumb for every shot and, while some gunslicks could do that fast indeed and nobody but a suicidal idiot ever tried to "fan" the old thumb-busting single-action of the era, a gunslinger of the same skill could get off four rounds, aimed, in the time it took to fire twice with single-action.

Young Henry McCarthy, William Bonney—or Billy the Kid, as he was known on various occasions—was no bigger than Alex Starbuck's somewhat tomboy daughter. So he had Colt pack a double-action .38 on a lighter, Lightning frame. A much larger Longarm favored .44-40 rounds to match his Winchester ammo, and fired double-action from the heavier Thunderer or Colt Model T frame. The antisocial Jesse James, who never in his life indulged in a quick-draw confrontation, eventually wound up with Smith & Wesson's version of double-action. He still needed all the edge he could get.

Jessie's father had gotten Colt Arms to split the difference in the Special he'd had made for his daughter. The .38 rounds it spit, fast, were heavy enough to do the job while still as gentle on a little gal's wrist as an adoring dad felt proper. Having the frame as heavy as the bigger Model T did a lot to cut down on the recoil as well, and made for a deadly shooting platform in the hand of a young woman who could easily have done as well with a .45.

Jessie and her .38 Special were a mite older and wiser now than the day she'd unwrapped it as a birthday present. Between them, they'd shot a lot of more serious targets than her late father had ever envisioned the day he indulged her in a gun of her very own. But the lady many had learned to fear wasn't thinking of gunplay at all as she strode down the plank walks of the sleepy little community. She was only afraid the infernal county J.P. her lawyers had lined up for her would be out judging a watermelon contest or maybe some purloined poultry. Mormons seemed to raise a lot of turkeys, for some reason. Maybe they did better than geese in such dry country.

She found the barbershop with no trouble. It was closed for the day. The sign in the window said something about a holiday. She didn't read it in full. She moved rapidly up the outside staircase of the frame building to see if Judge Reynolds had taken the day off as well. The old Mormon woman at the hotel hadn't said anything about this being a holiday. On the other hand, she hadn't said it wasn't, and Jessie had no idea when or why Mormons took a day off.

Upstairs, as she entered a dark musty hallway, Jessie sensed she had, indeed, come at a bad time. It was mighty quiet for an office building in midafternoon on a workday. It was, let's see, Monday? She knew folk of the Hebrew persuasion took Saturday instead of Sunday off. Some Christian sects did as well, come to think of it. But she'd never heard of anyone using Monday as their Sabbath. She moved down the hall, wondering why she was moving so quietly, even as she was doing it. The lettering on the nearest door said it was a dentist's office. She didn't have a toothache. She called out, "Hello? Anybody up here?" And, after a long, pregnant silence, the door facing her from the far end of the hall popped open and a man wearing a snuff-brown frock coat over a white shirt was staring soberly at her. He had a long-barreled dragoon conversion in his right hand, down at his side. It was easy to see he was worried about noises out in the hallway. Jessie smiled the length of the same and asked him, "Judge Reynolds?"

He seemed to hesitate before he asked her soberly, "Would you be the young lady who runs Starbuck Enterprises?" And as soon as Jessie said she was indeed, he swung the big .45 dragoon up to shoot her down like a dog.

It didn't work out quite the way he'd obviously planned. For before he could fire, Jessie had thrown herself to the left and had her own gun out. So they fired together, and her aim was a lot better. His round ticked the brim of the hat she'd hung on her back and took a few blonde hairs with it before it smashed the glass window set in the door behind her.

The lighter but straighter shooting six-gun in Jessie's hand put two rounds in the front of his white shirt before she'd even finished wondering what on earth could be going on. And then he crashed backwards out of sight and Jessie was running through the gunsmoke filling the hallway to see if he needed any more lead in his treacherous hide.

He didn't. As she stepped into what seemed to be the reception room of an office, she could tell at a glance that the man at her feet on the floor was as dead as he'd ever be able to get. His middle-aged face wore an expression of calm annoyance, as if he was about to chide her for raising an objection in court he wasn't about to allow. Jessie gulped and said, "Well, your honor, if that's who you are, one of us had to be drunk or crazy, just now, and I haven't had a drink all day!"

She turned and walked back the length of the hallway, reloading her six-gun without having to think about it as she tried to make sense of what had just happened. As she stepped back out on the landing of the outside staircase, she looked down to see men, boys, and even some women running her way from every point of the compass. A man with an Abe Lincoln beard and a brass star pinned to his vest paused warily at the foot of the stairs to call up, "Do you know where that shooting come from, ma'am?"

Jessie holstered her weapon and kept her hands polite as she replied soberly, "I fired two of the shots you just heard. I had to. There's a man up here who fired at me first."

As the town law came up the stairs, trailed by a buck-toothed younger rustic who had to be his backup, Jessie explained, "My name is Jessica Starbuck. I came here to see your Judge Reynolds. I fear someone must not have wanted me to see him."

As the law joined her on the landing he said, "Last I heard, the man you was looking for should have been over to the temple. It was him as called a special meeting of the Saints this afternoon."

Jessie said, "That accounts for how they knew they could get me alone up here, then. I'll show you the one who was laying in wait for me. I left him, dead, down at the far end."

As the two lawmen followed her back inside, the younger one said, "If this gentile gal has it figured right, Al, that could account for Elder Reynolds calling a meeting and not being there when everyone else traipsed over, right?"

The older lawman called Al said, "Maybe. What was this business you had with Elder Reynolds, ma'am?"

Jessie patted the legal documents she'd tucked in her waistband and replied, "I came to see him in his capacity as a judge. I don't know what that has to do with what just happened. But I just got off a train in front of your whole town, and if your real church elder didn't lure the whole population of this building away with a ruse because they wanted to trap me up here, I sure can't come up with anything better!"

The three of them came to the open doorway and paused there to regard the cadaver sprawled just inside. The town law called Al just stood there as his younger sidekick whistled and said, "Lord have mercy, little lady. You sure done a job on that poor cuss."

Al drew his six-gun but held it politely enough as he asked Jessie soberly, "You say you shot this man in self-defense, ma'am?"

Jessie said, "Yes. Wait, I'm not sure. The light's so tricky in here. The frock coat and shirt look familiar, but the *face* of this one doesn't quite match the one I met earlier and . . . where are the bullet holes I put in that shirt, if it's that shirt at all?"

Al said, "Cover her, Spud," as he stepped inside.

Jessie didn't resist as the bucktoothed backup relieved her of her side arm, saying, "Nice gun, ma'am. A mite heavy for a lady to pack, ain't it?"

She didn't answer as the older lawman hunkered down by the cadaver to gently roll it partway on its side. Then he told the couple in the doorway flatly, "This man never took no lead in the front of his shirt, ma'am. He was shot in the back, at close range, judging from the powder burns. I don't suppose you want to change your story some?"

"I didn't shoot anyone in the back at close or distant range!" Jessie protested. "We shot it out face-to-face, if that's who I shot it out with. I just told you his face looks a little different to me, now."

The older lawman got back to his feet, his gun still out, as he stared wearily at Jessie and said, "I don't see no sign of a gun on or about his remains, ma'am. What would you say he was pointing at you, his finger?"

Jessie insisted, "It was a .45 dragoon conversion. Take a look at that shot-out window at the far end of the hall if you don't believe me!"

Old Al said, "Oh, I believe a bullet went through that glass, ma'am. I noticed coming up the stairs. It seems sort of obvious a lot of lead was flying up here just now. You can still smell it. My point is that you would seem to be the only mortal with a gun to shoot up here."

She said, "Search the other rooms up here, then. If someone picked up that gun he fired at me they have to still be somewhere in this very building! Can't you see that?"

Al and Spud exchanged knowing glances. Then Al said, "I can see lots of things, ma'am. First you tell us you shot him in the chest, from the front, in a shoot-out that makes no sense at all, and then I see he was shot in the back, unarmed, which means someone has to be fibbing. And there ain't nobody but you to discuss the matter with."

Spud snickered and said, "I'll bet it was a lovers' quarrel. The old goat was two-timing his four wives with this young gentile gal. And when she couldn't get him to divorce his wives they got to fussing and—"

"Don't talk dirty about an elder of the church, Spud," the older man cut in as Jessie stared down in dawning horror at the dead man at their feet.

Having shushed his young sidekick, Al turned back to Jessie and said, "We can soon determine just how long you've been in town, ma'am. Now, how about telling us just why you come up here to see Elder Reynolds and how come you got so vexed with him."

She insisted, "I told you. I had legal matters to attend to with him. I can assure you I had no reason to argue with him. Before I could even meet with him this door popped open and . . . Dammit, I'm sure that's not the man I shot it out with!"

Al said, "I don't see nobody else lying dead on the floor up here. We'll be going over to the town lockup now, ma'am. I'd sure feel silly handcuffing a woman. So you just come along like a lady and—"

"On what charge?" she cut in.

To which the town law soberly replied, "Murder, of course. Did you really think you could back-shoot Judge Reynolds, an elder of our church, and get out of it by telling such a thunderous whopper as you just now tried to sell us? We got you, ma'am, dead to rights. If it's any comfort, Utah Territory gives a convicted murderer the choice of hanging or a firing squad."

Chapter 6

Meanwhile, back in Durango, the coroner's jury had finally met and, after jawing about it less than fifteen minutes, found the death of the late Buscadero Kid was a service to the community and offered Longarm its heartfelt congratulations for being so sudden on the draw.

Considering how long they'd made him hang around Durango until they could get around to it, Longarm felt they might have let him make a longer speech, at least. But he was glad it was over at last. For there were limits to how many positions a man could get into with a fat girl and, to tell the truth, both Peggy Gordon and her malt liquor were commencing to leave a cloying aftertaste by this time.

Longarm sincerely liked women and enjoyed their company even when they were just laying there. He liked to get to know a gal in the human as well as biblical sense, and few pillow conversations bored him. Or, when they did, he could usually put on his pants and get out of there with a graceful excuse about having to tend to a bank robbery in progress.

But old Peggy apparently didn't have a life story, or a past she wanted to talk about, and, worse yet, she'd known Longarm had to stick around until the local coroner got back. So Longarm had gotten to smoke more than talk, between times, and the Speyside Creature seemed to be an acquired taste he wasn't sure he wanted to acquire. It sure cleared one's sinuses and made gals with double chins look kissable, but it was mighty tedious to wake up every morning with a perishing thirst and your tongue tasting like smouldering wet peat. Switching to Maryland rye, once they'd at last drained that second bottle of hers, had only helped a little. He'd still had to spend the night with a gal who didn't tell interesting bedtime stories and was starting to screw predictable.

He didn't go back to their hotel right off. He knew he had to let her know he was leaving before he left, but the parting would be less sweet sorrow if he was able to keep it short as possible. Thanks to his misadventure with the Buscadero Kid, he was way behind schedule as it was. So whether Billy Vail liked it or not, he didn't intend to shilly-shally at the Indian agency to the south when plenty of folk had riding stock for sale right here in Durango.

By this time he was sort of famous in Durango and, since those mysterious sidekicks of the Buscadero Kid had failed to come after him after all, sort of popular as well. So the crafty-eyed old cuss who'd been touted as an honest horse trader greeted Longarm like a long-lost son and allowed he'd be proud to sell the U.S. government some riding stock.

As the old-timer led Longarm around to the corrals out back, Longarm said, "I've ridden the Four Corners range before. I found water harder to come by than browse. So, to tell the truth, I'd be more in the market for a couple of good Spanish riding mules than ponies."

The horse trader shook his head and said, "I feels for you. I just can't reach you, son. The mines all about buy mules as fast as I can get 'em. The best I can offer would be, say, three good Indian ponies, Ute bred and white broken. Two ponies can pack as much as one mule and no Indian pony eats much more delicate than a mule to begin with."

They came to the corral rails and both propped their elbows over the top one as Longarm morosely regarded the remuda of milling horseflesh inside. All the ponies had sense enough to know it was high summer, and none of them wanted to go anywhere with those pesky two-legged critters, so each one was trying to hide behind another, leading to considerable nipping and even more dust. Longarm pursed his lips and said, "Figuring ten pounds of oats a day, per pony, and water weighing eight pounds a gallon, I could likely get by, carrying

71

my own needs lashed to my saddle. But I dunno. That adds up to a snail's pace riding, and I am riding into Indian country."

The horse trader spat, hitting the horse apple he'd aimed at, and observed, "Hell, you can't *run* a pony in canyon country to begin with. The Indians know that, too. So none you might meet figure to make a running fight of it, son. When Utes spot easy pickings they generally try to circle round ahead and lay in ambush. Navajo fight more Apache style. They trails you, out of sight, 'til you stop to make camp. Then they dismounts and sneaks in on you. Neither nation is apt to come at you yelling and waving coup sticks, like Bannock or Sioux. It's a good way for either the chasers or the chasee to wind up down in the pumpkin. Not even an Indian raised in the Four Corners could know *all* the sinkholes and crevasses between the bushes."

Longarm fished out a cheroot as he muttered, "I said I'd ridden through them parts before." He saw no need to offer a smoke to a man who chawed, so he thumbnailed himself a light and got his cheroot going before he asked casually, "What are you asking for that barrel-headed buckskin with the one white stocking?"

The older man shot him a canny look and said, "I admire a man who knows horseflesh. That sweet little mare is less'n four years of age, and she don't need no ten pounds of grain a day. She's a war pony I got off a destituted Ute widow, and I still had to pay fifty dollars for her."

Longarm said, "You got gypped, then. Everybody knows a pony should wear four white stockings or none at all if you want its hooves to wear even."

The horse trader snorted in disgust. "That's just a fool superstition. But since everyone seems to believe it, and I can't afford to feed a pony that's selling slow, I'll tell you what I'm going to do. I'm going to let you have that pony you admire for just what I paid for her, fifty dollars. Deal?"

Longarm shook his head and said, "I never said I admired her *that* much. Let's talk about that brown and white paint. He looks solid, for Indian stock. How come he ain't been cut?"

The horse trader answered, "Bought him full-growed. He ain't as mean as some studs you might have rid. Steady under gunfire, too, as long as there ain't no mares in heat around him. How does thirty dollars sound to you?"

Longarm laughed rudely and said, "Awful. I was talking about riding him, not breeding him. Letting that discolored lop-eared brute cover a decent mare would be a crime against nature and, if I *was* willing to ride such an ugly mutt, I'd have to make sure the third scrub pony in my train was a gelding. I don't see no nuts on that rawboned bay with the white face. Assuming he ain't part Hereford cow, what are you asking for such an ugly critter?"

The older man cackled, "By swan, you surely do know which end a real horse shits from, don't you? I couldn't have chose out three finer desert ponies had you trusted me to pick 'em out myself. So I'll tell you what I'm going to do. I'm going to let you have all three of them ponies for an even hundred and that's my last word on the matter."

Longarm flicked the ashes from the end of his cheroot, put the cooler end back in his bared teeth, and said, "Four bits for the three of 'em and I don't want to talk no more about it either."

The old man blustered, "My three best ponies for fifty damn dollars? Surely you jest!"

Longarm removed his elbows from the rail as he replied, "I ain't got time for joshing. I got places to go in a hurry. It's been nice talking to you. But maybe I'd best mosey over to that other trader they told me about, Pop Ewing, and see what *he* has for sale."

As he turned away, the older man almost sobbed, "Ewing is a damned old thief and you can tell him I said so! You ain't about to get a better deal in thes parts, son!"

But as Longarm started to walk away the man held out his hand, palm up, and tried, "Six bits, because I admire you so for what you done to the Buscadero Kid."

Longarm slapped his palm and said, "Done," thus acquiring three good Indian ponies for twenty-five dollars apiece, which was about what they were worth this far from civilization, and if Billy Vail didn't like it he could lump it.

Longarm told the horse trader he'd be back shortly with a saddle and some bridles, digging out a ten-dollar gold piece as a deposit before he ambled back to the main drag of Durango.

At the saddle shop they'd told him about, he went through a very similar discussion before he wound up with a used but solid double-rig roping saddle made by Vadalia, along with three plain-bitted harnesses and plenty of trot line. When the saddler tried to convince him most gents led their pack animals bitless, Longarm just shrugged and said, "Some may not switch mounts as often as I do," and left to walk back to the horse trader with his purchases.

There, he laid out the rest of the money, and though the old-timer pissed and moaned about the cruel advantage Longarm was taking of his elders, the old buzzard helped him saddle the paint stud and bridle all three. Longarm asked him to hold the trot line for him as he gingerly mounted the paint to see how well they were going to get along. When the stud didn't buck, Longarm took the end of the lead with a nod of thanks and headed back to Main Street again.

He tethered all three ponies in front of a general store and went in to discuss the heavier supplies he'd need. The young gal minding the store looked like a schoolmarm but turned out to know her stuff as she helped him put his order together and even helped him carry it out and load it up. She was a strong little gal, he noticed, as she cinched one wooden pack-tree to the buckskin. When it tried to plant a hind hoof in her crotch she evaded it gracefully and punched some manners into the playful pony's barrel head with her little fist, asking, "Where'd you get her, Ewing or Hodges?"

Longarm said, "Hodges. Let's go back in and talk about that saddle gun, now."

They did. She didn't want to sell him a Winchester, used, for what he offered, and tried to steer him on to a Henry she promised him was just as good, saying, "The Winchester is based on the basic Henry patent in any case, you know."

But Longarm shook his head and said, "I don't want the basic action. I want all the improvements the Winchester company made when Henry sold out to them. Where I'm going, I need a carbine that throws seventeen rounds of .44-40 as fast as I may need 'em thrown. I told you I was riding down into the Four Corners."

She sighed and said, "I know. That's why I said this had to be a cash transaction. Let's wait 'til we tally up your whole order and I may be able to give you a price on the gun and ammo. I'm not sure two hundred pounds of oats will get you and three ponies there and back."

"Neither am I," he told her. "It's all I can afford to pack along. My ponies are Indian bred and might be able to get by on shorter rations. Indians don't oat 'em at all."

She said, "Indians ride bareback, and don't treat their women so good, neither. You'd best take enough oats to last you at least a week on the trail. You won't find much natural forage where you're headed, you know."

He replied soberly, "Might not find much water, either, and I couldn't get no mules. A pony dies of thirst lots faster than it can starve to death and, even empty, them water bags make quite a load. They'll be heavier than the oats by far, once I fill 'em. So let's not argue about the fodder and water for my brutes no more."

She dimpled and said, "Someone ought to argue with you about the way you're fixing to feed a growing boy. How long do you expect to get by on just those few cans of beans and tomato preserves you bought off us?"

He shrugged and said, "Long as I have to. Men are tougher than ponies. I get to sit down most of the way, in any case."

"You still can't hope to exist on a can of beans and a can of tomatoes a day," she insisted, "and that's all you'll have if you're down there among the canyons more than, say, a week."

He smiled thinly and said, "I could tell you a tale of going hungry for more than a week on canteen water and grass roots, if I wanted to brag on a dumb war I was in one time. Let's just say a man has to worry more about his ponies than himself if he aims to go on using 'em. I'd better take along more matches, though. Lucifer brand, waxed, if you got 'em."

She placed a brand he knew to be almost as good on the counter beside his stacked boxes of .44-40's. She hadn't been able to sell him any hollow points. But when he had time he could cut X's in the soft lead of the rifle rounds. At long range, Longarm like to know anything he managed to hit would really feel it.

He bought a whole box of cheroots for his saddlebag and a bar of naptha soap as well. When she suggested a little jar of glass beads and pointed out that both Ute and Navajo admired them, he shook his head and said, "I ain't going down to trade with either nation. I just have to find out what's eating 'em."

She said, "We'd heard there was trouble down yonder. Don't you think a few gifts for any redskins you meet might be a good idea?"

"Nope. I get along with most Indians because I savvy the way fighting men talk to one another. I know a lot of Indian agents play Santa Claus when they ride in. I know what most real warriors think of 'em, too. They've learned not to trust a white man offering 'em play-pretties and a new reserve a jackrabbit would have a tough time living on. I find they treat me and my badge with more respect if I just tell 'em who I am and why I've come and, if they don't like it, they can lump it."

She looked at him as if he was a pleasant village idiot and said, "I'd better let you have the Winchester. I don't suppose anyone's told you that more than one white man may have been lumped indeed, this summer, down where you're headed, alone?"

He nodded and said, "I've had little to do but talk in the last few days. I heard about the prospectors some law firm in Texas sent wires about. Didn't hear about any other missing white men, though."

She confided, "Nobody knows whether they're missing, official. But at least half a dozen strangers have passed through, recent, bound for the Four Corners. Nobody's seen hide nor hair of 'em since."

"They might have just ridden on through, right?"

"Where? The next town south of the Four Corners would be Winslow, Arizona Territory. And why on earth would anyone want to ride to Winslow across a good hundred miles of Indian country that's barely been mapped, when you can get to Winslow so much safer from the Gila Valley to the south?"

He told her that was another matter he might take up with

the Indians, and once again she helped him lug stuff out front and pack it aboard his ponies. She was a nice little gal, and not bad looking, either. It was likely just as well he'd met up with old Peggy Gordon first. If the sweet little store gal was this worried about him before he'd ever kissed her, he could well imagine the fuss she'd raise if he had to part any sweeter with her. She looked as if she was fixing to bust out crying when he simply paid her off and left with a tick of his hat brim to her.

Back at the hotel, Longarm tethered his three ponies on the shady side and went into see if he could say adios sweet enough to content Peggy Gordon without getting all hot and sweaty again.

He could indeed, he saw, when the big brunette rose from the lobby chair she'd been waiting for him in, fully dressed and with her bags on the floor nearby. "Oh, I was hoping you'd return before my train leaves, darling," she said.

Longarm shoved his hat brim back to kiss her in a more brotherly way than he could recall from recent memory, since the room clerk across the way was likely only pretending to read that newspaper, and told Peggy, "I didn't know you had a train to catch. What happened to that job you were after, honey?"

"I didn't get it. You know how many places in town I tried, whenever you'd let me out of bed, you horny thing. How did it go at that meeting you had to attend, dear?"

"About like I figured. They say that lady with the busted leg will likely make it, too. But waiting for that fool coroner to get back has sure slowed me down a heap."

She grinned up at him. "Really? I hadn't noticed. But I knew they'd let you off and I knew you'd be riding on the moment they did. So . . . I guess this is it, huh?"

He nodded soberly and said, "Yep. I wish there was some way to put it more mushy, Peg, but we both knew, from the first—"

"I told you I was a big brave girl," she cut in, though not able to meet his eyes. "It was grand while it lasted and, whether you believe me or not, I'll never forget you, Custis."

77

Then she brightened. "Oh, I almost forgot." She bent over to open one of her bags as she added, "I was saving this for a bon voyage present."

Then she came back up at him with yet another bottle, a whole pint, of that smoky Speyside Creature, saying, "Maybe, if you enjoy this on the trail some night, you'll think of me just a little?"

He chuckled fondly as he took the malt liquor from her. "If I enjoy it *too* much I might not be able to think at all. But where did you get this bottle, honey? I was sure we'd killed the last of it when I went out to get that regular booze the other evening."

"I was holding out on you. I wanted to give the last of it to you as we parted. I guess I'm just sentimental at heart."

He said he was sentimental too, and promised to think horny thoughts about her with every sip of her gift he took on the lonesome trail. Then she walked him outside. He offered to wait for her train with her, but she said she didn't want to tie him down any more than she already had. So he kissed her, more friendly, with nobody but the ponies watching, and mounted up to ride off, feeling a lot less tied down than he had for some time as Peggy Gordon waved to him from the shade of the hotel.

She'd been a swell pal, and he knew that some night, alone somewhere on a dry weekend, he'd no doubt regret not having her big sweet thighs wrapped around him some more. But he sure doubted it would be soon. For, toward the last, it had commenced to feel like work.

That was the trouble with spending too much time in the same company, he knew. Unless a man moved on before he'd worn out all the novelty with the average gal, he could get to wondering why he was putting all that effort into what was after all a fleeting pleasure when one was only doing it for fun.

As for the few gals he'd met who didn't make him feel like so, they could be, if anything, more of a bother. For Longarm knew that sooner or later he always had to be moving on, and when it did hurt, it could hurt like hell.

He wondered just where old Jessica Starbuck would be

bedded down later tonight, and told himself not to wonder about such painful subjects. For if there was one gal on earth he had no business messing with, it was sweet little Jessie, with all those charms and all that money. He'd never been pleased to part with her. But what sort of a skunk could stay with a gal who could buy and sell the whole department he worked for?

Chapter 7

Far to the west, in Richfield, Jessie felt neither desired nor prosperous as she paced the second-story cell they'd locked her in. Her supper sat untasted on the table that shared the modest space with a hard-looking cot and a chamber pot she just wasn't interested in, either. The sun had just gone down, as if to make her surroundings gloomier. They were already gloomy enough. The coal-oil lamp hanging just outside cast the shadows of her cell's bars in inky stripes across the gray, painted floor of boiler plate. The walls were solid steel as well. It was one of those patent cells small towns sent away for. Small towns knew what they were doing. Once it was riveted together, a patent cell could stand up to dynamite, and she didn't even have a nail file to work with.

But the sun had only been down a few minutes when she heard a soft hiss and turned from the inward bars to see Ki staring in the tiny barred window at her, upside down.

She didn't ask him how he'd managed to climb up there. The amazingly agile Ki had long since proven that if anything was solid he could climb it. But as she moved over to the window she did ask, "Why are you lurking out there like a bat? Wouldn't they let you in downstairs?"

"No. They tell me you're allowed one visit a day, and that the one I paid you this afternoon when they arrested you was it, for now. I've sent all those wires you wanted me to get out to the real world. Western Union tells me they close for the night here, so that's that, until tomorrow morning. How are they treating you, in the meantime?"

She waved a casual hand at the untouched platter behind her. "Remarkably well, when you consider they think I'm guilty of murdering an elder of the Mormon church. Some sweet little ladies came by just a while ago with some home cooking I wish I felt like eating. It smells delicious. I don't know whether they were behaving as good Christians or anxious to get a glimpse of the gentile hussy who shot Elder Reynolds in the back because he wouldn't leave his four wives for her."

"The whole town's buzzing, all right. But so far there's been no talk of rough justice. I guess they figure it would be unmanly to lynch a girl who's sure to hang once they can get another judge down this way. Meanwhile, that should give us a day or so to get you out of there."

She shook her head. "Don't you even think of busting me out, Ki. They know who I am, and Texas extradites murder wants. I mean to walk out of here free and clear of all charges."

Ki asked, "How? Peters and Cohan should be on their way right now, if they can read a telegram. But these Mormons have you dead to rights, in an airtight box. I'd think you were guilty myself, if I didn't know you better."

She asked him if he'd scouted the murder scene as she'd told him to, earlier. He answered, "Top to bottom, once everyone went home for supper. The doors were all locked mighty cheap. I had to break a couple of desk drawers open. There was no sign of that dragoon you mentioned, and I'm sure I'd have noticed an extra dead body. I can think of a couple of ways someone might have smuggled a cadaver out during business hours, but how are we to prove an educated guess in court? They've got a strong case against you, Jessie. I don't even think those lawmen who arrested you think they're lying!"

"I don't either. I'd have no doubt been killed trying to escape if old Al and young Spud were involved in some dark plot against me. I've had lots of time to think about what happened this afternoon since I've been locked up here, Ki.

The only way it works, for me, is that someone knew we were coming, got to Judge Reynolds first, and then spread that story about his calling a special Mormon meeting."

Ki nodded, upside down. "That accounts for the top floor being deserted when you came up those stairs. I don't imagine they planned on you winning against their hired gun, or did it really matter? If some really treacherous mastermind had already noticed that hired gun looked something like the older man you were expecting to meet—"

"Don't be so convoluted," she cut in. "Custis Long once told me it was easy to get in trouble thinking chess when the game was simply checkers. The vague resemblance to the hired killer and the man they'd already killed, in bad light, could have simply been a happy accident, for them. Did you send that wire to Custis for me, by the way?"

Ki repressed a grimace of annoyance as he said, "I did. He'd be getting it about now if one assumes he's in Durango. Marshal Vail never sent him to Durango. He sent him *by way of* Durango, remember?"

She sighed and said, "It was worth a try. Custis gets along with Mormons, for one of us. You're so right about my lawyers needing all the help they can get, once they get here. It's safe to assume the local Saints are mighty annoyed about all this, no matter how saintly they may still be acting. What have you done about Victoria?"

Ki frowned and answered, "What am I supposed to do with her? She's at the hotel, where I just left her, if she heeded my advice. I told her not to go out and wander about a strange town that could be on the prod about strangers."

Jessie nodded. "Good. You'd better take the same good advice, Ki. Everyone in this Mormon community seems to look seriously Anglo-Saxon. A lot of the sect was recruited directly from England. The folk at the hotel are already worried about your neither-nor appearance and, of course, Victoria can be spotted for a breed at a glance by anyone who's ever met an Indian. You know where my money belt is, if you run short. In the meantime, you two had better stay out of sight and mind as much as you can until someone from Peters and Cohan shows up."

Ki argued, "Jessie, that could take the better part of a week, and we might not have that much time. If some Mormon judge shows up first to assign you a Mormon public defender, well, a firing squad may be better than a hanging, but not really that much better. What if I just helped you escape a while and then, once you were ready to face them with a brace of good lawyers and even Longarm . . ."

She shook her head firmly. "No. That would make me look guilty for certain, and I'm not about to let those rascals get away with framing me so sneaky. You just do as I say, Ki. Like the Indian chief said, 'I have spoken.'"

Ki muttered *"Hai,"* and let go the drainpipe he was hanging from to twist catlike on the way down and land on his feet most lightly for a man his size falling that far.

As Ki strode off down the alley behind the town lockup, he was challenged by a burly dark figure, who called out, "I see you, mister. Who are you and what in tarnation are you up to back here with the other alley cats?"

Ki didn't answer. Answering argumentative drunks was, to Ki, a waste of time as well as a way to attract attention. After he'd knocked the noisy oaf unconscious with a ferocious but controlled chop with the horny edge of his hand, Ki knelt just long enough to determine the man was still alive and, from the smell rising from his gaping mouth, either a local gentile or a lapsed Mormon. People in small towns knew all the town drunks. So it seemed likely that even if this one recalled, later, just how he'd wound up sleeping it off in an alley, few locals figured to pay much attention.

But, to make sure nobody connected his tall feline figure with unseemly local gossip, Ki rejoined Victoria Miller at the Mountain View by scaling yet another drainpipe and simply swinging in the nearest open window of the top floor Jessie had paid for.

Victoria let out a startled gasp as he materialized from nowhere. She might have screamed, had she been a white gal, or had the room lamp been lit. For she was lounging on the bed, atop the covers, stark naked.

There was enough light coming from the open door across the bedroom for the two of them to recognize one another.

Victoria protested, "Don't you know enough to knock?"

Ki shook his head, tried not to bust out laughing, and said, "Not this early in the evening, as a rule. Do you always get undressed this close to sundown?"

She covered herself as best she could with a handy pillow, leaving a lot of tawny hide still exposed, as she answered with a pout, "I wasn't sleepy. I was feeling hot and sweaty, thanks to these windows facin' the damned old setting sun. Now that you've seen me, more than you should have, did you see Miss Jessica and find out when they are fixing to let her go?"

Ki sat on the edge of the bed beside her to say, "I saw her. They're not about to let her out. Meanwhile, her orders are for you and me to hole up here and stay out of sight until further notice."

The pretty little breed said, "Oh, well, all right," and tossed the pillow aside to lie back expectantly. Ki laughed incredulously, and started to tell her not to be silly. But then he wondered why any normal man would want to say a silly thing like that. For she was beautiful, obviously willing, and while Ki was given to more meditation than your average man, he knew he'd have more than enough time to meditate between now and the time help arrived. So he calmly but quickly climbed out of his clothes and mounted Victoria, who didn't seem to mind at all and said so, loudly.

Ki kissed her to shush her before he hissed warningly, "Try to keep it down to a roar, will you? The idea is for the two of us to stay out of sight and mind here, not to frighten horses in the street outside! You sound like a mountain lion who's just met the big cat of her dreams!"

Victoria wrapped all four of her tawny limbs around his paler body adoringly as she moaned, "I can't help it. I *have*! It's been nigh a year since I've had a man and, Lord have mercy if you ain't a lot bigger than I expected!"

As Ki started moving in her skillfully, she gasped, "Oh, dear God, careful with that wicked weapon 'til I get used to it, will you?"

Ki nibbled her ear as he assured her, "I expected you to be small and, by the way, as long as we're on such familiar terms right now, it's all right for you to call me Ki."

She didn't get it. Ki had noticed lots of women didn't have his dry sense of humor. But he had no complaints about the way she moved her compact muscular body under his, two strokes to each of his, until she suddenly flung her legs as far apart as they would go, moaning. "Forget what I said about taking it easy, sweetheart! Give it all to me, as fast as you can, for I am coming and I've never come so hard before, and if I die, I die!"

Ki did his best to please her, both ways. For in truth he knew his own strength, and how much damage he could do to man or woman if he failed to control himself at all times, even times like these. Few women understood, and some were hurt, if and when they sensed the reserve of steely control the big Amerasian, trained in the samurai's Bushido code, had over his iron-hard body at all times. Jessica, perhaps, understood how a man could allow himself to have human emotions without letting them take full command. If this had been the one woman he was really devoted to, right now, she would know just how to respond, and the two of them would share an orgasm to jar the circling planets from their appointed rounds. A man with a firm grip on his emotions didn't allow himself to even fantasize about things that could never be. So as Ki ejaculated in Victoria Miller, hard, he knew exactly who he was making love to, and that wasn't bad, either.

As they lay still in one another's arms, he told her quietly, "If you'd like me to show you some unusual ways to attain orgasm, we have plenty of time, and it's best to enjoy the pleasures of nature slowly, even when one does not have a lot of time to kill."

She crooned, "Ooh, keep twitching it in me like that. It feels so freaky. I'm sure glad you decided to kill time this way, Ki. Up to now, this trip's been more tedious than interesting."

Ki rolled partly off her, placing a stiff finger in her hirsute little lap, to either side of her more usual center of sensation, as he said, "I've been meaning to talk to you about that. You certainly have seemed disinterested, for a girl Jessie's been trying to stick with a gold mine."

Victoria spread her thighs farther and moaned, "Oh, I'd

85

rather you stuck it in me some more. What are you *doing* to me, lover? It feels crazy as hell!"

"It's a form of oriental finger massage I picked up in my misspent youth. Do you like it?"

She gasped, "Oooh, don't I ever! But it feels so teasy. Put them loving fingertips together, right in my tickle spot, and do me right, if that's what you want to do to me!"

He kept massaging her the same way, saying, "Relax. This way is slow but sure. Do you notice how this stretches the pinkness and gets it hotter without my really having to touch you there?"

She answered truthfully, "I just told you that you were driving me crazy, damm it! Do it *right*, or, better yet, put your big old love muscle in me all the way again! I'm right on the razor's edge of coming and if you don't get me all the way I'm going to just *die!*"

He went on teasing as he told her, "No you won't. I can hold you right here on the threshold as long as I want. Who sent you to Jessie with that story about a gold mine, Vickie?"

She moaned, "Do it! Do it! I can't stand it anymore and I just have to come!"

He said, "I'll make you come, eleven times in a row if you like. But first tell me who sent you to Jessie, back east."

She gasped, "Oh, Jesussss, I am coming, almost, and it feel so crazy that it almost hurts! I *told* you who sent me to work for Miss Jessica, you torturing heathen! I was sent as a maid by the employment agency and . . . faster, harder, don't stop!"

He did, holding her thrusting pelvis firmly in place on the bounding mattress as he demanded, "How did they come to choose you, of all people, when Jessie contacted them!"

To which she replied, with tears streaming down both brown cheeks, "I was the next in line for the job. Ask them if you don't believe me and, oh, shit, I don't know if I just came or tore something loose down there, but I hate you, hate you, hate you! So let go of me and get out of here!"

Ki did no such thing. He rolled gracefully atop her and, although she tried to struggle, soon had it in her again at an angle she'd never heard of before, albeit back in Dai Nippon it was a position favored by many court courtesans who occasionally found it desirable to climax with an assigned lover. The effect it had on the much less experienced and jaded Victoria would have alarmed Ki if he hadn't been expecting it. Her passion inspired his in turn, and so they were very good friends again by the time she'd climaxed, again, with him.

But as they relaxed once more, entwined in a postion that made her giggle, she said, "Fess up, Ki. Were you trying to torture secrets out of me, before?"

He rolled both her love-slicked nipples between thumbs and forefingers as he told her simply, "Yes. I think I'm beginning to buy your story. But for a girl with her own gold mine who's been forced to work as a lady's maid for eating money, I have to say you've seemed less worried about your inheritance than Jessie has, up to now."

She said, "That feels good. I'm sorry Miss Jessica got in all that trouble on my account. But to worry that hard about gold, I reckon you have to be white, and I'm half Paiute. My mother's people call gold, yellow iron and, to tell the truth, they'd rather have real iron. What's so funny?"

Ki said, "I just remembered something I read in a book about the Spanish conquest of Peru. It seems the captive Inca couldn't understand what drove the Spaniards so after gold. The Inca told them they already had glass and iron, and that both seemed a lot more useful than that soft yellow metal you couldn't make a sharp knife blade or decent needle out of."

Victoria moved her hips to inhale him a little more as she stretched and said, "Paiutes find lots of nuggets crossing dry washes, or they used to, before the saltu came and started digging all over the desert. I know what gold is, since I've had to work for my keep since Cousin Lavinia threw me out. But, I dunno, maybe you have to be pure white to go crazy *total* at the thought of being rich."

"Don't you want to be rich, Vickie?"

"Sure I do. It has to beat working. But I like this, better. Do you want me to get on top, if you're feeling tuckered?"

Ki felt just fine. But he enjoyed novelty as well as anyone else. So they were soon at it again, with her doing most of the work, until she suddenly stopped, with his reinspired erection throbbing in her, close to climax, and told him, "It's my turn to torture *you*. Coming out here on the train, Miss Jessica said something about incorporating my dad's gold strike as a joint whatever of her Starbuck empire. What did she mean by that? Tell me true or you'll never get to come again!"

Ki laughed up at her and said, "I could show you a yoga trick that might give me more pleasure than you. But I'll go along with this unbearable pain you're puttting me through and we'll just see who has the most will power."

She moved on him uncertainly and pleaded, "Come on, honey. I really want to know you and you know we both want to come."

Ki laughed again. "All right, I confess. Jessie meant a joint venture, with you owning the mine and taking all the profits, under the shield of Starbuck Enterprises, an outfit too big for many claim jumpers to mess with. We can assume your father had trouble holding on to his color, despite his mysterious trips in and out for the desert, and he was pure white."

"You mean someone might think screwing a half-Paiute girl-child out of a claim would be even easier?" she asked.

Ki replied, "I do. Jessie learned about such matters the hard way when *her* father was murdered by business rivals. They moved in like wolverines to divide up the pie her father left her. Thanks to me and other friends of Jessie and her father, she not only kept the pie but baked it even bigger by the time the gunsmoke began to clear. Most of the wolverines who took Jessie for a helpless young thing are dead, or still running, now. But it wasn't easy. It takes a lot of noise to scare wolverines away. So, if you know what's good for you, you'll operate your dad's claim as joint partner with the very noisy and powerful Starbuck Enterprises. You don't have to. I, for one, would just as soon Jessie didn't have that added worry. She's already got the worry of everything from cow thieves to Malay pirates on her plate. Making sure you're not screwed out of you inheritance is sure to take up more of her time than her far-flung business dealings may be able to afford."

Atop him, Victoria suddenly laughed and said, "Speaking

of screwing, how can you just lie there so calm? I can feel you're still stiff as a poker."

He shrugged his bare shoulders and asked, "Would you like me to make it go soft for you?" Then she was moving up and down on it as fast as she could manage, telling him not to be so cruel. So in the end she wound up in another position she'd never heard of before. For Ki had decided that as long as it seemed they could trust one another, as much as Ki ever dared trust anyone, there was no sense keeping secrets from a pal.

Chapter 8

So, as the captive Jessie tossed and turned in her dreary prison cell, and Ki taught Victoria sexual secrets ladies in the Orient had to pay good money to learn, Longarm was staring into the glowing coals of the thrifty camp fire he'd made just after sundown in a handy hidey-hole he'd come upon in the gloaming.

He'd bypassed the Indian agency south of Durango in favor of a more southwest route, taking advantage of a canyon he'd remembered from an earler ride through these parts, because he knew better than to light a fire atop a mesa in Indian country, and he'd been told the local Indians considered this canyon haunted.

It was easy enough to see why, as an owl hooted somewhere in the gloom. One of his ponies nickered nervously from where he'd tethered all three inside the shell of an old Hohokam, or maybe Anasazi, ruin. The Ho-speaking Indians said such long-abandoned cliff dwellings had been built by ancient folk, or Hohokam, while Na-Déné speakers called 'em the ancient strangers, or Anasazi. By either name they were long gone, save for a bone or a whole mummy, here and there, if you didn't watch where you were stepping. There wasn't even a whole unbroken pot or shred of basket weave in this modest old pueblo he'd come upon at dusk, sheltered overhead by a swell of pumpkin sandstone and perched on a ledge not too high above the brush-filled canyon floor. Longarm hadn't chosen to camp there because it looked like rain. He knew nobody would be likely to spot a fire even a mile away. So after watering and oating his ponies, he'd built this one, seated with his back propped against his saddle near yet another wall, and seriously considering Peggy Gordon's parting gift as he waited for his coffeepot on the coals to boil. He'd picked up a couple of pints of his own favorite snakebite remedy at that general store, not expecting to be given any more Scotch iodine. He'd meant to season his otherwise black coffee with a shot of Maryland rye, since black coffee, neat, was hardly a bedtime drink for a man on the trail who aimed to catch much sleep.

On the other hand, since he knew he'd likely wind up consuming all three bottles along the trail as long as he had three, it struck him as more sensible to swallow the Speyside Creature well diluted with black coffee. Maryland rye went down a lot nicer, pure.

The owl hooted again. Closer. Longarm muttered, "Aw, shut up, bird. Do I look like a ground squirrel out late?" Then he fumbled in the saddlebag at his elbow to get out the malt liquor. But as he uncorked it with his teeth he couldn't help inhaling some of the fumes, and they somehow made him queasy. He and old Peggy had parted friendly enough, and he'd even gotten her to take a bath with him a couple of times. But for some fool reason, he just didn't want to be reminded of her right now, and in any case, it made more sense to just turn in and the hell with it if he was worried about coffee keeping him awake.

He lit a cheroot to smoke while he made up his mind, casting a casual eye over his dimly lit surroundings as one of the ponies fussed again about something. Pack rats, most likely. None of the old dwellings barely visible in the firelight had been with a roof for sometime. But their free-stone walls and mystic nooks and crannies made a perfect site for a pack-rat town. He started putting everything small enough for a pack rat to pack away in his saddlebags. When he'd done that, he turned back to the fire to notice, for the first time, he was not alone.

There were four of them. All dressed Ute and wearing mocking smiles as well. They were all sixteen to twenty, a mighty dangerous age to be, or meet up with alone. Long-arm's side arm, cuss its hide, was hanging over the horn of his saddle behind him. All four of them had the drop on him, in any case, with B.I.A. repeating rifles some son-of-a-bitch Indian agent must have issued them to hunt with. Longarm felt sure not even an Indian agent could have other white men as their legitimate prey. But from the way they were grinning down at him, they might not know that.

He tried, "Howdy, boys. I'll have some coffee ready for us all in a minute. I reckon you kids ain't scared of haunted houses, eh?"

The older and meaner looking of the not at all pleasant gang replied, in passable English, "We are just as brave as any saltu who sits down to piss. I am called Captain Kidd. I can read. I went to the second grade at the agency. My brothers and I know evil spirits are just bullshit."

One of his companions, eyes sort of glistening, murmured in Ho to the no doubt aptly named English speaker. Captain Kidd nodded. "That looks like a bottle of firewater on the blanket beside you. Why did you offer us coffee if you have firewater? Are you trying to say we are children who should not be offered firewater?"

Longarm picked up Peggy's gift and held it out to them, even as he said, "I can see how you boys have grown. But take it easy on this stuff. It's three times as strong as trade whiskey."

One of them moved in to snatch the bottle from Longarm's hand with what sounded more like a wolf snarl than a gracious thank you. The young Ute put the bottle to his lips and swallowed a substantial slug of it before he had to wheeze, sort of glassy eyed, and pass it on. The next young tough tried to swallow more without stopping. But he couldn't. So it was Captain Kidd's turn. He said something that made the others cover Longarm as he tipped his head back to gargle some down, gasp, and hand what was left to the last Ute, saying, "*Wa*! That is real firewater! What else do you have for us, saltu?"

Longarm said soberly, "I didn't know I was on my way to a birthday party. But you boys are welcome to that malt liquor."

Captain Kidd snarled, "I know that. What *else* are you going to give us, aside from your guns and horses? We always take guns and horses. Maybe, if you have something else for us, we might not kill you slow."

"Do you really have to kill me at all?" asked Longarm, which his tormentor translated. It got quite a laugh.

"Of course we have to kill you. How often do you think we get a chance like this?"

He started to raise the muzzle of his rifle as Longarm tensed to at least go under as a moving target. Then the Ute blinked owlishly and muttered, "*Heya,* that's strong stuff in that bottle," before his knees buckled and he dropped to them to bend gravely over and lie facedown in the fire, spilling the hissing contents of the pot on the coals as his hair burst into flames.

Longarm rolled to one side, groping for the derringer he kept in his vest pocket for just such emergencies. But as he rose to his knees with it trained on the Indians, or where he'd just noticed a mess of Indians, he saw all four of them were down.

He got to his feet, muttering, "Jesus, I've heard some Indians can't hold their liquor, but this is just silly." Then he put the derringer back in his vest to bend over and haul Captain Kidd out of the fire by his bare ankles.

Neither the spilled coffee water nor the frying of Ute faces had done wonders for the small fire. But there was still enough light to work by and it only took Longarm a few moments to determine that all four Indians were stone dead. He picked up the half-empty bottle near the sprawled form of the last one to go down and sniffed. The pungent reek of the Speyside Creature served to hide the scent of whatever in thunder Peggy Gordon had bestowed upon him at the last, so lovingly, but he sensed that once again his instincts for survival had told him more than his common sense was able to manage at times. He muttered, "I didn't think her name was really Peggy Gordon, but I never guessed it might be Lucrezia Borgia! I somehow simply didn't feel up to drinking any of this shit this evening."

That owl hooted at him some more, somewhere down the

canyon. Longarm scattered the last of the coals with his boot and stomped them dead. Then, by the ghostly light of the rising moon he hooted back as best he knew how as he moved back to his saddle, put the bottle aside, and picked up his gun rig to strap it on, muttering, "I sure wish sneaks would come at me one at a time. It makes it hard to think when a man has to sort of juggle 'em."

There were two ways up to the ruin-haunted ledge he'd chosen as a night camp. He'd led his ponies up the ramplike trail from upstream. That mysterious owl was hooting from downstream and that meant a sheer drop. But as he recalled from the last time he'd been able to see anything around here worth mention, it was only ten or fifteen feet from the ledge to the hopefully sandy floor of the canyon. So he jumped.

He landed hard, since he'd fallen farther in the dark than he'd planned, but as he sat up, groping for his hat in the gloom, he decided he hadn't busted any bones and, when that owl hooted at him again, he refused to answer and simply got down to crawling through the bushes.

The canyon floor the long-gone cliff dwellers had once grown corn and squash upon had gone to a waist-high tangle of sticker bush that smelled like someone had burned down a drugstore. The rare but powerful flash floods through the canyon made certain nothing grew there long enough to qualify as a tree. The spaces between the gnarled roots and branches of the tangle were soft sand and Longarm could move silently over rock scree if he had to. The light seemed a little better, now. The moon was rising higher, even as his eyes adjusted to this game of cat and mouse.

He'd worked his way to the far canyon wall and was working down it when he heard the impatient stomp of a stationary pony's hoof and a low voice comforting it in Ho. When that was followed by a worried owl hoot, Longarm grinned wolfishly in the dark and proceeded to move in.

The Ute kid they'd left in charge of the ponies was about fourteen or less, and let out a girlish scream when he suddenly found himself flat on his back with the muzzle of a .44-40 shoved up one nostril and a big black giant sitting on his chest. Indians were only stoic when they saw pain coming.

But now that it was here, the young Ute recovered his manners enough to gulp and tell Longarm, in mission-school English, "Hear me, you are going to be sorry when my brothers find you sitting on me."

Longarm wasn't ready to inform the young tagalong about the fate of the bigger kids, yet. So he just said, "I'm glad you savvy my saltu, Big Chief. Let's see, now. Them five ponies you had tethered yonder adds up to a total war party of five. So I'd say I had you all to myself for now."

His captive replied, "You talk crazy. Are you the saltu we spotted on the canyon trail just before sundown?"

Longarm answered, "Yep. And I see you boys went to considerable trouble to circle wide on the mesa above and work your way down another way. Do you usually work so hard to nail one weary traveler?"

The skinny form under him shrugged, or tried to, and replied, "You were alone. You had three good ponies. Washka, you call him Captain Kidd, thought it would be fun to take everything away from you and maybe use you as a woman before we killed you. Hear me, I said I did not think it was a good thing to do to a blue-eyed saltu. Our nation is not at war with the Great Father this summer. Our old men have only said to avoid your kind, not to kill them."

Longarm eased his gun muzzle to a more comfortable position and said, "I reckon some old boys just pay no heed to their elders. How come you chiefs don't want anyone talking to my breed of late? Don't they like salt, tobacco, and other trade goods no more?"

The Ute kid said simply, "I don't know why the old men are afraid. They never tell us much."

Longarm pistol-whipped him gently and suggested, "Try for an educated guess."

His young captive hissed up at him, "You would not act so brave if I was on my feet with my knife in my hand!"

So Longarm climbed off, rose to his somewhat alarming full height, and said, "Try me, you little shit."

The small but wiry young Ute sat up and put a hand to the hilt of his belt knife. But he didn't rise as he stared soberly up at the big white man and decided, "I don't think it would be a

95

good fight. If I tell you what I know, and let you live, what happens, then, to me and my brothers?"

Longarm said, "I let you go, hoping you go home somewhat older and wiser."

"What about my brothers? Are you going to report them to the agency as renegades?"

Longarm shook his head sincerely and said, "I see no need to cause the B.I.A. more pointless paperwork, any more than you might want to tell your tribal council you were out to get 'em into another big fight with the blue sleeves by going into business on your own. I have no use for your ponies or your skinny red ass. But you leave your weapons here and ride back the way you came. That's if you tell me a tale I find worth hearing, of course."

The boy said, "The old men have not let us come to any of their meetings. But everyone hears things. There is talk among my people of bad saltu, many bad saltu, deep in the pumpkin. They shoot at anyone who comes near them with medicine guns. Guns that fire fast and forever, like the smoke that comes out of the top of the iron horse you people have. Maybe they bred an iron horse to a Remington repeater. Maybe they just have strong medicine. Either way, nobody can hope to win against them. All we can do is stay away from them."

Longarm frowned thoughtfully and decided, "Sounds like at least one Gatling gun, and you're right, they have to be crazy. Are we talking about saltu like me or could they be Mexican or maybe astoundingly advanced Navajo?"

The young Ute scoffed, "No kind but your own has guns that shoot faster than your own iron horse can puff. Do you think we would be afraid of mere Navajo or Mexican saltu? Hear me, even the ones to the south called Apache saltu wet their legs when they hear our proud name, Ute. We are strong. We are many. Our women can beat the men of any other nation, as long as everyone fights fair. I don't think it's fair to shoot at us with guns that are half iron horse!"

Longarm decided, "Whether it's fair or not, it can't hardly be lawful. Nobody's allowed to shoot nothing at the Great White Father's red children without a hunting permit. So

96

which way do I ride to have a word with the mysterious rascals?"

The kid answered simply, "I don't know. Some say their leaders live in a big pueblo, maybe built in the long ago by the Hohokam, near the place where the Chaco Canyon winds to meet the Mancos. Others say this can't be so. That place lies just inside the hunting grounds our Ute leaders said Navajo could use, as long as they strayed no farther north. If the crazy men with the medicine guns want that part of the pumpkin, why are they shooting at us all the time?"

Longarm said, "I mean to ask 'em. I suspect they've been scaring Navajo as well, and a private country set up on or near the treaty line between two Indian nations can't be constitutional. You'd best be heading for home now, sonny. It's getting sort of late and your mamma could be worried about you."

The young Ute rose gingerly to his feet, but answered, *"Ka!* I mean, no. I can't leave without my brothers."

Longarm's voice remained conversational as he told the kid, "Sure you can. Captain Kidd and the others are dead. So just toss that bowie to the sand, get aboard the pony of your choice, and we'll say no more about it."

The kid did no such thing. He threw a string of curses in his own lingo at Longarm, and then he proceeded to wind up for some knife throwing. The six-gun in Longarm's fist fired almost without conscious thought on Longarm's part, and the young but mighty deadly little cuss was back-flipped into a clump of chaparral as the big knife imbedded it's moonlit blade in the sand between them.

Longarm swallowed the green taste in his mouth and moved in to see what he'd just wrought. The kid lay sprawled in the tangle with a bemused smile on his face and a crimson rose pinned to the front of his white blouse by hot lead. Longarm sighed and said, "Well, you'd have likely grown up mean, and at least I won't have to explain all this to the Ute council, now."

He holstered his six-gun and moved away to untether the five ponies, muttering, "You boys are free to graze here all you like before you wander home. If I had a lick of sense I'd

97

shoot you, too. But I always was a sentimental cuss."

He strode back up the canyon to his night camp. The walking was quicker and the climbing was slower. Once back on the ledge, he found neither his own ponies nor the dead Indians gone. He got out his watch to check the time. The night was still young. The moon was still high, and he really wasn't up to explaining why he was camped with a mess of dead Ute in Ute country. So he sat back down and lit a smoke as he pondered his next move.

It was light enough for serious riding, provided one knew where he was going. Nightfall had caught him only a few miles out of Durango and, back that way, he hadn't noticed anything much to trip over. Deeper into the pumpkin, it sounded more spooky. He'd have to move at a walk, this side of sunrise, and that didn't add up to half the distance he wanted to put between himself and the nearby Indian agency before anyone came looking for those five mean kids.

As he stared morosely at the nearest moonlit corpse he told it, "You boys sure have complicated an already confusing job. But at least you didn't get to kill me, thanks to old Peggy's gypsy switch with that bottle and . . . son of a bitch! That has to be it!"

Longarm gave himself a mental kick in the ass as he rose to his feet, muttering, "I should have known right off. She said right out her folk come from Scotland, and I've never yet met a Scotch lassy dark enough to pass for a Spanish gypsy. It was right on that Wanted flier that the Wicked Watsons were said to be Scotch gypsies and you, you damn fool, were involved in the death of at least two Wicked Watsons just before she picked you up, so obvious, aboard that narrow-gauge!"

He saddled the buckskin, but left the pack-trees where they were. He needed time more than supplies he meant to charge to the department in the first place and could easily replace in the second. Then he led all three ponies along the ledge on foot until it rejoined the canyon floor. The smell of fried Ute made all three of them spook in passing, but not enough to be a real bother to a man who'd expected that.

Once he was mounted up and riding for Durango at a brisk trot, leading the other two ponies on the long line, he told the buckskin, "Yeah, I know we're going back the way we just came. But we got to put out an all-points on Miss Peggy Gordon. It just ain't fair to let lawmen great and small across such a vast expanse fall into the clutches of such a treacherous woman. There was nothing in them earlier wants about the Wicked Watsons being downright *murderous*. Everyone will be keeping an eye out for a drifting band of petty con men. News that some of their men may discharge firearms inside the city limits will have gone out, by now. But not a word about a gypsy gal who'll go to any lengths to kill a lawman dirty!"

As he briskly backtracked toward Durango, Longarm backtracked his mind over all the events that had transpired since the so-called Peggy Gordon had picked him up, days before. She'd doubtless picked the name knowing how wicked that gal in the old Scotch ballad was to poor dumb innocent men, the wicked sass. It made him feel dumb as hell as he recalled how hard she'd worked to find a job in Durango once they'd gotten there. He wasn't sure about the Buscadero Kid. There was nothing on the hired gun's yellow sheets to tie him in with a gypsy band. On the other hand, a hired gun was for hire by anyone who had the money, so . . .

"I reckon not," he confided to his pony. "Why lay out good money for a shootist when, all the time, you've been planning to *poison* your victim?"

He rode on, pondering the perfidity of womankind. If she hadn't been trying to hold him in one spot for maybe yet another gent with a gun, why had she waited so long to poison him? She could have done so any time they were alone and drinking together, right?

"Wrong," he muttered aloud. "It makes sense, sort of, if one recalls she sure enjoyed her pleasures sort of perverse, and that a lady who was sort of loco en la cabeza might have gotten a wicked thrill out of playing cat and mouse with a doomed lover. She did say, that one time she wanted it through the back door, that she doubted I'd ever get another gal to take it that way so enthusiastically. How was I supposed to know she meant I'd never get no gal but her for the rest of my impending life?"

The pony under him put a hoof down wrong and staggered a few paces as Longarm threw his weight the right way and steadied it, soothing, "Easy, Buck. You're supposed to see better in the dark than any human, so watch where you're going, damm it."

As they trotted on at a safer pace, Longarm muttered to himself, "Of course, whether she liked it as much as she said or not, there's a less-crazy answer. By waiting until all the excitement of that shoot-out back in Denver died down, and parting friendly with that thoughtful gift, she could have figured on being far off and as forgotten by the time her victim died somewhere off in the canyon lands, like them Ute just did. If and when them boys are ever found, nobody's ever going to accuse a long-gone gypsy gal of murdering 'em!"

Less than two hours later they rode back into Durango. He reined in out front of the Western Union and went in to send some night letters.

The sleepy-eyed clerk on duty scanned the first form Longarm had block printed, brightened at the return address, and said, "If you'd be U.S. Deputy Custis Long, I got a wire for you here. It came in late this afternoon, addressed to you. I was wondering why you didn't come by to pick it up."

"I was busy," Longarm growled. "Get that all-points out sudden. I'll read old Billy Vail's nagging wire as soon as I finish this form, telling him what I just found out about the case, so far."

The clerk handed the yellow envelope to him, suppressing a yawn as he said, "I ain't sure it's from your home office, unless you work out for Richfield, Utah Territory."

Longarm frowned. "I don't even know anybody in Richfield. Hold on, I'm almost finished with this report. I always report sort of terse when I don't know much."

He signed the short report to Vail about someone shooting at Indians with what sounded like a Gatling, leaving out any Indians he'd noticed already dead, and tore open the message Ki had wired from Richfield about Jessie.

His lips went white between his bronzed jaw and dark moustache as he grasped the context of Ki's relayed cry for

100

help. The helpful Western Union clerk asked, "Bad news? You look as if you just met a ghost, no offense."

Longarm said, "I wish that was all I had to worry about."

Then he tore off another sheet, picked up the stub pencil, and wrote, I AM COMING STOP HANG ON FOR FORTY-EIGHT HOURS STOP CUSTIS. Then he told the clerk to send it to J. Starbuck care of Ki and asked how soon they'd get it. The Durango clerk said, "Tomorrow morning at the earliest. We don't stay open all night in towns that rinky-dink."

Longarm nodded curtly. "It don't matter. There's no way in hell I can get there in less'n two days."

Chapter 9

Ki didn't see how that was possible when he delivered Longarm's wire and others to Jessie at the town lockup the next
morning. As they sat across a plank table with an armed deputy standing by in the visitation cell, Ki explained, "I came
here directly from the telegraph office, of course. But last
night I went over that desert route with Vickie again, in some
depth. Your knight in shining armor is talking about over two
hundred miles as the crow flies and one hell of a lot farther by
horseback. He must think he's the Pony Express. But not even
Wild Bill Hickok would have made such a brag when *he* was a
Pony Express rider. Say Longarm meant to ride flat out across
open prairie, changing mounts every few miles, his boast
would be an outside possibility. But there just aren't any re-
mount stations between here and Durango, and Vickie says
there are canyons even Longarm couldn't leap, a lot of them,
between here and there."

Jessie remained adamant. "Custis has never made me a
false promise."

"There's always a first time. You can run a horse fifty
miles a day, or maybe a little more, if you don't mind shooting
the poor brute when it drops out from under you and the desert
sun. What's he supposed to do then, run the rest of the way on
foot? Jessie, the Greek Marathon measures less than twenty-
five miles, and more than one runner's dropped dead trying
that, in cooler and a lot flatter country!"

"If he says he can make it in two days you'll just have to

ask him how he did it when he gets here in two days. What about those other wires, Ki?"

Her segundo handed them all across to her. "I took the liberty of reading them on my way here. I didn't know how soon they'd let me see you. Peters and Cohan say they'll have a defense team here about the time Longarm's due to come puffing in across the sage flats to the east. I guess your lawyers don't think they're wearing seven league boots. I don't understand what they mean about asking for a change of venue. I haven't been speaking English as long as most lawyers."

"I understand it and it sounds like a good idea," Jessie said. "I can't say I've been mistreated here in Richfield. When one considers what they think I did to an elder of their church, I have to allow they've been mighty good sports about it. But a change of venue would mean a hearing before some other Utah court, with a jury that might not have gone to meetings with the late Elder Reynolds, see?"

Ki frowned thoughtfully. "Not if we're talking about a Mormon jury, anywhere in this territory. They all behave as if they're suspicious of outsiders."

"I reckon they have a right to feel sort of persecuted. The young prophet who founded their faith, Joseph Smith, was killed by a lynch mob, along with his brother, back in the Midwest in the forties. The mob threw both of them to their deaths from the same high window. The army may or may not have had a just reason for hanging another Mormon leader named Lee, during the California gold rush. Custis says there's good and bad on both sides and that Lee was guilty as hell. But of course he's a martyr to many Mormons, and the eastern papers still print lots of lies about them. So who can blame them if they'd just as soon the rest of us stayed out of their dusty little promised land?"

"Let's not worry about whether we've been persecuting anyone for holding different religious views or not. I know for a fact you didn't back-shoot that holy man they say you did. But I doubt a Mormon jury, anywhere, is going to let you off with so much hard evidence against you. Why can't Peters and Cohan ask for this change of venue to a *federal* court?

Utah's still a territory under federal jurisdiction at the top, isn't it?" Ki asked.

Jessie sighed and shook her head. "Only at the very, very top. One of the things both sides agreed to when the short but bloody Mormon War of the gold rush days was called off was that the Latter-day Saints would get to run things pretty much their own way, with the cavalry at Fort Douglas dealing with any further Indian trouble and the federal courts only butting in when the rights of Mormons and us so-called gentiles came into serious conflict."

Ki shot a disgusted glance at the bearded stoic guard across the room, on Jessie's side of the center table, and asked the girl, "What do you call this damned frame-up, then? They're talking about standing you in front of a firing squad, Jessie!"

She smiled wanly and replied, "I get to ask them to hang me, instead, if I want. I don't think the law here framed me, Ki. I feel sure they're sincere. The rascals who *did* set me up so slick left no lawman with a lick of sense much choice. They did find me standing over that poor man with a hot six-gun in my hand, and I did admit I'd shot him. Or, rather, that I'd shot *some* damned body. The problem is simply to prove it wasn't their Elder Reynolds I shot."

"In front of a more tolerant federal jury," Ki insisted.

But Jessie said, "I don't see how even Peters and Cohan could get a local federal judge to touch the case. My constitutional rights as a non-Mormon are not in question. They haven't locked me up for smoking or sipping tea, you know. This is the county seat of the county a judge of said county was murdered in. The jurisdiction would be the same in any county in this country. It's going to be a tall order to get my case before another Utah court as it is. I frankly doubt a jury of strange Mormons would be apt to decide on the evidence against me any less justly than a federal jury that would likely be half Mormon to begin with."

She unfolded one of the other wires Ki had just handed her and swore in a most unladylike way, albeit under her breath, before she said, "I don't like this about impending labor trouble at my East Texas cotton mill. I thought we ordered that manager to offer those mill hands an extra two bits a day."

Ki shrugged and said, "You did. When the cat's away the mice will play. I warned you not to come out here on this wild-goose chase when you have a business of your own to mind, Jessie. That man knows textiles well enough. He just can't seem to get it through his head that President Lincoln meant what he said about slavery, and a lot of those mill hands are colored."

She pursed her lips. "Fire him. I never hired him to abuse my hired help, white, black, or lavender. That delegation of textile workers I received made a good case for the way food prices have risen since the depression of the seventies. So I *told* him to pay them the extra money they needed to feed their families. What do you suppose could have gotten into the fool?"

Ki said dryly, "You leaving Texas, for openers. I told you he was sort of pigheaded about paying colored men *anything*. I think young Jenkins would make a good replacement. He knows the business and, while he rode for Texas in the war, he seems to have adjusted to the way things just have to be since Texas lost."

"Good. That's settled, then. Oh, I see one of our tea clippers put in to Galveston with a spoiled shipment from Dai Nippon. The insurers ought to cover us. But that must have been one awful leak, to pickle a whole hold full of tea."

Ki sniffed. "A fire hose would have worked as well, and felt safer to old Captain Mason. I told you Mason was loco, or knew something *I* didn't about my own mother's country, when he said he could get a better price for you at Hakodate than at Nagasaki, remember?"

She asked, "How come? Don't they drink tea at Hakodate?"

"They drink it there," Ki replied. "They don't *grow* it. Hakodate is so far north of the tea country that it's as cheap for them to import it by sea from Mainland China. I've already wired our agents in Galveston not to dispose of that so-called ruined tea. Seawater-soaked or not, I'm sure I can still tell tea leaves from maple leaves or whatever Mason got Starbuck Enterprises to pay for in Hakodate."

She started to ask when he meant. Then she sighed and said, "It's my own fault for giving a skipper under a cloud a second chance. My insurance agent warned me about him, too. Have his cargo impounded and send him on shore leave until we can make dead certain he tried that old chestnut again. I know all too well what it feels like to be accused of something I didn't do, and clippers have been known to spring leaks, you know."

"Lots of skippers come back with the cargo a ship owner pays for, too. Meanwhile, assuming your *Delta Cloud* hasn't sunk at the dock in the meantime, who do you want to send her out under? You don't make money on a masterless ship tied up in Galveston, you know."

She thought for a moment. "Caleb Norris, that first mate on my *Comanche Warrior*. He's as honest a man as I've ever met and a mite overage in grade. Order him to inspect the *Delta Cloud* top to bottom and make sure she's shipshape before he takes her out again to . . . Nagasaki?"

"If you still want all that tea. The merchants there get it homegrown *and* Chinese. So they're always anxious for a big-bulk transaction. I'll take care of it. What do you want to do about that problem with your panhandle herd? Do we fight or negotiate?"

Jessie scanned the telegram from her worried ramrod. "I don't think a few sides of beef are worth bloodshed. Let's wire Uncle Quanah Parker at the ranch he lives on now, and see if he can get his Comanche kids to ask for grub politely instead of scaring my poor cowhands half to death with all that wild shooting and war whooping."

Ki said he felt sure the sensible and now much calmer Comanche leader could probably nip the trouble in the bud and suggested that, meanwhile, it might be a good idea to order the boys with the panhandle herd not to shoot back unless some Comanche kid drew blood. Jessie agreed and said with a sigh, "You're so right about mice when the cat's away. It seems I've barely turned my back on things and all sorts of petty details are getting out of hand back home."

She picked up the last telegram, read it twice, and shook her head with wonder, saying, "Now this is just too much! Has everyone back home been smoking loco weed?"

Ki asked if she was talking about the message from her

stockbroker in Fort Worth and she said, "Yes. Didn't you send that wire from Denver, ordering him to get rid of those silver shares and buy me some copper?"

Ki, who'd of course already read the sassy reply to a client's order, said, "I sent it from the Western Union office across from our Denver hotel, not five minutes after you wrote it. I don't understand that answer, either. What do they mean about a discretionary account, Jessie?"

"It's power over a client's money my dear father told me never to give a broker I was married up with. It allows your broker to buy and sell for you at his own discretion, of course. Dad said it was like giving a man a license to steal from you. So I've never done it. Now the damned fools say they can't sell my silver shares at a loss without a hand-signed order from me. So they haven't done so, and the silver market was dropping when I told them to dump that silver stock, way back in Denver!"

Ki felt better trying to understand the workings of another man's gun hand than the mysteries of high finance. But for once it didn't seem complicated, even to him. He grimaced and said, "Even I can see silver's in oversupply while all those wires they're stringing back east have to be made of copper. I'll wire them right away to do as you say, Jessie."

But she asked bleakly, "How? It says here in black and yellow that they refuse to be responsible for a client's losses unless they're covered by discretionary power or some dumb law papers they want me to sign, in ink, in front of a notary public. How am I supposed to do that if I'm locked up in jail?"

Ki didn't know. He said, "Well, as soon as your lawyers show up they'll be able to do something about it. Meanwhile you still own the silver stock, whatever it's worth, and, frankly, I think a stock market loss is the least of your troubles right now."

She laughed wearily and got up from the table as she told him to carry on as best he could, without her, for now. Then Ki left to send some blistering telegrams as the bearded Mormon deputy escorted Jessie back to her cell.

As he locked her in, the laconic local lawman shifted his

weight awkwardly and said, "I couldn't help listening in on some of your conversings back there, ma'am. Don't let 'em change venue on you. There's a chance you'll wind up with a hung jury here in Richfield. Lord knows what a jury of total strangers might decide. You was so right about the evidence. They got you dead to rights with the murder weapon in your hand."

She dimpled at him through the bars. "I sure thank you for that doubtless well-meant advice, sir. But tell me, if you think I'm guilty, how am I to hope for this hung jury of yours?"

. He said, "Oh, I don't think your guilty, Miss Jessie. Neither does my wife, Sarah Ann. She's one of the ladies as brung your supper last night. I'll allow I had my doubts, until I heard you talking to that breed gent just now. I've never heard an outsider talk so understanding about us and our ways. It just don't make sense to me that a lady as rich as you have to be would come all the way out here to murder a Mormon elder unless she hated Mormons just crazy. I don't think you do. I think you could be telling the truth. It's just that I don't see who else could have done it, or why, either. But my Sarah Ann's been taking your part and the folk at your hotel has spoke up for you, too. They say they heard you telling your friends you was leaving to see Elder Reynolds on some legal matters, and I just heard myself how much of them matters you has to worry about. They say you never left the hotel looking mad at anyone, and I say that even if you had, it don't seem likely an outsider gal could have called that meeting at the temple, and I know for a fact *that* was a big fib."

She favored him with a more hopeful smile and asked, "Then you think a local jury might believe me, after all."

He shook his head and said, "No, ma'am. Based on the evidence as I see it, I'd have no choice but to find you guilty if I was called for jury duty myself. But lots of folk around here ain't half as smart as me, and you only need one juror outta twelve to hold out and mess things up so bad the judge has to declare a mistrial."

She sighed and said, "I don't want a mistrial. I want to be found innocent so I can get out of here!"

He regarded her soberly though the bars and told her, "It

ain't no use hoping for the impossible, ma'am. But at least if it takes 'em longer than usual to find you guilty, that'll be all the more time you has to live. So you just do as I say and hope for a long-drawn out process and, oh, yeah, when they finally *do* get around to your execution, make sure you ask for the firing squad. Everyone does, as a rule. So our local executioner would be likely to botch a hanging just awful."

Chapter 10

The next two days seemed to take forever, even to Ki, who had a better way to occupy his nights than Jessie did in her tiny cell. When he wasn't in bed with Victoria, Ki struggled to keep Starbuck Enterprises from taking the bit in its teeth and going out of control in every direction. It wasn't easy, by wire, even with the powers vested in him by a lady everyone agreed was the boss, even as they ignored her orders. It reminded Ki of the confusion after Alex Starbuck had been murdered. Apparently some felt about a boss in jail the way they'd felt about a dead boss leaving the reins of his empire in the hands of a mere girl. It had been a hell of a struggle, convincing some stubborn men of the error of their ways. Now it seemed to be starting all over. Couldn't the fools see that Jessica Starbuck was still in the saddle, or at least still alive?

While just as worried inwardly, Jessie soothed Ki's rage when he visited her by telling him a story. She said, "My father knew a man one time, maybe even richer than him, who liked to play a little trick on his friends and relations. He'd noticed, coming home from the losing side right after the war, that a lot of folk who'd always called him Colonel and sort of bowed and scraped to him didn't act like that at all, once they saw him in a threadbare Confederate uniform with half the gold braid shot away, and heard his plantation had been burned. What they *didn't* know was that he still had a heap of money on deposit with the Bank of England, and owned a share in a South African gold mine as well as a considerable herd running half-wild in West Texas but still wearing his brand. My father didn't know this when they met up. He just staked the ex-officer enough to get his cows up the Chisholm Trail once things settled down a mite."

Ki asked, "Are you talking about that cattle baron, old Ned Eskers?"

"I am. Cattle are the least of his holdings, and it was him who tipped my father off on the Black Hills strike a few years back. He had lots of friends in places high and low. But, you see, a lot of folk judge a book by its cover, and so he learned who his *true* friends were fast when it looked for a time as if he was broke. He couldn't go on looking broke very long, of course. His wife wouldn't let him. But it's surprising how hard it is, today, to get an invitation to the grand parties they throw at their new mansion on the Brazos. You see, he doesn't just remember friends he's made since the war. Every five years or so he makes it his habit to show up at his fancy club, looking upset, to announce he's just been about wiped out of the stock market. Then he waits to see who still wants to drink with him or even offer to help him out with a loan if he could use one. My father passed that test, of course, and that's when he learned the story. A man has to tell you something when you're shoving money in his face and he doesn't really want it. I always thought it was a sort of silly way to act, but now that I've had time to study on it, I can see the point. You've often warned me I'm too good-natured, Ki. If ever I get out of this mess I mean to do some housecleaning back in Texas, starting with those damned brokers. A nice deputy brought me the Salt Lake papers this morning, and that silver stock I told them to get rid of has dropped even further."

Ki grimaced. "I've been getting defiance from other quarters as well. Your Galveston warehouse firm says I can't give orders in your name unless you give me power of attorney and send them a copy."

She shrugged and said, "I'll sweep that corner when I can get at it with my broom. Everybody knows you're my segundo. But I reckon they don't expect me to beat this murder charge after all. I can't think of anything else that might make grown men I hired act so willful."

Ki didn't answer. He'd already thought of that and had been hoping she might not. So far, the local population had been as decent to him and Victoria as small-town folk ever were to outsiders with unusual features. But despite what Jessie had told him about that one friendly deputy, the town sure seemed to be expecting a short trial and a quick verdict.

Hence, Ki was feeling mighty anxious by the time the train he was waiting for finally arrived late one morning, just before noon. Ki had left Victoria at the hotel. He was pacing the open platform like a caged panther, wondering why the devil somebody didn't get off, as, up closer to the engine, they were unloading some riding stock and a few crates destined for the local stores. Then the chubby, short Tom Cohan of Peters and Cohan detrained with a colored porter and a saratoga trunk, blinking around at his stark, sunbaked surroundings. He looked a lot happier when he spotted Ki approaching, and held out a hand to exclaim, "Jesus-Mary-and-Joseph, and is this where the poor lass has been locked up by them dreadful religious fanatics? I got here as soon as I could, Ki. Where are they holding poor darling Jessie?"

Ki said, "The lockup's not far. You look as if you were planning on staying a while, Tom."

The lawyer said, "I hope not. My plan is to get her transferred up to Salt Lake City, at least. Even if it take some time to get her off, the women's house of detention up there will be ever so much more comfortable for her."

Before Ki could answer, he spotted yet another familiar figure getting off the train, lugging a big sachel in one brown fist and the fork of a Vadalia roper in the other.

Ki gasped, "Longarm! I thought you were in Durango. Way the hell east across two hundred miles of desert."

As he joined them, Longarm said, "I was. Nobody but a natural fool would try to cross such disgusting country in high summer, even if he wasn't in a hurry. It was tough enough getting here by *rail* in just two days. I had to go the long way round and change trains considerable to get me and my ponies here when I did. Who's this gent in the derby hat, Ki?"

The tall Amerasian introduced them, and Longarm said, "I wish I'd known who you were on the train, Lawyer Cohan. We could have jawed about this mess poor Jessie's in as we rode down from Salt Lake together. I saw you in the club car, talking to that big red-headed gal, too. I could have told you she figured to be going on down the line with your free drinks in her. But I didn't know you, then."

Tom Cohan smiled sheepishly. "I had to pass the time some way."

Ki picked up Cohan's heavy trunk as if it was empty and said, "I'll take this to the hotel for you. You've just time to wash up before it's visiting hour at the lockup, and Jessie will sure be glad to see you both."

Longarm told them to go on ahead, as he had to see about the three ponies he'd haggled for once. He didn't want to go through *that* all over again. So Ki led Tom Cohan to the hotel, introduced him to Victoria, and after a short conversation checked the time and said, "Let's go, Tom. Vickie, you'd better stay here."

The pudgy lawyer didn't argue. He said he was anxious to hear Jessie's side of the story as well, adding, "I guess you know what the papers all across the country are making of this case, don't you, Ki? If ever you decided to shoot anyone at all important, make sure nobody's ever heard of you before."

Ki said, "Dammit, Jessie never shot anybody. I told you it was a frame-up in the first night letter I wired you."

Cohan said, "That you did, and I for one believed every word of it. But to tell the truth, I don't know how I'll ever get a jury to buy her story, Ki. Did they really arrest her with the smoking murder weapon in her hand and all?"

"No. If Reynolds was shot in the back, someone else had to be holding the murder weapon. Jessie says she'd just shot it out with another man up there. But let's let her tell you all that. What are the odds on getting her out on bail in the meantime, Tom?"

Cohan sighed and said, "On murder-in-the-first-degree? Not good, I fear. For what sort of bail could the court set that a very rich lady might not jump to save her own pretty neck?"

Ki grimaced and said, "They shoot you for murder in Utah.

113

But I see what you mean. That's the lockup ahead, gray building to the right."

But before they could get there, Jessie stepped out into the bright sunlight with the town law on one side of her and Longarm on the other. That would have been astonishing enough, but she was wearing her six-gun, as well.

Longarm greeted Ki and her lawyer with, "Howdy, boys. You got here just in time. Jessie, me, and old Al here were just on our way to the murder scene. Jessie's been released into my custody. So we better make sure she didn't do it, lest I have to arrest her some more."

Tom Cohan smiled incredulously and said, "That's impossible! I was just telling Ki that they never allow anyone facing trail for a capital offense to go free on bail."

Longarm replied, "Hell, I know that. You show us the way, Jessie. I'm sure anxious to see where they switched dead bodies on you."

Jessie pointed and said it was just a short walk that way, adding to her lawyer, "Hello, Tom. Isn't he marvelous?"

As Ki and Cohan tagged along, the bewildered lawyer said, "He sure is, and how did you do it, Longarm?"

The tall deputy answered modestly, "It was nothing. As I had to lay over in Salt Lake between trains, I looked up an old pal, a territorial officer of the court who also happens to be a Mormon bishop."

The Lincolnesque local lawman, Al said, "I still say Bishop Cosgrove must be out of his mind, and I can't wait to see what our prosecuting attorney is going to have to say about all this. But who are we to take on the U.S. government and the Salt Lake Temple, all at once?"

Longarm explained, "I got 'em to place the suspect in my personal custody so I could investigate the fool crime right. They know in Salt Lake that I'm sort of good at such things, even if old Cosgrove and me don't agree about sipping coffee and worse. Are those the outside steps you told me about, Jessie?"

Before she could answer, the bearded Al said, "They are, and as anyone can see, they're the only way up or down. Nobody else went up or down 'em after me and Spud heard

114

them shots and come running. We was on the walk, making our rounds, when we heard 'em. We never lost sight of them steps as we run this way, neither!"

Jessie said, "Nobody ever said you did, sir. I told you I was alone, upstairs, with the man I shot it out with."

"Or so you thought," Longarm said, and then took the lead as they reached the bottom of the steps. He knew it would have been more polite to let ladies go first. But he wanted to see just what Jessie had seen when she'd first gone up those very same steps. They'd fixed the window, damn their hides, and as he entered with the others in tow, he saw the dentist's door was open and a little kid in there was hollering fit to bust as his mama told him to be brave. Longarm waited until Jessie and the others had crowded in with him before he asked Al if he had the key to the late Elder Reynolds's office. Al said he had it, and didn't want to miss this for the world. So Longarm let him take the lead and followed Al down the hallway, casually asking Jessie along the way whether she'd noticed any other doors open that fateful day.

She said she hadn't. As Al turned the key in the lock of the last door down he said, "I can answer that one. All the others with business up here has been questioned by me, personal. They all locked their doors when they left for that fake meeting at the temple. This here is the only door any stranger could have opened. Only it wasn't no stranger. It was poor old Reynolds. He seems to have been the only person who wasn't told about that meeting he called."

Al opened the door. They all went in. Jessie pointed to the floor just inside and told Longarm, "That's where the man I shot was laid out when I last saw him. The next time I looked, it was Judge, or Elder, Reynolds. The rest you know."

Longarm said, "Not hardly. I just got here. Where does that door lead, Jessie?"

She looked blankly at the door across the room and said she had no idea. Al said, "It leads into the poor man's inner office, of course. This here's just his waiting room. Can't you see that?"

Longarm moved over, put a hand on the knob, and tried it as he asked, "Did you search in here the day of the shooting?"

115

Al could only reply, "There was no call to. The dead man lay out here, and you may have noticed that door's locked."

Longarm grimaced, fished out his pocketknife, and made short work of the slip latch as he muttered, "So much for all those other securely locked offices up here. Can't you see how cheap this place is put together, Al?"

The older lawman said he sure could now as he followed Longarm into the cluttered office of the dead man. There was a rolltop desk, a table, and a mess of shelves, all covered with papers, books of legal and religious persuasion, and a lot of dust. Al moved to open the window, commenting on how hot and stuffy it was in there. But Longarm said, "Don't. I smell how disgusting it is in here, too. I want to study on that before we stir things up."

Jessie, from the doorway, wrinkled her pert nose and said, "Good heavens, it smells like, well an outhouse in here."

Longarm spotted something glinting from the shadows of the dead man's desk and bent to scoop it up, saying, "An outhouse someone was smoking in, while they were waiting. Have a look at this, Al."

The Mormon lawman took the little paper ring and held it up to the light, apparently sincerely puzzled as he read off the gilt, "Daniel Webster, Longarm?"

The younger but more worldly lawman sighed and said, "It's what I get for expecting such a clean-living gent to investigate a murder scene. Daniel Webster is the make of an expensive cigar, Al. I forget what they cost, but I know *I* can't afford to smoke Daniel Websters, and Miss Jessie would be too refined."

Al handed the cigar band back with a shrug, asking, "So?"

Longarm said, "So are you content to have an elder of the Latter-day Saints caught smoking back here, private, when his parents weren't watching?"

"Oh, I get it. You're saying that since us Saints don't smoke at all, and ladies hardly ever smoke cigars, you think some other man must have been up here in this office at some time. What if someone was? All the clients poor Reynolds dealt with wasn't Saints."

Longarm shook his head. "First you accuse one of your

116

own church elders of having a secret vice, and now you aim to make him out as a lazy slob. Take a look in the wastebasket and tell me what you see, Al."

The town law stepped over to the wastebasket near a leg of the rolltop, glanced down, and said, "Nothing. There's nothing in there, Longarm."

Longarm nodded and said, "Right. That means someone emptied it, before Reynolds was killed. You can see by the clutter he wouldn't have worried about that himself. How often are these offices tidied up by the hired help?"

Al thought and said, "Three or four times a week, in the evening, I think. But . . . hold on, now. You're saying the charwoman tidied up in here the night before the killing, and that poor Reynolds didn't have time to toss nothing in his wastebasket before Miss Jessie shot him in the back, that afternoon?"

Jessie stamped her booted foot and told him she'd never done any such thing. But Longarm shushed her with a wave and told old Al, "You're learning. Anyone can see that, Saint or not, Reynolds was no fiend for tidiness. The only way a busy man could have avoided tossing one fool paper in his office wastebasket all morning was by not working here worth mention. I read it that he had an early morning caller, a gentile who smoked expensive cigars. That smell that's still lingering is what you get when, sorry, Jessie, a dying man craps his pants in a small closed room and spends a lot of time on the floor of the same."

Al said, "But we found him out yonder."

"I ain't finished. The killer done the deed in here. Then they sat about waiting, and since I just observed how disgusting some dead men can get, at least one of 'em lit a cigar to cut down on the stink."

"Hold on. Did you say killers, plural?"

"Had to be two, at least. One was the one Jessie shot, and the other was the one who switched the bodies on you all. Jessie says the one who greeted her with a gun already drawn asked who she might be before he started to aim said gun at her. That wasn't the way it was supposed to work out. But when she killed *him*, instead, his less-courageous sidekick did

117

the little he could to tidy up, and damned if it didn't almost work. I'm just guessing about this part. But I'd say he, or they, got the extra body out by way of that there window, later, after dark. It didn't hurt a man who was already dead to fall out a second-story window, no matter how he might have landed. After that, they just locked up. You can see how tough that must have been. Now all we have to figure is the who and how come. The who figures to be harder. Since the loser of that shoot-out was waiting to greet Miss Starbuck by name, I'd say they had to be waiting for her to show up. They knew she had an appointment to meet here with poor old Reynolds. They likely just killed him to keep him from warning her. Then they put out the word about a meeting up the way, taking place about the time she was due to arrive."

From where he stood near Jessie in the doorway, Tom Cohan said, "You were right. He's marvelous. Even if he's making it up out of thin air, that's going to be our defense and I'm sure to get you off!"

But even as her lawyer was saying this, another couple of fussy-looking gents, dressed for court or a funeral, bustled in to demand an explanation of the unusual situation.

Al introduced them as the prosecution team intent on having Jessie shot or hung, lady's choice. Then he told the county prosecutor, "Things are starting to look a whole lot different now, Morg. This federal man's got me about convinced the little lady didn't do it!"

Morgan Welch snapped, "I'll be the judge of that! Who let you all into this locked office without a court order?"

Longarm said, "Me. I don't need a court order when I got my pocketknife. I didn't bust nothing."

Al explained what they'd figured out so far, as if he'd had most of the grander notions springing from his own brow like old Athena from the brow of Zeus. Longarm didn't mind Al stealing some of the credit. He'd long since learned how handy it could be, in court, to have a lawman the jurors knew better on one's side.

The local prosecutor cut the town law off before he could finish by objecting, "That's all mighty fanciful, but let's stick to the facts, Al. You and Spud caught this young woman standing over the victim with a smoking gun and, by the way, what's she doing out of jail with that same gun strapped around her hips?"

Al protested, "It wasn't my notion," as he produced the court order from Salt Lake City and handed it over.

Longarm was too polite to tell the small-town prosecutor to read it and weep. So he said, "Why don't we talk some more about Miss Starbuck's gun? As I've just been told—and your jury is sure to hear in court if you don't behave yourself—Al, here, along with lots of other honest citizens the defense can call, heard three, count 'em, three shots before he ran up here to find the accused on the landing, repeat landing, with her gun in hand and a tale of a shoot-out on her sweet pure lips."

Welch almost snarled, "A tale that won't hold water. It takes two to gunfight, and it's been my experience that when people fight they generally face one another. The victim was found just outside this very room, unarmed, with a bullet in his back."

"That don't work," said Longarm flatly. "Let's all step back out there while we ponder the three shots that even you agree a mess of folk heard."

Once he'd herded everyone back into the reception room, Longarm said, "It's been fixed since, but I'm sure Al will agree the glass down to the far end had been subjected to gunfire. More than one pane, Al?"

The older lawman shook his bearded head and replied, "Nope. Just the lower right-hand pane."

"That accounts for one round," Longarm said. "Miss Starbuck, here, says that one was fired by her would-be assassin. But for the sake of argument, let's say she's lying. Let's say she was the only one up here that day with a gun. Al says, and your charges read, that the late Elder Reynolds was right there on the floor with one bullet in his back, with powder burns around the puncture in his dark coat, or dried blood smears if I'm guessing right about what really must have happened."

"What difference does that make, as long as she shot him?" asked the assistant with Welch.

Longarm said, "I'm coming to that. Meanwhile, see if you can count on your fingers with me. One bullet in Reynolds and one bullet through the window glass adds up to two of the shots you boys kept insisting this young lady fired. Where did the *third* one end up?"

There was a collective gasp from everyone but Longarm, who naturally didn't have to wonder why *he* hadn't thought of that. He just pointed at the four walls around them and went on. "If there's a .38 slug from Miss Starbuck's gun embedded anywhere on or about these premises, you'd best start searching for it before she stands trial, Lawyer Welch. For unless you can produce it in court, Lawyer Cohan here is going to make you look like the village idiot."

The cherubic Tom Cohan grinned like a mean little kid and said, "That I will, with the greatest of pleasure!"

Welch looked sick. Then he brightened and said, "Hold on. Who's to say only one bullet went through that one pane of glass down the hall?"

Longarm looked disgusted and said, "Now you're really reaching. But, all right, anything's possible. Let's say a gal with no motive had to fire three times to hit a man in the back, and only aimed good when she was missing him. I'm a fair-minded man, empowered by both the federal and territorial governments to investigate this case and see that justice is done. I sure hope old Reynolds ain't been buried yet."

Al said, "Well, *sure* he's been buried, Longarm. He got killed days ago and it's high summer. It wouldn't have been decent not to bury him."

Longarm nodded sympathetically and asked, "In that case, you surely have an autopsy report to show me and Miss Starbuck's defense, right?"

Al and the local law team exchanged stricken glances. Welch said, "There was naturally a death certificate, signed by his family physician. There was no mystery about the cause of death, dammit."

Longarm raised an eyebrow and asked, "Wasn't there? Seems to me that before I accused a lady of putting a bullet in a man, I'd want to make sure there was a bullet in him. Miss Starbuck's shooting iron throws .38 slugs. How were you aiming to prove in court that Reynolds wasn't shot with a .45, .32, a .22 or, come to think of it, no bullet at all?"

Morgan Welch snorted in derision and said, "Now you're just talking foolishness. Of course he'd been hit by *some* sort of bullet. How else would we have found a bullet hole in his back?"

Longarm replied grimly, "Before you call anyone around here a fool, I want you to consider that an elder of your own faith was murdered most foul by a person or persons unknown, and so what are you doing about it? You're trying to pin it on the first handy stranger, and a gal at that. Do you call that justice?"

"I think he's got you, Morg," said Al with a crooked grin.

Welch snapped, "It was your notion to arrest her, you grinning ape!" Then he turned back to Longarm and said, "Speaking of apes, if you're so smart, suppose you tell me how one goes about shooting a man in the back without a bullet, and how you know so much for a gent who wasn't in town at the time!"

"We'd best eat this apple a bite at a time. I have the considerable advantage of knowing Miss Starbuck hardly ever fibs to me. But, as a lawman, I still have to go along with solid evidence. Al, here, and everyone else in town at the time, heard gunshots just before Al and his deputy responded to the same. That's evidence, whether we buy Miss Starbuck's story or not. If she's lying, she fired three shots to kill a man once. If he was already dead before she got here, and that's the only way her story works, how come nobody heard gunfire, earlier? Silence is not only golden but evidence as well. It just plain wasn't possible to shoot Reynolds in the back before all them folk went off to that meeting at your temple. Before you ask why the murder had to take place earlier, ask yourselves why they'd murder a man they didn't have to."

Al stared at Longarm with open admiration as he opined, "That makes sense. They had to know it was safe to spread false rumors about a meeting. Reynolds might have told us different, if he was free to wander about. So before they done it they had to have him tied up secure or dead, and if they had him tied secure, why did they have to kill him?"

"They didn't bother with trying to hold him captive," Longarm explained bleakly. "They killed him early in the

121

morning just to get him out of the way. It was nothing personal. They were after Miss Starbuck. They didn't shoot him, though. The whole town would have heard that. They stabbed him, likely with an ice pick or one of them sneaky stiletto blades some professional killers favor. Then they left him dead in his own office and lay in wait for their more important intended victim, Miss Starbuck. It was likely the stiletto sneak who had the yellow streak. When his noisier sidekick lost the gunfight, he just lay low in the back, behind a locked door, until he saw the chance to switch the bodies and hole up some more."

He smiled thinly at Al and continued, "I doubt he planned on you jumping to such hasty conclusions, pard. That was pure luck. He was mostly out to keep you and me from identifying his sidekick. The man Miss Starbuck really shot was likely a hired gun with a record and known features. We all tend to judge a man by the company he keeps, and strangers stand out in a town like this one."

"That's for sure," Al said. "I see it all, now. Them hired killers got here ahead of the lady and just killed poor Elder Reynolds to lay a trap for her!"

Morgan Welch protested, "Soap bubbles! It's a pretty story, I'll allow, but you haven't said one thing so far that you can back up with a single shred of solid evidence! As long as we're making up fairy tales from thin air, how do you like the one *I* mean to tell in court?"

He pointed at the floor between them and said, "Fact: Elder Reynolds was found right there, dead as a doornail!" He pointed at Jessie and said, "Fact: This young woman was the only other person anyone saw on or about the premises at the time and, fact: She was holding the murder weapon in her hand!"

Longarm turned to Jessie's lawyer with a weary sigh and said, "I reckon you could get an exhumation order from a higher court if they refuse to give you one here, right?"

"That I can and that I shall. You have my word on it!" Tom Cohan said.

Morgan Welch looked sort of green and protested, "You

can't do that. It would be inhuman to dig the poor man up again!"

Longarm shrugged. "Not as inhuman as watching this poor gal die for a crime she may not have committed. You have my word I'll say I'm sorry as hell, in writing, if it turns out there's a .38 slug of her brand embedded in the carcass of that Morman elder. I can't answer for what others might say if it turns out he was killed with anything else. But I see no call to worry about *your* political future, you stubborn cuss."

Welch gulped. "I'm not trying to be unreasonable, dammit. I have a job to do, just as you have. I can see how you might feel a lady you admit to being friends with could be innocent, Deputy Long, but do we have to act so ghastly about it?"

"Not if you're willing to listen to me with your ears more open. I don't want to upset the dead man's kin any more than I want to see an innocent gal get shot or swung. So why don't we ask Al, here, to ask around town a mite more impartial?"

"Hold on, Longarm. Are you accusing me of sloppy methods?" Al protested. "I feel sure the lady will agree I treated her fair and square. I calls things as I see 'em, and as for asking other witnesses to come forward, even you admit nobody but the accused, a dead man, and maybe some mysterious strangers, saw one fool thing up here. So who in thunder am I supposed to question about what?"

"That meeting, called by a man I'm sure was dead at the time. I know it couldn't have been me or Lawyer Cohan, here. Miss Starbuck and her party hadn't arrived in town yet, either. So who's left?" Longarm asked.

Al frowned. "Let's see . . . I could not attend, myself, because I was on duty. I think it was the Addams boy who told me there was going to be a special meeting. But I've known him since he was born and . . . I see what you mean, Longarm. At some point in time some damned somebody had to be told to spread the word and, if I ask enough folk, someone might recall someone he or she didn't *know* telling him or her to pass it on."

Longarm turned back to the prosecution team to ask, "Deal?"

Welch replied grudgingly, "It has to be less disgusting than digging dead folk up. I'll tell you what I'll go along with. Since Miss Starbuck's been placed in your custody in any case, I'll leave the case on the back of the stove until we've all had time to calm down and dig deeper, above ground."

Tom Cohan said, "Hold on, Counselor. That's not giving my client the moon and all, you know. Just how long do you think Miss Starbuck can afford to be tied up in this one-horse town? It's a busy young woman she is and I'd like to know just how long it should take you to make up your mind one way or the other!"

Welch shrugged and said, "It's not for me to say. You and this other friend of hers were the ones who asked me to keep an open mind. If Al, here, or any other lawman can produce one shred of evidence that any other strangers were in town the day of the murder, I may just buy Deputy Long's alternative notions, wild as they still sound to me. I'm not about to fight Salt Lake if there's even an outside chance your client's innocent. But I feel it's only fair to warn you that should your client attempt to leave my jurisdiction before she's been cleared of all the charges, it will be my pleasure as well as my duty to charge her with flight to avoid prosecution."

He turned to Longarm with a grim smile as he added, "Correct me if I'm wrong, Deputy Long, but isn't it the duty of a federal lawman to track down men, or women, fleeing prosecution across state or territorial lines?"

Longarm said, "It is, you mealymouthed son of a bitch."

Chapter 11

Jessie didn't seem to want to flee prosecution or anything else he had in mind when she and Longarm were finally alone in her corner room at the hotel. It was still broad day and you really did have a view of the distant Pavant Mountains from one window, had either of them been interested in distant views at a time like this.

Longarm wasn't. His breath seemed to stick in his throat as the beautiful woman he was alone with undressed by the bed as calmly as if it was a chore she performed before him more often. But despite her outward calm, her breathing was sort of labored as well. For though they'd been lovers many a time before, and it seemed silly to be coy, she was as anxious as he was to make love again, yet aware, all too aware, of the awkwardness of their relationship.

As she finished undressing and lay back atop the counterpane, the sunlight through the west window highlighting the golden hairs of her head and other parts, it was all Longarm could do to keep from taking a running dive at her. He knew she was strong for a gal her size and shape, but she tended to call him a moose when he was trying to be gentle. So he just climbed aboard the bed beside her and took her in his own naked arms to kiss and fondle a spell. Then they were intermingled in sudden sweet delight and going deliciously crazy, as if they'd never been apart such a long torturous time.

For no matter how many times he made love to this one woman, it always surprised him to learn that no matter how

125

good the memories of the last time in her arms stayed stuck in his heart, each time he entered her it felt even better, as if a man was biting into a honeycomb, knowing how sweet honey tasted, only to discover it tasted better than he'd remembered. He knew, or thought he knew, that if there was one woman on earth a man could make love to twenty-four hours a day without it ever beginning to feel like work, it had to be Jessie. But wasn't it just his luck that of all the women he knew, she was the one he just couldn't spend that much time with?

For although she was perfection as a pal and even better in bed, there was just no way they could ever be more than occasional lovers. Their worlds were simply too far apart, most of the time. They'd met, it seemed so long ago, though it hadn't really been that long, when he'd been investigating the murder of Alex Starbuck and she'd been just a poor little orphan, or so he'd thought, fighting to hang on to the empire her father had left her. He and that infernal Ki had helped her avenge her father's death and hang on to the fortune he'd left his only child. So now, when she wasn't getting framed for murder in dinky western towns, she was doubtless eating fish eggs, and sipping French wines at governor's balls and such. He knew she gave away more in tips to servants than Uncle Sam gave him in a year, and he'd never forgotten how he'd felt that time he showed up with flowers and, even though she'd never let on they weren't grand, he'd followed her into a big fancy room at her home spread to see fancier ones, flowers so fancy he couldn't name 'em all, stuck all about the cavernous room in vases made by Ming and such.

But in the sweet here and now, she was his again, a good old gal who needed some backing in the sort of social scene he savvied. So he wasn't thinking of how rich she might feel in Texas as he came in her, hard, in Utah Territory.

As they paused to get their second wind, Jessie sighed and said, "Oh, damn, that was so lovely, Custis. I wish we could just stay like this, forever and ever, and not even have to get out of bed to eat."

He kissed a tear from her cheek and murmured, "I ain't

126

hungry right now. You're not fixing to blubber up on me, are you?"

She chuckled fondly, hugging him tighter with the strong shapely legs she had wrapped around his waist, and said, "You big goof. I just love it when you talk so romantic. I'm not going to blubber up on you. We both know the rules you seem to want to play by."

He kissed her and told her soberly, "You must not have been listening, last time, then. It ain't what I want, Jessie. It's just what has to be."

She moved her hips teasingly and replied, "Are you going to jaw at me about it, cowboy, or are you aiming to treat a lady right?"

So he laughed and said, "Powder River and let her buck!" before going crazy with her some more.

He didn't know, he didn't want to know, how a gal so young and unspoiled-looking could have learned to do it so good. She'd once told him that she had been taught some oriental skills by the erstwhile Japanese geisha her father had brought back from the Far East and installed as a governess for his only child. Thanks to motherly advice her father might not have approved of, and practice with oriental toys he'd have been downright shocked to find under his roof, Jessie could do things with her firm young body that could drive a man crazy even if she wasn't that fond of him. So when making love to a man she allowed herself to love, if only for the moment, it was small wonder that Longarm never found a single thrust into her loving and lovely body the least bit insipid. The only complaint he might have had with her, if any man had anything to complain of in such astoundingly delightful surroundings, was that she made him climax all too soon with a woman he felt like making love to constantly. She made up for that, in part, by making him come harder as well as more often, than any other woman he could recall, including not a few who'd been almost worth marrying up with. He didn't suffer false modesty. He'd been told how good he was in bed. But he didn't know his unusual stamina was a delight to Jessie as well. A woman who could bring the average lover to climax before he was really all the way in her had her own problems.

But with Longarm, Jessie could let herself go, and did, until, at last, she went limp as a dishrag in his arms and murmured, "My God, I think we just broke a record, even for us. Have you missed me, darling?"

He laughed boyishly. "I think I just threw my back out. Perhaps we'd best share a smoke while I work up my second wind."

She agreed he was crushing her and he rolled off to see if he could determine where in thunder he'd thrown that vest with the cheroots and matches. He had to sit up to explore the rug. She gazed up at him adoringly and said, "I'd forgotten what a lovely body you have."

"Mush. I'm just overworked. You're the one who looks like a Greek goddess, save for not having a dumb fig leaf where I'd surely hate to encounter vegetation."

She laughed and observed he'd need more than a fig leaf to get by in any museum open to the general public.

He said he'd make her pay for that remark if ever he could get it hard again. Then he found his smokes, lit one, and lay back down beside her.

As they cuddled and share the cheroot she asked him how long this was apt to last, this time. He answered, "Hard to say. I ain't supposed to be here at all. Billy Vail's going to have a pure fit if he finds out about it. On the other hand, I can't take you across a county line without getting us both in even more trouble."

She said, "Good," and cuddled closer, apparently less worried than he was about her current status as a suspect in his custody.

He patted her bare shoulder fondly and said, "In all this recent excitement I never got to find out what you and Ki are doing here in Utah to begin with, Jessie. Are you on one of your missions, hurling pinwheels at anyone I ought to know about?"

She told him not exactly and proceeded to bring him up to date on the help she'd been trying to give Victoria Miller when things suddenly got out of hand.

Longarm smoked his cheroot halfway down in silence before she'd finished. When she had, he still pondered silently for a time before he said, "If Victoria is that little breed gal I only got to howdy, down the hall in your hired sitting room, I have to allow she didn't strike me as a sneak. On the other hand, I've been lied to by lots of folk who looked as honest. So I dunno, Jessie. Her story leaks at least as much as a new Pima basket."

She asked him why and he said, "For openers, the Four Corners ain't where I'd look for gold."

"Custis, that country is barely surveyed," she protested.

"They got *some* of it mapped. Leaving out the details, that maze of canyons still runs through what geologists call the Colorado Plateau. That big rock sandwich runs pretty much the same, clean over to the Grand Canyon and beyond. I'm not a mining expert, but I have to know something about gold mines, for they attract crooks the way a dead cow attracts bluebottles. Different ores come in what mining men call provenances. That's a fancy way of saying you don't find silver in an iron lode or gold mixed with zinc. Where I just was, in Durango, the mining is mighty interesting because it's smack where two mineral provenances butt together. Northeast of where they do, the rocks are laced with silver, lead, copper, and even gold, like they mine all over the Colorado high country. But, to the southwest of the joint where two kinds of country crunched together, you get iron ore too far from the market to make it worthwhile, along with mica, vanadium, and uranium that ain't worth all that much when you do get it back east. I just rode over a lot of sandstone that they said was on the cheap side of Durango, Jessie. I can't say I got all that far, but it sure looked a lot like the rest of the pumpkin. Nobody's ever found any gold in it. Tiffany can't use five hundred pounds of uranium a year, and vanadium ain't worth much more. Has she told you she ever saw this mysterious gold mine out in the middle of country so awful that we're letting the Indians keep it?"

"No, but her father did come out of those canyons more than once with burro-loads of high grade. I've been through the Grand Canyon, Custis, and isn't it true that down under all that layered sedimentary rock you come to solid granite? And don't you find veins of gold quartz running through granite?"

He sighed. "Sometimes. And leave us not forget that before you get to the basement of the Grand Canyon you got to pass a whole damned mile of sandstone, shale, and such. The canyons east of the main one ain't near as deep, deep as they may feel if you step over the edge. So all you really have to go on is the word of a gal you don't know all that well."

Jessie began to toy absently with him as she answered, "That's what Ki says. He'll be so pleased to hear you finally agree with him about something, dear."

"Let's study on this, honey. You know me and that segundo of yours have never argued about looking out for your best interests as best as we knew how. It don't take a genius to see your heart may have taken the reins of your pretty little head again. I'm sort of fond of poor little orphans myself, and I'd be proud to help a lady get her gold mine back, if I thought there was an outside chance she *had* a damned gold mine. What did your lawyers have to say when you told 'em you were leading this crusade to the land of El Dorado, Jessie?"

"They said I was being foolish, of course."

"I thought your Tom Cohan looked sort of bright. If it was up to me, we'd hang all the lawyers and then go after the bankers. But fair is fair, and if he told you he thought you could be getting flimflammed, I reckon we may have to spare him."

Then he snubbed out the cheroot and rolled back atop her again. He kept his voice calm as he asked, "How come you've been going about setting up a mining claim all bass-ackwards if you got such good lawyers, honey?"

She asked him what he meant and he said, "You never needed a Utah mining claim if there's a mine at all near the juncture of the Chaco and Mancos, honey."

She stiffened in his arms, saying, "Wait. Calm down a minute, dear. My survey map puts that area just inside the southeast corner of Utah. Doesn't yours?"

"Nope. Mine could be more up to date. I bummed it off the Indian Fighting Army, and those old boys are too interested in where they might be going to survey casual. I make it almost smack where the four corners come together, but just inside New Mexico Territory, if Santa Fe had beans to say about Indian country. The whole damned canyon complex has been set aside as Indian reserve for one fool nation or another."

"Does that mean we have to ask *Indians* for mineral rights where Vickie's father found his gold?"

"Not hardly. If Washington thought Indians had mineral rights, George Armstrong Custer might still be wearing his hair. In the Black Hills, the old boys who found gold around Lead and Deadwood got permission to dig it from the federal government. It upset Red Cloud considerable, but that's the way Washington feels about gold. If your part-Indian protégée has any claim to a placer or mine in the Four Corners country, which raises a lot of other lawyer questions, she, or you as her purer pard, would first have to stake the claim, pin it down tight on a map of the proper scale, and file on it as a strike made on *federal land*. Don't worry about that part. I got lots of paper-pushing pals working for the same Great White Father. The B.I.A. won't be no problem. The Indians they're supposed to be in charge of might, but you got to eat the apple a bite at a time."

He started moving in her, but she insisted, "Wait, Custis, you've got me all confused. I can see how my Texas law firm messed up the paperwork. Texas took care of its own Indian problems Texas-style, before the Union had anything to say about it. So we may not know as much about filing on Indian land in other parts. But someone out this way must have thought Utah had more to say about the matter than you seem to think."

"How come, and, speaking of coming . . ."

"Now cut that out!" She laughed, explaining, "Vickie could be wrong about the location of her father's strike. She was never out to his diggings with him. If it turned out to be inside the Utah line, after all, wouldn't that account for someone wanting to kill Judge Reynolds, and me, before we could put our heads together?"

He said sincerely, "Jessie, it ain't our head we got together right now."

So she moaned, "Oh, don't I know it!" And so they didn't

worry about anything but racing one another to heaven for a spell. But later, she just had to dig up the bone again and ask, as if nothing had happened,. "I think all my recent troubles prove there's something to Vickie's story. From here we were planning to head out across the desert to where her father's own map puts his claim. If there's nothing there, why would anyone want to kill me to keep me from taking her there?"

He nibbled a turgid nipple as he muttered, "Half the gents I arrest are sort of stupid. If *I* was out to keep an heiress from claiming her inheritance, and wasn't worried about gunning women, I'd start by killing *her,* not her *pals.* Maybe they were after you for some other reason and . . . I'll be switched with snakes if that don't work!"

She asked what he meant. He propped himself up on one elbow to tell her, "If you'd gone about getting to the Four Corners more sensible, you'd have got as close as you could, by rail, and that would have taken you through Durango."

She nodded. "Ki said something about that being the shorter route. But since I didn't go through Durango."

"I did," he cut in, "and I'd no sooner got there than I met a hired gun, a hired gun from Texas, laying there in wait for somebody. I don't think it was me. He just thought I was after him. He could have been laying for you, Jessie."

She smiled up at him incredulously and objected, "They were laying for me *here,* over two hundred miles away, Custis."

"Don't you play any chess at all? There's only two ways by rail to get within practical riding distance of the Four Corners. So how many brains would it take to cover both squares on the board? What we got to figure, is who might have known for sure you were getting off here in Richfield when you were. They had to know what time you'd show up, ahead of time, to set that trap so neat for you, see?"

She said soberly, "I see that. But would you like me to list possible suspects in numerical or alphabetical order?"

He asked what she meant. She said, "I've been trying to run Starbuck Enterprises by Western Union. Ki and I have been sending out orders and questions almost everywhere we've stopped along the way. I told Lord knows how many

132

people they could wire me here, care of the last stop, and that's only the beginning. A lot of people take interest in those bright yellow telegrams, whether they have any business reading them or not. So any number of people could have read any number of messages, on a desk or even a wastebasket."

Longarm swore softly. "No sense even hoping the telegraph office would be able to help us with messages sent the other way, in code, to someone named Smith or Jones. It sure pains me to say this, little darling. But as soon as we get the local charges against you dropped, you got to beeline back home and fort up good 'til Ki and the rest of your boys figure out who's gunning for you, and why."

She shook her blonde head. "Don't be silly. I'd never get anything done if I worried about rascals out to do me in for business reasons. As I told you the first time you took me for a helpless child, I'd as soon go on about my business and let the rascals come at me. The one laying for me here in Richfield didn't get me, did he?"

"No, but at least one of his pals and maybe more got away, and they're still out there, somewhere, with the same working orders," Longarm warned.

"Good. Once I'm out in wide-open country, with you and Ki to back my play, I'd just like to see them *try* for my fair white body again and, speaking of fair white bodies, don't you like me anymore, darling?"

Chapter 12

By supper time, Longarm and Jessie felt sated enough with sex to try indulging their own appetites for a spell. They all ate downstairs, so the men had to forego caffeine and tobacco with their meal. Nobody minded until dessert was served with no coffee. But they finished fast and by mutual consent moved out to the front veranda to watch the sun go down and maybe sneak a smoke. Jessie and Victoria found wicker chairs out there to sit in. Tom Cohan sat on the steps. Longarm hooked half his rump over the rail so he could rest a mite and jaw with the gals at the same time. Ki just stood there. He reminded Longarm of a wooden Indian half the time. Longarm wondered if it just came natural to Ki or whether the big Amerasian was jealous and pouting in his stone-faced way. Jessie had intimated Ki had something good going on with the little half breed gal. But lots of gents Longarm had known to have their own fool wives at home had started up with him over barmaids in his time, and Jessica Starbuck was a lot better looking than any barmaid he'd ever had to fight over. Longarm had never quite settled in his own mind who figured to win if he and old Ki ever got into it hot and heavy. He wondered if the same thoughts occasionally passed through Ki's head. Since Ki was all man, and at least half American, Longarm figured it likely did.

Nobody was saying much when the Lincolnesque local lawman, Al, came striding toward them through the gloaming. Al didn't say anything until he reached the veranda,

134

propped a booted foot on the steps next to Cohan's plump behind, and observed laconically, "I thought you folk might like to know I take my job serious. I've been asking high and low all over town this afternoon."

The lawyer stared up at him like a pup who was dying to go outside and almost pleaded, "Not one person in town could recall who might have started that false rumor of a meeting at your temple?"

"I never said that. As a matter of fact, I found three kids, two boys and a girl, who told me that a growed man they didn't know asked the three of them, separate, to go tell folk about that meeting. He stopped all of 'em near the foot of them fateful stairs, around the corner from the barbershop, and said he was speaking for his pal, the elder, who was anxious to proclaim a vision or whatever. It was sort of slick of him to fib to kids. We raise our children not to question their elders, even when they've never seen 'em before."

"What time did he talk to the kids?" Longarm asked.

"I don't know, exactly. None of the kids he stopped remember what time it was. Kids seldom care what time it is. But it works out to well before Miss Starbuck's train arrived. Kids like to run over to the tracks and admire steam engines, too. Don't you want to know what the rascal looked like?"

Longarm nodded. Tom Cohan asked, "Were they able to *describe* the man?"

So Al said, "Sure they was. We raise our children respectful, not *blind*. The girl gave the best description. She recalled an elk's tooth on a gold chain he wore across his brocaded vest of maroon silk. The boys wasn't as sure about the vest. One said red and the other brown. But all three could agree on the black riding outfit he had on. A short-cut charro jacket and bell-bottom pants worn over high-heel boots. We get a difference of opinion on his boots and what sort of hat he was wearing. One of the boys thinks he was sporting a black Mex sombrero. The other boy and the girl recall it as more ten gallon. I'll go with the girl on the hat. She was the only one who recalled the elk's tooth, so she might have been paying more attention."

"What about arms?" asked Ki from his position closer to the door.

But Al shook his head and said, "None of the kids said he was wearing hardware. That's not saying he didn't leave a six-gun, somewhere, with his mount. None of the kids saw any pony, and he might have known that it's easier for a stranger to draw curious looks and questions in a town like this with a gun on one's mysterious hip."

Tom Cohan brightened and said, "Well, that lets my client off the hook, then. Those adorable children put a mysterious stranger in the vicinity of the murder scene and, better yet, they can testify to the fact that he was a barefaced liar!"

Al nodded but said, "None of them say right out they saw him kill nobody, though."

Jessie protested, "For heaven's sake, what do you want from that hired gun, a signed confession? By his own words to those children he stands convicted as a stranger up to no good. If they'd never seen him before he could hardly have been a member of your Mormon congregation. So how could he have been speaking for a Mormon elder when he ordered everyone to come to a meeting?"

Longarm shifted his weight and said, "That's easy. He knew old Reynolds was in no position to stick his head out the window, right upstairs, and make a big fibber out of him. Leaving aside pointless practical jokes, nobody but a man who knew Reynolds was already dead would have been standing there getting kids to spread false rumors, right?"

"That's the way I read it. I just now come from Morgan Welch's place, hoping to be the bearer of gladder tidings when I got here. Morg says that what I found out sure works in Miss Starbuck's favor, but that he ain't ready to drop the charges, just yet," Al answered.

Tom Cohan rose to his feet, protesting, "That's just plain pigheaded, dang it! Can't you see he's just a small-town lawyer out to make a name for himself with the only important case he's ever likely to try?"

"Yep. Morg was sort of spiteful when we was kids, as I recall. He just hated to lose at marbles, even though we wasn't allowed to play for keeps. Meanwhile, it ain't for the likes of me to say. I'll tell you true I surely doubt even old Morg expects it to come to trial, now. Like I said, he just hates to lose. But they are sending a circuit judge down the line to fill in for the only judge we had, the murder victim. So I reckon old Morg wants his day in court. But don't you folk worry. He'll get to play cock of the walk a spell. His wives, at least, will admire him. Then he'll no doubt move for a dismissal to show us all how generous he is."

Cohan said, "I sure hope so. Ah, was that *wives,* plural, you was just saying?"

Before the Texan could get his foot any further into his own mouth, Longarm cut in to explain, "The Salt Lake Temple's sort of met the rest of the country halfway on a sticking point to statehood. The Saints have agreed that a good citizen has to obey the law of the land, and Washington's gone along with the notion that it would be sort of cruel to turn extra women and children out of many a Mormon household to fend for themselves at this late date."

Tom Cohan said, "Polygamy or even bigamy is still unlawful, and here we'd be having a county prosecutor, living openly with more than one wife, giving my client a hard time over the finer points of the law!"

Al shook his head and said, "Fair is fair, Lawyer Cohan. Like Longarm just said, the former nation of Deseret, and the rest of these United States is working things out sensible. No member of The Church of Jesus Christ of Latter-day Saints ever broke no laws on purpose. Back in thirty-nine, when the Prophet Joseph was taking down the revelations of the Angel Moroni, it was writ that as the Lord commanded we go forth and multiply, it was jake with the Lord if a man took more than one wife to multiply with."

Cohan protested, "That's not what it says in *my* Bible!"

But Al just shrugged and said, "Nobody said you had to read The Book of Mormon if you had another book you liked better. To get back to the pragmatic here and now, the Prophet Joseph never writ it was a sin to have just *one* wife, either, if one was all you had in mind. So, since some men can't take nagging all that well, a lot of us never married up with more than one to begin with."

Cohan asked, "And didn't your Brigham Young make up for that by wedding a couple of dozen and all?"

Al said, "I ain't finished. Brother Brigham also said it was only right to obey the law of the land. So after we decided to come into the Union, after all, that left us in a sort of bind. Our book agrees with your book on divorce. It would be a sin, even if it wasn't cruel, to chuck a woman out in the cold after she'd been your wife and born your children twenty years or more. So the Salt Lake Temple decided it was all right to keep any extra wives you already had, as long as you didn't bring too many *more* home."

Longarm cut in to explain, "Federal statutes don't apply to matrimony or even morals, Tom, unless you mess with Indians or other wards of the federal government. Marriage rules and regulations are enacted by each separate state or territory. Since Utah's been trying to become a state, it don't issue multiple marriage licenses no more. But, since lots of Mormons married up with lots of folk under the statutes of *Deseret,* I wouldn't bring up Morgan Welch's troubles at home when next you meet. There's nothing us outsiders can do about 'em. He's already sore enough at Jessie, here, and Jesus, *duck!"*

Not everyone did as a lone rider whipped around the far corner of the hotel at full gallop, firing from the saddle like a drunk in Dodge on a Saturday night. Little Victoria hit the veranda deck, wicker chair and all, while Tom Cohan dove headfirst off the steps to flatten out in the yard gravel just before a bullet tore a big splinter from the plank his plump rump had been perched upon.

But everyone else chose to fight back. So the pony thundered on with an empty saddle, and it would never be known for sure who'd killed its rider first.

For as the dust cleared away and the survivors gathered round the black-clad figure sprawled in the roadway at their feet, he lay there with two .44-40 rounds fired by Longarm through his rib cage, a .45 slug thrown by Al had severed his spine, lower, and Jessie had poked a round of .38 in his left eye. The whirling steel shuriken that Ki had whipped out of nowhere to throw had cut, or buzzsawed, his guts open just above the belt line. Old Al hunkered down over the decidedly dead killer, muttering, "That ought to learn folk not to shoot up my town."

Then he fingered the elk's tooth hanging by a gold-washed chain across the now mighty messy silk vest as he added, "Well, I can't say I recall what's left of that face around town or temple. But he sure fits the description those kids gave of the man they spoke to at the foot of them steps the day of the Reynolds killing."

Longarm hunkered down to join the local lawman, striking a match to make sure before he said, "I know him. Not personal, of course, just by a photograph the Pinkertons distributed along with some reward posters. For whatever reason, we would seem to have ended the career of Rampaging Richardson, a homicidal cuss they've been wanting to hang in Fort Smith as well."

"Hired gun?" asked Al.

Longarm replied, "He'd been known to shoot cats and dogs just for sport, but, yeah, they do say he could act even meaner for money. The Pinks want him for robbing trains. Judge Parker, over to Fort Smith, had a bench warrant out for him for killing a slow-paying gambler for a tinhorn who confessed as much before he swung."

Longarm began to go through the dead man's duds as the now mighty dusty Tom Cohan joined them to opine, "That wraps it up tighter than I really needed to get my client off, then. For it just won't work any other way. We've the words of his very own mouth to prove he was a liar, intent on driving possible witnesses from the scene of the crime. We've his tacit confession, signed by his own last mortal moves in front of two peace officers and a member of the bar, that he was out to murder one or more people just now. Put a known killer at the scene of a murder, at the right time, together with a young lady of good reputation and no criminal record, and see how even a jury of *Apache* would have to add *that* up!"

Ki asked Longarm quietly, "Have you found the knife on him?"

"No. He never had a rep as a back stabber to begin with. I'd say he acted as their lookout, right?"

Ki nodded and said, "Two others went up to the office well ahead of Jessie, while this one made sure Reynolds had no other visitors. When he saw Jessie coming he ducked out of sight. She went up, beat that one killer fair and square in the hallway and then made the mistake of turning her back. The other in the back office with the dead man wasn't about to take on a girl who'd just shown how good she was with a gun. He switched the body of the man he'd knifed with the body of the one she'd just shot. As he'd hoped, once the town law had a body on its hands to account for all that gunfire, they didn't find it worth their while to force a door locked from the inside. He waited until after dark, dropped the other body out that side window into the dark slot between the buildings, and together with this one, disposed of their sidekick. He was probably a man with some paper out on him as well."

Jessie said, "That one's doubtless buried somewhere outside of town. The one who packs a stiletto and smokes expensive cigars sent this one back for another try at me. So he's still at large, and this one came closer than the first one to blowing my brains out. His first round hit the high back of the chair I was sitting in."

That thought made her turn to ask, "Are you all right, Vickie?"

But Jessie wasn't really concerned about it until the pretty little breed called back from the shade of the veranda, "No, ma'am. He creased me. Please don't make me say where, in front of all them gents."

Jessie ran back to the girl on the veranda and, as the chubby lawyer started to follow, Ki stopped him, saying, "Let Jessie look at her wound, Cohan. You just heard Vickie say it was a delicate matter."

So the men all stayed out in the street as Jessie and, by now, their landlady and a female cook from out back, gathered around Victoria Miller. As Jessie tersely explained all the noise to the bewildered women, she hoisted the little breed's blood-streaked skirts to see that the victim had been creased in a manner more undignified than dangerous. Jessie repressed a laugh as she told Victoria, "It's just a little divot out of the left cheek, Vickie. I don't think it will leave much of a scar, and

140

in any case, nobody but a mighty close friend is ever going to notice it. Let's go back upstairs. I have iodine in my first aid kit and we'll have you taped up in no time."

The hotel cook allowed she could boil some water. But Jessie shook her head and said, "She's not having a baby. She only got shot in the ass."

Then she took Victoria's arm to lead her inside as, behind her, the landlady observed, "I try to run a decent establishment here, you know. If there's anymore gunplay on or about my premises I fear I'll have to ask all you gentiles to check out!"

Meanwhile, out front, the sounds of gunplay had attracted more than a little attention from other quarters. Al picked up the dead man's S&W .45 lest it get trampled even dustier by the many boots gathering around. A teenager called out, "There was a dun pony running loose and wild up the other end of town, Constable. They got it tied up in front of the hat shop, now."

Al had just nodded his thanks for this information when Morgan Welch bulled through the crowd to demand, "What's this I hear about *another* murder here?"

Al pointed at the cadaver, now nearly hidden by the shade of the still-growing crowd, and replied soberly, "It was more like an execution than a murder, Morg. This cuss just tried to kill Miss Starbuck some more and you can see where that got him. I'd say the gentile gal has been telling us true all along. For this has to be that rumor monger I was telling you about earlier this evening. Longarm just identified him as a known murderer. Little Willa Thomas and the Lockwood boys will doubtless be able to identify him as the mysterious stranger who fibbed to 'em on the day Reynolds was murdered. We figure this one was acting as the lookout."

Welch said, "Oh, you do, do you? And just how do you mean to prove this dead man was upstairs killing Reynolds at a time three witnesses say he was downstairs on the street, telling fibs or not?"

Tom Cohan tried, "Be reasonable, dammit. You know I'll cut you in little ribbons in court if you're dumb enough to insist on my client standing trial with her alibi spread out, right there, like a damned rug!"

But Welch insisted, "This particular victim of considerable multilation can't alibi anyone. At the moment he seems to be dead and, on the day of the murder, he was downstairs in the street with a pretty good alibi of his own. Did anyone see him anywhere near Reynolds? Can anyone prove they ever met, at any time or place?"

Al sighed and said, "Dammit, Morg, you always was a spiteful little teacher's pet, and growing up hasn't improved you one lick! Are you trying to make this town look like a lunatic asylum to the whole outside world?"

Welch sniffed and said, "It was outsiders who killed one of our own. I'll allow the case against that gentile woman doesn't look as airtight as when I first drew up my brief against her. But someone has to pay for the death of Elder Reynolds and you still haven't arrested any suspects who fit the charges better!"

Longarm growled, "Aw, shit," and grabbed Welch by one arm to add, "you and me had best have some private words, you poor misguided mule head."

Welch really didn't want to go with him, judging from the way he kept trying to dig his heels in, but Longarm was used to leading average-sized gents where they might or might not want to be led. So he led the county prosecutor around the corner, lighting a cheroot as they went. When he got Welch alone in the shadow of the Mountain View, Longarm shoved the outraged legal eagle against the plank siding, blew smoke in his face, and growled, "I got better things to do with my time than shilly-shally here any longer. So listen tight."

"Cut that out. I don't approve of tobacco at all, and certainly not in my face, dammit!"

"I don't approve of some of *your* disgusting habits, either. But they don't allow me to pistol-whip small-town big shots, even though they will keep getting in my way."

"Are you threatening the prosecuting attorney of Sevier County, damn your hide?" demanded the same, as he tried to break free of Longarm's steel grip on his shirtfront.

Longarm slammed him against the siding some more and

told him, "Hell, no, I'm only trying to help you out. This is an election year, in case you forgot, and you wouldn't want to look like a *total* asshole even if it wasn't, would you?"

That calmed the small-town politico down considerable. But he still looked petty and stubborn as he asked, "What do you mean?"

"You want to strut your stuff in front of a court full of admirers and I don't blame you. It goes with the job. Folk expect a county prosecutor to take a dim view of murder-in-the-first, and they admire hell out of him when he can brag on seeing that justice has been done."

Welch nodded. "That's what I've been saying all along. So unhand me, dammit!"

Longarm said, "I'll blow more smoke at you if you don't simmer down. I've always found smoke handy in working around a beehive and I've noticed a beehive seems to be the emblem of you folk out here. I can go along with acting busy as a bee. I got a boss who expects me to work harder than I really want to. Your trouble is that you keep working against the rest of us, as if you thought just buzzing contrary to the rest of us bees was all there was to looking busy."

"I believe in working hard at my job," Welch replied.

Longarm nodded pleasantly and said, "Good thinking. Dumb doing. It's your job, and mine, I'm talking about. For each of us, in his own way, is sworn to uphold justice and the laws of the land. I don't expect you to believe this, but if I thought Jessia Starbuck was a lawbreaker, I'd arrest her, painful as it might feel to me, personal."

Welch sneered, sort of dirty, and said, "Oh, come now, the whole town knows how sweet you are on that pretty blonde."

Longarm sighed and said, "I sure wish walls weren't built so thin. I just said it would pain me personal. I'd hate to have you think me a kiss-and-tell, but as long as this is man to man, I'll tell you I *have* had to arrest women I was sort of fond of. My personal feelings ain't supposed to stand between me and simple justice. I fear yours do. You ain't out to pin the killing of that poor old man on Miss Jessie because you think she killed him. You're out to prove she done it because you got to provide a convicted killer or admit you got nobody for the county to hang or shoot, loser's choice. I can see how you feel. It pisses me off considerable when I have to come back empty-handed. It doesn't happen often, praise the Lord, but it does happen and, so far, I've never tried to pin a federal crime on any old cuss just to brag I always get my man."

Welch protested, "Dammit, I defy you to prove I've made up one false shred of evidence against that Texas hussy!"

Longarm smiled thinly. "Miss Jessie ain't no hussy. Maybe just a mite warm natured, and I see you do have a personal spite against a natural beauty you just can't have, as well. But sticking to the cause of blind justice, as we're supposed do, I want you to ponder some well-meant words of professional advice. Are you pondering, pilgrim?"

Welch snarled. "Get to the point."

So Longarm nodded and said, "There's no way in hell you're going to convict Jessica Starbuck in open court. The best you can hope for is a chance to give a beautiful stranger a hard time and allow a lot of ugly old biddies to enjoy her discomfort, if only for a little while. In the end, you know as sure as you know how jealous of me you are that she's going to walk free, and then where will you be in this chicken run?"

"I'll have done my duty," said Welch, prissy-lipped.

Longarm said, "I got a better duty for you to perform. That dead man around the corner is a federal want. The famous Judge Parker of the Federal District Court in Fort Smith, Arkansas, has already convicted him, federal, on Murder One. He's been looking high and low to hang him. They don't give you no other choice at Fort Smith. So what if you was to write or, better yet, wire Judge Parker that a notorious desperado who's eluded a whole posse of his deputies, has been brung to justice at last, here in your jurisdiction?"

Longarm could read the newspaper headlines in the small-town big shot's piggy eyes. But Welch only answered, "Well, of course it's my duty to inform another court that one of my own peace officers . . . Al *was* the one who got him, right?"

Longarm said, "Well, he put a .45 slug in the bastard's spine, in tricky light. That ought to read sort of good in the newspapers. Naturally, the story will surely make the front page in Fort Smith as well as here and Salt Lake City. But I ain't finished, pard."

"There's more?" asked Welch hopefully.

Longarm nodded and said, "If you play your cards right, Al was the one as brung Judge Parker's want to ground. It wasn't you. So if you just say the town law, here in Richfield, seen a wanted killer and killed him, Al figures to get admired far and wide. But to get your *own* name printed along with his, you got to provide what a reporter I know on the *Denver Post* calls a news angle, see?"

"How do I do that?" asked Welch wistfully.

"By using your head instead of just buzzing it, of course. The killing of a killer who was only passing through a small town reads one way. The killing of a murderer who was *resisting arrest,* local, reads another. Al says he told you earlier that he suspected that dead rascal took part in the murder of your own Elder Reynolds. So, even if that disgusting individual hadn't been shooting at Al and everyone else he could see in passing, wouldn't it have been Al's duty to bring him in, once you'd told Al to arrest him for the murder of poor old Reynolds?"

Morgan Welch hadn't gotten to be county prosecutor by being completely stupid. The gears were already turning in his crafty pig eyes as he started to ask a dumb question and then nodded to say, "Right, the well-known Texas heiress, Miss Jessica Starbuck, was a material witness in the case and gave us great help in solving it, as I recall. But, ah, just what did I solve, Deputy Long?"

Longarm explained how he and the others had put the probable details of the case together, and this time Welch bought it eagerly, adding, "By gum, the lawman I sent to warn Miss Starbuck there could be another attempt on her life got there just in time, didn't he? I'd better announce an around-the-clock police guard on the homes of those three children as well. For although two of the murderers have been brought to justice, a third one may still be at large, right?"

Longarm assured him that was the first sensible thing Welch had ever said to him, and they shook on it. So Welch got back out front to busy-bee about the dead man who still lay there while Longarm, not seeing anyone there he wanted to jaw with, went inside.

He found Ki and Tom Cohan seated in the little lobby, going over some papers together. Longarm said, "It's over. Welch has seen the light at last and so Jessie's free to go. I sure wish she'd go back to Texas. I'd best have a word with her about that."

He moved up the stairs, only to meet Jessie in the hallway, coming from Victoria's room. He stopped her there, saying, "I just got you off the hook. Welch has agreed to drop the damned fool charges and you ain't in my custody no more. How's the other gal?"

Jessie dimpled at him in the dim lamplight and told him, "She's going to be fine. Maybe a mite stiff for a few days and, well, she and Ki will have to find some position that doesn't rub her tape off on a pillow. But, speaking of interesting positions, isn't it sort of late for a boy your age to be up? I mean up out of bed, of course. I don't mind you being up in other ways."

He laughed and followed her back to her own bedroom door. But as they entered, he only took his hat off for the moment, saying, "Hold the thought, honey. First we got to talk. Your Paiute princess ain't up to much rough riding, and your notion of riding out after lost gold mines in Indian country sounded sort of dumb even *before* we knew someone was out to get you. So how do I get you to give up this fool notion and head back home, where you'll be a lot safer?"

Jessie moved over to her dresser, picked up her own Stetson, and stuck one of those wicked shuriken stars in the hatband as she told him sweetly, "You can't. My mind's made up. But I'll go along with any *other* suggestions you have to offer. So why don't you take off your pants?"

Chapter 13

Next morning, at the breakfast table, Tom Cohan took a crack at talking Jessie into coming back to Texas with him. Longarm and Ki were too talked out to do more than eat, and little Victoria just kept squirming on the pillow she'd brought downstairs to sit on. Cohan said, "My senior partners are never going to forgive me if I can't persuade you, ma'am. Starbuck Enterprises has been going to hell in a hack since you tore out here to get yourself arrested. Even with the signed orders you just gave me to carry back to Texas, keeping so many balls in the air at once without you there to put your pretty foot down now and again might not be possible!"

Jessie lowered her fork and said, "I told you who I wanted fired and I signed their dismissal notices and severance-pay checks. If that doesn't work, feel free to shoot them," Jessie added with a wink.

Cohan sighed. "If only we could. But Texas has gotten sort of sissy since President Hayes called off the Reconstruction. In any case, I fear my law partners and I just don't frighten stubborn lads as much as you and Ki can when you're both minding the store back home."

Jessie washed down some eggs with the ice water she could have, at least, in a Mormon dining room, and said, "As I told you, that outburst of independent thinking was no doubt the result of wishful thinking when I was arrested on a capital charge. Now that everyone back home will be reading it in the papers that I'm running loose again, I suspect most of the boys will get back in line."

Ki frowned across the white linen at her to say flatly, "You know that's not true, Jessie. Orders you issued by wire from back in Denver have been ignored. Tom's right. There's some sort of mutiny brewing back home. It started before that nasty Morgan Welch tried to frame you for killing Reynolds." ·

Before Jessie could reply, Longarm cut in with a shake of his head to say, "It wasn't the local Saints who tried to frame anybody. I don't like Morgan Welch any more than you do, Ki. I don't see how his own wives can stand him. But fair is fair and he, like old Al, was calling things as he seen 'em. Nobody would have had to arrest Jessie if she'd walked into that trap and lost. It was three or maybe more hired killers, unrelated to anyone in Richfield, as far as I can tell, who were *sent* to kill the owner of Starbuck Enterprises. I've reason to suspect they had Durango staked out for you and her as well, in case you came that way." He met Jessie's sober stare and continued. "I wouldn't fire anybody if I was running an outfit and had good cause to suspect one or more employees of the same had set me up for early retirement."

Tom Cohan gasped and sputtered, "Jesus-Mary-and-Joseph, are you saying someone's trying to murder my client and take over her vast holdings?"

"I ain't saying it. It just looks to me like that could explain why some old boys have been acting so independent. Jessie and her sidekick have wandered away from home before. Everyone who works for her knows that. They ought to know that, so far, she's come back."

"That's true," Jessie agreed. "Starbuck Enterprises has always almost run itself, since before I inherited it from my poor father. Between us, we've always hired good managers, paid them good wages, and kept out of their hair. Why would they turn on me just because I had to turn my back on them such a short while?"

Ki said, "I think I can answer that, Jessie. I've been doing most of the paperwork. We haven't been having trouble from the men you've had on your payroll long enough to matter. Most of them stood by you, you'll recall, when your father was killed and his enemies tried to move in on you."

She nodded and Ki continued. "Thanks to mostly loyal hired help, a few friends like this cheroot-smoking cowboy here, and that gun your father gave you as a birthday present with target practice in mind, you held on to your scattered holdings and, since the gunsmoke's cleared, you've even expanded Starbuck Enterprises in a way that would have made my old friend and your father mighty proud of you."

Jessie said, "Aw, mush."

Ki shook his head. "I'm not finished. To take advantage of the current business boom, you've hired a lot more help than you ever started out with. Your payroll's almost doubled and you've naturally had to hire a lot more management."

She protested, "Not that many, Ki. A lot of gents running different branches were promoted from lower positions as things opened up."

Ki insisted, "Not all, and who can say what a man who's been *taking* orders might feel about it when he finds himself in position to *give* some orders for a change?"

Before Jessie could answer, Tom Cohan asked, "Is it your position that some of the people who work for Starbuck Enterprises don't seem to worry about orders from the boss because they don't expect the boss to be around much longer and all?"

So Longarm observed, "You boys are talking in a circle, no offense. Rumors of such impending changes always get around. So I'd say it's the *dumb* rascals who've been jumping the gun, not the mastermind and his close confederates."

Jessie and her lawyer both asked "Mastermind?" at once.

Longarm said, "Has to be, if there's anything at all to Ki's suspicion. It could well be that most of the rascals acting so uppity could be simply stupid. Nobody would ever get fired if everybody paid attention to his or her boss and didn't sass back. I mind a trail boss one time who, even though the owner warned and warned him, persisted in thinking cows could be driven thirty miles a day. But that's neither here nor there. Why I say there'd have to be a mastermind if there was some sort of impending mutiny back where Jessie belongs, is that nobody would be making such awful plans just to wind up with his very own cotton gin or modest herd. He could just buy his own if he had the sort of money it takes to hire gangs of professional killers and send 'em all over creation. Ain't that right, Lawyer Cohan?"

Cohan nodded. "The game would not be worth the candle unless the prize was the whole pot. Such candles, as you just pointed out, are expensive. Even if some mad branch manager managed to kill my client for the modest slice of pie he might wind up with, who would he ever be able to do business with?"

"Are you saying I run a mess of penny-ante operations, Tom?" Jessie frowned.

The stout lawyer shook his head and told her, "Not at all. I can tell you tales of the Great Hunger, in the old country, that led to mortal combat over crumbs indeed. But Longarm is right about no criminal with any cunning at all risking his neck for, say, one of your ships, a mill, or even a herd of dear sweet cows. For his legal problems would only be beginning after he murdered the lawful owner of the property. Peters and Cohan would see to that, if Ki didn't cut their heads off first with them dreadful steel stars he seems to hide up his sleeve."

"I'd be sort of surly, too," growled Longarm.

Cohan shushed them all with a wave of his fork and explained, "You'd have to stand in line. They'd be in court the day they was after claiming property they didn't own. You can't just grab a clipper ship and go sailing off like a pirate and all. Who would ever trade with you? How would you ever enter or clear a harbor without the proper papers? To get away with such a grand quick-money scheme a crook would have to be a mastermind indeed. Do you mind if I mention your will in front of others, Miss Starbuck?"

Jessie said, "I don't have any secrets from my friends. I don't have any children, either. Since I know it would confuse my estate, if I should die intestate, I've left most of the future profits of Starbuck Enterprises to various charities and, well, a few close friends."

Tom Cohan said, "There you are, then. Even if that trap at the office building across town had worked as planned, my client's business empire would never go to her killers. To begin with, the whole estate would be tied up in probate for a time, until the courts decided who would run Starbuck Enterprises in the future. If anything, mere branch managers would be sobbing at the wake. For nobody would be after getting paid a nickel until we made certain everything was being run legal and aboveboard."

Longarm raised an eyebrow and asked, "In the meantime, is it safe to assume your law firm would be acting, and getting *paid*, as the executors?"

Cohan laughed and said, "Don't shoot. I'm not armed. If you must know, Ki here has been named as her executor."

Ki protested, "I don't know how to do . . . whatever it is such a freak of nature does. Do we have to go on talking like this at the breakfast table?"

Longarm said, "It gives me the creeps, too. So I'll end this grim discussion with just one more observation. If someone ain't out to murder Jessie for her fortune, they have to be out to do so for some other reason. Some gents in the lower ranks may or may not have heard rumors to the effect that she ain't long for this world. Or we could be making chess out of simple checkers and dumb employees. No matter why she's been having so much of this mysterious and recent trouble, she's having it, and I say she ought to go home and fort up."

Ki said, "I second the motion."

But Jessie said, "Overruled by the chairwoman. I came out here to help poor Vickie claim her father's gold mine and that's just what I aim to do."

She saw the look that passed between Longarm and Ki. So she quickly added, "Look, boys, in all this talk about murky plots back home, has it not occurred to anyone that nobody tried to get at me while I *was* back in Texas, running things my way, whether some of my management help liked it or not?"

Ki repeated, "When the cat's away the mice will play, and a lot of old Ranger pals of your dad are fond of you, Jessie. *I* surely wouldn't want to murder you in Texas. Maybe someone else thought this was a good time and place to try it."

Victoria suddenly blurted, "It was *me* that man shot last night. I've been telling you from the beginning that I fear someone's gunned my own poor dad and jumped his claim. How do any of you know it ain't me they been after all this time?"

Jessie nodded and announced, "There you go. That makes more sense than some mastermind trying to take over Starbuck Enterprises. Everyone who's tried that has wound up mighty sorry. But someone who doesn't know us that well might be trying to stop us from doing just what I'm fixing to do about Vickie's inheritance. I'm fixing to find her dad's color, stake it, and claim it for her. So there!"

Victoria was the only one who looked at all pleased, and she looked confused, as well. Tom Cohan said flatly, "I think you need your head examined more than you need a lawyer."

Longarm said, "Even if you were talking sense, Jessie, it's hot as Hell's hinges between here and the Four Corners at this time of the year, and rough riding in winter. If you just can't stand staying out of disputed Indian country, at least let me show you how to get there sensible."

She appeared to be listening. So he explained, "I got here from there the longer but faster way round, by rail. I know it looks way out of the way on the map, but it's faster and you get to sit down a lot more."

Jessie shook her head. "I've already considered that. Getting there sudden isn't half as important as getting there right and, in any case we'd only save a day or so, your way, when you consider how much shorter the distance is, direct. You said yourself the maps you can buy don't agree so good on that part of this world. The map Vickie's father drew reads a whole lot different. He was no survey engineer. He just marked landmarks as he saw them and sort of guessed at angles and distances."

Tom Cohan asked her, "What good would such a map be at all? It seems to me that if I wanted to lose myself forever in the great American desert, I'd just be after walking about in circles until I was lost. I wouldn't need a worthless map to be reading along the way!"

Jessie said, "The map Vickie's father made for his own use could hardly have been worthless. It got him in and out of the area with gold dust. I said he'd marked the main features as

152

one sees them coming or going from here in the Mormon Delta to wherever the gold he struck may be. It doesn't really matter if his hand-drawn route is fifty miles off one way or the other as long as it's clear enough to follow, see?"

She saw Longarm didn't look convinced and told him, "Mr. Miller never drew anything on his map between Durango and the circle on his map that *could* be the juncture of the Chaco and Mancos canyons. So it would be no good at all to us if we tried approaching the mine from the northeast. We have to eat the apple a bite at a time, as you're always telling me, by starting from a known point here in the Mormon country and picking up each landmark on the map in turn."

Ki shot Victoria a curious look but didn't say anything. As a man who'd spent more time than most with his sometimes mighty stubborn young boss, Ki had learned to keep lots of things to himself.

Tom Cohan had fewer reservations on expressing his opinions. He said, "Well, it's off to Texas I'll be, then. For I doubt even a good lawyer will be able to do much for a client in trouble with Apache."

Victoria said, "Ute and Navajo, not Apache this far north."

To which the lawyer answered with a laugh, "You see, I wouldn't even be knowing how to address the court. In the meantime, Miss Starbuck, about those employees who've been refusing to run things your way, which shall it be?"

"Fire them," Jessie said. "I've considered what Custis suggested about keeping them on the payroll until we can have them investigated. I see what he means. I still want them fired. For aside from the money they're costing me with their mischief, they're abusing other people who work for Starbuck Enterprises. Do you need any more letters of authority, Tom?"

He shook his head and told her, "Allow Peters and Cohan to earn *some* of their retainer, ma'am. The power of attorney you've given me to show your paymaster should be more than enough. For whether a man disagrees with his discharge notice or not, he'll see the error of his ways once he sees no more paychecks coming his way."

The lawyer checked his pocket watch and added that his homeward-bound train would be coming through Richfield in an hour and a half. Ki said he'd carry Cohan's saratoga to the platform for him when the time came. So, since all the ham and eggs were gone and they couldn't have any coffee, the breakfast and business meeting combined broke up.

Cohan said he wanted to send some telegrams to his partners while he could. Longarm and Ki walked him as far as the hot sun and cheered him on from the shade of the veranda. The dirt street out front had been swept earlier that morning but a swarm of flies still hovered over a dark stain in the packed earth out yonder.

Ki turned to Longarm and said, "As long as I have your ear, alone, we'd better have a private talk."

Longarm said, "I hardly ever talk with my ear, old son, but what's eating you?"

"I don't know where to start. What do you think of Victoria Miller?"

Longarm shrugged. "If we're talking about her character, I'd say she seemed a not too bright but well-meaning little gal. I've barely talked to her, up to now. But for what it's worth, I've spied no signs of either education or low cunning. What worries *you* about her?"

"Her story keeps shifting like a distant butte you're gazing at through hot air. Just now, Jessie said she meant to follow that lost prospector's map. Wouldn't that mean she must have gotten it earlier from the man's daughter?"

Longarm started to reach absently for a smoke, remembered where he was, and dropped his hand back to his side as he told Ki, "I can't see Jessie drawing that map herself. What about it?"

"Earlier, Vickie was talking about *leading* us to her father's gold strike. She seemed just filled with suggestions about the best route. Does that make any sense to you?"

"Nope. But, then, I ain't a female orphan out to be accepted. Jessie says the pretty little breed came to her as a serving wench. Vickie's no doubt used to making herself as useful as she can, even when there's nothing useful to do. I've been invited to grand homes on Sherman Avenue back in Denver now and again. Silver Dollar Tabor once had me and a Denver police sergeant to dinner, after we'd busted up a robbery in progress at his mansion while he was up in Leadville doing something else. He had more servants than you could shake a stick at, and they struck me as more in the way than helpful. It's a pain in the ass to have a snooty-looking gent run at you with a clean ashtray every damn time you flick your cheroot. But that's the way such hired help acts. Vickie could just be trying to make herself feel needed. Jessie don't allow nobody else to comb her hair or give her a bath, like some rich gals do, you know."

Ki didn't want to think about how Longarm might have learned all this. So he looked away and said, "All right, lets say the girl really believes that shifty story about a mysterious mine at the end of some desert rainbow. We both know Jessie just isn't going to give up on that until she satisfies herself it can't be there. What was your impression of Tom Cohan, just now?"

Longarm shrugged and said, "Never ask a lawman what he thinks of lawyers, old son. I've had too many crooks I knew were crooks walk free on me to admire his breed. I reckon I'd have to say I thought more of him just now than earlier, though. I ain't caught him doing anything awful since first we met. Why do you ask? Has he been crooking Jessie?"

"You just watched him walk away in one piece, didn't you? I thought he said all the right things while we were arguing with the locals about her, too. It's just that I felt it would have been rude, inside, to mention him and his firm when I pointed out that Starbuck Enterprises has been taking on new help faster than I can chew them."

Longarm whistled softly. "I thought the names were new to me. That talk about a last will and testament sort of put me off my feed as well. Their idea?"

"I don't know. Maybe Jessie's always had a few thoughts about the simple grim fact that nobody lives forever. I hadn't been thinking about anyone putting it down officially on paper, either."

"Well, Jessie's too smart to sign anything dumb. If I was worried about my lawyer, I'd be more concerned about giving such a scamp my power of attorney. I doubt it hurts all that much to be crooked after you're dead and gone. But I'd sure hate to have a lawyer dipping into my pocket while I was still around."

Ki smiled, a rare expression for Ki, even when he wasn't looking at Longarm, and said, "We seem to agree on that, at least. Cohan *did* ask Jessie for power of attorney. I persuaded her the regular powers the courts already give one's attorney are more than enough."

Longarm nodded. "I've seen 'em skin orphans and widows with that alone. But what was that letter of whatever she did give him to take back with him?"

"Just the authority to stop payment on claims of wages due people who don't work for her anymore. They've been telling *me* to go to hell, and demanding it in writing from the top lady, when I've wired them that they're out of a job."

"You're right." Longarm chuckled. "She must have hired a lot of gents, recent, who don't know you and her as well as they ought to. But Cohan makes a good point about 'em acting more like uppity fools than sinister forces, Ki. Sassing the boss or her segundo ain't the way a *smart* man goes about taking over the outfit."

Ki said soberly, "I was there. I heard him, too. I hope he's right. I'm not a lawyer. Neither are you. So how do we make sure Peters and Cohan aren't in on it?"

Longarm frowned thoughtfully. "First we'd have to get our fool selves another lawyer. Then we'd have to know for sure *he* was honest, which is just plain impossible, and then we'd have to tell him what in thunder we suspected anyone, anywhere, could be in on. Are you sure you ain't been seeing spooks in empty shadows, old son?"

"That attempted frame-up was hardly a figment of my imagination, Longarm. You say someone seemed to be laying for Jessie in Durango as well. What if this whole wild story about missing gold mines was just a plot to get her out in the middle of nowhere so they could have her killed or worse?"

"There's nothing worse than getting killed, and it works the other way as well. Nobody was trying to kill the pretty gal before she left Texas with a half-breed heiress. Last night that rascal came closer to killing Vickie than Jessie, and leave us not forget he almost shot Lawyer Cohan in the ass while he was at it. What if all this mysterious albeit noisy plotting was aimed at keeping that lost gold mine lost?"

"Do you really think a gold mine in the canyonlands is possible, then?"

Longarm had to honestly reply, "I'd say it was highly improbable, but anything's possible. The old goat who left that map and daughter did come back with gold, more than once. I ask questions, too, and I was in Salt Lake City a spell between trains. Isaak Miller never recorded no claim, federal or territorial. But he did peddle color, and it did assay as almost pure gold with a little silver and such rock as he couldn't wash out of it. I'd have expected vanadium, uranium, or even oil shale where he told everyone he'd been digging. But he must have been digging some damn where."

"What if he found color somewhere else in a very big wilderness and accounted for it with a false story and a fake map?" Ki asked.

Longarm sighed. "I thought I just said that. On the other hand, Jessie tells me the man's daughter told her that her old dad sent her the map, personal, just before he vanished on her. Unless a man was planning suicide and a mean joke on his own kid, at the same time, why in thunder would he do a crazy thing like that?"

"Maybe he was crazy," Ki suggested. Then, before Longarm had to come up with an answer to that, they both heard distant gunshots. So Longarm got out his gun and they started running.

The source of the sounds soon became evident to the two big men as they covered the distance in the hot sun on their long-striding legs. For others had beaten them to it. A goodly crowd had gathered in front of the Western Union office.

As Longarm and Ki joined the others, old Al, the town law, told them, "Put your hardware away. It's over, and this time there's no mystery at all."

Longarm bulled through the crowd with Ki in tow. When at last he could see the grim little scene in front of the telegraph office, Longarm swore and said, "Oh, shit, how are we going to tell Jessie about *this*?"

Ki didn't answer as they both stared soberly down at the

remains of Tom Cohan. The pudgy lawyer was sprawled face-down on the plank steps as if he couldn't make up his mind whether he'd decided to die on the plank walk or in the dusty street. His derby was in the street. His pudgy face was laying in some of the dust with blood running out of his nose and mouth. The hilt of a cheaply made but obviously serviceable stiletto rose from the dead man's back.

He wasn't the only dead man in sight. Up on the walk a stranger in blue-denim riding duds lay on his side with his knees drawn up and a hurt look in his glazed but open eyes. His hands had gone limp, now. But it was easy to tell, from the blood all over them, that he'd died gun-shot, albeit too fast for Longarm's taste if he'd just done what it looked like he'd just done. Old Al joined him and Ki to observe, "My kid deputy, Spud, got the one in the jeans. I sent him to fetch the doc and Morgan Welch. We're sure getting famous here in Richfield. Guess who Spud just nailed."

Longarm took a closer look, nodded, and said, "They send us Wanted fliers, too. That has to be Dago Dillon, wanted for stabbing some other gents in other parts with that pigsticker he just used on Lawyer Cohan. You say your deputy got him?"

Al said, "I did. As Spud tells it, he was just coming around from the alleyway, where he'd been sort of watering the weeds, when he seen the victim step outta yon telegraph office and, right in broad daylight, that other cuss just stepped in back of him and put that blade in his back before Spud could even yell at him to stop. Then he seen Spud and just stared at him, wild-eyed and grinning like a polecat. So Spud done what was only natural. You reckon Dillon was the one as put that hole in the back of Elder Reynolds?"

Longarm nodded and said, "I do. And even Morgan Welch will have to agree both you and your deputy have brung two of the murderers to justice. Lord knows where they buried their pal after Miss Starbuck ended *his* career."

Chapter 14

The sudden death of Jessie's lawyer delayed the expedition another full day. This time the county authorities made no fuss about an open-and-shut killing that even Morgan Welch was both satisfied about and didn't want to share newspaper space about with outsiders he couldn't accuse of anything. But Jessie wasn't about to leave the remains of a man on her payroll to the tender mercies of even nice strangers. Longarm helped a lot with the chores involved in getting a fat corpse back to Texas in high summer.

The local undertaker was reluctant to pump the body full of arsenic. He told Longarm, "I know they used arsenic embalming on the Union dead during the war, Deputy. It comforts some to know them dead youngsters will still be recognizable a hundred years from today, after most folk I bury won't be. But you see, since they found out you can detect arsenic in a body that no mortician *embalmed* that way, they've been asking us not to do it. It would just make things too convenient for a spiteful soul to feed a spouse flypaper soup. Once such a murder victim had been embalmed with arsenic, there'd be just no way the law could ever find out."

Longarm nodded understandingly but said, "Nobody is ever going to suspect the cadaver in question was poisoned, pard. He got stabbed in the back with the law watching. Meanwhile, he faces three or more days in an unrefrigerated railroad car, and folk of his faith favor open-casket services."

The Mormon undertaker grimaced. "Even if I used old

159

Union Army methods, he'd still arrive sort of dusky. Arsenic embalming preserves the features better than anything I know of, but, if anything, it makes 'em turn black even quicker."

"I'd like you to do it, anyway. Mourners who might suspect a colored grandmother he never talked about ain't half as likely to puke than if they had to approach an open box with half a week of summer-rotted meat in it."

The undertaker looked as if he'd just sniffed something as awful. "Look, I can pump him full of formalin and red food coloring. That ought to keep him almost two weeks, even in this weather."

"Make it straight formaldehyde instead of that watered-down corpse-juice and we got a deal. It's even hotter in Texas this time of the year. Lower altitude."

They shook on it and the undertaker said he'd send the bill to Starbuck Enterprises. Longarm had to agree. It made him even more aware of his own modest station in life, next to Jessie Starbuck. But, once he and Ki had tidied up as best they could, Jessie tried once more to convince Longarm how impressive he was to her—in bed, at least—and so he took advantage of their daytime quickie to try and convince her not to go tearing off into Indian country without at least a troop of cavalry tagging along.

He even got her to agree, while she was hovering on the razor's edge of orgasm and would have likely agreed to jump over the moon, if only he wouldn't stop. But as soon as she'd come, and had her wits about her again, Jessie pouted up at him and said, "That wasn't fair. Promises made under duress don't count."

He rolled off to light a cheroot. It was too blamed hot that afternoon to get really down and dirty, even with the most beautiful gal for miles. He got his smoke going and insisted, "Dammit, honey, I'm already in trouble with Billy Vail for messing in affairs I wasn't sent to mess in. I got to get back on the mission he sent me on and I told you it's important."

"Good. You can ride with us, since we both have business in the Four Corners country."

"Not the same kind of business," he protested. "I got to contact as many Indians as I can. If there is one thing you and your party wants to avoid, it's Indians. Both the Ute and Navajo are already vexed about something over yonder. If there's one thing *they* don't need right now it's more strangers poking amongst their canyons for lost gold mines or anything else!"

She snuggled closer, despite the way he was sweating and she was glowing, to say, "You said yourself that once we find Vickie's inheritance we'll have to talk to the tribal councils and such about it, right?"

He shot a smoke ring at the hanging lamp above the bed and answered, "Later, after me and the B.I.A. gets a handle on what's going on in them parts. You'd be surprised how many Indians can read. Sitting Bull subscribed to the *Washington Post* and *Army Times*. They gave him lots of visions about what the Great White Father meant to do next. Any Ute or Navajo leader who knows his stuff already knows that the Lakota might still own the Black Hills if white folk hadn't noticed there was gold in them. Red Cloud and his braves went about it all wrong. They started killing whites *after* news of color in Deadwood Gulch got out. The way a smart Indian hangs on to his land is to make sure none of us consider it useful."

She asked, "Do you think Vickie's father was run over by Indians, then?"

"It happens. You don't see a gold rush to the Four Corners country, save your own dumb notions, do you? If local Indians killed Miller to keep some local details secret, it's a good bet they were smart enough to cover up all traces of his camp, mine, or whatever he was messing about on their hunting grounds. That's another good reason you should back off, honey."

She shook her head and said, "I wasn't raised by Alex Starbuck to back off. He taught me to read sign pretty good, as well. If there's anything there, buried or not, I'll find it. Then we'll pinpoint it once and for all and see that Vickie never has to be a servant again."

Longarm shrugged the bare shoulder under her damp gold hair and said, "Well, I'll allow that if you get her killed out yonder she won't have to pick up after anybody anymore."

161

"You don't have to come with us if you're so set against the idea, you know."

Longarm knew, but as Jessie had hoped and as he suspected she'd hoped, he found himself saying, "Oh, hell, I got to go that way in any case. I got my own three ponies and I can easily replace the supplies I abandoned on the far side of your rainbow's end. But, once we're in the canyonlands, I got to tend to my own chores. I mean that, Jessie. And while I know how tough you and Ki are, I doubt there's much fight in Victoria, even if you *had* me as well as Ki to back your play, we're talking two whole Indian nations and maybe worse. I told you those Indians who came close to killing me said something about a *white* gang hiding out around there someplace, remember?"

"I remember, dear. Vickie thinks that's who may have done her father in. She says he always got along well with most Indians."

Longarm chuckled and said, "She's living proof of that. But being part Paiute won't help her worth mention if you all run into Ute or Navajo. How can I convince you both nations are on the prod this summer, dammit?"

She said, "I have no call to doubt your word, darling. You've yet to lie to me, and you told me you'd been jumped by Ute toughs. But you're still alive, which is more than they can say right now, and you managed to cope with them all by yourself. With Ki and me taking turns on guard, knowing there might be trouble—"

"Dammit, woman," he cut in, "there's no *might* about Indian trouble over that way. Everyone but you seems to *know* there's trouble. Maybe a three-sided war between Ute, Navajo, and Lord knows who else. I was wide awake with my back to solid rocks and they still got the drop on a stranger to country they knew like their very own palms. And leave us not forget there was only five of 'em, or that they were kids, not a war party led by an old, foxy fighting man. You ain't seen that maze of rock- and brush-filled canyons, Jessie. It's natural ambush country, where one fair gun hand could hold off a whole army!"

She began to fondle him again as she observed, "Good. Ki

162

and I are both fair gun hands. So we ought to be able to hold off anything that comes at us and, aren't you finished with that stinky cheroot yet?"

He wasn't, really, but it wouldn't have been polite to tell a lady that while she was pleasing you. So he muttered, "Waste not, want not," and got rid of his smoke to enjoy hotter pleasures for a sweet if sweaty time.

Then they took a bath together. That was a cooler way to do it, at least, even if it was sort of awkward and Jessie got to worrying, at the end, about slopped-over water running through to the kitchen down below. So they finished back on the bed, which saved them some drying with towels, and then she insisted on him getting dressed again so he could help her buy some horseflesh. He didn't want to. He kept trying to talk her out of it. But by that evening, as the moon rose, the expedition was on its way, to wherever in hell Jessie thought they were going, cuss her pretty hide.

Victoria's personal advice and her late father's crude map agreed fairly well as they rode out from the Mormon Delta by moonlight. When Ki commented on this to Longarm during a trail break, the tall deputy said, "It hardly matters whether she recalls this stretch from childhood or whether she memorized a map she's been packing a spell. This far west, we don't have to worry about riding off a cliff or down a crevice by the light of the silvery moon. Once we're closer to the river, all riding has to be by daylight. There's many a split in the pumpkin a horse and rider could fall into at high noon. The damned juniper and lesser shrubbery can grow right to the edge, with the far roots hanging out over nothing. So be careful about riding through chaparral in any hurry, while you're at it."

Ki asked dubiously how rimrock vegetation could grow with roots exposed to the dry desert winds.

Longarm explained, "They don't start out with that in mind, old son. You see, the canyon walls can be crumbly and the winds ain't always dry. Juniper in particular grows mighty slow. It can take a human lifetime to get as tall as you or me. Meanwhile, many a winter snow and many a summer thunderstorm can eat away at a flower bed that may have started out a safer distance from the edge. Sooner or later the poor juniper gets to take a fall it never planned on while it was still a seed. You find a hell of a mess of mighty fine firewood down in the pumpkin. Meanwhile, like I just said, watch where you're riding. I found out about such treacherous shrubbery the hard way, first time I rode through canyon country, sort of expensive. I managed to save myself, as you can see, but it cost me a ten-dollar horse and a forty-dollar saddle. Had to buy a new Winchester, too. Falling a mile against solid rock can sure throw the windage off on the barrel, even if the stock don't shatter."

By this time both the gals had come back from some gal talk they'd likely had to have in the brush on that side of the trail. So they mounted up and rode on. Longarm didn't feel he had to warn Jessie against charging blind through brush in rough country. He knew she'd hunted stray longhorns on the Staked Plains in Texas as a kid a mite young to be riding so rough. Ki was the worry, even if he did sit his horse pretty good. Jessie had likely taught him how to be a cowhand while he was showing her how to fling them steel stars and play other Ninja tricks on folk. Longarm could only hope that last trick she'd shown him in bed back there had been her own discovery entire.

The night was cool, and the ponies Longarm had helped Jessie choose in Richfield were good. So they were making good time. Longarm preferred to travel lighter and Vickie looked uncomfortable, riding sidesaddle with a hotel pillow lashed under her. Longarm knew it was more to protect the pretty little breed's injured buttock from bumping the cantle of her stock saddle as she rode with most of her weight on the one that hadn't been creased. Aside from Longarm's three ponies from Durango, Jessie had purchased a dozen, or four for each of her own party, at prices Longarm was still brooding over. He hated to see a pal taken advantage of. She didn't seem to feel she had been. He had to admit all the mounts they'd bought off that grandfatherly Saint were good stock. But the way Jessie had laid out all that money without even one sob of mortal anguish served to remind him again of the vast financial gulf between them.

They rode through most of the night, changing mounts and resting all of them a spell, once an hour. It was Longarm's idea to go easy on overwatering them. Even though she'd grown up West Texas style, Jessie was just naturally more tenderhearted about dumb brutes than Longarm thought she should be, himself excepted, of course. He warned her that waterlogged ponies moved slow at times slow might not be called for and added, "They ain't sweating much in this cool night air. Once we're on the far side, they're going to need water that might not always be there, Jessie."

She asked, "Don't the Indians who live in those canyons have to water their ponies, Custis?"

"Whenever I see canyons that look like Indians live in 'em, I've found it a lot safer to go around. I don't *want* to meet no Indians before I see you pilgrims off in Vickie's pot of gold, or talk you into turning back. So, meanwhile, we'd best ride high and dry where Indians may not be interested in riding."

Ki called out to inquire just where that might be. So Longarm told them all, "In winter, spring, and fall, the hunting is fair amongst the brush atop the mesa lands. This time of the year, all the critters with a lick of sense are either down in a shady canyon or up atop some piny ridge. The flats between canyons are deserted by game right now, and hopefully by anyone interested in hunting them, or us."

Jessie asked, "Won't we be more exposed, riding higher atop the flat mesas, Custis?"

"Yes. What do you want, egg in your beer? The whole damn country ahead is a death trap. I tried riding below the skyline, coming in the other way a few days ago. It didn't work. I don't know if them Ute kids spotted me in the open and moved in on me once I was more boxed, or if they were down in the pumpkin laying for me to begin with. But the more I study on it, the dumber I feel. I reckon, this time, it may be best to keep as much nothing as we can all about us as we ride in. They can surely see us a lot farther off, that way. On the other hand, we can see *them* long before they can get to us. So it more than evens out. Neither Ute nor Navajo enjoy charging across open ground half as much as Comanche or the Lakota Confederacy, and them old boys would rather lay in ambush for you, as old Custer found out a few summers ago."

Ki told Jessie, "He's right. When do we turn back?"

Jessie said not until they found Vickie's gold mine, and the pretty little breed protested that she didn't want anyone put out, or killed, on her account.

But, naturally, they rode on, and on, until the sky ahead was starting to pale near the horizon. Longarm caught up with Ki, in the lead, and said, "You'd best keep an eye peeled for some shade. Any trees worth mention, this far east, ought to mean water, as well."

Ki growled, "Longarm, I may have been born in a place where rain is more common. But this isn't the first time I've been out in dry country."

Longarm smiled sheepishly and replied, "I know. We surely had a swell time fighting all them outlaws and Mex troops in the Baja that time. But I've ridden this particular range before, and it's sneaky as hell. It ain't true desert and it ain't true mountain country. It tries to kill you both ways. So if I tell you something you already know, don't act so disgusted. My heart is pure and I'd rather bore you some than fail to warn you about something your mamma forgot to mention."

Then Ki said, "Forget your apologies and take my word without turning around, Longarm. We're being followed."

Longarm kept his head turned the same way as he replied, "You'd best go on talking back to me, then. How many and how far back?"

"I make it two riders, just at the edge of visibility. Wait, they're dropping back. A couple of cowhands, just out for a morning ride?"

Longarm said, "It ain't that close to dawn yet, and even if it was, we haven't passed any spreads for hours. I ain't noticed no stray stock around here, neither. I'd say they just noticed it's gotten a shade lighter in the past half hour and so they've dropped back to keep us from doing what you just done, you sharp-eyed rascal."

Ki said, "Right. They have us outlined against the coming dawn. They can afford to keep their distance, the bastards."

Longarm thought before he said, "Make for that tall clump

of juniper to your right. See if you can swing us between that patch of blackness and them sneaks. As soon as you do, I'll just roll out of this saddle and we shall see what we shall see."

Ki started to object. Then he nodded and said, "It might work. Our fifteen sets of hooves must be blurring us at least a bit with dust, and even if they see we're on to them, it ought to keep them back until, as you said about Comanche, they'll have to come in openly or give up on their plan. What do you think their plan coud be?"

Longarm said, "I'll ask 'em," as, judging their present view of the eastern horizon was about as tricky as it was likely to get during the remaining darkness, Longarm drew his Winchester from its scabbard and quietly rolled out of his saddle to land on one hip and the gun stock.

The unexpected move spooked Jessie's pony and surprised her some as well. As she steadied her mount in passing, she called down to Longarm in a whisper. "What are you doing down there, dear?"

"Keep going," he hissed, "I ain't supposed to *be* here." So she did, leading Victoria and the considerable train of pack mounts after her as Longarm saw, to his satisfaction, that it really was hard to make out any detail between him and the dawn's early light.

Hoping his ruse had worked, Longarm crawled into a clump of rabbit bush and levered a round into the chamber of his saddle gun while, behind him, the others rode on as if nothing had happened.

It seemed like a million years went by. Longarm was beginning to curse Ki as a nervous nelly with disgusting night vision when, out of the night, he heard the jingle of a rider's spur against dry brushwood. Then, although they were walking their mounts with some care, he could make out the sandy crunch of steel-shod hooves. But strain as he might, he couldn't see them against the darkness back that way. Not well enough to draw a bead on either, that was. He could only make out that there were two of them, as Ki had said, riding side by side about three paces apart.

Had there only been one, Longarm would have had much less of a problem. His Winchester threw lead fast enough to make up for an occasional miss in the dark. But, wanting to make sure, he held his fire and, sure enough, the damn fools rode right past him. So now he was the one with the black wall of night at his back, while they were outlined sharp as black-paper cutouts against the paler sky to the east.

Longarm had always noticed it was easier to hit close targets than distant ones. So he rose to one knee, Winchester muzzle trained, and called out, "Freeze! I'll only say that once!"

One reined in. The other spurred his pony and was off and running a race he knew he was running with death. So Longarm killed him first. Longarm knew he'd killed the fleeing rider when he saw the gent's hands fly out and up, stiff, while his hat flew even higher. Nobody acted that way unless he'd taken a round in the spine.

As the man he'd shot tumbled from the saddle, the one closer in swore and drew to fire at Longarm's muzzle flash. So Longarm, who'd naturally crabbed sideways after firing and wasn't there anymore, fired from his new position and another saddle was suddenly empty.

As Longarm moved in gingerly, levering another round into the chamber, he heard Jessie bawling his name as, farther off, Ki yelled for her to come back.

That made two of them. Longarm yelled, "I'm all right. Stay back, goddamn it! Ain't you ever been in a war before?"

But as he reached the last man he'd shot, sprawled faceup in the cheat grass just off the trail, Longarm called out to her again, "Well, I reckon you can peek if you just have to."

As Jessie rode on in, gathering the reins of one of the now extra ponies in passing, Longarm hunkered down over the one he hadn't spine-shot and asked conversationally, "Are you still with us, you mysterious cuss?"

The dying owlhoot rider fluttered his eyelids and told the man who'd shot him to do something just awful to his mother.

Fortunately he was only able to whisper it. So Longarm told him, "Watch your manners. Ladies present. I'm sorry as hell about all this. But I did warn you to freeze and that meant *stay* frozen. Who are you and how come you've been trailing us so sneaky through the dark?"

168

The man on the ground blew some bubbles up at Longarm before he said, "You kilt my brother and I'll get you for that!"

Longarm closed the man's eyes for him and told Jessie, "I hope he meant them last words. I doubt it hurts as much to die when you don't know you're dying, and he sounded serious."

Jessie said, "Get up and grab these reins. I'll go after that other pony, lest it get away!"

"Let it go. By the time it strays back to Richfield we'll be long gone from here, honey."

She asked when he'd learned to read the minds of horses, and as he continued to search the man who'd just died for clues to his identity, Longarm said, "That dapple gray you're already holding was one we considered while you were gathering the remuda with us together. So the one as just lit out has to be a stablemate."

He found some change and a wad of silver certificates but no I.D. on the body as he explained, "Them Mormom lawmen back there would have noticed if even more strangers had been in town long. So this old boy and his pard, yonder, must have come in by train, recent, and naturally picked up their mounts from the same old horse trader as skinned you. He might or might not recall some names they gave him. But it's too far back and they likely fibbed to him anyway."

As Longarm rose, Ki rode in alone, saying, "Vickie and the remuda are tethered on the far side of those junipers. We're not going to find a better spot for a day camp. What have we got here, Longarm?"

The man who'd downed the two strangers said, "I ain't done looking, yet," as he strode toward the site where the spine-shot one lay, with Jessie and Ki following him on horseback.

When they got there, the first one Longarm had shot lay facedown, draped over a stubby but stout clump of brush. It was starting to get lighter by the minute. So it was easy to tell, when Longarm rolled him off and over, that the dead man had distinctly Mexican features. As he patted the cadaver down, Longarm said, "I'd hardly say these last two could be close relations. Yet the other accused me of killing his brother. He

169

must have meant one of the dreary rascals who died earlier, back in Richfield."

Ki pointed out, "You only shot that one in front of the hotel, yourself."

Longarm replied, "I even had help blowing *him* off his pony. Them last words was likely meant in the plural sense. If he was talking about a brother he lost in town he could have been cussing us in general."

Jessie broke in, saying, "Or he could have been talking about a brother of his you personally killed at some other time and place, Custis. You've killed many an owlhoot in your day and the breed tends to be vengeful."

"She's right," Ki said. "Who's to say they weren't after you personally?"

Longarm grimaced and said, "Common sense. The one Jessie shot it out with couldn't have been after me because I wasn't in Utah, yet. The one who smoked up the front of the hotel came closer to killing Vickie and Tom Cohan than any of the rest of us, and that last one killed in town by the town law had to be after Tom Cohan, not me, unless he was blind as well as surly."

Longarm got back to his feet, pocketing a little more pin money, as he added, "No I.D. and no cigar. Flattery will get you nowhere, Ki. The straw boss of these rascals smokes Daniel Webster cigars. He *has* to be after Jessie, and so far nobody's been able to shoot him."

He stepped over to take the reins of the leftover pony and swing himself gracefully up into the saddle with the Winchester in his free hand as he continued, "Vickie will be getting lonesome. We can leave these last two for the buzzards or, maybe Daniel Webster will send someone out after them once the other pony wanders back to town."

As his companions fell stirrup-to-stirrup with him, Jessie said, "We'd best not wait for next sundown to mosey on, in that case. It ought to be cool enough after five or six. But tell me something, Custis. I'm sure getting confused about the true aims of that mysterious cigar smoker. Every time I think I know who the gang's after they aim at someone else! I mean, sure, I had to be the target when I went to see poor

Reynolds, and it looked as if I was the target at the hotel. That rider did put a round through the back of my chair, and the lead thrown at Vickie and poor Tom could have been just wild shooting. But if they were after me, alone, why did they murder my lawyer? *That* certainly couldn't have been a stray shot intended for me!"

Longarm said, "It was more like a stiletto, and I'm still working on that. I had a discreet discussion with Western Union about the last batch of wires old Tom sent. It's against company policy, if not the law, to reveal private messages of even a dead customer. but I'm good at twisting arms and the forms old Tom penciled were still on hand."

Ki asked what Jessie's lawyer might have wired anyone a few moments before he was stabbed to death. Longarm shrugged and replied, "About what you'd have expected. He'd wired his law firm he was headed back with the case against Jessie dropped and the papers his senior pards had asked him to have her sign in his briefcase. He wired some gal his wife might not know about that he'd be there with love and kisses and not to plan on a weekend with anyone else. The only sinister thing he wired was that Jessie meant to go on with this fool treasure hunt. But I doubt Dago Dillon was reading over his fat shoulder when he wrote it and, in any case, Dillon died, as well, before he could have passed on such information."

Then they swung around the junipers and Longarm said, "Howdy, Miss Victoria. Been waiting long?"

The pretty little breed just looked confused as she looked up at them from where she'd squatted to put a camp fire together. The extra stock was already tethered to graze on cheat, farther east against the dawn light. It was Jessie who told the other young woman, "Don't light that, Vickie. We'd rather let them guess where we might be right now than send up daylit smoke signals."

Victoria asked how they were going to cook breakfast without a fire. Jessie sighed and said, "We'd best eat cold from the can until we camp somewhere with better cover."

Victoria didn't argue. She could see she was outvoted. So everyone else dismounted, and as Jessie helped Victoria set up the day camp, Ki and Longarm unsaddled the ponies. Long-arm suggested watering and oating the extra dapple gray and just turning it loose, explaining, "It ain't much of a pony to begin with, or no doubt Jessie would have bought it back there."

Ki said, "We have about as many pack brutes as we can handle. But, as Jessie's segundo, I say we just give it some water and let it rustle up its own grub."

Longarm shrugged, told Ki he sure was cheap, but that, looking on the bright side, the dapple gray might take longer getting the word back to Richfield if it had to graze all the way. He pointed at their other grazing stock and explained, "You don't have as much cheat grass in Texas. So you may not have noticed them ponies are getting more exercise than nourishment, chawing cheat."

Ki grumbled that he already knew what cheat grass was, but Longarm continued amiably, "The useless stuff sneaked into the U.S.A. as weed seed mixed with Lord knows what and busted loose out California way during the gold rush they had back in forty-nine. The prevailing winds and railroads have it almost to the Mississippi, now. But of course it don't compete so good against real grass, east of the Great Divide."

Ki asked wearily, "Were you studying to be a schoolmarm before you took up working as a lawman? I just told you I knew what cheat grass was. It won't hurt the ponies any more than chewing beeswax would, and I don't eat any kind of grass at all. Why do you persist in treating me like a green-horn from back east?"

. Longarm said, "Hell, that's fair, Ki. Ain't the land of the rising sun about as far east as you can get?"

As he went on rubbing down the last pony, Ki muttered, "If you want to play reductio ad absurdum, I distinctly recall sail-ing *into* said sunrise when I left Dai Nippon for the land of my father. So let's not argue about who might have been brought up east or west of whom. Do you think someone smoking a Daniel Webster could have intercepted that wire Tom Cohan sent, saying we were all riding east from Richfield?"

Longarm went on watering the dapple gray from a nose bag it wasn't going to get to keep as he shook his head and said, "I had a hell of a time getting Western Union to show me Cohan's blanks, and I pack a federal badge. I'd say they figured it out for themselves when they just *saw* us riding out last night."

Ki nodded and said, "In that case, they may not know exactly where we're going. Neither Jessie nor Vickie have shown that map to any strangers. Doesn't that mean we only have to worry about them trying to overtake us, rather than ambushing us along the trail as we ride on?"

Longarm said, "Maybe. It don't matter who may or may not be set up to ambush you, if they manage to do it. So we'd best keep a sharp eye, both ways, old son. Aside from Indians, the gents who vanished Vickie's father could still be most anywhere up ahead."

★

Chapter 15

They all managed to catch a little hot and fitful sleep, but not any warm kissing, as the hot Utah sun beat down on the piss-poor shade they were camped under, taking turns at standing or in this case sitting guard. By supper time, supper consisting of cold beans washed down with tomato preserves, the sweaty and restless Jessie insisted on pushing on and to hell with the sun.

So they did, and it wasn't so bad once the sun went down once more. The next moonlit neck of the expedition went somewhat the same albeit not exactly the same as the night before.

Nobody seemed to be following them, now. They stopped now and again on rises to make sure. As the night wore on, Jessie, at least, was almost wishing someone *would* attack them so she could get her mind off the effects such constant riding had on a young lady's libido in the company of a man she wanted but couldn't get at. Victoria was riding sidesaddle, and in truth, she was feeling some hankerings for Ki, now that her rump was commencing to feel a mite better.

Jessie was naturally riding astride, a position many of her Victorian elders found improper for a woman. That night, she couldn't help thinking about sex, with a lover as good as Longarm riding next to her. So, while they'd gotten an early start, Jessie just had to call a final halt a good hour or more before anyone expected the sun to rise again.

Nobody objected. Great minds tended to flow in the same

channels. So once they'd made camp again, under the north-facing overhang of a granite outcropping that promised at least some shade, Jessie assured Longarm that Ki loved to tend to the riding stock by himself and led her lover out to maybe forage for mushrooms or whatever among the waist-high sage they'd come to, now.

As the two of them dropped down out of sight amid the pungently scented sage, Longarm chuckled and observed, "Vickie will no doubt give him a hand."

Jessie giggled as she unbuttoned the front of her shirt and said, "I doubt it's her hand Ki wants her to give him, right now. I wish we could take everything off. But we'd better not. There's no place around here to bathe the sand off our bodies."

He settled for just getting the more important impediments to intimate contact out of the way and, looking on the bright side, knew that at least they got started faster. After all this time spent in each other's company, so chaste, neither felt the need for any foreplay. One of the things he enjoyed most about her, and vice versa, was that lovers so tailor-made by nature for one another could get as much or more out of doing it old-fashioned than a couple who didn't agree so well could have gotten out of doing it in, say, a steam bath, with a mess of gymnasium equipment. But when he told her that, Jessie laughed like a mean little kid and said, "Hmm, that sounds sort of interesting. Have you ever made love to a ballerina at the barre?"

He naturally assured her he hadn't. That old dancing gal with the Omaha Ballet hadn't let him *finish* in her that way. Watching herself get diddled in the practice mirror with both of 'em stark and her one old toe-dance shoe hooked over that practice bar had gotten her so excited they'd wound up on the hardwood floor.

As if she might have taken ballet lessons in her mighty interesting youth, the gal he was on the floor of the desert with at the moment did a sort of upside-down split and an amazing rendition of the Sandwich Island Hula at the same time. It had about the effect on Longarm she no doubt intended it to have, so as he pounded them both to glory he forgot all about that

Omaha gal and even poor old Roping Sally, the only gal he'd ever met who could give back this hard, until he met Jessie. Poor Roping Sally had been murdered up in Blackfoot country just a spell before he'd met Jessie and discovered he didn't have to go through life without a gal so enthusiastic, ever again, after all.

Later, as they lay side by side in the sand, allowing the dust to settle, she asked him what he was chuckling to himself about. He knew she'd never forgive him if he told her. Women were like that. He said, "I was just now thinking that if anything ever happened to you, I'd grow old and gray wondering where on earth I was ever going to get treated so right again."

She wrinkled her nose and said, "I doubt that very much. If I know you, I'd be barely in my grave before you were doing what you just did to me to some painted hussy."

He assured her, "Not until the funeral was over, and she'd have to be more decent than a painted hussy, honey."

She sighed and said, "I'll hold you to that, then. So if by chance, some night you're in the Denver Silver Dollar or some such place, and you feel a cold wind on your bare wicked rump, you'll know it's me, haunting you. I might or might not forgive you if my ghost catches you with a sweet little wife and seven kids."

He said, "I don't like ghost stories, Jessie. Not about folk I'm fond of, leastways."

She shrugged, staring absently up at the winking, uncaring stars, and said, "Whether it's as a ghost or not, I can still see that sweet little wife, down the road ahead. For how long can this tumbleweed life you live go on, Custis?"

He reached for a smoke as he said, "Until I get shot, or they make me retire, I reckon. I just can't see myself behind a desk like poor old Billy Vail. So maybe when they say I'm too old to hunt outlaws I'll take up raising beef. We're talking about another century, I hope. But folk will always eat beef and there's no better place to raise it than anywhere west of Kansas, right?"

She nodded but said, "I already have herds grazing just about any sort of range a man might want to settle down on,

Custis, and you know I pay my foremen more than Billy Vail pays you."

He lit his cheroot, shook his match out with a grimace, and told her, "Billy Vail don't pay me. The taxpayers of this great land pay me, to keep 'em safe. When I see bad stuff going on, it's my job to stomp it out or at least haul it before a judge so *he* can do something about it. Meanwhile, as long as Good and Evil let me go on tumbleweeding, as you call it, I don't want no other job, hear?"

She sighed, lay back, and said, "Consider my job offer withdrawn, then, and, speaking of withdrawals, darling, do you think we could do it again before sunrise, or would that be adding to the wickedness of your imperfect world?"

He laughed, got rid of his smoke, and rolled back between her welcoming bare thighs as he assured her, "Us heathens don't consider this evil. Nothing that feels so good could be. But we'd best make this the last one, lest old Ki haunt my poor bare rump with a cold stare indeed."

Longarm would have been less worried about that had he known what the sometimes severely staring Ki and the more openly hot-blooded Victoria Miller were up to at the same time, on the far side of the outcropping. As worried about Longarm and Jessie as they were about him and Vickie, Ki had the pretty little breed bent over with her bare hands braced against the sloping granite and her bare behind and tawny lower limbs exposed to his admiring gaze and almost brutal thrusts. The patch of white tape on one dark buttock, even darker by starlight, made it easy to avoid aggravating her minor but embarrassing wound as Ki gripped her bare hips to either side and penetrated her petite form. She sobbed, "Oh, it feels so big, this way!"

Ki assured her, "I know. That's why I thought you'd like it. Tell me when you're about ready. This one has to last us all day."

She giggled and wigwagged her derriere teasingly, or like a friendly pup wagging its tail, as she said, "I'll bet the others are behaving just as naughty, don't you?"

"Don't talk dirty about Jessie. It's not your station, or mine, to speculate on such matters."

She arched her spine to take him deeper, even as she told him, "Pooh, it's not always that easy, for a servant. Some act as if we're some sort of moving furniture they own. I mind this high-toned lady I once worked for who could do the damndest fool things in front of her whole staff. I came into the sewing room one afternoon, figuring it was empty and might need dusting, and I caught her in this very position."

Ki didn't answer. He just moved faster. Victoria gasped, "Oh, that's just swell, and that's how she was taking it. She just looked up and told me she didn't need me just then and that she'd ring for me when she did. She acted just as calm the time I served breakfast in bed to her and her husband's best friend. She sure was a marvel, and it's just not true that servants never notice such goings on. Are you saying you never wonder what Miss Jessica might be up to, on the far side of a closed door?"

"It's not my job, so I don't," Ki lied, only too aware that Jessie might well consider him a sort of moving household fixture, or perhaps a mobile weapon. He was vexed with the pretty little breed for making him think of Jessie while he was about to climax, and she'd done that before. When he stopped with it half in, the excited Victoria bit her lower lip and pleaded, "Don't stop! Not at a time like this, dammit!"

So Ki asked her calmly, "Do you really want to? I thought you were only in the mood for gossip about other people who might or might not be acting wicked."

She gasped, "Oh, wick me some more! I was almost there, you fiend!"

"Are you sure you don't just want to *talk* about the subject?" he insisted, making himself go stiffer in her with an effort of will as he refrained from moving it in or out.

She moaned, "Jesus, no! Right now you're the only man on earth and I'm the last woman in the world, and if you don't treat me right I'm fixing to just die!"

He said he didn't want that to happen. So they finished right and it even seemed to Ki, for at least the fleeting moment, that they were, indeed, the only creatures in the universe.

But a few minutes later, when Longarm and Jessie strolled

into camp, trying to look innocent by the dawn's early light, they found Victoria preparing their cold breakfast as Ki lounged calmly under the overhang, sharpening the points of a shuriken with a lump of sandstone he'd found.

As Jessie knelt by the little breed, both of them looking as if butter wouldn't melt in their mouths, Longarm sat down closer to Ki, braced his back against the rear wall of the rock shelter, and asked, "Don't you ever get them throwing stars sharp enough to please you, old son?"

Ki said, "No. Steel can never be too sharp and, as you'd know if people in this country made really good steel, a real edge needs occasional touching up if you really want to cut with it."

Longarm reached for another smoke as he said, "I reckon I can whittle pretty good with my old pocketknife, if I put some wrist into the effort."

Ki shrugged and said, "I have a double advantage at whittling, as you call it. Thanks to my father's lineage, I have pretty good wrists as well. But, thanks to my mother's side of the family having smaller bones, as a rule, Japanese smiths learned long ago to make tools and weapons that are easier to cut with. Have you ever used a Japanese saw blade, mighty whittler?"

Longarm surprised him by saying, "A time or two. Them whispy saws you make pagodas and such with are sort of tricky to use until a man gets the hang of 'em. You saw by drawing the teeth toward you instead of the sensible way, right?"

Ki nodded grudgingly and said, "You seldom have to sand a saw kerf made that *wrong* way, either. I've yet to figure out why my American relations saw backwards and then sand the rough results. My point is that a Japanese saw can be ribbon-thin and cut cleanly and with half the effort. It's true that naturally bigger people can get passable results by sort of hacking with duller tools. But I still prefer to keep my own weapons sharp, if you don't mind."

Longarm lit his cheroot and said, "I don't mind. That backup cutlery you carry has come in handy now and again. I ain't even worried about the throwing star old Jessie packs in her hatband, as long as she don't leave her gun behind. It just seems to me you spend more time fussing with that stuff than I spend fussing with my guns, and I clean them every damned day."

Ki smiled thinly and said, "There you go. Some might say a gun you haven't fired can go days with no further attention than a good coat of gun oil. So, in your own way, you have a proper samurai attitude toward your own weapons."

"That'll be the day. But do you want some oil to rub on your hardware collection? I can spare you some. I try to always have a can of gun cleaner amongst my possibles as well."

Ki smiled but said, "No, thanks. I prefer to keep my own steel sharp and naked." So Longarm observed that was likely why Ki had to keep honing it all the time, and then the gals had their cold rations open and so they ate. Ki didn't argue when Longarm said he'd stand first watch, atop the rock above them.

The first watch wasn't bad. It was just staring to warm up. The sage flats all about this one lone bump in an otherwise featureless plain made it easy to see for miles, even when the horizon hazed and the gray sage all around commenced to shimmer as if the Ute and Navajo together were creeping through the fool bushes from every direction. He knew the only Indians they were apt to run into this far out in the middle of nothing would likely be Diggers, and no Digger with a lick of sense ever approached white travelers, creeping. The big blue lake that was starting to form way out there, now, was just silly. Longarm was content to hand the Winchester over to Ki when the big Amerasian crawled up there to join him, saying, as he felt the sunbaked granite with a bare hand, "Thanks. I was afraid you'd forget to light a fire in the furance this morning."

Longarm told Ki to think nothing of it as he slid down to ground level and circled the big slab to see Jessie and the half-Paiute gal sleeping like babes in the cool shade. They'd both turned in under blankets, this time. Longarm didn't need to ask if they'd been sensible about trying to sleep with boots and duds on. Victoria's bandaged rump and more of Jessie's upper torso than she might have covered to begin with were exposed to broad daylight. He muttered, "Decisions, decisions," and lay down between them, fully dressed, to see how much shut-eye he might be able to steal from the desert sun before it got much higher.

It seemed as if he'd barely dropped off when Ki shook him awake to whisper, "Your turn again. Jessie told me to wake her first, but don't you dare. It's too damned hot up there for a lady, no matter what she said."

Longarm nodded and slid out from between the two sleeping beauties. They were both modestly covered, now. Longarm didn't know whether that had been their own sleepy notions or whether Ki had covered them more modestly before rousing another man. He consulted his watch as he joined Ki farther from the girls. He said, "You gave me an hour more than I had coming. Thanks."

Ki shrugged and said, "Thank Jessie. I gave her the extra time. I was afraid that if she woke up, just now, she'd insist on taking her turn up there. Wake me when she'd be finished, and since even she will have to agree it's time for my turn, we might not get as much of an argument out of her."

Chapter 16

Crossing what Victoria Miller insisted on calling the Green River would have looked complicated enough if it had been the Green River. But as the four of them stood near the rim, gazing down and down, and then some, at the ribbon of swirling muddy water below, Longarm explained for at least the fifth time, "Vickie, it don't matter what your dad's map says or even what your mother might have told you at her knee. That there is the plain and simple Colorado."

"It's the Green," Victoria pouted.

To which Ki could only reply, "I knew it. We're lost. That map has led us into fairy land, as I said it would."

Longarm said, "Not exactly, Ki. There's more Paiute than fairy folk in these parts and, so far, the landmarks on that map have matched up pretty good with what we've passed. I suspect this confusion is occasioned by the late Isaak Miller coming down this far from his mountain-man days. Anyone working his way down from the north to where we're standing right now would have thought he was indeed following the Green River. She starts up Wyoming way and runs almost due south. But up around the Orange Cliffs the Green meets up with the Colorado, which of course commences in the state of the same name. From the Orange Cliffs on down to the Sea of Cortez the results are the Colorado River, official. But I can see how a less official cuss could decide just as easy that the Colorado joined the Green or the Green joined the Colorado.

In any event, it's one river, here, thank God. I'd hate to consider doing this twice."

Jessie, who was holding the questionable map drawn by a semi-illiterate, said, "This says there's a trail down the cliffs, starting from . . . Mushroom Rock?"

Longarm had already stared about some before dismounting when he noticed how close the sky seemed to be to the ground ahead. So he pointed south, squinting against the sun, to remark, "The only mushroomy rock I see anywhere near the edge would be that one, about a quarter mile out. You all stay here with the ponies and I'll scout for a trail. There ain't one closer and this is no time to argue with a dancing pony."

He turned and walked that way, Winchester in his hands at port arms. To his mild annoyance but hardly displeasure, Jessie caught up with him, saying, "Dammit, I'm supposed to be in charge here. Must you have all the fun?"

He said, "Stay on my far side, then, and we'll both have fun. It does look as if some stock has passed this way, maybe a rain or more ago. You can see the tracks on the far side of the smaller rocks ahead. Unless some ponies were bent on suicide, I'd say they circled that big mushroom-shaped rock and— Oh, damn, *down!*"

They both dove facedown in the dirt behind the nearest rocks and only cover for a hundred yards or more as the rifle hand behind the mushroom rock put a volley through the space their heads had just been in. Longarm glanced back to see Ki was already moving Vickie and the spooked remuda farther back from the cliff. Beside him, Jessie bounced a pistol round off their side of the big boulder. Then she said, "I make it one man, an Indian or Mex in an old army jacket. I don't think he wants us using that trail down the cliffs, do you?"

Longarm scanned their surroundings grim-faced as he told her, "When you're right you're right. Ain't you glad I got sharp eyes? The question before the house, now, is how either side gets to move from cover without getting shot. This is mighty close range for swapping rifle shots. If I could circle him while you kept him pinned behind that rock . . . But I just can't crawl worth a damn over canyon air and, the other way, it's open ground without a lick of cover."

As if to prove his point, the tormentor forted up behind the cliff-side boulder popped up just long enough to bounce a slug off the rocks they were pinned behind, and of course dropped back out of sight before the two of them could aim and fire.

Jessie murmured, "I've had just about enough of this," as she put her .38 aside and removed the star-shaped shuriken from her hat. As she did so, Longarm said, "Hell, Jessie, there's no call to kill him sneaky. He knows we're here. We know he's there, and that toy ain't about to go anywhere I can't put a bullet, if only the bastard would show himself a second."

Jessie asked, "Want to bet?" as she gripped the razor-sharp shuriken in both hands and began to twist.

Jessie Starbuck's hands were feminine enough and even manicured when she wanted to look gussied up. But in truth they were stronger than the hands of many a man. So Longarm wasn't too surprised to see she could bend thin steel with them. He asked her what she thought she was doing, aside from busting the fool thing. She said, "I'm not sure it will work. I've only tried it a few times for the fun of it. Move over and give me some room, dear. I don't want to move the *other* way without a pair of angel wings."

He grasped her intent to throw the fool thing, if not her fool reason, so he made room and covered the mushroom rock with his more sensible weapon as Jessie took a deep breath, rose higher than he'd have let her if he'd known what she intended, and as the rifleman behind the better cover exposed himself just long enough for both he and Longarm to fire in unison, Jessie sent her shuriken pinwheeling through the air.

Longarm grimaced as he followed the glittering path with his eyes, too polite to comment on Jessie's aim. For he knew she could see, just as well as he, that she'd flung the fool star way wide of the mark. It sailed out to one side of the rifleman's cover and then, to Longarm's astonishment and no doubt to the other man's chagrin, the shuriken was spinning the other way, smack at him, and as it vanished behind the

184

mushroom rock they heard a scream of pain, followed by the sound of falling rocks and maybe more.

Longarm leaped to his feet and charged in as Jessie bounced .38 rounds all over the big boulder ahead of him. But when Longarm whipped around the safe side of the mushroom rock, firing for luck as he rounded it, he saw there was no-body there.

He moved gingerly to the far edge and looked over it. As he'd surmised, the mushroom rock guarded the beginning of a narrow but negotiable trail clinging to the otherwise vertical cliff. The rifleman's canteen had remained on the trail just below. But it didn't really matter where Jessie's shuriken had hit the cuss, now. Just getting hit by it had sent him over the edge.

As Longarm swallowed and moved back, Jessie joined him to ask, "Well?"

So Longarm answered, "The goblins got him. He wasn't there no more. How did you get that throwing star to think it was a boomerang, honey?"

She told him simply, "I told you I wasn't sure it would work. I noticed back at the ranch, when Ki was first teaching me the art, how one cuved a lot if it was bent at all. Just for fun I bent some more, to see what would happen. How do you like what just happened?"

He laughed and said, "A lot more than that other cuss must have. Can you do that every time, Jessie?"

"No. There's an element of luck in it and, unlike a real boomerang, I've never been able to get a shuriken to come all the way back to me."

He laughed again and asked, "Who'd want one to do a thing like that?" Then he added, "We'd best see how Ki and Vickie are making out."

As they stepped back around the mushroom rock, Ki had already moved in gingerly to ask the same sort of questions. The breed gal followed afoot, leading the remuda as if she thought she was Little Bo Peep and all those ponies were docile sheep. Longarm waved her back and told Ki, "The trail down is yonder. The cuss who didn't want us to use it ought to be on his way to the sea or raspberry jam, now, depending on whether he landed on rock or water. So, either way, we're free to head on down."

"Easy for you to say, up here. What if they have someone posted farther down, to pick us off as we play flies on the wall?"

Longarm sighed and said, "You sure are a cheerful cuss. Do you get your sense of humor from your father's side or your mother's?"

Ki answered stiffly, "I don't know. Unlike your own, my mother and father were married. But I can't recall anyone in my family laughing like a jackass under sniper fire."

Longarm replied, "That's what I was just saying," and then Jessie got between them to point out that they were both supposed to fight the other side.

So the two big men both grinned as sheepish-schoolboy as the situation called for, and Jessie said, "That's better. Now help us girls get down the durned old cliff, and if you drop us we'll never speak to you again."

They didn't. With each of them leading their own section of the remuda on foot, the narrow trail down to the river was more frightening than difficult. Getting across the river was the difficult part.

The Colorado was at low water that late in the year, but it *never* thought it was a dry wash or even the Rio Grande. The map drawn by Victoria's father said there was a river ford at the bottom end of his scary trail. But about all that could be said for the satiny sheet of rapidly moving brown water was that it ran wider and hence less deep, there, than it seemed to upstream or down. They still had to swim the ponies across the midchannel stretch, one at a time, of course. Longarm and Ki agreed the gals should only do it once. Jessie and Victoria still got good and soaked, trying to steer a pony by the tail as it towed them behind it through the deeper parts.

Longarm and Ki were even wetter by the time the last pony was across, shaking itself like an oversized bird dog. As Longarm put his gun and dry vest back on he gazed thoughtfully up at what came next. The ground rose more sedately albeit just as high, in time, to the east. The map called the results clay cliffs. They reminded Longarm more of the Dakota badlands. There seemed to be uncountable gullies running down to the riverside through the big layer cake of multicolored clay. He fished a smoke from his vest, lit it absentmindedly, and asked Jessie to pass him that map as he told her, *"All* them ways up can't be right. I've been in such cut-up claylands before. Such twisty-turny gully-washes can take you all around Robin Hood's barn before they take you to any sensible top."

When he had the map to work with he saw the dotted line did some serious zigs and zags between the so-called ford and an X described as "The Bighorn," whatever that might be. If Isaak Miller had thought he was anywhere near the Custer battlefield he was lost as hell.

The map didn't detail any other riverside features to indicate which of the multiple-choice erosion channels the primitive mapmaker had meant anyone else to choose. Longarm refolded it, gave it back to Jessie, and told her, "I just hate guessing games. But we can't stay here. Why don't we turn back?"

She told him they were dammit more than halfway there. So he was just asking her where she thought "there" might be when Ki called out, from the far side of the ponies, "Longarm! Over here!"

So Longarm jogged over to join him, saying, "I thought you liked to piss in private. What else have you been up to?"

Ki pointed at the sunbaked clay fanning out of a nearby cleft with little more to recommend it and suggested, "See if you read that streak the way I do."

Longarm did, after moving closer and hunkering down to run a finger over the dry surface of the redistributed clay. The windblown dust of high summer had coated everything but that one long smooth streak with gritty dust. Longarm said, "This clay's just a mite moist under the surface. It must have rained within the last few weeks. Some poor wayfaring stranger came down outta yonder gully, on foot, and got to skate a ways when he put a heel through the crust and into butter. I see he caught himself without falling on his ass, though. Must have been a sort of surefooted son of a bitch."

187

Ki said, "We've been wondering where the pony of that breed or pureblood you and Jessie sent over the far edge could have been tethered."

Longarm replied, "You just heard me call him a son of a bitch, didn't you? I think it was likely the same gent, too. He came down off the flattop to the east on foot. He would have had to know where in thunder he was going, even mounted. He was sent to block that trail we just negotiated down off the far side. If he came down that gully, that gully ought to take us to the top."

"To the top of what?"

"I can't say. I never been there, yet. I just now tried to talk Jessie into turning back. You know how she is, once she's got the bit in her teeth, and I was bound for the Four Corners to begin with. I reckon we may as well head up that way before the sun dries us total and then some."

Ki protested, "That sounds crazy, even for you. Didn't you just say that rifleman in the blue jacket was probably *sent* by someone to head us off?"

Longarm shrugged and replied, "I doubt he volunteered. After that it gets more confusing, Ki. We can't say he was sent to head us off in particular. Someone topside might not want *any* strange folk using this trail. Except for that uniform jacket and ferocious attitude, all I can really say about the rascal is that he smells more Indian than Mex. I know he wasn't a Swede."

By this time Jessie and Victoria were drifting over to join them. But it was Ki who asked Longarm, "What makes you so sure he was an Indian, then?"

Longarm nodded to the gals as he told Ki, "The considerable footwork. No decent Mex peon would be in these parts, and no Mexican bandido would ever travel half so far afoot. They consider dismounting for anything less important than rape sort of sissy. On the other hand, Paiute walk just about all the time, and other desert nations are used to scouting and fighting afoot."

He turned to Jessie, pointed his cheroot up the gully in question and told her, "We think we've found the usual way up. If you have a lick of sense you won't go up it."

She asked if he meant to and he said, "I got to. Billy Vail wants me to look up the Indians in these parts. That's my point. Once you start knocking off Indian scouts it's a safe bet you're fixing to meet up with Indians, and we just knocked one off in the literal sense."

But, as he'd expected, cuss her pretty hide, Jessie said that if he was going up that gully she and her pals were going up the same, adding that it hardly seemed fair he should hog all the fun.

Ki suggested, "What if we made camp here and left the girls and ponies safe by the river while we did some scouting?"

Longarm shook his head and said, "The bottom of a canyon ain't my notion of a safe campsite, no offense. If they're good enough to take you and me out, Ki, what sort of a fix would that leave these gals in, stuck down here in this slot with everything from boulders to bullets raining down on them?"

Victoria gulped and said, "I want to go home."

But Jessie told her to just hush and added, "We're trying to get you home. Or to your family gold mine, at any rate. Let's mount up. What are we waiting for?"

So they did, each on a fresh pony, and as Longarm took the lead, they followed him into and up the narrow break in the clay cliffs, strung out Indian file and still brushing a stirrup now and again against the steep clay walls to either side.

Since running water channels widen as they run downward, the gully narrowed even more as they followed it upward. Thus it came to pass that by the time they'd followed the passageway all the way to the top, they'd had to dismount and lead their riding stock up the steep incline on foot. The gent who'd slid down it on his heels, going the other way, was beginning to make more sense.

And when they got to the top, at last, it wasn't too clear it was exactly the top. A geologist might have found it interesting to note how layers of various resistance to weathering had left high pillars and blocks of baked clay standing all about under patches of the original desert pavement. All Longarm cared was that he'd been expecting things up here to be more wide open. The resistant layer that made a sort of lower level of the more or less flat mesa covered most of the space around. But he didn't like the look of all those clay castles, eroded to fairy-tale shapes no matter which way you looked.

Remounted, Longarm rose as tall as he could in his stirrups to just make out the hazy purple peaks of the San Juan Mountains to their northeast. So he and that home-brewed map agreed they had to be somewhere, anywhere, between the San Juan Mountains and the river-canyon of the same name. It was over thirty miles between the San Juan foothills and the San Juan River, with a mess of natural bridges and other loco riding between. Government survey teams were inclined to name things unimaginative by the time they were feeling worn out.

There was little vegetation on the clay flats they'd come to, and while there were streaks of harder packed clay running off in all directions, most were more likely the results of sheet erosion rather than game trails. It was the sharp-eyed Jessie who first spotted a distant dot of chalky white against the duller clay rising all around and asked what Longarm thought it might be. He told her and the others to stay put and rode forward for a look-see, drawing the Winchester from its saddle holster as he approached it. But as he did so he saw it was the skull of a desert bighorn, staring sightlessly back at him from where someone had stuck it like a wasp's nest to the side of a sort of witch's clay cottage. Longarm turned in the saddle to wave the others in. As they joined him, he said, "Old Isaak might not have been lost, after all. For this bighorn skull is about where he put that X on his fool map and there does seem to be a trail, or at least a streak of less windblown dirt, headed east-southeast toward the Four Corners."

Jessie asked, "Won't we come to the San Juan Canyon before we make it that far, Custis?"

"We're likely to come upon many a canyon that ain't been mapped yet, first. So it had best be daylight riding from here on."

Nobody argued. They'd just all seen how steep cliffs could get in these parts and they hadn't even seen what the Indians called the pumpkin, yet.

Longarm took the lead again. Or the lead of the main party in any event. He saw no need to object when Ki commenced riding off hither and yon, vanishing and then popping back in sight as he scouted ahead and to their flanks on his loping buckskin. He didn't seem to be raising any dust, and scouting wasn't a bad notion in country as strange as the Clay Hills.

But as they forged on the country began to open out more and rises ahead were acting more like true hills as the clay got to sunbake farther from occasional running water. So after Ki had sat his mount atop the gentle rise ahead a spell he rode back to them to announce, "We seem to be approaching more fertile ground. The flat ahead is dotted with scrub and there may even be some grass."

Then Longarm told him, "I don't doubt you, but don't make any hasty moves when you look back at that skyline you just rode down from, old son."

Ki turned casually in his saddle and went even more poker-faced than usual as they all regarded the dotted line of riders outlined against the cobalt sky.

It was Victoria who gasped, "Oh, where could all them Indians have come from?" For, despite her Paiute blood, Victoria hadn't fought as many Indians as Longarm, Jessie, or even Ki.

Ki said soberly, "Sorry about that, Jessie. I just didn't study any of those clumps ahead for feathers. What do we do now, Longarm? You know Apache better than me."

Longarm lit a thoughtful smoke as he studied the eighteen impassive cusses staring back at him from the rise ahead. They were wearing paint. White streaks across their dark faces, just below the eyes, and it was true they wore cotton blouses, boot-moccasins halfway up their bare shins, and no feathers in their wide headbands of red to indigo-calico. But Longarm decided, "Navajo. We're a mite far north for Navajo, but Apache this far north makes even less sense."

Jessie said, "They sure *look* like Apache."

Longarm nodded but said, "The Kiowa-Apache you get over Texas way are kin to them old boys yonder, Jessie. The whole nation calls itself Na-Déné, talks the same lingo, and has the same morose customs. But since Kit Carson gave the

191

Na-Déné clans the B.I.A. designation 'Navajo' on their ration rolls, they've took to behaving a mite less ferocious than the old boys we still call Apache. Apache is a Mimbre word meaning enemy. Navajo means the same sort of critter with more peaceful intentions, most of the time."

Ki said, "Whatever they are, they seem to be waiting for us to make the next move. Do we circle up, run for it, or take them up on their dare?"

Longarm had already been pondering on that. He said, "All of them choices could get us killed as dead. I'd rather at least have them admire me as I went down. So I'd best go up and see what they have in mind."

Jessie said, "I'm going with you."

"No you ain't. Sit on her if you have to, Ki. I know what Miss Virginia Woodhull's written about women's rights of late. But few Indians are as advanced as me about such matters. They don't even allow their *own* women to join in discussions of blood and slaughter. So they'd call me a sissy if I let a woman tag along and, if there's one thing I don't want them thinking I might be, right now, a sissy would have to be it."

Ki reached out to grab Jessie's reins and say, "*I* mean it, too."

Longarm rode on, alone, with his drawn Winchester riding politely across his thighs behind the saddle swells. He packed it southpaw so he could keep a casual hand on the trigger as he raised his right palm, halfway up the slope. Not a mounted man in paint moved a muscle in reply. Longarm reined in at easy conversational range and said, "I am called Longarm. I ride for the Great White Father. Does anyone here follow my drift at all?"

Nobody answered. So he tried saying the same thing in Spanish. A morose-looking individual with a jagged scar running down one cheek in and out of his war paint replied in passable English, "Your Spanish is terrible. I speak three languages, good. If you are so important, why are you so stupid?"

Longarm smiled thinly at the obvious leader and replied, "I

192

may not be as educated as you. But I ain't lost. What are you up to on this side of the San Juan?"

"Killing enemies," the one with the scar replied. "We had a good fight, two days ago, with crazy Paiute."

Longarm raised an eyebrow and asked, "Do tell? I thought you Na-Déné were too proud to hunt down the poor Diggers this serious. Ain't the Ute willing to fight you no more on this side of the San Juan?"

The war chief looked at Longarm half a shade friendlier as he said, "You know my people well enough to call them Déné. That is good, even if you say it wrong. The northern bands just say Déné because that is what we are, real people. Paiute are not any kind of people at all. They are animals who grub in the earth for worms and rabbit shit. Their men have nothing to steal and their women are too ugly to fuck."

Longarm said, "I'd heard your nation didn't admire Paiute all that much. But you just now said it was your notion, not mine, to ride so far out of your way to fight 'em. No offense, but I seem to be missing something here."

The Navajo leader grimaced and said, "We have agreed you know very little. Hear me, I am called Many Sheep. My band was awarded land in the pumpkin, much land, much, after we gave Kit Carson such a good fight that time."

Longarm was in no position to point out that the army version was a heap different. Despite his beat-up face, this particular leader would have been a small boy the time Kit Carson kicked the liver and lights out of the Navajo, murdered all their sheep, and marched them to Fort Sumner to plant peach trees and pull K.P. 'til they agreed to mind their manners. Many Sheep was getting mighty ill-mannered, it seemed, as he told Longarm, "The Indian agents are weaklings who lie as much as women. They have allowed others, rabbit-eating Paiute as well as white eyes, to settle in our canyonlands to the southeast! The Paiute would be bad enough. But at least we could let our young boys track them down for fun. It is the way you white eyes give the Paiute weapons, and even teach them how to fight, that is making us weep blood!"

Longarm said, "Hold on, Many Sheep. Are you telling me

white settlers have invaded the pumpkin, then allied with Diggers they're arming and training to take on folks the B.I.A. has already reserved that land for?"

Many Sheep scowled at him and asked, "Don't you even speak English? Are you calling me a liar? By the four hundred gods of real people, if you work for the B.I.A. as you say, pay *attention*. We may let you live if you can convince us you are not in with the white eyes who have been abusing us. But not if you don't pay attention. Hear me. I have a message for the Great White Father. Are you paying attention?"

Longarm scowled back just as ugly and said, "I surely am, if you have anything sensible to say, damn your eyes. I got the part about white land-grabbers with a private army of armed Indians. What comes next, dammit?"

Many Sheep said, "We have been trying to resist them, you fool. What else would you have real people do? Now and then we have been able to pick a few of them off. The one or two we are tracking right now were dumb enough to patrol far from the pueblo they fight out of. But when we try to get close to their main camp they shoot at us with a gun that spits bullets in a steady stream, too many bullets, coming too fast, for even real people to stand up to!"

Longarm whistled softly and replied, "That's the second time I've had what sounds like a *Gatling* gun described to me. The last old boys who told me about strangers with such an awesome weapon fought and spoke in Ute. So I'll be switched if I ain't starting to take such a whopper *serious*."

Many Sheep said, "The ones we cut off from their main camp do not have such weapons. Only rifles. We have trailed them almost this far. We don't know where they might be, now. Paiute are hard to track, even over softer ground. They ride no horses and have feet as soft as women."

"Might at least one of the old boys you've been tracking have been sporting a blue jacket and high-powered rifle?"

Many Sheep's eyes lit up wolfishly as he answered, "All of them did! The bad people who've taken over some of our best canyons issue blue jackets and red hats to their Digger soldiers, along with rifles. Funny rifles with a reloading knob on

194

the side. How did you know this? Have you seen any of the mangy rabbits?"

Longarm nodded soberly and replied, "One. He wasn't sporting a red hat. But he came close to getting me with his rifle, and he did have on a blue jacket when last we seen him, flying off the far rim of the Colorado without so much as a feather to slow him down."

Many Sheep relayed the news down the line in his own lingo. The other Navajo grunted comments at Longarm that could have been taken for admiration or disappointment. Longarm said, "Now don't get upset, boys. We only counted coup on one of them odd Paiute. One was all we met. We thought he was guarding the trail we had to follow down the cliff. It could have been we only met him on his way back to Paiute country and he just acted natural. On the other hand, we could have met another private army man entire. It's been some time since any B.I.A. agents have been able to get in, or at least get in and *out* of these parts. Anyone setting up a private empire in the canyonlands would likely know it would be frowned on by my nation as well as your own. They must be crazy as bedbugs, unless they have an even better reason than I, for one, can fathom. I've also heard tales of, ah, yellow iron in your part of the pumpkin, pard. Can you tell me anything about yellow iron?"

Many Sheep looked disgusted and said, "Yes. It's called gold in English and oro in Spanish. What do you think I sell my wool for, those silly little glass beads you people seem to think we have some use for?"

Longarm chuckled and said, "That's one on me, then. But now that we agree on high finance, what's the story on color over in the pumpkin rock?"

Many Sheep said flatly, "There isn't any. Many of your gold seekers, many, have passed through the pumpkin, in less troubled times. Some took rocks away with them. None came back."

Longarm nodded and commented, half to himself, "Makes no sense to stake a claim on uranium and such in hard-to-get-at places." Then he insisted, "Nobody's ever been up every side canyon of the pumpkin, right?"

Many Sheep shrugged and answered, "Only the Anasazi of long ago, if even they explored *all* of it. But hear me, the white eyes who looked for gold, not quite as long ago, told us there was no sense looking farther through the pumpkin rock. They told us gold was not to be found in such rock. If they had been lying to us, somebody would have come back to dig for the gold by this time, wouldn't they?"

Longarm said, "It seems someone just has, with a Gatling gun and a private army of Indian outsiders. Could you locate this big pueblo you mentioned on a paper map for me if I showed you one?"

Many Sheep shook his head and said, "No. Nobody I know has ever been able to get within a day's ride of it and return alive. We only know it is somewhere deep in the pumpkin, close to where ourselves and the Ute agreed nobody should herd or hunt if our nations couldn't fight anymore."

Longarm knew that about agreed with Victoria Miller's map. So instead of pressing for a tighter fix, he asked, "How do you know about pueblos and such if none of you can get near the main camp?"

Many Sheep explained, "One of our young women escaped from them. Before we knew they were there, they caught her alone and tried to make a slave of her. They should have known better. But she was their captive almost three nights before she killed the man they'd given her to and got away. She told us they took her to some Anasazi ruins they've fixed up. She said it was high up a canyon she had never been through before. She said it was a good place to hold, even without a medicine gun. The ruins were built into the rimrock of a sort of island mesa, with canyon walls guarding every approach. There is no way, none, to sneak up on them. They didn't see her getting away. She would not have gotten away if they had."

Longarm nodded understandingly and said, "She sounds like a spunky little gal. Did she say whether they handed her over to a white man or someone else as a play-pretty?"

Many Sheep answered gravely, "Nobody asked her. It would be very rude to ask a woman of my people to talk about a man she killed for abusing her. If the man is dead, her honor

196

has been satisfied. All of our young women are considered virgins unless some man lives to say this is not so. Isn't this the way *your* people deal with such matters?"

Longarm said dryly, "Not exactly. But there's a lot to be said for hanging rapists when you study on it." Then he got out another cheroot and said, "I don't have enough tobacco for all your boys, Many Sheep, but shall we smoke?"

Many Sheep hesitated, then nodded curtly and said, "We shall smoke. If you say those crazy people are your enemies, too. We shall ride against them together. Maybe you can show us how to get past that funny gun that throws so many bullets."

Chapter 17

Longarm had long suspected that his own race got into lots of misunderstandings with others because men of good will on both sides figured anyone with a lick of sense could see that their way of looking at things was the only sensible way and, ergo, anyone who saw things another way was out to pick a fight. Ki said he'd noticed too, and that he feared someday his father's folk and his mother's folk were just bound to get into an awesome fight, with each side accusing the other of spiteful insanity or worse.

They felt free to express such opinions on race relations because Many Sheep was the only Indian riding with them who spoke a word of English, and Many Sheep insisted on riding point, lest anyone mistake him for a private in the ranks.

Longarm and his companions, one of whom was already Indian by half, knew Indians better than most. Someone greener might well have thought the Navajo who'd joined them, or vice versa, were acting sullen as they rode along as if they were practicing to stand in front of cigar stores in the near future. Longarm knew this was partly because Navajo didn't think it polite to openly admire another man's pony, guns, or gal, and partly because they were as confused about white folk as most white folk were about them.

They knew that while whites were dumber than them about a lot of things, whites knew lots of things they didn't, and the way a noble savage could best hope to avoid a spelling bee or

198

geography exam was likely by just not acting interested in the world of what they liked to think of as an inferior species. Longarm could recall Indians who'd asked more questions, when he'd first come west. For, back then, most Indians had still felt they *were* top dogs. Getting licked, over and over, by greenhorns who tended to get lost and could hardly steal a horse without getting caught, had no doubt confused the hell out of them. So, save a few who'd jumped in with both feet and learned to live more white, most kept retreating further and further back into a blank-faced mask of pretended indifference. This particular bunch was busting a gut pretending not to notice the two good-looking gals or even so much fine horseflesh. But no man born of mortal woman can completely hide his thoughts from your average woman, and Jessie was above average in her understanding of the stronger but dumber sex. So after it had been going on a spell she rode up beside Longarm to say quietly, "I know Kiowa and Comanche better than these boys, Custis. Are you sure you know what you've gotten us into?"

He replied conversationally, "I didn't see no way of getting us out of it. These old boys are wearing paint. I'd rather ride *with* a war party than the other way. Old Many Sheep was spoiling for a fight when we met him, and, hell, how do you get out of riding against the same enemies without a mess of tedious argument?"

She nodded but said, "We don't even know who Many Sheep might be talking about, Custis. So how can we say they're our enemies?"

"Easy. I just did. From the little Many Sheep could tell me, some white rascals with a Gatling gun have taken over some cliff dwelling in some canyon I feel sure they never filed a proper homestead claim on with the land office. For if they had, the land office would have turned 'em down."

"What about a mining claim?"

He told her with a shake of his head, "The B.I.A. would know about it, and Billy Vail never would have ordered me to find out what's going on in these parts. I've already found out more than I started out knowing. The reason both the Ute and Navajo have been acting so proddy is that someone has been prodding them without a permit from the Great White Father. Doing so with a private army of armed outsider Indians sounds loco enough without that Gatling gun both Ute and Navajo agree on. We're talking about real money, here. Even if you can get Paiute to work free, and they ain't that dumb, it takes money to issue 'em repeating rifles and, for God's sake, uniforms!"

Jessie tried, "Well, Vickie's been telling us from the start that her dad struck plenty of color, somewhere in those canyons ahead."

But Longarm shook his head again and said, "Even if the pumpkin rock was famous for showing color, which it ain't, neither an eccentric old prospector nor a more serious gang of claim jumpers makes sense."

She protested, "Oh, come now, I've dealt with claim jumpers myself, Custis."

"I wish you wouldn't do that when my back is turned on you, little darling. My point is that to jump a claim you have to find a claim to jump."

"But Vickie says—"

"That's only the first part that makes no sense. Let's say Isaak Miller wandered into the pumpkin a total nitwit and just started producing gold dust without even considering a mining claim. The Comstock Lode was stumbled over by a drunken old prospector known to history only as Old Virginee."

She brightened and said, "That's who they named Virginia City after, right?"

Longarm nodded and said, "They did. It was just about all the poor old gent ever got out of his discovery. Smarter and meaner gents screwed him out of his strike. But, you see, that wasn't claim jumping, Jessie. Old Virginee was too stupid or too drunk to file a proper claim. So they just rolled him out of the way and claimed it for themselves. It was ornery, I'll allow, but it was still *legal*. Had the poor old cuss who found the lode come bitching to me about it, personal, there wouldn't have been a thing me or any other lawman could have done about it, see?"

She frowned and said, "*I* might have, had I been there. But what has the Comstock Lode got to do with the Miller mine?"

Longarm said, "Common sense. I told you whites were allowed to stake mining claims on Indian land or, hell, under a homesteader's outhouse if they struck *color* there. It don't sound fair to me, neither. But that's the way the mining laws were written. The first jasper who files has full title to the gold, silver, or whatever. So, you see, it wouldn't matter if Vickie's father had been there first. He never staked a claim. Anyone else who wanted to could have simply done so and told the old cuss to get off their damn property. They wouldn't have to act so all-fired mysterious about it. We know neither Miller nor anyone else has staked claim-one in or about the canyonlands ahead. So why is everybody acting so mysterious?"

She suggested, "Maybe they're just afraid of Indians. You know how some folk are, and it's easy to mistake these Navajo for Apache or worse."

He said, "I ain't sure there's anything worse than Apache. Yaqui, maybe. But nobody could have drug a Gatling gun in and recruited a mess of other Indians just to hold the Indians who already live around here away. Don't you see, honey, that if anyone had any sensible reason to set up shop on land set aside by the B.I.A. they could just get permission from the same and hire all the Ute or Navajo they wanted?"

She nodded confidently, and decided, "It's like I said. Someone's up to no good and the only thing worth fighting for, up ahead, would be Vickie's inheritance."

Ki, on Longarm's far side, had been paying more attention to their surroundings as they plodded on through ever rougher looking country. So he chimed in with, "Longarm, where are these newfound friends of yours taking us? I thought you said Navajo belonged south of the San Juan."

Longarm said, "I did. They do. I'd best ride up ahead and see if Many Sheep is lost."

He loped the bay he was riding at the moment up to the head of the column. He reined in beside Many Sheep, studied the sandstone cliffs moving in on them from either side now, and said, "I thought the canyon of the San Juan was over to our right a mite more, pard."

Many Sheep said, "It is. We have no enemies to fight down

201

that way. Only my people, real people, live south of that canyon."

Longarm felt sure at least some Hopi might dispute that. But he didn't want to argue the point. So he observed mildly, "We seem to be getting deeper and deeper into Ute country, old son."

Many Sheep grimaced and said, "That may be what you and the B.I.A. says. Hear me, I am Many Sheep. When I am on the warpath, nobody tells me where to ride. My people are not at war with the Ute this summer. But if they want to do something about me and my braves, let them."

Actually, the Ute waited until the racially mixed column was deeper into the natural ambush before they decided to do anything. It might have gone harder with Many Sheep and his boys if the Ute hadn't been confused or perhaps curious about the saltu riding along with their old enemies. It's hard to ask questions of the dead. So, up ahead, a grave-looking Ute on a black pony rode out from behind a big orange boulder to just sit there, staring, as Many Sheep and Longarm rode to meet him. Longarm raised his palm in the universal peace sign. Neither Indian leader did. So he assumed they were still studying on that.

Many Sheep finally had to rein in, since the older and sadder-looking Ute on the black pony didn't seem about to make way on the trail, and it would have been undignified to ride around a man without at least trying to kill him in the process. Many Sheep raised his Henry rifle to shake it above his head as he said, in English, "I am called Many Sheep. When Ute hear my name they all fall down in fear and wonder."

The Ute had to answer in the same lingo, since neither understood a lick of the other's native tongue. He said, "I am called Stone Hand in the saltu manner of speaking. I am only afraid of Navajo women. Everyone knew they all have pus as well as sand up their disgusting holes."

"Be careful, little buzzing fly," growled Many Sheep as Longarm began to sincerely wish he was somewhere else. For he'd spotted the other Utes up on the rimrocks, to both sides.

Stone Hand went on behaving as if he was all alone down

202

here as he said, "If I seem a buzzing fly to you, it may be because I smell shit. You wouldn't notice, of course. Everyone knows the only children of your nation who survive birth have to do so by escaping the womb through their mothers backsides."

Many Sheep replied, just as sweetly, "At least Déné can say they have mothers. Everyone knows Ute come into the world when a Paiute abuses himself with a squash. A rotten one."

Longarm cut in with, "I sure hate to bust up this mutual admiration, gents. But I was under the impression that some cuss with a private army and a Gatling gun was giving all of you a hard time."

The Ute stared soberly at Longarm and told Many Sheep, "It talks. What is it?"

Many Sheep said, "My friend. If you say one bad thing about a friend of mine you shall die. And you can tell those women up on the rimrocks what I just said. I would spit on Ute who are afraid to fight like men, if spitting on any Ute was not such a waste of Déné spit!"

Longarm said, "Aw, cut it out, you two. I never came all this way to listen to flattery."

He saw he had the Ute leader's attention and added, "I am U.S. Deputy Custis Long. Some call me Longarm. I was sent to find out about *other* saltu causing trouble in these parts."

The old Ute regarded him a long hard thirty seconds before he said soberly, "I have heard of you. It is said you arrested a wicked Indian agent who was stealing from some Ute to the north."

Longarm nodded and said, "Up to the Ouray Reserve. He's still making army boots in Leavenworth Prison, too."

Stone Hand said, "That makes my heart soar. It is good that you didn't just kill him. But if you are the good saltu, Longarm, why are you riding with these shit-licking Navajo?"

Longarm replied, "I am looking for a good fight with saltu who have no business in the pumpkin and, hear me, if my Ute brother keeps calling my Déné brother a shit licker, I won't invite him to ride with us against a common enemy."

The two Indians stared at him thunderghasted. Finally the

older and thus maybe wiser Stone Hand said grudgingly, "The prophet Wovoka keeps saying all the red people should join forces against all the white people and make them leave us all alone."

Many Sheep made a wry face and said, "Wovoka is not even a real person. He is only a *Paiute!*"

Stone Hand answered grudgingly, "That is true. But at least he talks to the spirits in *Ho.* Everyone knows the spirits with the best medicine are the Ho spirits. How could a Paiute have the imagination to make up clever lies? Hear me, the words of Wovoka make sense. He must have learned them from wise Ho spirits. Is it not true that Lakota and Cheyenne, people who speak different tongues and follow different medicine, were able to beat Yellow Hair and all his blue sleeves when they joined forces on the Little Big Horn that time?"

Many Sheep nodded soberly and said, "That was a very good fight. How many young men do you lead?"

When Stone Hand allowed he had two dozen rifles covering this friendly conversation, it got friendlier. Many Sheep said, "If either of you ever tell anyone I said it, I will have to call you both liars. But since no women are listening, I can say I think two or three Ute might be able to fight as good as one of my real men. I only lead sixteen, and that medicine gun we all have to worry about spits that many bullets at once. I think that if all of us charged it together, one or more of us might get to the white eyes behind that gun."

Stone Hand said, *"Ka,* that is a stupid way to fight, even for you sheep fuckers. If I had that many young men to lead all at once, I would use no more than eight or twelve to draw medicine fire as they shot at the bad saltu from cover. Then I would have everyone else circle out, both ways, and hit them from all sides at once."

Many Sheep shot an inquiring glance at Longarm, who nodded and said, "Makes more sense than Pickett's charge ever did. And them Union troops Pickett charged wasn't raking that slope with automatic fire either. The Gatling came out just too late to see much service in the war, thank the Lord for small favors."

He turned back to Stone Hand to ask, "Do you and your

folk know just where and how these mysterious land grabbers might be set up, old pard? My other old pard, here, only has their general direction figured out."

Stone Hand said, "We can't get too close. They have scouts, many scouts, Paiute, out on all the rimrocks. But we know the place well from before those crazy saltu came. It was holy ground to my people. The dream singers say it was one of the first parts of the pumpkin the Hohokam settled when Spider Woman led all human beings up into the sunlight from where they had been before, down, down, down in the earth with the worms and mole crickets."

Many Sheep protested, "That is not true. You Ute have no right to claim the Anasazi as ancestors. Those ruins one sees up on the canyon walls were empty, empty, when the first Déné came down from the darkness of the north to this, our own true land!"

Longarm sighed and said, "Dammit, boys, this is no time to argue theology! Whoever built them ruins in the first damn place, the question before the house, right now, is who in the hell has occupied 'em more *recent*, and how we're going to get close enough to find out."

Stone Hand nodded grudgingly and said, "If you and my Navajo brother want to follow me, I will lead you to the place. It is a good place to fight, for them. Two canyons come together in a way that leaves one mesa standing alone, with cliffs all around them and broad flat canyon bottoms one has to cross under fire to get at them. The Hohokam pueblo of thick stone walls is not what you call a cliff dwelling. They learned, later, to shelter their rooftops by building in under overhanging rimrock. This even older place I am leading you to is on top of the mesa, the way Hopi still build their pueblos. The entrance to the ruins guards the only path up the cliff sides. That is where they have mounted the gun that shoots so fast. Aside from the ruins, they have much flat land up there in the sky with them. Even some trees and, out in the center, a big water hole where all the rain that falls on the mesa can run to. I know all this because I climbed up there one time, in my youth, seeking a vision so that I would know the adult name the spirits wanted me to use. Nobody was living up there then, of course. But I was brave, even as a boy, and so I wandered freely through the haunts of the long-dead Hohokam. I did not meet any ghosts. Everything else I saw was just as I have told you."

Many Sheep couldn't resist opining, "We know you saw no ghosts. You would not be with us, here, if you had. Everyone knows how many Ute have died of fright at the sound of even a small owl. My young men and I know better than to follow any Ute into battle. So, hear me, if we ride together, Longarm, here, must be our war chief!"

Stone Hand scowled at both of them. But then he shrugged and said, "My Navajo brother makes sense, for a Navajo. My young men would speak to their mothers-in-law before they'd obey orders from a Navajo, and I can't be everywhere at once. We know Longarm is a good saltu, wise in the ways of fighting his own kind. I think we should make him our leader, too!"

Many Sheep smiled in a surprisingly boyish way for a man with a saddle-leather face streaked with war paint and said, "Good. Now that we have settled on a leader, when are we going to fight those crazy white eyes?"

They both stared at Longarm like a couple of overgrown schoolboys anxious to get started on some fiendish pranks. Longarm turned in his saddle to wave Jessie and the others up to join them, even as he wondered, numbly, what he'd gotten them and his own fool self into. For Longarm would be neither the first nor the last man empowered to start a war, only to wonder, before it was over, just how one might stop a war once he'd started it. Longarm was just a cut above average in knowing this in advance.

As his friends approached, Jessie called out, "What's going on, Custis?"

To which he could only reply, "I ain't sure. But it sure sounds ominous."

Chapter 18

As its name and geological description agreed on, the Colorado Plateau was in the main a big flat block with its bedding planes running more or less level. If the old fossils who jawed about fossils knew what they were jawing about, it had all been sea bottom, long ago, give or take a few million years. But now, despite the seashells one could find in the damnedest places, the surface of the monstrous block rose more than a mile above sea level. After one said that, the geology got more complicated.

For one thing, Mother Nature had cracked her big mud pie considerably as she'd lifted it. So there were places where fault lines had left awesome cliffs or cockeyed layers, even before Father Time and rare but patiently running water had nibbled at the original results.

Running water and busted-loose rock agreed the only way to go was *down,* as deep as water could run or rock could fall. So even where the going looked fairly flat, it wasn't. As Stone Hand led them eastward, it got easier by the mile to see why so much of the fine detail and even canyons deep and wide enough to hide Manhattan Island in didn't seem to be on the official survey map, or why such maps didn't agree with one another so well. It would take a mess of hot air balloons, or perhaps those flying machines Jules Verne kept dreaming up in his futuristic books, to ever map such wild country halfway right. Their Indian guides led them past thundering wonders that would have been wonders of the world if they'd been in parts of the world more folk could *get* to. They rode under natural bridges that made the famous one in Virginia look like a croquet hoop, and not one Indian bothered to look up. They passed time-carved monstrous shapes that were more spooky as well as lots bigger than that famous sphinx over in Egypt. As the Ute led them through broad flats cut lower than the average grade of the plateau by weathering, they passed whole fault-block mountains carved to look like everything from shipwrecks to camels, elephants, and critters that were just plain impossible. The route Stone Hand had chosen had them below the limestones, shales and such that lay atop the main formation of Navajo Sandstone, or pumpkin rock, now. The stuff carved smoother than most rock. Channels wide and narrow cut deep into the orange cliffs all around and pillars stood free, here and yonder, looking like they'd been whittled and sanded in that whiplashy Art New Vogue style that was just starting to catch on with the arty folk back east. They passed one old skinny pillar of orange rock, capped by a big flat mushroom of something harder that reminded Longarm of a Tiffany lamp he'd seen that time he went back east to pick up a want, save that this one was a heap bigger. And as if she knew about that Eastern society gal who'd shown him such fancy furniture, as well as a good time, Jessie rode forward to fall in beside him, saying, "I don't know about you, darling, but I'm just plain lost. The map Vickie's father drew fails to mention twenty-story Tiffany lamps or even that stone Fu dog we passed about a mile back."

Longarm said, "Well, he might not have been as familiar with Art New Vogue or even Oriental art as you and me."

"Or he might not have passed this way at all. As near as I can make out, his dotted line runs more or less this way, but farther south."

Longarm started to ask her how on earth she could know that. But then he recalled a rock formation, eight or ten miles back, that had sort of matched an X marked "Salt Lake Temple" on the crudely drawn map. So he nodded and said, "Yep, we did pass north of the lopsided version of the main Mormon temple in Salt Lake, and old Isaak did say to swing *south* of it. But we ain't steered all that far, either way. You can't, without bumping noses with a canyon wall. Besides, Stone Hand says he's been to them old ruins, personal."

She shook her head and said, "There's nothing on the map about a cliff dwelling. We're looking for a gold mine, Custis."

He shrugged and said, "*You* are, maybe. I was sent to find out who's been upsetting Indians in these parts. Both the Ute and Navajo agree some whites in or about them old ruins have them upset as hell. So that's where I'm going, Jessie."

She looked a mite hurt. So he added, "Look, Stone Hand says we ought to reach *my* goal by sundown. We ain't that close to where the Chaco and Mancos meet on *any* map. That has to mean any claim Vickie has in these parts has to be on the far side of whatever. So I'll be proud to ride on with the rest of you after I wrap up my main mission, closer."

Jessie nodded and then took another throwing star from her saddlebag to stick in her hatband. The motion was not lost on Ki, who'd been riding a few pony-lengths back, with Vickie. Ki loped his paint forward to ask what was up. Jessie said, "Nothing, yet, I hope. We're going to help Custis settle the hash of other claim jumpers, first. Then he's going to ride on with us as we track down Vickie's gold mine."

Ki frowned and asked, "How do we know we're not all talking about the same place?"

Longarm shook his head and told them both, "Wrong kind of country entire. We ain't just riding between pumpkin rock. This trail we're following is *paved* with the same, under no more than a few inches of dust. I'll allow there has to be granite under us, if you dig down deeper than any fool prospector ever dug alone. But, like I keep trying to tell everyone, you just don't find gold in rock like the rock all around us. The Indians say them ruins are perched on a sort of island in the sky, made out of the same orange stuff. The only place there'd be an outside chance of striking color would be if there was, say, a reef of crystalline bedrock cropping to the surface or at least a canyon bottom, farther east, where this pumpkin rock might not be so thick."

Jessie asked, "Have you asked them if it's like that where the Chaco and Mancos meet, Custis?"

"No. But I can ask. Stay back here with Ki and Vickie.

Indians don't like to discuss business in front of gals, and I don't want 'em noticing how pretty you are, anyway."

She didn't argue as he loped up the double column, Ute to his left and Navajo to his right, both sides trying to pretend they were riding alone.

When he caught up with Stone Hand the old Ute looked injured and asked, "Why do you spend so much time back there with your women if you are leading this war party? Hear me, not even the Navajo we usually fight with take women along, even hunting for meat. I will never understand, never, how you people have beaten us so many times. You don't do *anything* right."

Longarm said soothingly, "I was just making sure the gals wouldn't forge ahead of us. The one with yellow hair is sort of tough."

Stone Hand sighed and said, "I just said you were all crazy. Why do you let her wear a gun on her hip, like a man? Have you no control over her? You should make her act like the darker one who looks more like a real woman. If I had a woman who wanted to follow me into battle with a gun on her hip, I would beat her, beat her, until she learned to behave."

Longarm said, "I don't know if she'd stand still for a beating. She might fight back, and she was even smaller the first time she counted coup on Comanche."

Stone Hand gasped and demanded, "That little thing with the star-shaped concho on her hat was allowed to fight *Comanche?*"

Longarm replied, "Kiowa, too. It wasn't a matter of allowing. It was their notion to come after her. Our gals ain't as willing as some to be taken captive. It happens. But most white gals would rather fight, and they don't have to ask our permit when the time comes. You might point that out to any of your young men who might be curious about either of them gals back yonder."

Stone Hand said, "I have already told them that anyone who bothers the women of my brother, Longarm, would have me to fight as well. But this is all very discouraging. It's bad enough that you people outnumber us to begin with. It's just not fair if you let your *women* fight us, too!"

Longarm said, "I don't make the rules. Let's change to a more cheerful subject. I think I told you, earlier, about a prospector called Miller who's missing or worse, somewhere in the pumpkin up ahead. His daughter, the darker gal riding with us, had him located last about where the Chaco joins the Mancos to form the San Juan. Do you know the place?"

Stone Hand didn't answer. So Many Sheep, who'd been riding off to one side in offish silence, pretending they might not be there, drifted over to ask, "How could he? Can't you see he was gray in his hair? What Ute could grow so old if he dared to ride that far into *our* hunting ground?"

Stone Hand growled, "Navajo don't hunt. They herd sheep and, hear me, I have been there many times, many. Even the B.I.A. agrees everything north of the Mancos belongs to us. One time I rode way up the Chaco, just to see if it was true about your people and those sheep. To be fair, we didn't catch any Navajo in the act with a sheep. But of course we killed the ones we did see, and got back with all their ponies, many ponies!"

Longarm raised his free hand for peace and said, "Let's not argue about it, boys. You've convinced me that any white man who *did* spot color in such hotly contested territory would be well advised to just ride on. You'd both know, for certain, if anyone sharing my taste in hats had a gold mine going anywhere near the junction of them two canyons, right?"

They both nodded. Then, as if upset to find himself in agreement with a traditional enemy, Stone Hand growled, "No saltu, red or white, have ever camped there. We scouted the place, not long ago, when the B.I.A. asked us to look for a missing agent. We did not find him. We did not find so much as a lump of charcoal. It has never been a good place for anyone to camp. That place is where our warpaths cross."

Many Sheep added, "There is no gold there, either. We Déné are not as stupid about such matters as this Ute. Haven't you ever seen the fine jewelry our metal smiths make?"

Longarm nodded and said, "Your blankets ain't bad, either. I've always figured you got that turquoise and jasper natural. But is it a secret where you mine the silver?"

Many Sheep shrugged and said, "We don't have to mine

silver. We use the silver coins you white eyes give us for our fine wool and pretty blankets. Didn't you know that? Did you think we had our own silver mines?"

Longarm smiled thinly and said, "I knew most of it was coin silver. I was just making sure. The one thing we all seem to agree on is that the country ahead is distinguished for lots of carved-up orange rock, but not precious metals."

The three of them rode on in silence for a spell before Longarm said, half to himself, "All right, say that map the old man drew, freehand and not bothering with scale, could be off a day or more's riding. Say he was wrong about the names where two big canyons meet, well this side of where he may have thought he was. Say he found *something,* something worth mapping, right about where them old ruins are, and put that circle around it. It just stands to reason that what one man felt like leaving his daughter might make others feel it was worth stealing. Do either of you think it's possible the ancient whatever as built them ruins to begin with might have left, say, at least a few burro-loads of gold dust behind when they had to move away, sudden?"

Stone Hand frowned thoughtfully and said, "I told you I have visited those Hohokam ruins. There were many rooms, many, but I looked in every one of them. There was nothing of value to be seen. Here and there a broken pot, a bone that could have once been that of a person, or maybe just a deer. I told you the ancient ones had been gone a long, long time. Even the wooden beams of their roofs had crumbled to dust."

Longarm asked if he'd *dug* for treasure anywhere. Stone Hand just looked disgusted. Many Sheep said, "That would be a terrible thing to do, even for a Ute. I know some of *your* people poke at places better left to the spirits. But, hear me, nobody has ever found gold among the ashes of the Anasazi. I don't think they had any metal at all. If they did know what gold was, why would they have stored it as dust? What good would gold dust be to anyone but a crazy white eyes? When real people find native metal they pound it together into something useful, like a weapon or even a pot. Are you sure you know how to lead us? You talk as crazy as other white eyes!"

Longarm said, "Gold seems to drive at least some of my

kind loco. I know it was before your time, boys, but a Spanish gold seeker called Coronado once led an armed expedition through these very parts, all the way from Mexico, looking for the Seven Cities of Cibola. All he found were some pueblos, and they say the Grand Canyon discouraged him so much he turned back. But somebody, at least one Indian, had told Coronado there *was* gold in at least some of the pueblos up this way. It's a plain fact he never found any. On the other hand, who's to say he got to every one? The old-timers you call Hohokam or Anasazi were long gone before Coronado got to pester Hopi, Zuni and such. So nobody can say just how advanced they might have been. The Aztec, down Mexico way, *did* have gold, a heap of it, and they spoke a lingo related to Ho, if you follow my drift."

They didn't. Worse yet, Stone Hand suggested, "What if there was some gold, a long, long time ago, in that Hohokam town? What if they took all the unbroken clay pots and stone tools with them when they left, long, long ago? How much gold could even crazy Ho leave in one place?"

Many Sheep nodded and said, "It hurts to say this, but my Ute brother is right. You say this old white eyes took burroloads of gold out of the pumpkin, many summers ago. How long would it take even one old man to carry away *all* the gold he might have found where this old Ute was too blind to see it?"

Longarm whistled and said, "Nothing but a mine, a rich one, would produce even a trickle of color it's taken years to get to the bottom of. But you say that sky island's made of plain old sandstone, right?"

Stone Hand pointed at a sort of naked stone lady they were passing and said, "Like that rock. The same color, from top to bottom. Maybe that old man stole his gold somewhere else, and just said he'd found it here in the pumpkin."

Longarm thought about that before he said, "I don't want to discourage you natural born raiders, but anyone losing that much gold would have surely reported it to the law, and nobody ever did. There was lots of poorly reported looting during the war, it's been said. But that was over a dozen years ago and mostly back east. We're still talking long ago and far

213

away if we get into the casual looting, down Mexico way, when Juarez had it out with the so-called Emperor Maximilian of Mexico. He wasn't Mex at all and, anyhow, they shot him in sixty-seven and his wife, who was already sort of odd to begin with, went home to Europe to go crazy total. We'd have heard about any *recent* serious looting down that way, since. The dictatorship they've had since Juarez kicked the bucket takes stealing chickens serious as hell."

"We had some Mexican war refugees come through one time," said Many Sheep cheerfully. Then he added, "We had lots of fun with them. While they lasted. They didn't stand up to torture half as well as even a Ute."

Stone Hand yawned and said, "I was given a Navajo captive to play with when I was little. He cried like a woman when I got to his balls and died before I could get him even half skinned."

Before Many Sheep had to make up a more ferocious brag, Longarm said, "Simmer down, boys. We could *all* be in for some fun. I don't recall seeing that fluffy little white cloud creeping along them rimrocks to our north, do you?"

Nobody stopped riding forward. But after a time Stone Hand decided, "None of my people are hunting deer atop that mesa in this weather. I don't think that is a rain cloud, either."

Then, as the first fluffy cotton ball drifted off, thinning out as it rose, a second one, smaller and denser, sort of sprouted like cauliflower to take its place.

By this time others back along the double column had noticed the smoke signals as well. So Longarm wasn't too surprised when Ki caught up with them, calling out in a casual tone, "Do you know how to read that smoke, Longarm?"

The tall deputy answered, "I can guess. One puff usually just means some old boy posted in an eagle's nest has spotted someone coming. The other puffs are often meant to indicate how many. So shut up and let me read."

Ki did. After a time all the smoke had drifted off into the clear cobalt sky and no more seemed to be rising. Longarm nodded and said, "Most Indians count by fours, four being a medicine number. There's forty-six of us, and I made it eleven puffs up yonder. I don't know whether that means there's no way to divide a smoke puff or whether they don't count the two gals riding with us as serious. Either way, I'd say the rascal tallied us close enough."

He turned to Stone Hand to ask, "Is that island in the sky up ahead close enough for them to see what we just seen?"

The Indian nodded, grim lipped, to answer, "Yes. It is no more than three or four hours' riding, as you saltu count time. Maybe we'd better ride slower, now. I know where they will try to ambush us. It is not a good place to fight, by sunset light."

"Is it a good place to fight any time?" asked Ki.

The old Ute shrugged and told him, "No. But at least we might have a chance if we can see to shoot back at them, *ka?*"

Chapter 19

None of the Indians present could recall fighting General George Washington or, indeed, who he might have been. So the foxy old Indian fighter's advice on taking the high ground fell on deaf ears.

Even if they'd been willing to listen, Longarm would have had to yell. For some Ute had taken to tapping a tom-tom while, not to be outdone, four Navajo were banging on a bigger one, in unison, while everyone else proceeded to make camp.

Jessie and Vickie, at least, seemed willing to listen to Longarm as the three of them cut open cans, apart from the others and closer to the cliffs across from the smokier ones. Their own riding stock was tethered nearby but neither unsaddled nor unpacked as Ki played scout or ninja among the orange rocks above.

Even the part-Indian Vickie nodded understandingly as Longarm elaborated, "Old George made mistakes like everybody else. But it can't be said he ever disposed his forces across the bottom of a soup bowl and left the higher rim to the Redcoats. It don't take a military genius to see that, full of beans or bullets, an attacker can charge downhill thrice as fast as he can go the other way."

Jessie suggested, "These Indians know this country, high or low, Custis."

But Longarm snorted and replied, "That's no doubt why both nations have been pushed back so deep in it. They ain't

216

bad fighters but they're awful field tacticians. Many Sheep and Stone Hand don't have more than a rifle platoon between 'em, and a full regiment could get in trouble camped so dumb."

He pointed his can opener blade at the rimrocks above to add, "The berm of even a gentler crest offers natural cover to a marksman firing prone, while poor moving targets under his gun can't even hide behind your average rock! Why can't I make them poor moving targets see that?"

Vickie suggested, "Maybe they fear their night fires would be seen a long way off if they camped on higher ground."

Longarm finished opening his tomato preserves as he shook his head and growled, "Night fires are dumb in enemy territory even when it's cold out. But the other side don't need illumination to know where we are. We'd have never spotted that smoke if they didn't already know. The only question left is whether they mean to let us make the next move, or whether they can see they'll just never have a better crack at us than them tom-tom-banging idiots are offering."

Then Jessie waved. So Longarm turned to see Ki coming to rejoin them. As Ki hunkered down, Vickie handed him an open can and he inhaled some refreshment before he nodded at Longarm and said, "You were right. Those solid-looking cliffs are riddled like Swiss cheese. Anyone attacking this unwisely chosen campsite after dark could pour out all along the bases of the cliffs like mice popping out of a baseboard."

Longarm said, "I told you I'd wandered through the pumpkin before. Did you find any wormholes we could drag our ponies along to the top?"

Ki nodded and said, "Dragging is the word you were searching for. But at least one route is wide enough all the way." He turned to Jessie and added, "Wait 'til you see what running water does to that soft sandstone. Fortunately, most of the bends are smoothly rounded off. The best route to the top that I could find looks as if it was laid out by a sidewinder with a drinking problem."

Longarm said, "The gals will have to take your word on the natural beauties of that riddled rock, Ki. It would be dumb of us to move from here before dark with Lord only knows how many pairs of eyes watching from the smoky side, yonder. Even if we take the high ground, the four of us don't add up to all that big a boo. So let's not tell 'em where we might be found, ourselves, if they decide to rush this dumb camp." He wet his whistle with more tomato goo and asked Ki, "How does it look up on top if we should have to make a stand?"

"All things considered, I wish I was in Texas. But, thanks to the way the caprock is crevassed, I doubt anyone who's at all afraid of heights would charge faster than we could pick them off."

Then Ki swallowed another mouthful and spoiled it all by adding, "As long as our ammo holds out. And of course we only have enough water to last us a few days, once they pin us down. If they spot us, they will. So I have an even better suggestion. I think we ought to simply ride back to civilization while there's still time. We know about where those white land-grabbers are. The Indians have told you what you were sent to find out, Longarm. So what's wrong with getting the girls to safety and, if you like, I'll come back with you and that column of cavalry you ought to consider."

Longarm shrugged and said, "I've already considered calling in the War Department. I consider it unwise. Two reasons. For openers, we're talking about one long running gunfight across unmapped country with even *these* Indians sore at us. And, just as important, I don't work for the War Department. Justice and the B.I.A. asked me, discreet, to see if we could leave the army out of this deal. If they'd wanted some peacetime officer, likely overage in grade and spoiling for an all-out Indian war, they'd have already sent in the troops. Since they never, I figure it's my job to clean up the mess with as little fuss as I can manage."

Ki stared over the rim of his can in the direction of the throbbing tom-toms and muttered, "You've always been so subtle. Having seen you rake a Mexican army column with cannon fire that time in the Baja, I'd hate to hear what you call noise!"

Jessie smiled at both of them and said, "Oh, come on, boys, you both had fun that time and you know it."

218

Longarm nodded and said, "We'd have had more like another war with Mexico if I'd been fussing with them federales official, in army blue. That's likely why the B.I.A. asked for me and my delicate hand, hereabouts. Once you get the army and the pesky newspaper reporters they haul along into taking the field, it's hard to get things back to normal. Old George Armstrong Custer just loved to send newspaper dispatches from the fighting front and, while I hate to speak ill of the dead, I've often wondered how many fights old Custer tried to avoid with a bugler riding on his one side and a newspaper reporter on the other."

He stopped talking and got back to eating as old Stone Hand came wandering over, wrapped in a blanket now that the sun was going down. The old Ute said, "I have sent for more young men. They should be here by sunrise. If they are, we will hit those tame Paiute with many, many. But I am still worried about that medicine gun these crazy saltu have."

Longarm said, "You ought to be worried. This is not a good place to spend the night. My friends and I are going to camp up on the higher ground. We'll talk some more about it in the morning, if any of you are left down here."

Stone Hand looked hurt and said, "You may be able to get your*selves* up there. We know those scouts who gossiped about us with smoke must have made it far along the rimrocks, on foot. Nobody rides *ponies* up there. Where there is not slick rock under a pony's hoof, there is a hole. A deep hole. Deep. Are you sure these women have not nagged you into running away? I know you are brave, Longarm. I am brave, too. But my women nag, nag, nag me, too. So I know how it can make a man act silly."

Longarm said, "These gals are brave as half the men around here, at least. We'll see how brave our ponies are about mountain climbing as soon as it gets dark. You can run away if you've a mind to. If you don't, like I said, we'll see how things are, come sunrise."

Stone Hand turned and walked away, muttering to himself. Old Vickie, who savvied his lingo, blushed and murmured, "Oh, what a dreadful thing to call two ladies he's never been properly introduced to!"

Longarm chuckled and told Ki, "Finish your grub, old son. I'd like you to show me the route you found, afoot and discreet, before I have to haul two ladies and other critters up it in the dark."

Ki put his can aside, saying, "Let's go, then. It's already late in the day, and a man would really have to be hungry to finish a whoie can, after eating nothing but cold beans and tomatoes all this time."

So they left the girls to keep an eye on their belongings and riding stock as they strolled casually in among the rounded boulders at the base of the cliff, as if they were only going to take an after-supper walk. When Longarm followed Ki into what appeared as just a vertical fold in the sort of orange drapery, he whistled and stared up at the curvaceous streak of sky, high above them, and said, "So far so good. Does it ramp so steep all the way?"

Ki took the lead up the twenty-degree floor of the deep but narrow and twisty cleft, saying, "No. It's steeper in places. But no fallen rocks big enough to block a pony's passage if you haul from the front and shove from behind."

As Longarm followed, he thought it was sort of a shame the gals would have to pass through here after dark. For women enjoyed pretty sights and there was a weird sort of beauty to the way the pumpkin-colored walls had been carved in sensual curves by time and water. Ki commented that he could see why the Indians called this sort of progress crawling through the pumpkin. As he steadied himself with a palm against the smooth rock to negotiate a tricky twist in the passage, Ki muttered, "I'm glad I'm not a pumpkin worm. I'd hate to have to do this all the time."

Then, suddenly, they were atop the original surface of the huge tableland, feeling sort of like a pair of bugs that had wandered out into the light. The cloudless sky was starting to go purple over toward the enemy lines. Behind them, the setting sun threw their twin shadows far out across the dead flat, or apparently dead flat, surface all around them, as far as the eye could see. Some of the ground under them was wind-washed gravel, bird cage to coarse. But as Stone Hand had warned, a lot of the surrounding surface was wind-polished bare rock. Longarm scuffed up some gravel with a boot heel and decided, "Right here's as good a spot as any for us humans to bed down. I see no grass or anything else to keep the ponies close, unless we hobble 'em."

Ki said, "Hobbles should do it. Horses see good in the dark and the moon will be half full. They won't wander across any crevasse they can't jump easily, and there's one of those not too far in any direction."

Longarm stared thoughtfully at the string-straight feature-less horizon to the east and said, "All right. Time I can have the gals and ponies up here, it'll be dark. You'd best stay put up here and let us know if you see even a fly speck coming over the skyline, from any direction. One shot?"

Ki sniffed and asked if Longarm meant to teach him how to conjugate Japanese verbs, next. So Longarm chuckled and said, "Don't be sure I can't. One just never knows what an-other man might do or not do. So keep a sharp lookout."

Then he dropped down into the cleft again. Getting down was a heap easier than getting up had been, even though the passage was getting mighty murkey as the sky above grew darker. Not much daylight ever got down this way, even at high noon, he suspected.

By the time he'd rejoined the girls, there was barely enough gloaming light to read large print by. He knew nobody scouting from clean across the flats could see them that good, now. The fool Indians had built a string of glaring fires be-tween them and anyone they really had to worry about. So Longarm gathered the girls and the riding stock together and herded them all to the miniature side canyon Ki had found. It looked even spookier after sunset. But nobody but the ponies seemed scared.

With the help of the expert horsewoman Jessie was, they soon had their remuda string on one long lead. Longarm handed the end to Victoria and said, "You go first. Jessie and me will get behind and push."

The pretty little breed protested, "I don't know the way."

But Longarm told her, "Sure you do. There ain't but one way. You just keep climbing, keeping some pressure on that end of the rope, and old Ki will haul you out and give you a kiss for being such a big brave gal. The first three or more ponies on your side don't figure to balk. It's the ones further back as get to feeling independent when they suspect nobody but another dumb brute might be leading 'em. Jessie and me may have to remind 'em with a little lashing and a heap of cussing. But you'll see how it works once we get going. So get going, or do I have to lash and cuss you, too?"

The little breed giggled and moved into the cleft, calling back, "Ooh, it's *dark* in here!" But, to her credit, she kept going. Her dearly departed dad had likely taught her more than most Paiute knew about handling stock.

As Longarm and Jessie followed the last pack ponies through the seemingly solid surface of a sandstone cliff, she blinked and said, "I thought Vickie said it was dark. This is more like wading through India ink. I can't see my hand before my face!"

Longarm suggested, "Put one hand against that pony's rump and use the other to brush the wall. Then it won't matter if you can see, see?"

She replied, "I just said I *couldn't* see!" But she followed his suggestion and so, though it seemed to take forever to the girls, it seemed a shorter climb than before to Longarm because it worked that way, once you knew where you were and where you might be going.

They heard Vickie's voice, up ahead, distorted by echoes in the narrow passage as she called out, "I can see the stars and, yes, I'm out of that awful ditch at last!"

The ponies must have been anxious to stargaze as well, for Longarm and Jessie had to scramble some in the dark to keep up with them and, lest Vickie and Ki have trouble handling the excited brutes without help, Longarm and Jessie wasted no time popping out of the rocks to join them. But when Jessie called out, "Ki? Vickie?" and got no answer, Longarm hissed, "Hit the dirt and fill your fist, Jessie!"

But it was too late. Something at least as big and mean as a steam locomotive hit Longarm right behind one ear and filled his eyes with more pinwheeling fireworks than information he could use. Then four of them grabbed Jessie, and when they saw four might not be enough to pin such a spitting and

222

scratching wildcat, one of them pistol-whipped her across the nape of the neck and she was unconscious, too.

When Longarm opened his eyes again at last, he couldn't make much sense out of the little he could see, and he had even less information on how come he kept bouncing on his belt buckle so hard without even trying. As he fought the waves of concussion sickness that he'd have simply puked out, if his head hadn't been upside down, it came to him that he was lashed facedown across the saddle of a trotting mule or pony. He started to call out, but he decided not to. It might be more interesting to keep the sons of bitches guessing as to just how thick a skull he had. He experimented with the wrists they'd lashed behind his back. They'd lashed him good with what felt like rawhide. From the way his ankles kept bobbing in unison on the far side of this critter, they were lashed as well. So, all right, they'd slickered the keen-eyed Ki by playing sneaky gopher in that erosion-riddled sandstone they likely knew better and, where in thunder was everybody, now?

Longarm didn't even know where *he* was. He tried twisting his neck for an upside-down look-see at his surroundings. All he could make out was that the dark blur leading the critter he was on seemed to be trotting ahead on foot. That had to mean an Indian. Likely a legged-up Digger. The trail they were on ran through another cleft or maybe it followed a cliff. He couldn't tell what might be on the far side with his boots.

Then he was led around a bend and there was light up ahead. He could see now that the gent leading him at a trot had long stringy hair and bare brown legs, but he was wearing a turkey-red military kepi at a jaunty angle and, even more interesting, had his rifle slung across the back of a dark-blue jacket with red wool epaulets. Longarm grimaced and muttered, "I'll allow the steel butt-plate of that Lebel matches up with this nasty headache, you ornery bastard. But if you're trying to tell me you're a frog legionnaire, I'm just going to have to imply you are full of shit. The foreign legion can't be desperate enough to recruit wild Indians and, even if they was, they got no business in these United States, even the unmapped parts!"

223

He could also see now that the light came from either side of an imposing gateway with thick stone walls rising higher on either side. An impressive or at least fancy coat of arms had been painted on a sort of wooden inn sign over the gate. But Longarm knew they weren't entering any old castle. The masonry spelled Hohokam or Anasazi workmanship. Longarm sighed and muttered, "Well, I was planning to investigate these old ruins, anyway, albeit not exactly in this style."

His captors led him, facedown, into a sort of courtyard where the light wasn't quite as good. Then somebody cut Longarm loose from the saddle to dump him on his head in the dust. As he rolled over and tried to sit up, someone threw his hat in his face. They hadn't left him his gun rig or even his watch and derringer, the slick bastards. A voice behind him moaned, "Oh, Custis, did they get you, too?"

So he grunted, "Why, hell, no, Jessie. I just came along on my own to keep you all company. What about Ki and Vickie?"

Ki replied from a shadowy corner of the walled-in open space, "We're over here. I can't begin to tell you how sorry I am about this." Then somebody kicked Ki to shut him up.

Longarm didn't say anything as he sat there in the dust, watching a funny-looking gent stride out a low doorway across the way in polished boots and an officer's full dress, medals and all. After that he didn't look quite as silly. He was big, for one thing, and wore a horse pistol on one hip and a military saber on the other. He put a white-gloved hand to the peak of his red and gilt kepi, clicked his heels, and said, "Welcome to the Chateau du Montrouge. I am Colonel Trepont, commander of the garrison. You shall all find me most charming, as long as you obey. Any other attitude will be dealt with *très* severely. Your gracious hostess, La Baronne Du Montrouge, is expecting all of you to join her for a late repast in her dining hall. My soldiers shall untie you, now. The house servants will do their best to make you all more presentable. I feel it is only my duty to warn you all that should you attempt to take advantage of a not too well but kindly noblewoman, I, Marcel Trepont, shall see that your last

224

hours on this earth are painful as well as final. You have my word on that."

Nobody felt like arguing. So Trepont spun on one heel and marched out of sight while Indians in more shabby military kit moved in to cut all four captives loose.

Longarm picked his now even more battered Stetson up, banged some of the dust out of it, and jammed it on his head. Jessie let her hat hang down her back, Mex style. Neither Ki nor little Vickie had any hats to worry about, now.

As the four of them moved instinctively closer together, some more Indians, dressed more Indian, came out to join them, led by an old gray man in a sort of butler's outfit that didn't fit him worth mention. As she saw him, Victoria Miller called out to him, "Daddy?" and since he replied with a croak of, "Daughter?" they were soon hugging and kissing fit to bust as everyone else just watched, bemused. Then old Isaak Miller untangled himself from the weeping girl to tell her, and the other captives, "We don't want to keep the baroness waiting, and she can't abide dirty fingernails at table. She threw a prospector over the side of the cliff for forgetting to wash for supper, one time. I mean, she didn't throw him, personally, but—"

"Daddy, we all thought you were *dead*," his daughter cut in.

To which the long-lost father replied, "Sometimes I think I am as well. But you and your friends come along, now, Victoria. We'll have plenty of time to talk about all this later, if the old gal likes you." As if he thought the others had any idea what he was talking about, the major domo or whatever of the chateau or whatever added, "The baroness either likes you or she doesn't. I hardly ever worry about her killing *me* anymore. But for God's sake, don't any of you vex her by disagreeing with a word she may say."

Ki said, "That sounds easy enough, if we just keep quiet."

But Miller shook his head and said, "That can vex her even worse. You see, she's lonesome. If it was up to that Colonel Trepont, alone, all trespassers would be killed on sight. But the old lady does like company, as long as it doesn't cross her. So. . . . In here is where you can wash up. Here, Daughter, let

225

me borrow you my comb. Don't mention your dear mother at table. Tell her your mother was Mex, no doubt ravaged and buried alive by that disgusting Juarez."

As the girls got first to the one washstand set in the corner of the rock-walled chamber, Longarm reached absently for a smoke, saw he didn't have any on him, and asked old Miller, "Let's see if I got this lunacy straight. Are we talking about some old lady of the Emperor Maximilian's Mex court, who got mighty lost on her way home?"

Miller nodded but said, "The baroness doesn't have a home in the old country, now. Her man got killed down Mexico way, leading a dumb but gallant charge. His widow was a lady in waiting to the Empress Carlotta. Lord knows where *she* lit out to when Juarez won and shot her emperor. But, since then, the Emperor Louis Napoleon got whipped by the Prussians and lost *his* job, too."

Longarm nodded and said, "So both Mexico and France are republics right now, in theory, at least. I ain't so sure some poor Mexicans wouldn't settle for old Max, next to Diaz."

Ki frowned thoughtfully and put in, "Some of the old war-lord types in my mother's country had a hard time adjusting to the new constitutional monarchy. But I can't say any of them were crazy enough to run up a mountain and go into business for themselves!"

Miller repressed a shudder and almost whispered, "What-ever you think, don't you dare even hint at it to the baroness. You see, she holds that since she's a genuine aristocrat of the Mexican Court, and that since Mexico has just claim to all of New Mexico, Arizona, Colorado, and Utah *combined*—"

"Hold on," Longarm cut in to protest, "Uncle Sam took all the territory you mentioned away from Mexico back in forty-eight."

Isaak Miller made the sign of the cross and said, "I wasn't sprinkled Roman Catholic, but you pick up such habits around lunatics of that particular persuasion. Don't even mention that treaty Mexico signed under duress, as she puts it. You see, she blames agreements between earlier Mex governments and the U.S. for lots of what happened, later."

Ki, who naturally knew less of U.S. history than Longarm,

seemed to be having a hard time following the discussion. So Longarm explained, "After we all kissed and made up after the Mexican war, one of the terms both sides agreed to was to stay pals. So when Louis Napoleon took advantage of the fighting between the North and South to set up his puppet empire in Mexico, in sixty-four, Washington couldn't do much about it until they could finish up with the South. But then, after they had, old Louis Napoleon found out what an awful boner he'd made. The Union Army was still at the peak of its strength. The Confederate Army was in worse shape, of course, but a lot of boys in butternut gray were still under arms and looking for work. It might have healed some wounds indeed if the blue and gray, together, had had a good excuse to march into Mexico side by side and kick old Max and his French Foreign Legion galley-west. More than one old reb seemed anxious to offer his experience and service. But then old Louis Napoleon got scared and pulled his legion out to go kill Arabs some more. So Juarez was able to finish off the few stubborn imperialists with his own Mex troops and a heap of gringo ammunition on easy credit terms."

As Jessie turned from washing up to rejoin them, Longarm had time to add wistfully, "It's too bad Louis Napoleon was so smart, 'til he tangled with Bismarck, leastways. For I've always wished we *could* have marched against him, blue and gray together. If we had, it might be safer to whistle 'Dixie' in Wyoming or 'Marching Through Georgia' in Texas, these days."

Jessie said, "Nobody will ever get to whistle 'Marching Through Georgia' in Texas while *I* still live there. What are we talking about, boys?"

Ki said, "About the French Foreign Legion in Mexico. I can see how they got there. I can't see who got to fight whom, for what, after the French pulled them out."

Jessie said, "Oh, I can answer that. My father sold some beef to dear Uncle Benito Juarez that time. Uncle Benito was very nice. His only social gaffe when he had dinner with us, the first time, was mentioning how much he admired our Abraham Lincoln. My poor father looked like he was drinking castor oil. But he had to go along with it when Uncle Benito raised a toast to Honest Abe at our table. I think it was just about the time of the Battle of Gettysburg. I was sort of young. But I could tell, even then, what a sport my father was."

Longarm said, "Tell him about the legion," as he moved over to wash up.

So she said, "Maximilian was some kind of out-of-work Austrian archduke. So he had no troops of his own when the French set him up as a puppet emperor to help them collect money the Juarez government owed and just couldn't pay. But he must have been mighty willful, too. Because he refused to *act* like a puppet when the French withdrew their support for him and poor old Empress Carlotta. She was even crazier than he was. Her daddy was King Leopold of Belgium, the only king Queen Victoria ever called a disgusting brute in public. Anyway, Max, Lottie, and their court tried to hang on. I don't know what Custis means about the French Foreign Legion. They were supposed to clear out before the fighting got ferocious."

Isaak Miller shook his head and said, "Not all of 'em. The French left a token force, hoping the imperials could grow a real army around 'em. Maximilian hired other soldiers of fortune. In the end it was an awful mess, with men changing sides as old Max and old Ben outbid each other and, well, when the smoke finally cleared, old Max had been shot by a Mex firing squad, old Carlotta had run home to her daddy, and those imperialists left, like the baroness you're about to meet, had to fend for themselves as best they could."

Victoria had rejoined them in time to catch the tag end of her father's words. As Ki moved over to the washstand with Longarm, Miller's long-lost daughter said, "Never mind about her. What about you, Daddy? All this time we all thought you were dead, and that mean Lavinia threw me out on my own as soon as you stopped writing and sending money."

The old man in the ill-fitting butler's livery sighed and said, "That's why I sent a treasure map home, hoping for a gold rush. I always knew that child had a selfish streak. I had to quit writing home when they told me I couldn't no more. Colonel Trepont said that even if I fibbed about the gold dust I was cashing in for 'em, I was bound to attract attention."

Vickie pouted and demanded, "Ain't we got no gold mine, after all?"

Her father replied with a sad little smile and an expansive sweep at the surrounding stone walls, "I thought I had a good job when they first recruited me. The deal was for me to cash a heap of Mexican color for them and recruit a mess of Indians for 'em while I was about it. They knew I had a rep as a prospecting man, and I told 'em I could talk Ho. I tried to tell 'em they'd do better setting up this imperial outpost in Paiute country. But, as you'll soon see, the baroness has a mind of her own. Someone told her about all the impressive stone ruins up this way and, well, I reckon once you're used to living in a castle, a Paiute lean-to ain't your style. So here we are and here we'll stay, as long as we don't make the baroness cross with us."

Jessie, feeling angrier by the minute as the outrageous situation sank in, asked old Miller, "Do you mean to say *you're* a prisoner here, too.'

Miller nodded sadly and said, "Nobody goes in or out without the colonel saying they can, and he's mighty tight with overnight passes. Like I said, I had a more free hand at first. They let me do all sorts of dirty work for 'em until they had things set up here to suit her nibs. Then one day I said something about riding up to Durango and posting a letter to my child, here, and the colonel said I'd never make it to the bottom of the canyon, if I tried. They ain't paid me since then, neither. I tried to tell 'em what Lincoln said about even colored salves, but they just told me this was the Barony of Montrouge, not the U.S. of A., and that I'd best not give them any more sass if I wanted to go on living, even as a sort of pale slave."

Longarm rejoined them, wiping his hands on his pants as he allowed that was about as clean as he could manage. Jessie told him, "It's worse than we thought, Custis. The lady of the house is even madder than the Empress Carlotta she used to pick up after. She and her crazy colonel, for he has to be crazy, too, have set up a private feudal barony here!"

Longarm said, "No they ain't. This is Indian land. And

229

how come even the Indians have just heard about it? I can wash and listen at the same time, Miller, and, no offense, your yarn don't make much sense. Neither the Ute nor the Navajo got to acting upset until recent. You say all this nonsense has been going on for years?"

Miller nodded and said, "Damn it, I *told* you they was *crazy*. I reckon nobody noticed at first, because it was only a crazy old woman and a handful of crazy retainers lording it over a few Indians who wasn't supposed to be here to begin with. These ruins are strong medicine to the Indians who know where they are. The canyons all around, for at least a few miles, have been off-limits to both Ute and Navajo for generations. The baroness could have ruled here all she wanted, for a coon's age, if ruling a few haunted canyons was all she had in mind."

"What *does* she have in mind?" asked Longarm suspiciously.

Old Miller said, "Conquest. Don't look at me like that. I never said it was *my* fool notion. You see, they started out up here with plenty of loot from the imperial Mex treasury, and there was enough fertile land to feed a few folk. But our private Paiute army keeps having babies and sending for kin from back home. I tried to warn 'em there ain't enough food and fodder for that, here. But the colonel just loves to drill troops and the Diggers would rather play soldier than dig and duck stronger nations. They've gotten uppity as anything since the colonel taught 'em to shoot and salute. The baroness was the one who decided that since all this land belonged to Mexico and that she was a baroness of the Mexican empire, it was time to expand her domain."

Longarm said dryly, "That accounts for sullen Ute and Navajo, then. There's barely grub to get by in these canyonlands as they was. I can see how being pushed by whites and uniformed Indian auxiliaries must have added to their confusion. French blue and U.S. Cavalry blue ain't all that different. They'd have heard of fighting outfits like the Apache Scouts and so, no matter what their agents told them, they'd be inclined to think the Great White Father was doing them dirty, again, and just avoid all the whites they could. What's the story on that Gatling gun the Indians tell about?"

Miller said, "That was Colonel Trepont's notion. Maximilian bought a few batteries of the same, too late to do him much good back in sixty-seven. Man, them Juaristas must have been really sore. At any rate, Trepont hung on to two such weapons as well as the gold he and his boys could get at, leaving Ciudad Mejico one jump ahead of Juarez. He drug the baroness along as well, of course. They all hid out in Utah for a spell while I helped the colonel set up this little private estate for her nibs, cuss me for the fool I was. You know the rest."

Ki rejoined them near the doorway, saying, "I can wash and listen, too. We *don't* know the rest. How many men do we have to beat to get out of here?"

Old Miller gasped and said, "You can't be serious!"

So Longarm told him, "If Ki ain't, I am. So let's have some figures on the opposition, pard."

Miller said, "The Colonel and an eight-man squad of white legionnaires, for openers. Four of 'em man each Gatling, unless they need help with it. All of 'em are trained gunners. They usually keep one Gatling over the gate, covering the steep trail up the cliffs. But they can move it anywhere they want, if they want to. It's on a light gun carriage. As for the armed and legion-trained Indians, we're talking a full company of riflemen, good with the bayonette as well, along with again as many servants, dependents, and so on."

He put a protective arm around Vickie's shoulder and went on soberly, "Add them figures up and you'll see why me and my long-lost daughter ain't about to join a jailbreak off an island in the sky. There's only one way down, slow enough to get you there alive. Our best bet is to do nothing to upset the baroness. She gets upset easy and, when she does, you can wind up going down a cliff the sudden way. So let's not keep her waiting, hear?"

Chapter 20

The four captives, or honored guests, depending on how the lady of the house felt about it at the moment, were ushered into a dining hall with mighty fancy furnishings and mighty crude walls. The ruins had been built at a time when ancient whatevers had barely commenced building with stone and hadn't even thought of mortar. One of the reasons all the walls had to be so thick was that freestone masonry was held together by no more than friction and gravity.

As if to make up for the rough walls and new ceiling of unplanked pine, the doorways at both ends were draped with red velvet and the coat of arms painted over the gateway, or one mighty close to it, hung behind the head of the table as an even fancier tapestry, worked with gilt thread between the other, somewhat faded colors.

Jasmine-scented Mexican candles burned in two big silver candelabras on a linen-covered table in the center hall. The table was big enough for an officers' mess but looked sort of lonesome with so much rug around it. The carpeting was either Persian or a damned good imitation. It didn't quite make it to the walls. So some of the flooring under all the fancy show was visible. It was tamped clay, mixed with wood ash and who could say what else from the time of the long-gone canyon dwellers.

Despite the size of the table in the center, there were only six high-backed chairs and five place settings of silver. The fancy dinnerware at the head of table looked like gold. Old

232

Miller told the four of them to be seated across from one another, leaving both end seats vacant for the moment. Then a couple of white legionnaires came in with their rifles at port, with fixed bayonets, to take up positions against opposing walls, as if to make sure nobody left the table without permission. Old Miller in his ill-fitting livery found himself a corner to stand in. Jessie, with her keen eye for fashion, noticed both the legionnaires wore full-dress blue tunics and red trousers that, while spiffy enough at first glance, had been mended and patched to the point where she'd have bought the boys new duds, had they been on her payroll. The table linen had seen better days as well and, while each napkin was neatly tucked through a silver band, they failed to match. It was Longarm who noticed his fancy china was chipped. Old Miller had told them it was an old-money family, sort of living on the past.

Then another servant in livery, with a Paiute face, popped through the far doorway to announce a circus coming to town or that the dam was busted. It was hard to make out his attempts at whatever white lingo he was aiming for, and then Colonel Trepont came in with a tiny white-haired woman on his arm.

After all the ominous things they'd been told about her, La Baronne du Montrouge would have been a pleasant surprise, had she not been loco en la cabeza. As the men at her table rose, they could see she'd once been a little beauty. Even old and prune-faced, she still had a nice figure under that black dress of satin and old Spanish lace. She was smiling sweetly at everyone as the colonel seated her at the head of the table and then moved around to take his almost as thronelike position at the far end. Longarm and Ki figured it was safe to sit down when he did. Now that they could see him better, he made up for the faded beauty of their hostess by being ugly as sin. His bullet head was shaven, so you couldn't tell what color his hair was, or whether he'd ever had any. His face was so beat up it was hard to judge his age. He'd lost at least a couple of sword fights and a bout with smallpox in his time. Someone had once busted his nose as well. It was easy to see why. Trepont had one of those snooty faces most men just itched to plant a fist in.

233

But it wasn't the colonel who first showed them just how snooty a born snob could get, before the wine had even been served. The baroness was smiling but her faded blue eyes were cold and dead as she stared down the table at Victoria Miller and asked her butler, as if there was any doubt in her mind, which one of the young ladies might be the daughter he'd mentioned. When Miller indicated Vickie, the baroness said, "How curious to find the daughter of a servant seated with ladies and gentlemen. She belongs in the servants' wing with you and the others. See to it, my good man."

Miller gulped, waved Vickie to her feet, and led her off somewhere as their gracious hostess sighed and said, "That's better. You must forgive poor Miller. He's only been with us a short time and good help is so hard to find, these days."

Jessie, who'd noticed the slight accent coming from the head of the table, tried her finishing-school French on the old woman. But the baroness looked pained and said, "One prefers to use a language everyone present has in common, my dear. For one thing, it affords more privacy. The legion deserters here to see that our little gathering goes smoothly speak no English and, if the truth would be known, their French is abominable as well."

At the far end of the table the colonel's accent was thicker as he protested mildly, "My men may be of peasant stock, Madame La Baronne, but do you really think it just to refer to them as *deserters?*"

The old woman smiled almost fondly back at him as she nodded and replied, "I do. What else would you call men who, like yourself, survived my husband, your commanding officer, in battle?"

The colonel almost snapped, "Survivors, Madame. All that was left of the old brigade in the end."

"You ran away," she said with a shrug. "Shall we have the wine, now?"

They did. Yet another Indian produced an earthenware jug and naturally poured for the baroness first. She tasted, grimaced, and murmured, "Oh, well," so he could pour for the rest of them. Longarm didn't consider himself a wine snob, but this was awful. As if she'd read his mind, the baroness said,

"One hopes it may improve with age. Colonel Trepont assures me the wild grapes one finds up this way are, indeed, grapes. But there are times one wonders."

Longarm said, "You folk were lucky to find any sort of grapes in the canyonlands, ma'am. This ain't bad at all, for homemade."

The old woman stared thoughtfully at him before she decided, "You must be the one our retainers caught carrying a badge. It says you are some species of policeman, *non?*"

Longarm nodded and said, "I'm a U.S. deputy marshal, ma'am. Maybe we ought to talk about that. I'll allow your boys got the drop on me, in the end, if you'll allow I got pretty close and had this place located pretty good, despite all your earlier moves to stop me."

The old woman raised an eyebrow, told Longarm he was droll, and asked Trepont if he had any idea what the species of cowboy was talking about. So the colonel asked Longarm what he was talking about.

Longarm addressed him, then, to say, "I don't know how you knew we was coming. But you must have, if you went to all that trouble to stop us. As you can plainly see, however, we got through all your stakeouts, and found our way to almost here, so your game is up, no matter what you do to us. For Uncle Sam is sure to send others, just as he sent me to look for earlier federal agents who never came back. I want you to study on that before you do anything mean to anybody here."

Trepont sipped some wine as he tried to digest what Longarm had just said. Then he told the old woman, "I assume he refers to those trespassers we dealt with earlier. One did say something about some sort of Indian agency as I was adjusting his blindfold." Then he turned back to Longarm with one eyebrow cocked to say, "Repeat the business about our retainers trying to intercept you, earlier. My Paiute scouts assure me they got you on their first try."

Jessie was trying to kick Longarm under the table but the table was too wide, and Longarm was more curious than worried about his table manners, in any case. So he cocked an eyebrow back and said, "Come on, don't you have some old boy on your payroll who smoked Daniel Websters and knows a lot of hungry gun hands?"

Trepont grimaced and said, "I do not smoke. I do not have much patience, either. Explain yourself in plain English, if it's not too great an effort for you."

So Longarm did. When he brought them up to date on how hard a time they'd all had getting here, the colonel shook his bullet head and said, "Someone else must have been after the four of you. It is not difficult to see why. It was Madame's idea to receive you rustics so graciously, not mine. But I do find it interesting that someone else seems to know where we are, and it's even more interesting that they, too, seem to want to keep our little secret a secret."

Longarm suggested, "Well, they might have shared our view that there could be a gold mine in these parts. You'd know if there was one, right?"

The old lady at the far end sighed and said, "Alas, if that were only true. We've asked the local Indians for the usual royal fifth of anything of value. But they keep insisting, even under torture, that the natural resources of my domain leave much to be desired."

This time Jessie tried harder to kick him, and Ki was tempted to throw at least a fork when Longarm said soberly, "That's something else we ought to study on, ma'am. The U.S. Homestead Act allows almost anyone to claim federal land that ain't being used by anyone else. So you could find plenty of places out this way to file on and fence yourself a domain and, while U.S. laws don't recognize patents of nobility, coats of arms and such, they don't *forbid* folk calling themselves fancy names or hanging up a family coat of arms, if it makes 'em happy. I doubt one Kentucky colonel in ten ever even asked for a real commission, and I know another madame in Dodge City who sports a coat of arms on her carriage. But you're just going to get in trouble if you keep trying to use these Indian ruins, on Indian land, as a fairy-tale castle."

The old lady somehow grew taller in her thronelike chair as she sniffed grandly and said, "Explain my feudal rights to this barbarian, Colonel."

Trepont nodded, turned to Longarm, and said, "We are aware of the spurious claims of the United States to this part of the old Hapsburg Empire, *mais*, naturally, we do not recognize them, *hein?*"

Longarm frowned and said, "You don't have to. Mexico and the U.S. of A. agreed on it, in writing, more than thirty years ago."

Trepont looked pained and insisted, "The Republic of Mexico had no right to cede anything to anybody. It did not exist as a legal entity. Neither the Spanish nor any other crown worn by members of the Hapsburg Dynasty ever recognized the formation of a so-called Independent Mexico in 1821. The war your people fought with Mexico, and we don't blame you at all for that, was really a punitive expedition against what *we* have always considered a band of unwashed half-breed rebels."

Jessie said, "Uncle Benito was a full-blooded Indian. He told us so. He was proud of it."

Longarm said, "Whatever he was, he was the president of old Mexico. But get back to the government we licked, fair and square, to take this very real estate from, years and years ago."

Trepont looked pained and insisted, "You did no such thing. You forced illiterate rebels to cede you land they held no title to. These canyonlands were first explored and claimed by the Coronado Expedition, under the rule of Karl of Austria or Don Carlos of Spain. He was the same person. His empire spread from Hungaria to the Philippines and it was said, with some truth, that the sun never set on it!"

Longarm smiled thinly and said, "I heard the Hapsburgs was a big family. Are you saying old Maximilian came up with that grand notion he was the emperor of Mexico because he was a Hapsburg with nothing better to do?"

Trepont snapped, "Let's have a little more respect for yet another martyred fighter for the cause of monarchy. Of *course* our late emperor was the lawful ruler of Mexico by virtue of his noble birth. He was a Hapsburg, and the Hapsburgs never recognized the independence of Mexico. He was only reclaiming his birthright, which of course included all the lands ever claimed by Spain, you fool."

Before Longarm could say *he'd* like some respect around here as well, the baroness chimed in with, "My late husband's family had the same difficulties with the *French* rabble. They cut off his father's head, but naturally there was no way to change the fact that the Du Montrouges were *très* noble. The Great Maximilian and my lady, the Empress Carlotta, were able to rectify the distressing matter by restoring the title to us, as *Mexican* nobility, and of course that gave us the right to our own feudal domain, so—"

"So this ain't going to work," Longarm cut in, staring at old Trepont, who didn't look quite as crazy. "I ain't no lawyer. I know land claims are tricky and I know some of the old Royal Spanish land grants here in the southwest have been recognized by the U.S. government, provided someone pays taxes on the same and behaves halfway sensible. But you can't just squat on Indian lands set aside by the same U.S. government and lord it over everyone like this."

Colonel Trepont shrugged and said, "We have. We may have to claim more, as the feudal property due a noblewoman whose family bore arms before your so-called United States existed."

Longarm snorted in disgust and growled, "You can call Uncle Sam anything you like. But sooner or later he's sure to *gitcha,* if the Ute and Navajo combined don't gitcha first. You don't *look* half-witted, Colonel. How come I have to tell you what ought to be plain as the nose on your face?"

Trepont shrugged and said, "I am a soldier. It is not my place to reason why. My men and I serve Madame La Baronne as we served her late husband, our commanding officer. I do not wish to discuss the matter further, *hein?*"

Longarm said, "Well, somebody better. You and your boys ain't ancient knights. You're over-the-hill French troops. Even the French emperor who loaned you to a Mex emperor has been put out of business. There just ain't no French or Mex nobility no more."

The baroness looked upset and said, "Take them away, Colonel. I don't find them amusing, after all."

So that's what the bullet-headed officer and his armed men did, as Longarm muttered, "Hell, don't we even get no supper?"

Longarm was even hungrier by the time they finally came back to lead him from the tiny cell he'd spent what seemed like a million years in, in the dark. As they led him outside it was just getting light enough to see. As he saw four other guards frog-marching Ki his way with fixed bayonets, by the dawn's early light, Longarm said, "Morning, Ki. Where do you reckon the gals may be?"

Ki growled, "I don't know, thanks to you and your big mouth. I just spent the night, alone, in some long-dead Indian's root cellar, or tomb, for all I know. Couldn't you have been more diplomatic? We already knew that old woman was a dangerous lunatic."

Before Longarm had to answer, they'd both been led outside the walls. As they were marched off across soil and slick rock with clumps of wind-gnarled juniper here and there, Longarm could see why the crazy old lady thought she needed a few more quarter sections, at least. He figured there was no more than a full section or one square mile to this island in the sky, and none of it he'd seen so far looked too fertile. The uniformed Paiute herding them under the direction of one white corporal took them maybe two hundred yards out across the flattop of the mesa to where Colonel Trepont stood alone near a piñon tree twisted almost as wildly as that old woman's imperious mind. When they got to him, Trepont nodded curtly and said, "If it was up to me, I'd just have the two of you shoved over the edge. But your rudeness at the table last night caused the baroness great pain. She does not like to dwell upon the fall of the court she and her gallant husband served."

Longarm said, "Well, if that means someone else has to be caused great pain, I'd like to remind you I was speaking for myself, as an agent of the U.S. government. So why can't you be a sport about my friends, at least?"

Trepont looked away and said, "It is *not* up to me. I only obey orders, and the baroness was *très* annoyed at *all* of you, she said."

Longarm tried, "That was last night. Can't you ask her how she's feeling this morning, pard?"

He noticed Trepont spoke English as he told the Paiute to follow with the prisoners and turned to walk on, staring down at the ground, as if he was looking for something. So Longarm edged closer to Ki, or tried to, and muttered in Spanish, "I don't think these Indians speak anything but Ho or English. I can see why, if Miller recruited them from over to the west."

Ki growled at him to shut up, in the same language. But Longarm insisted, "We have to speak *something*. I don't want anyone listening in. I fear that officer is hunting for insects. So whatever you do, don't let them tie you down where you see red ants with black behinds. The pure red ones are bad enough. But those black-tailed little bastards are the *real* killers. A man might hope to get off with just a few nips from the all-red ants they have out here, but those others . . ."

Ki lapsed back into English to almost shout, "You stupid son of a bitch! Now you've really done it!" as their French guard trotted forward to say something to the colonel, grinning back at them sort of dirty. The colonel started grinning too.

So Longarm smiled sheepishly at Ki and said, "Oops, I should have figured even a Frenchman who'd served in Mexico might savvy some Spanish."

As they rejoined the sadistic officer, Ki said, "Pay no attention to this idiot. He's always trying to tell stupid jokes."

But the two legionnaires were rattling back and forth in French too fast for Longarm to more than follow the drift as Ki groaned and said, "Now you've done it, you asshole!"

It took their captors a little more time to find a big anthill inhabited by the black-tailed variety, since they were less common than the all-red variety. But the colonel was a man who enjoyed his work and so, though Longarm and Ki both struggled, they were soon sharing the same big pile of sand grains and twigs, about the size of an overturned and somewhat flattened bathtub. As the grinning Paiute lashed Longarm's last sweaty wrist to a stake driven deep into the earth,

Longarm writhed and gasped, "Ouch, you sons of bitches! I'll get you for this!"

Right next to him Ki snarled through gritted teeth, "Lay still as you can. You fool! It's still cool. Most of them are still numb from the night air. If you just lay still and let them get used to us being here— Jesus Christ and Buddha's balls!"

Longarm smiled weakly and said, "I *told* you they was mean little bastards. Just wait 'til the sun warms us all up."

Colonel Trepont looked willing to wait. But then another of his French-speaking followers came running to yell something in that lingo and Trepont seemed to think it was more serious than executing prisoners by ant fire. So the whole bunch lit out for the stone ruins. Longarm waited until they were well out of earshot before he said conversationally, "I talk a little Canada-style French, but I wasn't sure I could follow that. Could you?"

Ki grinned and said, "Enough to assume Stone Hand must have meant what he said about sending for more troops. I hope he has a lot of them. The colonel just said something about moving a Gatling gun down off this mesa to ambush them in some narrow passage. How are you doing with your bindings, Longarm?"

The slightly taller but no stronger prisoner tied across the ant pile said, "Not so hot. But at least we slickered them about the fool ants. I was afraid you'd be slow catching on, old son."

Ki chuckled and said, "I've been in this country longer than they have if they haven't noticed, by now, that black-tailed harvester ants *don't* sting."

Longarm said, "They're the only ants I know of in these parts as don't. I was hoping that infernal furriner wasn't as interested as us in the local flora and fauna. I wish he hadn't been so good at tying knots, though."

Ki said, "You're talking funny again, and there's nobody here but us, now. Trepont didn't even risk his twinkle toes on this ominous mound of vegetarian ants in ferocious war paint. It was those damned *Indians* who tied us down, damn them."

Longarm replied, "That's what I just said. I'd have slipped

241

most knots a white man would have tied by now. You can't hardly beat a Digger who hunts rabbit with big string-nets when it comes to tying knots. But keep working on yours while I keep working on mine. For even if them bastards don't come back before we can bust loose, we got to find the gals and make sure they ain't in an even worse fix!"

Chapter 21

The answer to Longarm's question, although neither were in any position to answer, was that Victoria Miller, as the child of a still useful servant, had been spared, to the crazy old woman's way of thinking, to work as yet another house servant, or slave. The baroness found the distinction a bore to consider.

But, as if to make up for it, or perhaps because the baroness herself had once been young and pretty, the beautiful Jessica Starbuck had been placed in a big woven basket, her wrists and ankles bound as skillfully by Indian hands, and then hung out to dry, as the colonel had put it.

Actually, Jessie's open basket was suspended on a rope, fastened like a fishing line, to a log beam they'd swung out a window in the stone walls, to dangle her way in the middle of the air, ten feet out from the sandstone cliffs and over a thousand feet above the rocky canyon floor below. Other than that, she was unharmed. For as the colonel had explained when he'd forced her into the basket at gunpoint, the delicious torture lasted longer when the victim started out feeling up to par.

They'd suspended her down the south face of the cliff, where the sun could get at her most of the day, with neither food nor water. The colonel had assured her, based on earlier experiments, that thirst would drive her mad long before she had to worry about losing much weight. She was feeling a mite dry already, albeit not yet ready to roll out of the basket to her death. Colonel Trepont had told her most people did by the second or third day, faced with dying slow or sudden. The beauty of this form of punishment, as he called it, was that either way the victim had so much time to *think* before they finally did what they knew from the beginning they'd have to do, sooner or later. There was no other choice to dwell on, over and over, as the thirst got more horrible and the only way to end it slowly sank in, every horrible screaming second to the bottom.

But Jessie wasn't ready to commit suicide just yet. So she just hung around up there, trying to examine her surroundings without making the damned basket swing so sickeningly.

From her unwanted vantage point, out there, she had her first good view of the cliff-top ruins. They were impressive in their own confusing way. Most of the split-level complex sprawled along the rimrocks still lay roofless and deserted, with blue sky showing through many a gaping window. Those parts had more dignity than the parts clustered about the entranceway with its pretentious coat of arms and curtains hanging in the windows never intended for such flimsy finery by the long-gone and hard-working builders of the majestic ruins. She wondered what earlier, more-dignified women who'd ground corn, woven baskets, and worked at other sensible chores behind those thick walls, would think of one old woman lolling about to be waited on hand and foot while she drooled over the past and plotted future mischief. Custis had said they'd likely spoken a lingo something like Comanche. Whatever their ghosts could have said to her, she felt sure she'd understand them better than that crazy old baroness.

There was a tinny blast from an unseen bugle and Jessie turned that way to see movement on the trail over to the west. The trail ran down the cliff side sloping the other way. So she could only make out some of what seemed to be going on. But it did seem that crazy colonel was waving his sword about as some others wheeled a sort of shiny cannon out and down the trail. The colonel went back inside, the brave thing. He hadn't even looked her way. So she knew that whatever was going on had to be more important to him right now.

Before he remembered her, she had to really start thinking

about getting out of this fool fix. So she got to work.

Getting her hat off was the hardest part. It was easy enough to get the braided cord it hung from between her teeth. But try as she might, she couldn't work it back up over her head that way. So she started chewing. It was well-tanned leather, and chewing it didn't help her thirst at all. She knew she could be wasting body fluids she'd sure miss later if this didn't work. But her saliva seemed to soften it some as she ground her healthy young teeth back and forth until finally one strand and then two gave way. She had no idea why the third strand held out so long, but it did. It took her the good part of an hour, all told, before at last the hat was free to slide down her back, between her body and the basket, until she could get her hands on the felt brim.

The next part was really tricky and called for some care as well as enthusiasm. For if she dropped it to the bottom of the basket she'd be right back where she'd started. But she never. She got to the steel throwing star the colonel had taken for some female notion. Then she carefully wedged one sharp point into the basket weave behind her. After that it was duck soup to cut her wrists free and even easier to slash through the thongs binding her ankles. Then came the hard part. She was still out there in the middle of nowhere, a thousand feet above the canyon floor.

On the far side of the ruins, it had just occurred to Longarm and Ki that, since two of their wrists shared one stake in common, they might do better working together. So they did, both strong men straining like hell in a series of jerks until, at last, the stake came free and Ki could get at the knots with his own sharp teeth. Once Ki had one hand free, it only took him a few moments to free both himself and Longarm, although he did say it was a shame he couldn't take advantage of such a glorious opportunity.

As they rose cautiously behind the scrub between them and the rear of the ruins, Longarm said, "I don't see anyone posted out back. Maybe they didn't know as much as you and me about ants. Let's go."

Ki said, "Walk, don't run. It's broad daylight and sudden movements catch the eye quicker."

To which Longarm could only reply, "Teach an old dog how to scratch fleas, why don't you?"

So they sort of mosied almost to the rear entryway they'd been marched out of before a sleepy-eyed Paiute, with his rifle slung stepped out back to piss or whatever, shot them a startled look, and might have made it back inside if Ki hadn't nailed him with a handy rock that made hash out of the back of his head.

Ki growled, "Teach an old ninja new tricks while you're at it."

But Longarm was already running and didn't stop until he was inside, pointing the fallen guard's bayoneted rifle down the gloomy corridor as he muttered, "Now we're getting somewhere!"

Meanwhile, Jessie was getting from the basket to the beam above the hard way, by climbing the rope hand over hand and not looking down. The rope was thick and slippery. Many a man could not have climbed it and Jessie might not have been able to, either, if she'd had any other choice. But she had no other choice, so she did it.

When she finally managed to haul her head above the beam she locked both elbows over it for a breather, then swung one leg up to lock an ankle over as well. As she started to inchworm along the beam to the opening it jutted out from, she made the mistake of looking down. She gagged, swallowed the big fuzzy cat in her churning innards before it could claw its way all the way out, and told herself it was only a few yards, now.

So she was staring ahead at the opening hopefully when a Paiute wearing a red kepi appeared there, grinning at her like a shit-eating dog as he started to unsling his rifle.

Then his grin was replaced by red ruin as Jessie threw her shuriken. As the spinning blades buzz-sawed him out of sight behind the stone sill, she grunted, "I knew it might come in handy again before this day was over." And then she was over the sill as well, armed once more with the dead man's rifle and her blood-slicked throwing star.

Not far away but feeling as lost, Longarm spun in the semi-darkness to confront the sharp crack he'd heard just in time to see another Paiute going down with his neck twisted at an odd angle. As Ki scooped up the dead man's rifle Longarm muttered, "Spoilsport. All right, you see if you can find the gals and old man Miller. If he has any control over these Paiute he recruited, we might not have to kill every damn one of 'em."

Ki growled, "Now who's being a spoilsport? Where will *you* be all this time?"

Longarm said, "Got to do me some sniping. I got a rifle. The Indians on our side got rifles. We'll have to get that Gatling gun crew between us since it can only fire one way at once."

"Didn't old Miller say they had *two* such weapons, Longarm?"

"I doubt they'd take both out of this stronghold. If they did, and I wind up dead, Durango's the nearest place you and the gals want to head for. It's been nice talking to you. I got to get on down the road now."

Ki didn't argue. He knew the passageway Longarm was following led more or less due south. So he followed a turn to his left, hoping he remembered the general direction of the living quarters correctly. He hadn't gone far when two more uniformed Indians met him, going the other way. Ki got one with his butt stock and ripped the other one open with the bayonet before prowling on, muttering, "Someone had better have a word with these Indians before I get all sweaty and blood splattered."

Meanwhile, Victoria Miller was looking for her daddy after finally busting through the wall of the chamber they'd locked her in the night before, a loose rock at a time. Finding herself in a gloomy maze, she could only grope her way toward that end she figured her friends might be at. She doubted they'd still be supping with that old crazy rich lady. But if she could find that big dining hall, they'd likely be nearby.

But she was more turned around than she thought, albeit headed in the right general direction. So when she saw light through red door hangings up ahead, the pretty little breed just busted through them, a big rock she'd armed herself with in one small brown fist, to find herself in the bedchamber of the baroness, with the baroness still in bed.

The old woman sat bolt upright, gasping, "How dare you! I'll have you punished!"

Victoria Miller snapped, "You already hurt me and my poor daddy all these years, you crazy old bat! For it was thanks to you I thought I was a poor orphan, forced to work for other old rich-bitch crazy ladies! You think poor folk don't have feelings, damn your hoity-toity hide? You think it was *fun* to make me toil and scrub all this time while you made a slave out of my daddy, *too?*"

The baroness gulped and said, "Now, my dear, I feel sure we can talk this over. Your own father can tell you how kind I have always been to the lower classes."

But Victoria hit her with the rock, knocking her off the far side of the bed and then, seeing the old madwoman was still not only alive but conscious, Victoria moved around to that side, grabbed the baroness by the scrawny ankles, and proceeded to haul her, kicking and fussing, toward the nearest window as she told the baroness, "I've *heard* how nice you are to the hired help you've ever been too cheap to pay. You got everybody scared because they're afraid you'll chuck 'em down the cliff."

"What are you doing? Where are you dragging me, you horrid child?" the old woman babbled in sheer terror. For she feared she knew and it didn't help at all when the strong young Vickie told her, "To the window, of course. I aim to chuck you out it."

"Oh, no! You can't! That would be inhuman!" sobbed the old woman.

To which Victoria replied, Apache-eyed, "This is a poor time to consider folks like me could be human, ma'am. I figure you like to chuck us subhumans outta windows because, deep down in your twisted soul, you've always thought

248

that would be an awful way to go. So here you *go,* you mean old thing!"

She didn't want to. She fought like hell. But Vickie was twice as strong and at least as determined. So the baroness went out the window, screaming all the way down the cliff, until she hit the bottom with an awesome smack for such a dried-up old prune. It seemed to Vickie to take no time at all. As she stared down, she muttered, "Hell, that wasn't as much fun as I thought it was going to be."

Longarm and Jessie were more than good friends, but they still came close to killing one another until they recognized each other in the gloom. Jessie said, "Howdy, pard. Where are we going with these repeating rifles?"

Longarm said, "Those Indian pards of ours are headed this way some more. Trepont knows it. He's setting up an ambush with one or more Gatling guns."

Jessie nodded and said, "Just one. I saw his crew taking it down the trail a spell back. They were manhandling it on foot. So they couldn't have meant to haul it far, and the steel rims of that gun carriage ought to be easy for us to follow."

Longarm answered, "Us? Well, all right, as long as you keep your pretty head and ass down. Did the colonel go with 'em or is he still up here someplace?"

"He's holding the fort. Where's Ki?"

"Likely *taking* the fort, if I know Ki. Let's worry about eating this apple a bite at a time. We got to take out that infernal gun before Many Sheep and Stone Hand walk into it!"

They found their way to the gate after a couple of wrong turns. As they stared across the courtyard toward the exit to the trail, they both gasped. Then, as one, they both raised their captured rifles to blow away the four men posted by the other Gatling perched on its carriage just inside the gate. As Longarm levered another round into his chamber he laughed and said, "Now, this is just too good to be true. But I'll steer her down the trail by her tongue if you'll man the brake lever!"

So that's just what they proceeded to do. They didn't know that up above them, from a corner window, Colonel Trepont was trying to draw a bead on Jessie's back as she bobbed back and forth to hold the wheels steady but not too steady for Longarm, farther down the steep grade. Trepont had just decided he was never going to get a better shot when the door behind him opened and Ki said, "Drop it."

Trepont did, turning with a click of his heels to say, "I see you have the advantage on me, for the moment. *Mais* enjoy it while you can. I am not alone up here, you know."

"I wouldn't bet on that. I just heard a voice that has to be Victoria Miller's, yelling a lot in Paiute. If your Indian recruits pay attention to one of their own, you could have less backing and I could have more than we started out with this morning."

The older but meaner-looking man shrugged and said, "Such are the fortunes of war. If you were a gentleman, you would at least allow me to defend my honor, at the last, with cold steel."

Ki said, "I didn't know you had any honor. But if you want a fight, that's all right with me."

The colonel raised an eyebrow as Ki tossed his captured rifle away, to face him bare-handed. Trepont asked, "Don't you suppose you ought to find a sword, as well?"

Ki said, "I don't need one," as he crossed the space between them, much as a sidewinder might have, purring, "After what you tried to pull on Longarm and me with those ants this morning, I don't owe you any favors."

Trepont grinned wolfishly as he drew his sword, saying, "*Eh bien,* this shall give me the greatest of pleasure."

But, actually, Ki had all the pleasure as he proceeded to kick the liver and lights out of a brute who knew a lot more about sword fighting than the oriental martial arts.

By the time Trepont had died, slow, Jessie was pleading with Longarm to stop cranking that infernal handle so she could see. He did and, as the smoke cleared between the muzzle of the Gatling gun they'd hauled a mile to cover the other one set up to ambush their Indian allies, they both shared a long low whistle. For, down below, the other Gatling rested on one shot-up wheel, surrounded by what looked like five piles of bloody rags. Longarm patted the warm brass breech of the Gatling he'd just been spitting a thousand rounds a minute with and told her, "Wars sure figure to get messy, if ever they get these things light enough to pack around easier."

She wrinkled her nose and said, "Nothing could get messier than what you just did to those poor boys."

"They was planning to be just as mean to our pet Indians. All that noise must have run Stone Hand and Many Sheep back a ways. They won't move closer before they scout here some. Meanwhile, we'd best go back and see if old Ki needs any help."

She said, "If we can make it back up that trail without drawing fire, it will mean Ki needs no help, dear. Either way I vote we wait here for those Ute and Navajo."

So they did. They didn't dare get too friendly while they waited. So to pass the time, Jessie said, "I'm still confused about all this, darling. After all these attempts on our lives, I still don't know who on earth has been trying to kill us!"

Longarm said, "I'm dying for a smoke, and old Trepont couldn't have been the rascal who smokes Daniel Websters. But there may be another way to skin the cat, Jessie. You know we're still alive and I know we're still alive, but could Daniel Webster know we're still alive?"

She asked him what he meant. He said, "First we'll see if we're still alive. If the fighting here is over, it might be sort of interesting to have old Ki stagger out of the wilderness, sobbing he was the only survivor."

Chapter 22

Longarm never would have gotten his crusty boss to go along with it. Jessie might have found it easier to pull hens' teeth. But in the end she got her dear Uncle Billy to go along with what he still called tea-total lunacy and, once U.S. Marshal William Vail of the Denver District Court made up his mind to issue a false press release, he dictated one to Henry that made the prissy office clerk suffer alternate fits of pallor and the giggles.

When poor folk die that's about the end of it. But life can get really complicated when someone dies with money in the bank. So that's what happened when it was reported far and wide that Miss Jessica Starbuck of Starbuck Enterprises and, oh, yes, some deputy named Custis Long, had been slaughtered by maniacs in the Four Corners country.

Most people are familiar with the scene in the lawyer's office where the attorney for the estate takes his copy of the last will and testament from his safe and reads it to the friends and relations of the dear departed.

That's about the end of it for anyone who got left out. They are free to go home and sulk. But things are just starting to get interesting for those *named* in said will. For before anyone left a penny gets a penny they have to go through the whole thing some more in probate court.

Most such hearings are pro forma, as long as nobody seems out to dispute the will and the probate judge can read and sees no bloodstains on the paper or other indications that the will might not be exactly what the dear departed had in mind. The job of probate judge is a political plum, often awarded to old party hacks who made it through law school with a C average and never wound up in jail.

But the presiding judge at the hearing held on the top floor of the Fort Worth Federal Building was an old pro who'd once ridden against Comanche with Billy Vail. The Honorable Frank Dickerson had distinguished himself more for hanging than messing with probate. Federal judges were seldom called upon to deal with such matters unless the person who'd made the will got to dearly depart under federal jurisdiction, which the Indian lands the crazy old baroness had been trying to steal had been, of course.

The law firm of Peters and Cohan were sports about it. The Fort Worth Federal Building was just a hoot and a holler from the local county courthouse they were more used to. The hearing was held in Judge Dickerson's chambers with just a court stenographer and Billy Vail backing the judge on the federal side. The young gal taking down all the words of wisdom looked cool and collected despite the heat outside. Billy Vail looked rumpled and weary from his train ride down from Denver. The judge was no fool. He'd long since learned a man could look just as dignified in a Texas courtroom in summer with no more than an undershirt under his black robes. But his crotch still itched as he sat behind his desk with the steno on his left and Billy Vail perched to his right and just behind him, seated on a cold steam radiator.

Since Tom Cohan had only been shipped back to Texas so they could bury him, the firm was appearing before Probate in the person of Cornwallis Peters, Esquire, a tall, thin gent in a well-cut gray suit that just about matched his thinning hair. He'd brought along a shorter and somewhat younger gent he introduced as his law clerk. Billy Vail was more impressed with the very good-looking brunette with a big hat and a small husband, introduced by Lawyer Peters as the principal heirs or, to be exact, heiress and spouse. The lady in the big hat appeared to be distant kin to the late Jessica Starbuck on the maternal side. Her married name was Riggins, Flora Riggins, née Davis. She modestly allowed that like her poor little kissing cousin, Jessie, she was related to Jefferson Davis, President of the C.S.A.

When she did, Billy Vail said, "That's odd. I knew Alex Starbuck well enough to drink with and he never mentioned being kin to old Jeff Davis, ma'am."

Judge Dickerson told Vail to shut up and suggested everybody else sit down. As they all took his suggestion the judge said, above the scraping of the chair legs, "Nobody never said Alex Starbuck was related to anyone, Billy. You know Jessie's poor *mother* came from a fine old southern family."

He turned to Lawyer Peters with a cocked eyebrow to ask him, "Are you satisfied as to identity of these folk, Counselor?"

Peters nodded curtly, snapped his fingers at his backup, and when the latter handed him a brief case, Peters hauled out a sheaf of folded bond paper, bound together with a rubber band. He hauled out those he wanted at the moment and handed them over to the judge, saying, "You'll find everything in order, there, Your Honor. As attorney for the estate I naturally made certain everyone named in poor Miss Starbuck's will was the very person named. You'll find all the identification I insisted on when these relations of the late Jessica Starbuck came forward, from Miss Flora's own birth certificate to that of her late mother's, who, as you can see, was a first cousin to Miss Starbuck's mother."

As the judge leafed through the imposing documentation, Lawyer Peters smiled up at Billy Vail to ask, "Where's that segundo, Ki? Poor Jessica left him a tidy sum as well. So I expected to see him here today."

Vail said, "He was feeling poorly. Ant bites. I told Ki that I'd look out for his interests here. Him and my deputy, Longarm, was pals." Then Vail asked casually, "Wasn't Ki named exec of Jessie's will, by the way? He said something, up in Denver, to the effect he might be running Starbuck Enterprises, now."

Flora Riggins sniffed and said, "That will be the day, I'm sure. I hear the man's a Chinee!"

Peters shushed her with a warning frown and said, "He may be an American citizen. Then again he may not. It would

254

be up to him to prove, should he care to contest the will."

"Can he do that?" asked Vail innocently.

Peters didn't know what a sly old fox the somewhat rustic ex-Ranger really was. So he nodded pleasantly and in a tone usually reserved for explaining birds and bees to small children, said, "Anyone can contest anything in court, if he can afford the legal fees. I don't see why Ki would want to, however. His late employer left him well provided for, with a pension for life."

"No gold watch?" asked Vail dryly, going on to mildly protest, "We ain't talking about a faithful old darky, you know. Ki was Jessie's *segundo*. He just about ran Starbuck Enterprises for her. She had lots of other hobbies that took up a great deal of her time. Are you saying that, now that Jessie ain't with us no more, you mean to put poor Ki out to pasture?"

"Such matters are not for me to decide," the lawyer protested.

But his somewhat firm-jawed female client told Vail, "It's for me and Melvin, here to decide. I don't know about you all, but I was raised in the tidewater and I'll not have an uppity nigra in charge of *my* affairs!"

Her husband nodded and said, "Me neither. Is it all right if we smoke in here, Judge?"

The pert stenographer grimaced, but Judge Dickerson nodded as he went on reading. So Melvin Riggins hauled out an expensive smoke and lit up to lean back, feeling rich.

Judge Dickerson finished reading and put the papers to one side on his desk blotter, saying, "Well, I can see you went to a lot of trouble gathering proper identification for your clients, Counselor. We'd best get on with the last will and testament out of your office safe. You say Miss Starbuck named your firm as the executor?"

Peters nodded modestly. Billy Vail said, "Hold on. How come Ki told me Jessie told him she'd left that chore to him if it wasn't so?"

Peters shrugged and said, "Knowing nothing about her exact relationship with that odd Oriental gentleman, I can only hazard a guess that he may have felt, as Miss Flora puts it, a bit uppity about his position. No matter how she felt about him, she'd have hardly left her considerable estate under the management of a mystery man who wasn't even *white*."

Vail scowled and said, "Ki's always acted white enough for my tastes. I've never caught him in one lie, neither. So why in thunder would he say one thing when you say that will Jessie left with you says another? Am I supposed to believe she was loco en la cabeza?"

Judge Dickerson turned to Vail to say, "Simmer down, hold hoss. I see no issue of a sound or unsound mind while signing one's last will and testament, here. As long as a will's been signed in front of proper witnesses I only have the power to question the sanity of the dear departed when they put down something *stupid*."

Everyone calmed down. So the judge went on, "It just ain't true you can leave money to an heir providing they do something weird. I have been known to set aside a will leaving more money to a goldfish than any fish could have any possible use for. But as long as the late Jessica Starbuck drew up a sensible-sounding will with her own attorney, here, as witness, the only call this court would have to refuse probate would be if this Ki gent or anyone else could prove she was loco, acting under duress, or not signing it at all when she signed it."

Flora Riggins said, "Good. When do we get the money?"

Judge Dickerson said, "When I finish probating, of course."

Then he turned back to Peters and said, "I don't doubt it's your handwriting where you signed as a witness, Counselor. What about the other witness, Thomas Cohan, Esquire?"

Peters dug into his briefcase again as he said, "Knowing you might ask that, Your Honor, I took the liberty of bringing along some other documents signed by my late junior partner. I dug some signed letters from the late Jessica Starbuck from the files while I was at it. But surely her signature on that will before the court, as witnessed by two members of the Texas Bar, could hardly be at issue, here, could it?"

Judge Dickerson said, "Well, I'm no handwriting expert.

But if you say that's the will Jessica Starbuck signed, that ought to do it. What do you think, Billy?"

Vail stood up and said, "I got a better way to make sure that there will is worth the paper it was written on. Let's just *ask.*"

Then he stepped over to a side door and pulled it open to let Jessie, Ki, and Longarm into the already somewhat crowded inner chamber, asking, "I hope you kiddies was paying attention to all this grown-up conversation?"

Jessie pointed at the woman calling herself Flora Riggins and said flatly, "My cousin Flora died of the yellow jack when both of us were no more than six or seven. I don't know who this woman is, but she sure can't be any kin of mine!"

Longarm shot a more startled look at the red-faced gal with the big hat, recovered, and grinned at her somewhat sheepishly as he said, "Howdy, Miss Peggy Gordon. *I* thought you was a gypsy gal. Now I see your taste in malt liquor was even more sinister than I imagined."

Then all hell broke loose.

As the court stenographer screamed and dove under the desk with the judge, Longarm fired the derringer he'd been palming ever since he smelled that Daniel Webster cigar smoke through the door crack. So that was the end of the so-called Melvin Riggins, and Billy Vail beat the young tough backing Peters to the draw in the meantime. Vail had been planning on putting his first round into Peters—he just couldn't stand lawyers. But Ki was in Vail's line of fire because he was doing something awful to Peters himself, barehanded.

The lady in the big hat, whoever she was, made the mistake of going for her garter gun instead of simply diving for the nearest exit. So she wound up diving out the window, through the glass, when Jessie pumped two rounds of .38 into her junoesque breasts. She hit the hot pavement three stories below with a mighty loud splat, being sort of on the chubby side, as Longarm recalled, and so he never had to explain *all* the details to Jessie, after all.

As the noise faded away and the gunsmoke began to clear, His Honor gingerly rose from the floor behind his desk to stare down in wonder at the mess they'd made on his rug. Longarm had put out the Daniel Webster cigar with a boot heel, but there wasn't much he could do about the big sticky puddle of blood old Mel now reclined in with two derringer rounds in his rib cage.

The so-called law clerk reclined in a far corner with the grips of his .45 still gripped in one lifeless hand and a little blue hole in his forehead. Vail had aimed high to avoid hitting Ki. The lawyer Ki had hit, Peters, hardly had a face at all, now that Ki had worked him over with the iron-hard edges of his chopping palms. Judge Dickerson heaved a mighty sigh and said, "Well, I was worried about a slick lawyer pleading Entrapment, anyways. But you and your pals sure play rough, Billy Vail."

Vail growled, "I told you to begin with, they was playing a mighty rough game for mighty high stakes. Explain it all to the judge, Longarm."

So, as the pretty little stenographer gal got out from under the desk to take it down, Longarm did. He said, "Some of the confusion was occasioned by there being two sets of homicidal lunatics after Jessie, here, at once, Your Honor. I'd have figured things out sooner if only one team had come at us at a time."

Judge Dickerson nodded and said, "Billy told me the crazy old lady holding court in a cliff dwelling had never heard of this bunch, and vice versa. But it seems to me Peters and his pals was working at cross purposes long before you all met up with the baroness and her own hired guns."

Longarm nodded but said, "The plan Peters and Cohan started out with was simple enough, it just got out of hand in the execution."

Jessie protested, "I'm still not sure poor Tom Cohan was in on it, Custis. We didn't murder him. They did."

Longarm shushed her with a weary smile and said, "I'd have never treated his corpse so tender if it hadn't taken me some time to add it up. Like I said, things got out of hand and I'll never get finished if you all won't let me just tell it from the beginning."

Nobody argued. So as the stenographer gal took shorthand

258

he went on to explain, "In the beginning Jessie, here, made the mistake of hiring a new and hungry law firm. Please don't tell us why, Jessie. All that matters is that they just couldn't stand the notion of one young gal having all that money and power when they felt sure they could handle it better. But even a crooked lawyer has to study some on crooking a client half as smart as they knew you was. So they behaved themselves until the day you came to them with Victoria Miller and her wondrous tale of gold mines in unmapped Indian country. You asked them to check out her story. When they did it sounded even wilder. They knew there was a good chance you'd just vanish into the pumpkin the way others had before you. So naturally they done all they could to encourage you to act silly."

Vail cut in to observe, "We just noticed how good Peters was at documenting records to make things look more sensible than they was, Longarm. But why didn't they leave it at that, once they had Jessie hell-bent on self-destruction?"

Before Longarm could answer, Jessie said, "Fair is fair, and you were there when Tom Cohan tried to talk us out of riding into the pumpkin, Custis."

Longarm shot her a disgusted look and said, "Well, of course he told you it was dumb. What kind of a lawyer would want to say, later, that he'd *advised* a client to commit suicide so he and his pards could produce a fake will for probate? They knew it was safe to warn you, for the record, not to do what they knew you meant to do. For they knew of your adventures with Ki. That part was nothing but an act. Can't you see that?"

The door behind Longarm popped open so a sweaty faced copper badge from downstairs could stick his head in and say, "Your Honor, there's a dead lady on the sidewalk under your window. I thought you'd like to know."

Then he glanced down at the corpse-littered floor between them to gasp, "Oh, Lord have mercy!"

Judge Dickerson nodded and said, "You'd best get some of the other help to tidy up, Ryan. We're still working on how these chambers came to resemble the last act of Hamlet."

The uniformed guard ducked back out. The judge told

Longarm to go on. So Longarm said, "Knowing Jessie could take care of herself when even Comanche messed with her, they decided not to leave it to the Indians alone. Having established their client was off on a mad adventure, against their good advice, they hired some folk they knew to be deadly to see that she wound up dead for sure. The lady who just went out the window was staked out in Durango to supervise a hired gun called the Buscadero Kid. They knew he was just wild and woolly. As the gal they'd set up to be the fake heiress to most of Jessie's fortune, they figured they could trust her to see he done things right. Her husband, old Melvin, there on the rug, was sent to supervise in Richfield in case Jessie got off the train there, like she did."

Longarm reached for a cheroot as an excuse to avoid meeting Jessie's eyes as he continued. "The Buscadero Kid was wilder than expected. As a wanted man he just did what he thought he had to when he recognized a lawman, me, coming at him. The gal was just as cool and professional as Peters and Cohan had hoped when they recruited her. We'd already, ah, met. So she knew that while I was a lawman, I was on another case entire. I'm still working on why she decided to kill me, after all, in the end. I may have mentioned knowing Jessie in some conversation I can't recall."

"A pillow conversation?" asked Jessie sweetly.

Longarm lit his cheroot and took some time to get it going before he told the stenographer, "Don't put that down, miss. Let's just say I got stuck in Durango a spell for shooting the Buscadero Kid and, well, a man talks a lot to the few folk he may know in a small town. She may have just wanted me dead because I said I might be coming back any time, and didn't want me to be able to place *her* there when and if Jessie wound up dead in Durango as well. She knew me and the local coroner was on speaking terms."

He was able to meet Jessie's eye as he said, "Meanwhile, Jessie, Ki, and the Miller gal had arrived in Richfield. They knew she meant to look up a local Mormon J.P. when she got there because they'd given her bum advice on mining claims."

Jessie asked, "But why did they have to murder that harmless Elder Reynolds, Custis? Couldn't they have ambushed me most anywhere in town?"

He shook his head and said, "Reynolds wasn't harmless to their devious plan. He was when they killed him. But later, after you was dead, he'd have recalled having an odd conversation with you about mining claims. He did know regular law, as well as the Book of Mormon. So how was Tom Cohan to deny giving you a bum steer if Reynolds bragged on setting you *right* on mining Indian land?"

Longarm pointed his cheroot down at the body of Melvin Riggins and said, "That rascal got to supervise the action in Richfield. Lord knows the glorified saddle tramps a couple of crooked lawyers had recruited from the dregs of Texas needed supervising. Old Mel got there well ahead of the actual killers to case the layout. I don't know whether he just dropped that cigar band in the office of old Reynolds while he was setting Reynolds up with some fool story, or whether he liked to hand out cigars to the hired help. Either way, we know about what happened when you walked into the trap they laid for you and so there's no sense going over all that again."

Ki said, "There's no argument about the way they murdered that Mormon elder and framed Jessie for it. But explain that wild shooting at the hotel, with Cohan in the line of fire. Or how *he* wound up murdered, himself, in front of the telegraph office."

Longarm shrugged and said, "You just said yourself it was wild. Old Mel, there, wouldn't have hung about to supervise the rascals, once he saw they'd locked Jessie up for murder. That was where things started falling apart on the plotters. Nobody set out to *frame* Jessie. They was out to murder her entire. But her unexpected arrest, instead, called for Riggins to haul himself and his Daniel Websters out of there, sudden, before anyone who might recognize him, later, when he got so rich, turned up to cover the trial of such a famous long-lost relation."

He pointed at the battered corpse of Peters and explained, "As Jessie's attorney of record, this sly cuss just had to send his junior partner, at least, to go through the motions. I have to say Cohan behaved about the way any honest lawyer would

261

have. He had to, with you and me watching, Ki. But, naturally, the hired killers still about were not as sophisticated as you and me. All they knew was that Peters and Cohan had recruited them to lay for Jessie and kill her. Only she killed one of them instead, their supervisor had lit out, and here came yet another member of the team doing his best to bail her out!"

"They suspected a double cross," said Billy Vail, who was used to how much honor among thieves any lawman worth his salt had seen on the job.

Longarm nodded but said, "I wish I could get more words in edgewise, here. As I was trying to say, at least one of the gang got excited and tore past that hotel, acting ferocious, if only as a hint to Cohan that the boys wasn't happy about the way things seemed to be going. We all know what a bad move that was. They had no way of knowing Tom Cohan and Victoria Miller were the only ones present who didn't put a bullet or worse in the cuss. So now they must have really been worried. Dago Dillon, the one who'd stabbed Reynolds and knew Cohan knew it, panicked when he noticed Cohan sending a telegram to Lord only knew where about what, or who. So he done what comes natural to a congenital back stabber, and I have to say that confused me pretty good for a spell."

Ki nodded and said, "I had my doubts about that slick-talking lawyer, even before you pointed out he'd steered us wrong about filing on Indian land. But, once he'd been killed the same way as Reynolds had—"

"I just said that," Longarm cut in. "The last ones left either wired Peters, there, to get things straight in their fool heads, or came after us, free, because like that one old boy said, at least one of the others who'd wound up dead in all the confusion was kin. Let's not worry about every infernal loose string. We got them instead. So that's that, and I'd say I just wrapped it up for that little lady's shorthand pad."

Billy Vail said, "Like hell—sorry, ladies. I know how you got shed of the killers hired by Peters and Cohan, only to wander on into an even worse gang. Coming down on the train to attend this masked ball, here, I read the depositions of Jessie, Ki, and them Millers, along with your infernally short official report, you long-armed but shortchanging cuss. There wasn't word-one to indicate how you connected all them murderous folk out west to that poor cuss Ki just beat to death."

Longarm sighed and said, "I didn't put nothing on paper before I could *prove* it, boss. That was the whole point of telling old Peters that Jessie and me was dead and then waiting to see what he'd try to pull next. I didn't know for sure he'd produce a fake will and made-up heirs. All I knew for certain was that the firm had talked Jessie, here, into leaving a last will and testament with 'em and, of course, what she'd *really* signed."

"I told him," Jessie said. "I knew all along there had to some *motive* behind all this madness."

Longarm shushed her and said, "Me too. I couldn't come up with one less obvious. So like I told you all, before we set things up so neat, all Peters had to do to prove his innocence was show up here with the paper Jessie signed and left in his care. He proved his guilt, just as easy, by producing forged documents along with old Flora and Mel, the slimy rascal."

Judge Dickerson stared down at his desk to observe, "Oh, he didn't have to resort to too much outright forgery. I see this marriage certificate is dated recent. Nobody would have asked a blushing bride-to-be to produce any proof as she filled her side in. Saying her name was Flora Davis to go with the real birth certificate of a cousin who died back east in her childhood was sort of raw. But of course they assumed neither the late Alex Starbuck nor a late Jessica Starbuck would dispute a legal document indicating a common maternal ancestry."

The chamber door opened again so that the same copper badge could stick his head in again to announce, "The morgue wagon's come for the mortal remains, Your Honor. They already loaded the lady who went out the window. They'd like to know if you're about done with the ones up here, now."

Judge Dickerson nodded and suggested they all step into the main courtroom so the boys could tidy up in here. So they all had to.

Longarm was starting to find the proceedings tedious. He saw Jessie and Ki were starting to look fidgety as well. So, knowing how old men liked to drone on and on after the tale had been told, he cleared his throat to gain Vail's attention and said, "I got a few errands to attend to here in Fort Worth before I head back to Denver, boss. You don't really need us here no more, do you?"

Vail glanced at Dickerson, who shrugged and said, "You young folk run along. I know how to get in touch with you if we need more fool paperwork. But I'm sure vexed with you all for what a mess you made of my rug, hear?"

Longarm and Jessie grinned at one another and walked out, arm in arm. Out in the corridor, Jessie confided, "I can't wait to ask you about that fat brunette. But such pillow talk can wait until after. I know this darling little hotel just down the avenue, you brute!"

He looked sheepish and said, "I was never half as brutal as she was, damn it. For she was out to poison me, steal your fortune, and even fire old Ki!"

Jessie sniffed and said, "I'd have never forgiven her if she'd done half she set out to do. Now that I suspect I know what else she might have done, as well, I'm glad I got to shoot her."

Longarm said, "Don't speak ill of the dead, and, speaking of old Ki, where is the cuss? Didn't the judge say Ki was free to go, too?"

Jessie nodded but said, "The judge had a mighty pretty court stenographer as well. Didn't you notice how attractive she was, darling?"

"I hadn't noticed," Longarm lied. Then he laughed like hell and said, "Well, I never. You mean her and old Ki?"

"Why not? Did you really think you were the only man in town who might want to get some down-home slap and tickle?"

He gripped her arm tighter and started walking her faster as he assured her, "Honey, nobody could want that half as much as me right now!"

Watch for

**LONGARM AND THE NEW MEXICO
SHOOT-OUT**

one hundred eighteenth novel in the bold
LONGARM series

and

LONE STAR IN THE BIG THICKET

seventy-fourth novel in the exciting
LONE STAR series